ALSO BY
WILLIAM SCHLICHTER

NO ROOM IN HELL
The Good, The Bad & The Undead

THE SILVER DRAGON CHRONICLES
Enter The Sandmen
The Dark Side

Since it began, who have you killed? You wouldn't be alive right now if you hadn't killed somebody.
~ Major West, *28 Days Later*

WILLIAM SCHLICHTER

400 MILES TO GRACELAND

NO ROOM IN HELL
BOOK 2

LIVONIA, MICHIGAN

NO ROOM IN HELL:
400 MILES TO GRACELAND
Copyright © 2017 William Schlichter
All rights reserved. Except as permitted under the U.S. Copyright Act of 1976, no part of this publication may be reproduced, distributed, or transmitted in any form or by any means, or stored in a database or retrieval system, without prior written permission of the publisher.

This book is a work of fiction. The characters, incidents, and dialogue are drawn from the author's imagination and are not to be construed as real. Any resemblance to actual events or persons, living or dead, is entirely coincidental.

Published by Umbra
an imprint of BHC Press

Library of Congress Control Number:
2017936841

ISBN-13: 978-1-946848-03-1
ISBN-10: 1-946848-03-4

Visit the author at:
www.bhcpress.com

also available in ebook and hardcover

NEVER TRUST A SURVIVOR UNTIL YOU KNOW HOW THEY SURVIVED
KURT VONNEGUT

NO ROOM IN HELL

400 MILES TO GRACELAND

CHAPTER ONE

METAL PIPES IMPACT his upper torso.

Each new blow pulsates through Ethan, activating his muscle memory and bringing back to life every physical pain he's ever experienced.

If they were smart, they'd whack my wounded leg—send me to the ground instantly. A strange thought, as he should do something with his arms to prevent hit after hit. Higher order thinking—animal instinct, anything to remove him from the situation.

Four pipes bounce off the Kevlar pads in his vest. No matter how fast they swing, the velocity pales in comparison to bullets he took to the chest two weeks ago. The shots were over in seconds. The constant beating wears him down. Ethan has one advantage over his assailants; the only reason he has yet to receive a blow to the head—they are too short to reach his skull. Part of his brain attempts to count the pelts against his body.

He fails.

His knees wobble.

If I collapse, my head will become their target. I doubt the g contusions and the following hemorrhages will be a quick death. Then again, if they don't bash my skull in...

Vagrants, vagabonds, and venomous villains remain in the world of walking undead, and he has faced them down to be beaten by these shits. *Decent people don't have the heart to make tough choices need-*

ed to survive. How does one put a bullet in their child even if their child hungers for flesh? He has no answer. His brain searches ten-thousand synapses for a route of escape from concussions.

They want what I have. My supplies. My guns. My fortitude. They can't. I need it to survive—to finish my task. My job of keeping people safe—my last promise made. I will find—

Thigh.

Damn!

One of them figured out to strike my thigh. At least it wasn't the bad leg. His right knee buckles. *If they bash the left knee, it'll be over. My hard head won't take blows like my chest does. Kevlar allows for a bit of a cheat.*

Aroused by the torture, the attackers dance and release wails of pleasure with each new impact.

A lead pipe fails to find its destination. The glancing slap allowing Ethan to redirect it through the mouth and out the back of the closest attacker's brain pan.

They stand still.

Ethan finds a moment to draw in one breath. His chest tightens—constricts. Bruising.

Shocked, the three men back away—a moment of reprieve.

They didn't expect me to be able to kill one of them during the beating. They've practiced on travelers before me and always got it right.

It took four to get the jump on me.

The blows stimulate the fading bruises under his chest armor. *Bulletproof vest lacks the truth in its name. 'Might stop a bullet, but you're still shot, and it hurts like FUCKING hell!' must be too long to place on the label.*

Ethan's eyes water from the next impact.

Before he's able to reach for a weapon, a fresh blow glances off the back of his head.

Rather than slumping to his knees, he falls over into the dirt. More blows thump his back.

Images flash, overlapping his thoughts of escape.

Emily.

The next blow cracks against his right shoulder.

Even if not dislocated, my quick draw speed might be permanently hampered.

Facing down dozens of undead with a mere handful of rounds never sent full body shivers quivering to his toes like this assault. His thoughts wander from overcoming his attackers to the fate of his fellow survivors. *Will they learn of my demise? Will they just speculate? It will be a grand story! It only took a thousand undead to bring him down. No, ten thousand. My work will continue. They'll prevail, if they keep to my doctrine of survival methods.*

Two more impacts.

Fuck.

His favorite weapon—Smith & Wesson M&P 40—soaks moisture from the grass.

I had the drop on three attackers but missed the fourth. Under their campfire, they had dug a pit allowing number four to lie in wait. Even with my expensive, student loan-funded brain, I didn't expect anyone would hide under the campfire. If the material between the fire and the attacker failed...there are no more burn trauma wards to repair a face.

Ethan wishes the hidden spring-loaded knife device he sported for a while had worked better. *Stabbing just one of the three remaining bastards would give me a second to reach my M&P.*

Two more blows fill his eyes with wet stars. The M&P rests out of reach. Tomorrow disappears from his thoughts. His body no longer registers pain.

One good blow to my skull will end it—keep me from returning to life. Unlike Emily and Hannah, I was unable to rescue my daughters.

His last thoughts drift—

"Stop!" Not a call for mercy from a female voice. "He's got gear in his pockets we don't want to damage."

Pressure.

Tenderized from the beating takes his brain a moment to realize they are rummaging through his vest pockets. The Kevlar plates smoosh against his bruising skin.

Jerking at Ethan's sleeve ensues. "I want his coat," demands a gravelly-voiced man.

Ethan's boot separates from his leg. "Man, this dude has big feet." The scrawny man lines the bottom of his foot up with the sole of the boot with five inches of overhang. "These are military."

The gravelly-voiced man corrects him, "They aren't. Military boots don't have zippers down the sides. They're nice."

"They're mine," the scrawny man hisses.

"Keep them. I want his guns." The tallest attacker with droopy earlobes racks the M&P slide. A bullet flings out. "Fully loaded."

A woman with knife-cut hair yanks an emergency battery jumper from Ethan's backpack. "This dude was prepared. We start cars with this." She fidgets with the power cord used to charge the device. Her eyes shift, revealing a quizzical thought.

The gravelly voice questions, "This guy's too well equipped."

"You can never be too well equipped." The tall man attempts to twirl the gun but it flounders around his trigger finger.

"He is. He's prepared more than most. It's been ten months, and his boots look fresh—store bought."

"The battery jumper has a full charge, like he has a generator or something," adds the girl with the knife-cut hair. "He has full gear, clean clothes." She sniffs him. "I smell shampoo."

The scrawny man jumps up. "You mean this fucker still has electricity and running water?"

The tall man extends and twists the Smith & Wesson M&P as if he were in the hood. "It's possible. Nuclear plants would never run out of power. Radiation lasts forever."

The knife-cut-haired girl shoots him a derisive glance. "Someone has to maintain the plant or they shut down to prevent a meltdown. I saw it on *The Discovery Channel*. He's got gas generators stashed in a secure location. With enough gas to waste on running a washing machine."

"Make him tell us," demands gravelly-voiced man.

"We beat the living hell out of this dude and he didn't beg us to stop. What are we going to do to make him talk?" asks the tall man.

The girl offers, "Take his pants off. When he wakes up, cut off his balls if he doesn't tell."

The three men involuntarily clamp their own legs together in a motion of protection.

"He's too big to move."

"He may not be able to walk. I cracked his leg but good."

"We can't stay in the open long," gravelly-voiced man says.

"Make a litter and we'll drag him." The girl spits. "Do I have to think of everything?"

"You seem to know a lot," says gravelly-voiced man.

"I'm first in this dude's shower. God, I hope he has hot water. I'd kill for a hot shower."

"You're going to kill him. Once we get to his hideaway, you'll kill him."

"If he's got hot water I will," she says. She kicks at the overgrown grass with her foot wondering how much noise they have created. The noise drives off any animals, however, attracts predators—the undead.

CHAPTER TWO

AMANDA ALWAYS WANTED great legs. Boys in high school thought she had a fantastic ass, but she desired sharply stems, gams—Beyoncé dancing legs. Ten months of daily jogging granted her wish.

Every day she runs.

Not for health, but to stay alive.

The tight, well-formed calves lack any adipose tissue or traces of cellulite. Had the world not ended she'd be assured a job as a leg model or maybe a body double for a scrawny, overpaid actress in a feature film. If the next home they raid has some baby oil or lotion she'd like to shave and rub them smooth.

Theo gawks every chance he gets. If they encounter a home with running water she might let him help her groom. She misses the rough touch of a man's hands on her legs. Since their group thinned she's not felt safe enough. It doesn't take much to stimulate her pleasure centers to distract her from even a full out nuclear attack. Desires embraced every cell of her body leaving her vulnerable. Even feelings incited by some one-night drunken grope-fest could produce screams of passion, attracting the infected.

Theo's stolen glances are as far as he dares. He remains a gentleman, as much as possible when she must pee under guard, or he must retrieve tampons because monthlies attract the undead. If they find a location she finds appealing she may discover if Theo's a world rocker. Now Jarrod exerts the manly talent of fire building. He used a hunk of ice last winter to ignite flame. She'd never believe it had she not been there.

Twigs and dry branches shatter at the approach of undead. They shamble through the underbrush, snarling the distinct moan-howl haunting every survivor's dreams.

Amanda flips open the cylinder on the snub-nose .38.

Four live rounds.

She'd been saving the bullets—one for herself.

Jarrod clubs an undead with a log he ignited. The rags of the infected spark. Flaming undead are frightening because they don't stop, drop, and roll like a living person. They don't stop. Just burn and eat.

Intended or not, the flaming corpse illuminates the immediate area giving Amanda light enough to take careful aim.

Bam.

RATTTTTTTTTTTTTT.

Machine gun fire sprays through the encroaching infected. They fall with moan-howls, ceasing as soon as their heads explode.

Amanda shoots the burning corpse only to have headlights blind her night vision. Forced, she shields her eyes with her forearm. Men in military fatigues hustle her into the front seat of a Jeep.

More gunfire erupts.

As her eyes adjust to the false daylight, Jarrod climbs onto the bed of a truck. She whips her head around—no sign of Theo.

"Herd!" a soldier's voice warns.

Not surprising, being this close to Memphis means more undead. She'd seen two herds and lived. Thousands, maybe ten thousand undead moving as a wave of rotten flesh devouring any animal it encounters, especially man.

"Where's Theo?" she demands.

The soldiers ignore her.

Within seconds, the machine gun fire ceases.

Her ears ring.

The vehicles speed along the highway. Escaping the herd, the male soldiers still refuse to speak to her.

Not sure where she stands, Amanda hikes her leg allowing her foot to rest on the dash. She attempts to enjoy the moment. She's had little time to let her hair down, and in minutes, her world could return to violence. Most likely with her at the head of a train of men. Their peeks lose their flatter after the first few refused to glance away.

She smells their lust. Hunger permeates toward her. Behaving like a nun won't protect her nor will flaunting herself. She slides her bottom over, using the dash as leverage to prep her body for a leap from the moving Jeep. If she lands on her toes she can out sprint any of these men. If they shoot her...well...

They'll do what they want with my body anyway.

She keeps her eyes forward. No chance of inadvertently inviting the driver. "We haven't seen military in months. Rumors of a withdraw circulated." She didn't want to say *retreat* or the insulting *defeat.*

A few months ago, her group contained ten survivors. *I'm the only original member left of my merry band.* Everyone she met before the apocalypse—dead. Those banding together after—dead. Dead. Dead. Dead.

Down to three affiliates, she doesn't want friends. They keep dying. They avoid encountering other survivors. The last group they were lucky to miss was a traveling motorcycle band and another group keeping a harem of women in a tractor-trailer. Only luck found them on the opposite side of a river where the women bathed. She guessed the men killed other male survivors and persecuted the women into servitude.

Somehow, in the last ten months, she's never been forced to sleep with anyone she didn't desire. A few of the men didn't have any idea what to do with a woman. She might have been willing to educate them if time permitted, but when she could be eaten by undead at any minute, she demands instant gratification. Fulfillment. When she allows herself to be so vulnerable as to enjoy a man she needs him to be successful. Not like before when she grew with the relationship and could explore her partner and teach him how to pleasure her.

Floodlights break the darkness.

They blind Amanda. She covers her eyes with her forearm. Peeking through the glare she spots twin guard towers. The Jeep barrels between. More flood lights click on.

A distinct lack of a humming generator means somehow this place has electricity. Amanda considers willingly opening her legs for a hot shower.

Part of the wall of concertina wire reminds her of a prison and even not knowing exactly where they are she still doesn't think they are near one. *A prison would make a great hideout. It already has walls and security measures. Most people avoid them; they wouldn't think to go there to save themselves.* She wishes she'd considered Corrections ten months ago. In all her meetings of survivors none of them were medical people and even fewer were cops unless they went rogue. No one ever said they had been a Corrections Officer.

Prisons, like hospitals, may have been overrun quickly once the plague spread.

Reunited with her fellow survivors, all three are escorted inside. The communal living area was once a warehouse and now home to bunks, washing stations, weapons storage, and a half dozen poker games. All the men halt their activity to admire Amanda's legs. She spots no women among the soldiers. Under guard, they reach a pair of double doors. There, someone who could only be defined as a super nerd scientist greets them in a hailstorm of handshakes and apologies.

"You're the first survivors we've discovered in two weeks. We were so worried."

"Worried?"

"Yes. When we couldn't find survivors, we became concerned we were all that's left." A shiny gold name badge reads Ellsberg.

Amanda has many questions, but Jarrod beats her to the first one.

"Who are you?"

"Introductions are in order. I am, or was, the CDCs top virologist in Nashville. Now I supervise this camp. Where we've been perfecting a cure."

"Impossible," says Theo.

"Even if you did cure those walking dead, wouldn't they die from the rotten flesh and holes in them?"

"Cure isn't an accurate word—vaccine. We are perfecting a vaccine. So, those bit will not turn."

Amanda legs numb. "You mean this could all be over?"

"We're close. A few test trials remain. What we can offer you is a warm meal and hot shower. A place to get some clean clothes. Food. We do insist on some blood work."

Amanda remembers the camping trip her dad dragged her on when she was ten. Bug bites, poison ivy, and squatting to pee. Not that she didn't hover over public toilets as an adult, she never splashes piddle on her shoes. The best part was the first shower when she got home. Water never felt so warm or so...comforting. Hot water consumes her, protects her. Safe is something she has lacked. Now, Irish Spring suds and flowing water as near boiling as she can take comforts her. The scientist said they have an auto ten-minute max. She lathered herself in the sink so she could just stand under the flow for as long as she could. The heat releases the tension in her shoulders. Constant lack of sunscreen and opportunities to tan has left her with white patches on her skin, but she doesn't care. She wouldn't mind a pedicure, but never can she remember feeling so clean.

The shower beeps a thirty-second shut off warning. Amanda spins around one last time to ensure no soap was missed before the drip, drip, drip replaces the waterfall she enjoyed.

Sniffing the clean towel, she pats her face, choosing to air dry. The beads of water on her skin keep her clean—fresh. They give her papery scrubs to wear. No underwear. No bra. The hospital socks have the gripper pattern to prevent slipping because they left her no shoes.

Some tests and food are next and then she wonders if she will be able to sleep. Not some half-an-eye-open sleep but peaceful, safe sleep knowing nothing could harm her here. Amanda attempts to slide her feet on the floor, gliding as if ice skating, but the gripper socks keep her toes in place.

Jarrod waits for her on a bench.

"Where's Theo?"

"They took him for blood work. Said the sooner they draw some vials the sooner we eat."

"It's going to be MREs," Amanda notes.

"Don't care. They won't be rancid like the ones we found."

"With a vaccine, the world could return to normal."

"Not right away. They'll still have to clean up a lot of undead, but at least their numbers are depletable. No more worried about being bit," she says.

"What a fantasy to rebuild the world. How long do you think it will take?"

"Years. The country will become a new frontier and have to be explored all over again."

A man in white scrubs waves at Jarrod. "We are ready for you now."

"Where's Theo?"

"Getting a bite."

Amanda nods at her friend. Too bad when they numbered nine people they couldn't have found this place. Fourteen or fifteen was as large as the group got but some of those people... Some people were made for the end of the world and others need to be destroyed. It took her a time to accept the apocalypse means new beginning, but not for everyone.

The male nurse waves, demanding Jarrod to enter a room down the hall.

He brushes the top of Amanda's shoulder in a good luck, goodbye sort of way.

Alone for long minutes, she wonders. *Why does no one wants to speak to me? Survivors tend to want to exchange information. Everyone wants to know if it is as bad where they came from as it is here. Even the mongrels who plan to kill you for your last MRE talk first.*

The male soldiers' stares confirm not many women are around. She's surprised none of them have requested a date or offered to assault her. One crazed survivor once attacked her group spouting how he was going to drill her until she needed a new hole. He was one of the living people she was forced to kill. Since she seems to be a lone woman—why? Plenty of women outlast men in this new world. After food, she's going to have to demand some answers from the nerdy scientist.

The nurse waves for her turn at health inspection. Her memory plays tricks on her—she swears Jarrod went into a room across the hall.

The male nurse pumps the sphygmomanometer until the pressure cuts into Amanda's arm.

"I'm sure I'm malnourished." She flashes a smile before realizing she can't recall the last time she brushed her teeth. There was no toothbrush in the shower room.

"When was the last time you ate—anything?" He keeps a surgical tone while twisting the knob to release the air from the blood pressure cuff.

"Yesterday. Food's been scarce in this area."

"The soldiers didn't feed you?"

"No. The soldiers haven't even said hello." She quickly adds, "We were promised food after a blood draw."

He refuses to lock eyes with hers. Amanda accepts trust must be earned, but she's done nothing but cooperate.

After he draws three vials of her blood she finds herself alone again now with a rumbling stomach. She had pushed food from her mind until he asked about when she last ate.

Her head slams against the table. Three—no, four men grab her. Amanda somehow knew having not seen any women she'd become the object of unwanted affection for many.

She kicks, but even her muscularly-defined legs strike nothing as she's lifted into the air.

They slam her into a hard-backed chair and secure her right forearm in clamps on a metal table. The last soldier tears away the paper gown covering her right arm. One clamp prevents her wrist from moving her elbow. Both bands prevent her from leaving the chair. Two of the four walls are a hard-clear plastic. Men in lab coats scribble on clipboards. The wall adjacent to the metal table raises.

The two lab coats enter. Ellsberg prepares a syringe injection.

They disregard Amanda's protests, questions, and curses. She kicks at them but they seem to stand behind an invisible border just out of her reach.

Familiar moan-howls jerk her head to an opening wall. The scientists ignore her. Secured by a steel Trapline Catch Pole, two soldiers force a snarling dead man at the table.

Screams pitching high enough to bleed eardrums emanate from Amanda.

Ten months to shape her lower body into the perfect dancing legs—gone. Five family members demanding she survive to carry on their memory—over. Three living people she was forced to kill to survive—all for nothing.

The teeth grip her skin.

They clamp.

With her arm secure, her instincts to jerk away are prohibited. This prevents the monster from tearing flesh. It must bite again. It chews at her flesh unable to break the skin immediately.

More chewing.

Fear swells in her. Each bite failing to break the skin draws out the inevitable. She will soon be one of the undead. Her flesh buckles and a bloom of blood mushrooms from her arm.

They yank the undead creature away before it eats anymore.

Amanda closes her mouth. No point in screaming. It's over. She's dead. Everything she fought to keep—stolen.

The glasses-wearing scientist clicks a stopwatch. Ethan inserts the needle into her left arm vein. Any desire to fight him off leaves her. She could scratch him. For some reason, she focuses on his golden name tag.

Logically, she assumed they drew blood to check the growth rate of the germ-filled bite. She has seen people turn seconds after a bite and others take days. Only stinging warmth itches her right arm.

They injected her!

"What the fuck?"

"Female subject has received full dose of Kalocin."

They step back as the clear wall lowers, sealing Amanda's last few minutes as a lab rat. "I've never heard of this drug, Dr. Burton."

"My great uncle was made aware of it during a microbe outbreak in Arizona during 1969. It will cure cancer."

"They keep it under wraps to increase research funding?"

"In this case, no. It cures at the cost of the host's life."

"But in our subject's instant she's doomed to die anyway."

"Not if the cure works, Dr. Ellsberg."

CHAPTER THREE

PRIVATE AMIE SANCHEZ steps off the running board of the semi as the air brakes hiss. Noise undoubtedly attracts unwanted guests. A second semi towing a flatbed screeches to a stop followed by a military Humvee.

A dark, short-haired girl jumps from the Humvee, drawing a Glock.

"Karen, this the place?" Amie draws her own Glock.

"You've made enough noise to bring the dead," Karen snaps. *It took me all winter to convince Ethan to let me lead a scavenging team and now this military tramp—in camp less than a week—has a command position. She must have found a way to convince Ethan she has the skills.*

Frank crawls from the passenger side of the Humvee in his EMT BDUs. Kalvin, the third member of her team, scales the semi-trailer ladder. Unslinging a rifle, he assumes a lookout position. Others disembark from the back of the semi strategically assuming defensive positions around the vehicles.

"Let's get the trucks loaded." Amie waves her index finger in a circle above her head, sending those not on guard duty toward the Orscheln's Farm and Home store.

"It may be on the edge of town. Nothing to draw a lot of biters, but we've got to be careful," Karen reminds her. "We don't have tanks and gunships to back us up."

Amie senses animosity from Karen, not sure what she did to earn it. She marches toward the store entrance. The glass under the door handles has been smashed to allow entry by looters. She nods at Herman.

The tall, dark-skinned man jams a crowbar in between the downs and cracks the bolt.

"This place still has a lot of supplies. After we sweep for biters, move in filling the totes with items on your list first. If the trailer has room, we'll empty the store starting from the back. You'll only have natural light so be careful. Questions?"

"We've all done this before," Herman reminds her. "With Ethan."

Amie now recognizes the source of the animosity. *I'm not a part of this team. I shouldn't be spearheading a mission yet. Not even in the military would I be given a command. Why did Ethan think it was a brilliant idea to insert the recent military additions into leadership roles? Didn't consider the seniority aspect, or did they? I must gain respect of these people more qualified to be outside the fence among the undead than me. All my training as a soldier gave no prep time in dealing with the undead.* If possible, without losing face, she will defer to suggestions of her team.

"While we sweep the building, load the fencing supplies on the flatbed." Amie draws a flashlight in her left hand. She flicks it on, resting her right wrist over her left so she can swing her arm, illuminate, and be ready to fire her Glock.

Following her with an MI6 at the ready, Private David Combeth notes, "They aren't happy you're in charge of this operation."

"Karen and her team scout a location. Then bring back a crew to pilfer the place. No telling how many times they've completed such a task in the last ten months." She takes each step down the aisle with caution. Her eyes have yet to fully adjust to the dim light. "I wouldn't be happy if a less experienced recruit—" *having never faced down the undead* "—was promoted over me."

"They're not military," Combeth says.

"We have to work with these people. They've their own command structure. Technically, we aren't military anymore."

"We didn't come in and take over. Their own leader put you in charge of this operation. He has worked us in where we'll do the most good. Other than the doctor, we all sleep in the community center. People here before us get priority on the next available houses. That would upset me more than who leads the grocery runs."

The shelves remain full of items. A rat scuttles away from the light.

"A good sign there are no biters in here."

"Don't count on it." He snatches a dust-covered bottle of Bronco Equine Fly Spray. "Not much call for fly spray."

Amie side steps down the aisle, swinging into the next. "This place is packed. The candy at the checkout's gone, but there are racks of winter clothes. Good work overalls. They'd keep you warm."

"I don't think people had time to ransack. They just ran."

"Someone came back for the food, but who wouldn't want a rack of Snuggies?" She draws the gun barrel across the shirt rack. No empty hangers.

"From my talks with the scavenging team, many places have been left untouched and other areas are burnt to the ground. With no reasoning as to why."

"People, as a general rule, don't maintain reason during a crisis." Amie snatches a screwdriver from a rack of tools at the checkout. "Clear?"

"Clear," he confirms.

"Private Combeth, patrol the aisles, in case they need you, but stay out of their way." *Let's make friends.*

The sunlight blinds her for a moment. She flips off her flashlight before jamming the screwdriver under the door to keep it propped open. "It's clear." Amie holsters her Glock.

The people each grab an empty plastic tote from the trailer before entering the store.

Karen escorts Amie as she heads toward the Humvee. "I guess you'll be all right at this."

"Thanks." Amie remains unsure of what to make of the dark-haired girl.

"I'm just glad you military people want to work *with* us."

"Why wouldn't we?" She must build trust in her command.

"You're the largest group brought in and that concerns some people. One or two blend well, but fifty people...they could attempt to take over," Karen explains. "We may have to work hard, but we like how we are surviving."

"Most of the people on the trucks were civilians and have specific skill sets your leader requested."

"Dartagnan requested them," Karen mumbles. "Fort Leonard Wood was our last chance to easily find trained personnel. Everyone else we bring into the camp from now on will be random survivors."

"Your system works. You outlasted Fort Wood."

"You haven't dealt much with people living outside the wall of your base the last ten months." Karen decides later she'll share some Ethan stories about the kinds of people existing in the post-apocalyptic world.

"We've had our own issues, but we could sleep secure in our bunks." Kalvin raises his rifle.

Both Amie and Karen jump at the report.

"Hold your fire! SITREP!" Amie orders the men on top of the tractor trailer.

Kalvin fires again. The second man, Clint, calls down to her, "Herd!"

"What does that mean?" Amie asks.

"Nothing good." Karen pops a biter staggering around the semi-trailer. The half dozen people loading fence panels onto the flatbed clamber onto the trailer. They draw their weapons waiting for orders to fire.

Amie breathes deep for a moment. Panic will get them killed. *The safest place is locked inside the cargo trailer, but there's no time to get everyone in the store out.* She moves fast. *I can't lose anyone. I can't afford to lose anyone on my first command.* "Get inside!" she shrieks at the people handing totes to the two men loading the cargo trailer. "Lock the doors!"

"Karen, get on top of the cargo trailer and cover me." Amie jumps into the Humvee.

"The 50 cal will draw more attention!" Karen decides whether she trusts Amie or not.

Amie guns the motor, and the beast lurches forward.

Uncertainty holds Karen in place for a second, but the flood of shambling undead sends her legs into a sprint to the trailer. She counts five people getting into the truck as one cargo door swings shut. She hears the bolt snap, securing it. They modified all the doors to open from the inside. She grabs the rung welded to the side of the trailer and pulls herself up.

Bruce decides he must be inside the trailer instead of on the flatbed.

Even with the growing moan-howls of undead, Karen hears Bruce's ankle pop. Instead of turning around and climbing back up on the flatbed, Bruce hobbles toward the cargo trailer.

Amie smashes the Humvee through the child-enticing game machine stationed at the store's entrance sending dozens of plush stuffed toys raining everywhere. She slams the Humvee against the building, indenting the door frame but effectively blocking the entrance with the vehicle. She leaps from the Humvee and fires at the closest biter.

The thundering crack of her weapon gives ankle-boy a moment of reprieve as the undead turn their attention to her.

Karen reaches for the next rung. She admires Amie for entering harm's way to save someone she's just met. "Bruce, get back to the flatbed!" Fingers grasp her arm as Clint helps jerk her on top of the trailer.

Bruce continues hobbling toward the cargo trailer. The second door slams closed and bolts shut. Five are more important than one. Everyone on the flatbed takes aim with their weapons. Some biters remain limber enough to climb onto the bed. No one fires. Multiple gun shots will charm the biters who have failed to notice the people on it.

Bruce limps away from the shambling biters. Rotten skin dangles from festering muscle tissue. Coagulated blood stains the ragged clothing. They reach with emaciated fingers.

Karen waves for them to scramble on top of the semi pulling the flatbed. The roof will be crowded for five people but safer. Even if the biters ascend onto the flatbed she doubts they scale the semi.

Amie sprints toward Bruce. She wants to scream at him, but she wants to hold back on the noise. The orchestra of moan-howls lacks a unifying purpose. Once she fires it all goes to hell.

Why hasn't the fool drawn his own weapon? He has a pistol holstered on his belt. Fear will be the death of this idiot, not the bites he's about to receive.

She fires.

A biter's shoulder explodes in a mass of inky oil. Congealed body fluids spray surrounding biters. The wound would have incapacitated a living person and bleed out. The biter merely continues his shuffle-drag step toward its meal, unnoticing it now has only one arm.

Clint takes aim, popping a biter in the skull. He aims again. Head shots are the most difficult, but if he remains calm and take his time accuracy is assured. Firing blindly into this growing herd does nobody any good and wastes his limited supply of ammo.

Amie prays Combeth keeps those inside the building calm and alive. Dozens of biters now stand between her and Bruce. Worse, twice as many biters stagger between her and the rung ladder to the top of the cargo trailer. Returning to the Humvee would be a death sentence. The other entrance doors are blocked from opening to prevent any biters from crawling through. The cab of the truck hauling the flatbed is higher and lockable. No matter what choice she makes, she must abandon Bruce to the biters.

Amie won't let that bother her. If she makes a command decision, it must stand. Bruce has made a choice.

The good of the group outweighs the panic of some dumb manchild. Amie knows Bruce wasn't from the military base so he's managed to survive for ten months. The surge of stupidity makes no sense.

Putrefaction of once-people fills the air. More and more undead stream into the parking lot creating a river of moaning rot. Amie bolts for the semi-truck. She scampers into the cab as flesh-peeled hands grab her legs. Together, dozens of corpses are stronger than the Private. She kicks, smashing a biter jaw. The crunching bone and torn skin would send a living man to the ER, but this creature continues to reach for her. It has no pain receptors only a hunger for living tissue. Amie holds onto the door frame for her life as dozens of hands tug her out the door.

A shot rings out from above. Hands release her leg. Another shot. The release of pressure on her body allows Amie to grab the steering wheel and pull with every bit of fear-inspired strength she has. A third shot removes another set of hands from her legs, allowing her to heave herself inside but not before the door slams. Warm goop soaks her leg. She can tell it's not from a bite, but the smell of fresh blood chums the wave of undead.

Moan-howls pierce the air. They grab and paw at the door. Amie seizes the handle and slams it on the arms reaching for her before any of the undead figure out how to crawl into the cab. She slams the door again. The crunch of fingers and bones echo around her. None of the biters flinch. She slams the door again. This time some fingers break off and sprinkle on the floormat. Her final slam smashes through an arm and the door seals. She thumps the lock and scoots away from the door, finally able to breath.

Amie jerks a bandana from a pouch in her uniform and ties it around her leg. She hopes to staunch the bleeding with pressure, avoiding tying a tourniquet. She had only days of battlefield medic training, but knows a tourniquet is the last resort. Amie doesn't have the allotted time to reach a doctor if she does. She thinks just skin layers were torn open and prays the blood will stop soon. She pops the clip from her Glock making sure she still has plenty of loaded ammo. She now must figure out how to save her team as an endless flood of undead fill the parking lot.

If she had time, she'd pull the cross from around her neck and kiss it thanking the Virgin Mary for not getting bit. A tapping on the passenger side glass draws her attention. None of the biters have made it to this side of the vehicle yet. She rolls down the window. A young, thin woman with chestnut hair braided into a whip-like ponytail flips inside.

"Too many of us on that roof." Someone hands down a rifle to her through the window. "What's the plan?"

"Becky, isn't it?"

"Good memory. Now, remember how to get us out of this," the thin girl blasts.

Amie draws in a breath. Calm is key. But none of her combat training has prepared her for this. She has to remain in command or this group will fall apart and they will all die.

"We have four options." Amie's mind comes up with four ideas quick. "We thin the herd. We drive this truck out of here, shoot the biters from down the road and draw them away from the building allowing our people to get out and into the semi-trailer."

"That's actually a sound idea," Becky praises.

"You haven't heard my other ideas."

"Do I need to?" Becky asks.

Amie didn't have any more plans. This one seems sound. "I can't drive the semi."

Becky sticks her head out the window. "Kenneth, we need a driver," she calls.

The slender, beak-nosed man slides in. He crawls over the two girls into the driver's seat. "Where we going?"

None of these people question her. It makes Amie wonder why Bruce panicked. These non-military people trust the person Ethan placed in command without question. "Drive over these biters and down the road. I want to pick as many off as we can, give our people a chance to evacuate from the building to the cargo trailer."

"Why not just use the 50 cal. on the Humvee?" Kenneth asks.

"You dumb nut. It will cut through those biters and the tires of the cargo trailer. You want to change one of those out here? 'Cause my road side assistance has expired," Becky snaps at him.

Amie doesn't admit she hadn't thought of that. She had considered trying to reach for the 50 cal. She must forget military tactics. They only work on the living.

Becky pounds the roof yelling, "Hold on."

Kenneth grinds the truck into gear. The crunching of undead turns to splatters as the truck picks up speed.

As they barrel down the road, loose fence sections are flung from the flatbed. Rolls of woven wire bounce off and land on the undead. Arms fail and legs kick but without the weight smashing the skulls, the creatures remain animated. All the racket confuses the biters. Some lumber after the truck. Others investigate the newly-splattered bodies for sources of nourishment.

Amie's vest pocket beeps. *How could I forget?* She fumbles for the radio.

"What the hell are you doing, Private Sanchez?" screams the voice.

She presses the button, shouting back, "Saving you asses. Don't fire on the biters. I'm going to draw them away. When it's clear, you get everyone in the cargo trailer and haul ass back to Acheron, Combeth."

"Copy."

Becky hangs out the window. Her rump and top of her red thong exposed to the world. She lines up each one of her shots before squeezing the trigger. Biters slumping to the ground—officially dead. Two more turn from Orscheln's parking lot and scramble toward the flatbed. Amie orders, "Make every shot count." She turns to Kenneth. "If we get overrun, drive further down the road. We'll keep doing this until we draw them all away."

"Is this going to work?" Kenneth asks.

Fuck if I know, Amie thinks. "They like noise. We'll give them enough noise to follow."

The air horn bellows.

Warm, coagulating blood pools in her boot. Since Amie doesn't have access to a window to fire she has a moment to examine the wound. The door slammed on her hard. *Hard enough to crush the bone, maybe, but it doesn't feel broken.* She removes the first-aid kit from the glove box.

"Did you get bit?" Kenneth slams on the breaks grinding the gears into park.

One of the three people on the roof topples onto the hood rolling off onto the pavement before the semi.

Becky catches the rifles knocked from her hands from the instant jolt. Had it hit the pavement she doubts she could help whoever fell off the roof.

"What the *fuck*, Kenneth?"

"Amie's bleeding."

Becky grabs at Amie's Glock with her left hand. During the tussle, she demands, "Are you bit?"

"Door crushed my foot. It's bleeding."

Becky raises her hand. "Are you positive?"

After the "everyone works or they don't eat" rule of Acheron, the second, and unspoken, is we shot all those who are bit.

Pounding echoes on the roof followed by panicked calls for assistance.

"We've got someone on the ground. I'm not bit."

Becky accepts Amie's response as gospel, crawling halfway out the passenger window.

"Clay's on the ground!" Jason hollers.

Biters flood from the tree line.

"Cut the engine. Becky, wait to fire."

Mark climbs from the roof to the hood peering over the front of the semi.

Rifle reports.

Clint fires with less accuracy at the biters cleaning the flesh from Bruce's bones. Kalvin fires into the massing throng of undead. Those chasing the semi turn back toward the cargo trailer. Once the herd shifts toward them they both drop flat out of sight and keep their weapons ready making as little noise as possible. When the moment comes, they must destroy any straggling biters to protect those about to flee the store.

"This has gone cluster." Becky flings open the cab door. "Mark, you have thirty seconds to get Clay." She raises her rifle. "Count to thirty," she orders Amie.

Amie accepts Becky's order. *I should not allow an underling to have control in this situation.*

Kenneth leans out the window waiting to pop any biters reaching the flatbed.

Biters scramble, surrounding the flatbed, attracted to the blood from Clay's road-rashed body. Mark struggles to drag his companion to the flatbed.

To staunch the bleeding, Amie cuts her pants along the seam. *I hope I can repair them. The combat fatigues are functional and comfortable, and I won't get another trip to the PX to replace them.*

Her handheld walkie chirps with Combeth's voice, "The biters have moved away from the door."

"Wait," Amie barks back into the radio. She reaches twenty-nine in her head. "Thirty."

Becky drops a biter. "Get your ass on the truck."

"Kenneth, get us moving." Amie clicks her radio. "We're going to pull further down the road. When the parking lot clears, get those people into the cargo trailer and haul ass home, understand?"

"Understood," crackles back.

She taps Kenneth on the shoulder. "Pull us down the road. Blare the horn."

"Wait!" Becky protests.

Mark flips Clay's legs onto the flatbed. He leaps up, avoiding a biter.

"There're on." Becky empties her rifle.

"Go."

The young man does as he's instructed. Blaring the foghorn sound until it deafens all of them.

Amie slaps pressure pads on the wound. She was afraid to examine it too close, but it looks like part of the door cut her deep. And blood loss has lightened her bronze skin.

Kenneth allows the truck to roll forward at a speed the biters keep pace with.

The repeating thundering boom of a .50 cal rattle through them. Combeth fires away, incinerating mostly chest cavities of the undead, sending streams of bloody confetti. Frank pulls the Humvee between the building and the cargo truck. Combeth uses suppressive fire to prevent the biters from getting at the people escaping into the cargo truck. Many of them carry the last tote they packed.

Amie clicks the radio mic, but screaming at Combeth about the waste of ammo won't be heard. She needs to salvage this mission.

Despite the metal shield constructed to deflect the empty brass ejecting from the cannon back into a metal box welded to the Humvee, only about seventy percent of the smoking hot empty cartridges land in the box. Someone will reload them. Combeth lowers the barrel, decimating legs of the dead—slowing their attack.

The cargo trailer doors snap shut.

The road is besieged now with the beleaguered and tormented bodies of still functioning undead. Many have lost limbs, but with intact brain stems they keeps crawling toward the loudest noise source.

The semi pulling the cargo trailer roars to life. Speeding from the lot, crushing dozens of the fallen undead. The Humvee follows through the goop. This location will be a draw for more biters for days as the massive amounts of noise will have attracted every biter in the county. Combeth doubts anything else will distract them from that path. He pops a biter in the head as they speed away.

CHAPTER FOUR

DANZIGER YANKS THE kitchen drawer open. He fishes through the junk finding nothing of use. He clicks the front stove burner on. Blue flames pop into existence. Taking a pot from under the sink, he shoves it under the tap before flipping it open. Water trickles out. Filling half the vessel before the pressure ceases, he places the pot onto the crackling flame.

No sense in watching water boil. He locates a bathroom. He swipes a bottle of Tylenol, some feminine hygiene pads, along with cotton towels. *Why don't people have medical kits? Even the stupid miniature ones from the dollar store? So damned unprepared.*

Using a serrated steak knife, he cuts the cotton towels into strips. He drops two cloths into the boiling water—using salad tongs, he retrieves one rag, dangling the dripping cloth over the pot. He has little water to waste. Danziger holds out his left forearm. The heat stings, scalding the flesh—and he hopes—the infection.

The scalding water flushes away the dirt and caked blood from the lacerations induced by the modified bear trap Levin used to secure him. Slices of flesh if laid open would reveal bone. The damaged tissue swells red, but any further contagion should be forestalled. He picks a large flake of rust from the cuts with tweezers. Once clean, he staunches any fresh blood flow with a feminine hygiene pad and ties it down with the cloth strips.

Those undead bastards love the smell of blood.

Flipping the flames off, he pulls out another rag. It's harder to work his left hand to flip the cloth onto his right forearm. He manages to clean most of the wound, scalding it to kill the infection. He presses on the large cut, pushing the pad against the gash. *I nearly severed my hands to reach Levin only to have the bastard escape in a military convoy. It traveled away from Fort Leonard Wood. Where would they go? Why would it go? The man who seemed to lead them wasn't military. I should have ran to them. Fuck, they'd have shot me as a crazy mother.*

Danziger secures the pads using his teeth to tie the strips. He takes a pitcher with a plastic lid from the dishwasher. *It will take time for the water to cool to drink but it's sterile.*

If they only knew what kind of man they rescued.

Danziger would start with the love for his daughter and how that bastard stole her. It wasn't just his little girl, it was other teens too. The bastard put them down first. Danziger was so close to identifying the serial murdering rapist. Then his girl went missing. Fucking law. His own daughter and he had to cease police work on the case. Conflict of interest. Nothing would allow him to work his daughter's disappearance short of quitting the police force. He needed to be a cop. Nothing prepared him for when they found her body.

He takes a scrap of towel to wipe away the bubbling snot from his nose.

He dry swallows some Tylenol. He glances around the kitchen one last time, spotting a broom with a wooden handle. He snatches it up. Danziger swallows some of the lukewarm water to unstick the pill lodged in his throat.

Once outside, he slams the broom end against the porch, snapping off the straw end. The bristles flip over and over down the porch slamming against the tire of a bicycle. He admires the splintered point and then stares at the bike.

Dragging the bike down the steps before straddling the seat, he attempts to figure out how to hold the lance and ride. He fills the squeeze bottle attached to the frame. Danziger wheels the bike down the gravel lane.

His first few pedals are shaky, but within ten feet on the blacktop he steadies. Keeping the broom handle as if he were a jousting knight, he gains speed.

I'm healthy. Able to ride some fifty miles in a day—in a fantasy. Those vehicles had a tow truck, so even stopping to clear the highway they will disappear long before I catch up. And the undead and a safe place to change the bandages. Infection may take my hands. As he sweats, his arms itch under the pads.

Foolish. Danziger debates with himself over his course of actions. *Yesterday, I was willing to lop off one of my own hands to kill the man who murdered my daughter. It took the end of the world for me to find Levin. Now he's escaped in those trucks and my actions will kill me.*

Focus on the road.

Besides possible DK attacks or pot holes, some living person may want my bike. Steal what I stole. Half a jug of clean drinking water is all I own. People have killed over less. He doesn't count the stick.

Danziger brakes. Had he been on any vehicle other than a pedal bike he'd have miss the broken tree branches. The torn green bark dangles from splintered limbs. A truck had turned from the road to the dirt farm field, cutting ruts in the grass and ripping limbs from a tree hanging too low.

Lacking other evidence, the cracks were caused by the military convoy. Danziger decides the risk is justified. *How many trucks large enough to cause this damage are on the road?* All the armored vehicles, including an army tow truck, attracts more attention than the undead. Cutting cross country provides cover, less living to avoid, and masks the noise.

Tracking the truck's possible route with the ruts in the field. Without anyone to cut hay, the growing stalks remained massed and bent from recent wheeled travelers. Too rough for a bike designed for blacktop, Danziger hops off and pushes it through the grass following the smashed stalks.

Western or easterly direction, I'm not sure which way this group will end up, but whichever way they zig-zag to conceal their destina-

tion, the convoy's heading north, and they'll have to return to the road if they plan to cross the Missouri River.

Danziger jerks at the new lock on the chain before lifting the bike over the gate. *Even if they wanted to conceal their trip across country by padlocking the chain, the muddy ditch has fresh Grand Canyon-sized ruts leading to the blacktop which gives them away.* He straddles the bike. His forearms blaze. Little needles peck at the gashes. Never one for praying even when his little girl was stolen by the Blonde Teen Slasher. Even when Levin taunted him with envelopes full of his little girl's body hair was he ever tempted. *God, just allow me enough life left to eliminate a child slayer.*

In a world bound in constant cruelty, grant me this one desire. I promise it will be the only thing I ever ask, God, even if it means my own demise at the hands of the undead.

Guessing he's been on the pavement for five miles, Danziger notices displaced gravel on a county turnoff. Not enough to be the entire convoy but one truck. He sips at his remaining water, heavy with decision. *I may never be able to keep up with the vehicles, a wrong choice now certainly will end my chance of finding Levin.*

The choice hinges on why one truck would leave the group.

After a full minute of contemplation, the former St. Louis police detective bets on the full convoy. *Even if by some miracle I find them, odds are the large assembly will know where the single truck is.*

No more signs of anything leaving the blacktop as the sun crests on the horizon. As much as he hates to, Danziger must find shelter. Any longer on the road and he'll miss valuable clues in his pursuit in blackness.

The first rays of morning sun poke through the woodshed wall slats. Danziger flips over. Before he rubs his bloodshot eyes, he forces his fingers to cease as they dig into the bandages. The urge to rip and tear at the itching scabs drives him to his feet. His thoughts swim. *Even the night I slept in the tree belted to a branch wasn't as uncomfortable as sleeping on those woodchips. Lack of proper medical*

care may cost me a hand, or both. He touches the back of his arm to his forehead—fever.
If I could just properly clean the wounds caused by the bear trap I'd improve my odds. Maybe I should locate some maggots in the wood.

Dilapidated with age, the woodshed seemed safer than the half-collapsed barn next to it. No farmhouse in sight or any kind of water well, Danziger wheels his bike to the road. He'll have to search the next home for some supplies.

Three days of scavenging and guessing, the last road I recognized was parallel to Highway 50. The convoy appeared to head toward Jefferson City, but there would still be ten-thousand DKs to battle through to cross the Missouri River. Hermann, the winery town, would be the next bridge. All these country roads mean little to a native of the city and the cross-country jaunts throw me off my bearings.

As the infection spreads, his body temperature rises and his thoughts cloud.

Hermann seems logical now I've lost the trail.

Danziger skids to a stop as the front bike tire shreds. Dismounting, he realizes that age has ruined the rubber. Grateful he noticed before he face-planted, he dumps the bike in the ditch.

As he surveys Hermann from the top of the hillside, Danziger wishes he had the bike for the trip down. At least he could coast until he had to start back up the main street toward the bridge.

As quaint as the town appears, it must have had a population in the hundreds, maybe thousands. Once down there if I encounter even a small herd my stick won't last.

Plenty of homes left unransacked—I hope. A police or fire department with medical supplies, maybe even an urgent care center, someplace to treat my arm damage. If nothing else, wine—enough wine to kill any pain. Danziger was never much for drinking beyond the celebratory glass when a case was closed. If I thought I had no shot to find Levin, I might.

Many DKs must be in this sleepy village. Hell, if someone was smart they'd turn the bridge spanning the Missouri River into a toll route. Collect supplies to cross.

Eventually, bridges across even small rivers will extract a price. If the military's plan pans out, all the major bridges spanning the Mississippi River border states are now defunct. Making this place one valuable piece of real estate.

Tom.

Tom went south, after all those people fleeing the sweeping hoard overwhelmed the convoy to Fort Leonard Wood. I abandoned him. He knew. He was helping me find my daughter's killer. I broke Tom's arm. I had to so we could escape the family who attempted to feed us to their undead relatives. The fever must be getting worse. Tom is south. But I am betting my hand the trucks went north.

As Danziger makes the jaunt down the hill, he decides he must get through the town quickly. The fallen population sign reads 2,431.

Way too many undead to deal with on this side of the river.

Pain radiates from his arms. They itch. Demanding he scratch open the cuts.

If you don't take care of your arms, what good does getting to the other side of the river do? You don't even know where to go once you get across.

Northeastern Missouri's sparsely populated. Large farmed areas and no bustling metropolises. A lifetime of searching.

Screams of...pleasure.

Voices. Must be in my head. Full on hallucinations will be next. Maybe I'll wake and the plague will be a dream.

Danziger wishes he'd paid more attention to the rest of the world falling apart. Instead, he and his partner spent time doing their jobs as cops. He assisted in keeping order as St. Louis prepared for a siege. A siege no one fully understood.

It took months for St. Louis to fall to the undead. Stories filtered in from other locations of the infection spreading swifter causing communications to be censored and nothing outside the city was reported to the masses or most of those keeping order.

400 MILES TO GRACELAND

He never had time to listen.

Levin caught a ride in the caravan fleeing St. Louis to Fort Leonard Wood. His murderous tendencies overwhelmed him and he caught a teenage girl to act out his sick fantasies.

Danziger was careless in his pursuit and was captured by Levin who took sick pleasure in forcing Danziger to watch his unnatural acts on the teen. The perverseness extended further as Danziger knew these same transpiring events were performed on his own child.

Danziger stumbles. *In this new world, no one will ever think to stop a serial killer. No one would even notice another mutilated corpse. I'm the only one. God. I'm the only one left to stop him.*

New motivation propels him forward. *Search some houses. Clean my wounds. Find something for the fever.*

The river wafts on the breeze but along with the scent of water a more manmade smell brings him pause.

Camp fires have an aroma unlike a house or car fire—a pleasant, intentional smell.

No melted plastic or charred electrics in the fragrance, but a peaceful relaxing bouquet. Anyone brazen enough to create a campfire also lacks fear of the undead, which means weapons or numbers. Could mean medicine. Danziger has nothing to offer any group except a dirty appearance resembling more undead than a police detective. With blood-stained bandages, they may shoot him before they care to find out if he has a pulse.

He moves low through the tree line in the hopes not to catch a bullet. Screaming about his approach might also cost him, but he needs to know what sort of people are nearby before he reveals himself.

The overgrown park has a two-stall restroom bunker in reach of the trees. The fecal stink might mask his blood scent. Danziger worms his way toward the structure until his picture of the group focuses. Three people wail on a man in a black duster. He spots a corpse on the ground with a lead pipe embedded into its skull.

He eyes the group from behind the concert bunker restroom. They scatter leaving the tall man on the ground bootless and beaten as they scavenge his equipment. He wonders how such a stupid group has survived for so long. A man traveling well-armed and equipped should have his hands bound before they wandered away from him.

The bludgeoned man on the ground sounds as if he may be a part of an organized group. Makes him valuable alive. Any well-provisioned individual might have knowledge of the military convoy. Danziger prays his thoughts are not fever induced.

He contemplates letting them complete the litter. *I can't carry this monster-sized dude by myself, but I could drag the litter. I've to get the gun away from the leader.*

Danziger uses all his cop experience to size up the greasy-haired punk with tattooed arms and drooping earlobes where he once had huge gauges in them. *He can't be educated beyond high school, if he ever graduated. The scrawny man cares only for the oversized boots he tromps around in. It's the girl with the short, choppy hair who will be a problem. She's smart. The real leader of the group. She lets the droopy earlobe kid think he's running the show while she pulls his strings.*

Watch out for her.

They drag some long branches back and the knife-cut hair girl lashes them together.

"How do you know how to do all this?" the scrawny man asks.

"I read a book once," she snaps. "Just entertain yourself with Cybele." She jerks a thumb at the concert bunker where a mousey girl staggers from the stall.

She smooths out her kilt.

Five.

I missed her completely. Despite her weak appearance, I doubt she'd have lasted this long if she were helpless.

"You'll get her in a minute." The kid with droopy earlobes drags the mousey girl by the arms to a picnic table, bends her over, and flips up her kilt so he has access to her.

Disgusted, Danziger understands how the knife-cut hair girl controls the group. While engaged in lust, the droopy ear-lobed kid will be distracted.

The knife-cut hair girl ties off the end of the triangular litter while the scrawny man lashes a rat-eaten blanket.

None of them notice Danziger until he slams the Beretta scooped from the grass into the droopy-eared kid's face.

The gun has enough weight to have rounds in the clip—one in the chamber?

Danziger smacks the hilt of the gun into the kid's face again.

The mousy girl slumps under the table without a sound, her lower body uncovered as her *lover* collapses. Danziger keeps the gun on the knife-cut haired girl and one eye on the fallen man with the pipe through his face. At the moment, no one seems to care if he's dead—his brain intact.

"Who the fuck!" she demands.

Blood squirts from the fountain replacing the droopy eared kid's nose.

Danziger fights his natural urge to answer *police. I haven't been a cop in months.*

"Just walk away, lady. I need to question this guy." He nods the gun at the beaten man.

"You want his hideout. You *fucking* want his hideout!" she screams.

"I need him." The cop in him—the person who seeks revenge for his daughter—keeps him from pulling the trigger in cold blood.

"We share his hideout. We can share all we've got. Take a turn on Cybele and help us carry him," the scrawny man offers.

There's nothing to consider. The choppy haired girl will kill me the first chance she gets. No hesitation. I spotted it in her eyes. She's hoping I'll want to pump the mousey Cybele and gut me while I'm distracted. I'd bet she stabbed dozens of men while they raped the poor girl.

The knife-cut hair girl takes a second option when she notes Danziger doesn't even glance toward Cybele. He hasn't even reflected on the girl's exposed ass.

The shiny .357 magnum is too heavy for her to swing quickly. Danziger puts one bullet in her chest before her arm fully rotates. A second bullet in the scanty booted man and a third kills the ear-lobe kid. Knife-cut hair girl gurgles a bloody breath. He puts a round in her forehead. Before he gives death to the scrawny man, shots ring out.

Danziger swivels on his heels and crouches low. Cybele bleeds on the grass, a lead pipe in her hand. The man he intended to rescue holds a smoking .22 pistol nearly hidden by his large hand.

Danziger's police training reminds him why they pat down suspects. *This guy probably has another gun or two on him. How did they get the jump on such a well-prepared individual?* He wonders, *Maybe the naked girl's ass distracted his eye?* He rolls Cybele over to put a bullet in her skull and spots the tiny red dot exactly in the center of her forehead. *The badly beaten man with a swollen eye has deadly aim. If he had wanted me dead, I would be.* Danziger ends any chance of the ear-lobed boy raising from the dead.

Trust might be too much to ask for from the beaten warrior. His gun and canteen are military issue. He could have taken them off a dead soldier. Danziger assumes the man came from a well-stocked camp. He's recently shaved and lacks body odor.

Ethan drops his arm still clinching the .22. He coughs. His body spasms. Pain finally escapes him in a whimper.

Danziger's certain this man never cries in pain. Not so much as a single moan emanated from him from the seconds of the beating he witnessed.

Ethan coughs up sputum.

Danziger forces himself to glance at the mucus pile. *No red means no internal bleeding has manifested, yet.*

Something makes Danziger ask, "Do you want your pack?"

The beaten man whispers, "What did you do before...before the biters?"

Of all the things to ask. "I was a cop. Detective. Worked homicides." Puzzled, he asks, "Do you need me to help you?"

"There are rules at my camp."

"You're concerned about this now? I'm offering to help. I could've slit your throat and be on my way." Danziger scoops up an unopened water bottle from the grass.

The beaten man clinks the barrel of the tiny gun against something metal in his pocket. "I've access to supplies."

A trade. "I'll get you back to your friends. You stock me with gear. Then I'm on my own. I've got to find someone."

"I'll make sure you're well supplied. Whatever you can carry. Or you stay...and work." Ethan's breathing labors.

Danziger takes a drink, letting some of the water splash from his mouth onto his face and neck. "Water?" he offers.

"Your arms?"

"I'm not bit. I escaped a human attack. The wounds are infected." Danziger swallows some Tylenol.

Ethan's body tightens as he reaches into his coat pocket. He produces a plastic-covered map. "Find Highway 19. Follow it north." He gives into the pain, passing out.

Danziger grabs the map.

"Follow 19."

He doesn't bother to correct the wounded man about Hermann being on Highway 19. "Not quite the same as follow the yellow brick road."

Eating a protein bar pilfered from the man's gear gives Danziger the energy to complete the litter. He rolls the fallen warrior onto the nasty blanket. Collapsing next to him, he drinks deep from the canteen. "You're one big dude. Not much of a talker. I wish you were. You've got folds in this map not along the factory ones. They reveal a planned route only you understand. I need you to get you back."

He splashes a small amount of water onto his neck. "If those bandits had killed you the map would have meant nothing to them. It would keep your friends safe. I figure you've got a few. You do supply runs for them. You're too clean not to have a safe haven close by. I hope they have meds for my fever." *God, let the convoy have gone there.*

Underbrush rustles.

Danziger grips the .357 now holstered on his hip. A rabbit darts across the road. "Glad I don't have to fire this hand cannon of yours. It will attract the entire neighborhood of those undead bastards. Why aren't there more staggering around?"

He grabs the ends of the litter poles and marches on. "You could wake up long enough to make sure I'm heading where you want me to go. I could use help. I'm sweating from this infection. I'll follow 19 north like you said. Your people better be there."

CHAPTER FIVE

EMILY PULLS CLUMPS of her blonde hair away from her head in order to glare at the brittle strands. She'll dump the expensive conditioner she liberated from the canteen on some unsuspecting girl. Back to dollar store cheap stuff to liven her hair again. Maybe she'll trade it for some fingernail polish. Her toes are in desperate need of color. She'll have to remember not to wear her sandals when Ethan returns. He'll berate her again for using her free time to beauty herself.

At fifteen her entrusted responsibly at Acheron leaves her feeling less important than those securing the gate. Some surely consider hers a cushy job especially if they knew she had time to consider painting her toe nails. But dispensing books, movies, and working electronic devices allowed people to relax and stay sane during their down time. Removing a few hours of worry from each day about the millions of undead wandering outside the compound was what had been lacking in the military refugee camp.

Others in the camp might be qualified to operate a lender library. She knows of two teachers, but one was a crack shot. Emily qualified to carry the .22 on her hip, but not accurately enough to guard the fences. Her failure with the posthole digger was epic since she lacked the muscle tone to carry the tool. Days of lugging it around might pack on some meat to her arms, but the work quota expected would cost her meals defeating the purpose of the hard labor.

Given time allowed for reshelving and checking out DVDs, she contemplates why she was given this job at fifteen. Her best answer—not many viable fifteen-year-olds are left in world. Everything in this camp must work as the mantra states, 'You don't work you don't eat.' Even the well-fed cattle serve as meals. Eventually, her value as a mother will take precedence over librarian if humanity continues. She's old enough to become a mother, so why wouldn't Ethan make her a woman when she offered herself to him? He balks at her age. A poor excuse when living people are needed to make this camp work and those born into their world will learn to survive its dangers quicker than those forced into it.

Maybe at fifteen she only crushes on the man who rescued her from certain mutilating rape instead of being in love with him. A good reason to love someone. Her assignment to merely track and rent out books and DVDs for entertainment has spiraled into whispers she was given the task for an exchange of personal favors to the boss. The most popular and her favorite rumor by the plethora of women who attempted to win his affection but got nowhere. Uninterested in any romantic entanglements with women inside the fence, people figure he visits Emily secretly. She wishes. She offered herself to him fresh from the shower in naked unspoiled glory. Despite clear interest from the bulge in his pants, he refused her. She doesn't understand how not bedding her keeps him noble in a world when the old rules no longer apply. He's older; no one seems to know exactly how old, and she's fifteen. None of which should matter anymore. She's bled for over a year now and when people's life expectancy was age thirty-five it qualified a girl to be married off.

Emily wonders what the average life expectancy is now. *Does age even matter? The biters don't care about age. They only seek food.*

Rocked from her thoughts by the library door slamming open, Emily drops the stack of DVDs she was cataloging.

"Sorry, Emily. I didn't realize it would open so fast when I kicked." Major Ellsberg carries a cardboard box.

"The top bar thingy that automatically closes it broke. Now it takes the slightest push to move." She picks up her stack of fallen movies.

"Where can I work?"

"Pick a table. Shouldn't you be allocated an office?"

"They are building one as well as a radio room in one of the empty classrooms." He places the box on a table. "Do you have a laptop for me?"

Emily places her DVDs on the workstation before pulling out a laptop. "It should still be connected to the Wi-Fi printer. I tested it. It still works. Too bad all websites I've tried pop up error."

"I'll need to print photos of the fences where reinforcements are needed." He places a digital camera on the table. "Do we have area maps and any books on trains? I think we should add defensive spikes at the entrance."

Emily takes folded road maps from the top drawer in the workstation. "I've lots of state maps. Ethan raided a visitor center. He lives by these things." She waves a pamphlet. "I've got some local lake maps for fisherman as well."

"Road maps won't be out of date until we defeat the vectors and rebuild."

Emily types on her computer. "I have *The Big Book of Trains* and *The Bedtime Train* book. This was an elementary school."

"If you run across anything more adult on trains, bring it to me." Ellsberg unfolds the map. "Do you have any maps of this county?"

Emily jots down *trains* on a sticky note. "Dartagnan has constructed the best map of our compound."

"No argument there," Wanikiya says at the entrance. The Native American's one of the tallest people Emily's ever seen. He ducks under the door frame in order to enter the library. He's the best cook, feeding the camp and leading when Ethan scavenges, but he paints his face with John Wayne movie war paint. His face terrifies her. The way she expects an Indian seeking scalps would decorate his face. Wanikiya claims it's the warrior way of his people, which she's not sure if it's true or just Hollywood in order to scare the white people of the camp. Certainly, the polished silver tomahawk on his belt does.

She's secretly thrilled leaders of the camp use her library for discussions giving her access to information others in the colony aren't privy to. Ever since the fall of Fort Leonard Wood more former soldiers seem to be helping with camp operations. Many of the camps long term residents discuss heavily at dinner how much they disapprove.

Wanikiya spreads out a map with black marker outlining part of the camp fence. "Dartagnan's model representation of the camp is more accurate."

"I've inspected the fence, and drawn up where we need to reinforce immediately. I suggest you stop moving your west fence line," Major Ellsberg says.

"We need the land and the houses outside the fence," Wanikiya protests.

"I didn't say we stop reclaiming territory. We stake off a wall and put up several checkpoints to close off if needed in case of a breach. If the perimeter wall fails, the infected will flood the entire camp. This way we can shut off sections and maintain control."

"It will take a lot more fence."

"Yes. We keep everyone else safe in a breach event."

"You're not talking about full airlock security like our main gate?" Wanikiya confirms.

"No. Swinging or sliding gates. Some of them wide enough the cattle herd just move through if they are going to openly graze. We build tracks so even a four-year-old could pull them closed."

"The current scavenging team was designated to collect fence material from the farm supply store. The plan is to herd the cattle into smaller grazing areas and clean off the grass before moving them to a new section, utilizing as much fresh feed as possible," Wanikiya says."

I'm no farmer."

"The fencing crew's current expansion project will cut through the houses we desperately need to acquire."

"Populated areas need to be isolatable in case of breach," says Major Ellsberg.

"Dartagnan says we need more grass. But they're too cooped up in the community building. We need housing for all the new people first."

"Our food supply must have a food source. I can't believe you defer to a retard kid," says Major Ellsberg

Emily reminds the two men she's present. "He's not retarded. He's some kind of savant, of sorts."

"His ability to calculate in his mind what we need has made sure we survive," says Wanikiya

"I would not ever let the boss hear you call him anything but 'Dartagnan'," Emily advises.

The Major defers, "I shouldn't have called him a name. Any person who survived without fences can't be mentally challenged." He moves on. "In my examinations of the compound and the area we are expanding toward, are these railroad tracks." He thumps a location on the map. "I need a team to inspect them."

Wanikiya rubs his chin. "Trains make a lot of noise. It will attract more biters than those driving trucks deal with now."

"We'll work around that problem. I want to build our network of fences toward them. We build a supply station, put together a few cars, and use a train to cover longer distances safely. Freight trains run all over the country. Stop the train before a town, the noise will draw infected, and send a team into the town with less chance of danger."

"Portable scavenging teams," Wanikiya considers the Major's plan. "It will take some logistics and well-trained teams."

"We build our secure fence to the tracks then work our way back to the current compound. The teams will always have a fence to their backs and sweeping the newly fenced-in areas will take less time allowing the movement of people and cattle."

"I agree. But you are asking for a lot more fence we don't have and must scout to get," Wanikiya says.

Ellsberg explains, "At first we use the bigger single pieces of chain link for outer security. What will become the inner fences—we use what people put around their yards—and tie it together. It's not as strong but we are not expecting it to face the brunt of a herd like the outer fence. It is to prevent walkers from moving into the next section if something goes wrong. By that time your security forces should retake the area."

CHAPTER SIX

KAYLA OPENS THE window, letting sunlight into a twelve-bed hospital unit, converted from a former classroom. None of the privacy curtains are pulled as she has only one patient. He turns his head away from the light. She uncuffs the shackle around his wrist.

"I understand why you handcuff wounded, but am I not off the critical list yet?" asks Levin.

"The doctors are concerned any patient could die in the middle of the night. Camp rules you sleep in chains. Sorry. I do have good news. Today's the day, Mr. Smith. After you eat. We go outside."

"Call me Levin." *Smith as a last name is an easy lie to remember. Apparently, I gave away my first name under the medications they gave me when they repaired all the wounds from Danziger. I'll see many pretty blonde girls suffer for his attack. If I can't find one in this camp maybe nurse Kayla will satisfy my urge. She's older, but she's still pretty. Her scrubs hide her figure, but I'll transform her.* "I'm ready to stay out of this bed."

"I know, but some of those gashes could break open and bleed if they haven't been given time to completely heal first. So, we'll start slow." She brings him a tray of food, which includes scrambled eggs, potato cubes, and toast cut from a loaf of homemade bread. "I convinced them to give you some extra eggs this morning. You'll need the protein for energy with all the walking you are going to do."

"I thought I was getting off easy?" He spears an egg on the metal fork.

"The definition of easy around here is not the same as before the rise of the undead." She inspects the larger of the dozens of bandages protecting the holes where chunks of flesh were carved from him. None of them show signs of having bled through. "Tomorrow some of the stitches come out."

I've been out of bed. A paper clip allows for easy picking of the cuff lock. I've planned my own recovery therapy to rehabilitate myself and return to my passion without the knowledge of these overly helpful survivors.

They have built a secure compound preventing any infected from getting inside and when my health was questionable they kept me handcuffed to the bed. Now they make mistakes many living make—trust of a fellow human. My wounds left them with sympathy and I won't allow my advantage to slip by.

The armload of books hide the figure of a blonde-haired girl entering the room. Levin quells his excitement. *She is the correct age.* He won't tip his desires. *Before the end of the world I could go months without collecting a victim. I should heal and stalk them at my leisure. They have nowhere to go.*

"I brought some books for you to pick from. Might pass the time." Emily places them on the tray table. "I'll bring you something else if you don't like these. A few classics but mostly adventure stories."

"Thanks. Are there a lot of teenagers here? You're a little young to be a librarian." Levin's careful with his questions to prevent damage to the trust he's built with Kayla.

"Many older teens survived, especially those not spending all their time playing video games," Emily knows she sounds like Ethan.

"People are given jobs suited to their skills. Emily was selected based her aptitudes."

"Or lack of," she pats her .22. "I shoot well enough to carry, not well enough to be a fence guard."

"Books must be vicious here."

"Everyone carries." Kayla props her foot on the bed and rolls up her pant cuff to reveal an unshaven leg and ankle holster. "Once you are certified you will as well. And you'll be given a job."

Kayla chops up a weed with a long-handled hoe in an herb garden constructed outside the kitchen entrance.

"Is tending this garden part of your nursing duties?" Levin shifts his weight so most of it leans against a garden rake. A wheelchair rests behind him.

"Not really, but we don't have patients every day, so I like to help Wanikiya with it. The man's a genius chef, but some basil and dill improve the taste. He's got some peppers over there. When fall comes I can't wait to enjoy a hot bowl of spicy chili."

"Is this part of my therapy?"

"Getting out and moving is part of your therapy. We don't have the machines a sports rehab place would use. And hard work is the new norm here."

"Tending garden?" Levin asks.

"It can be relaxing. You move your entire body and you help with making our meals better."

"Sounds productive to me." He exaggerates his leg movement, thrusting it stiffly out. He tills the ground with the rake between two plants. "You have a lot of space between these plants; couldn't you fill it in with more?"

"If it were corn, but herbs need lots of breathing room and they are only harvested as they are needed."

"A nurse with a green thumb."

"Not really. I just listened as one of the gardeners who planted them."

"Does everyone here work together like this?" Levin asks.

"What we've built here hasn't been easy and there have been a few incidents. Mostly we've had a few people slack in their work and they lose a meal. After missing food for a day no one seems to fall out of line. People like to eat."

"I guess Mom was onto something when she sent me to bed without supper." Levin smiles. "Other crimes like stealing, muggings, fighting?"

"There's nothing to steal. No money is exchanged. We have more televisions and VCRs than people. Everyone carries a gun once they have been certified, and with everyone working there's not much time for fighting."

"Sounds utopic."

She pauses before saying, "For the most part."

"So, it's not perfect here?"

"If you break the main rules you could be exiled, but we do have one cardinal executable sin." Kayla doesn't share what she witnessed a month ago with the young Kyle.

"Are you not going to explain? I want to make sure I don't break that rule," says Levin.

"You don't look like a rapist."

CHAPTER SEVEN

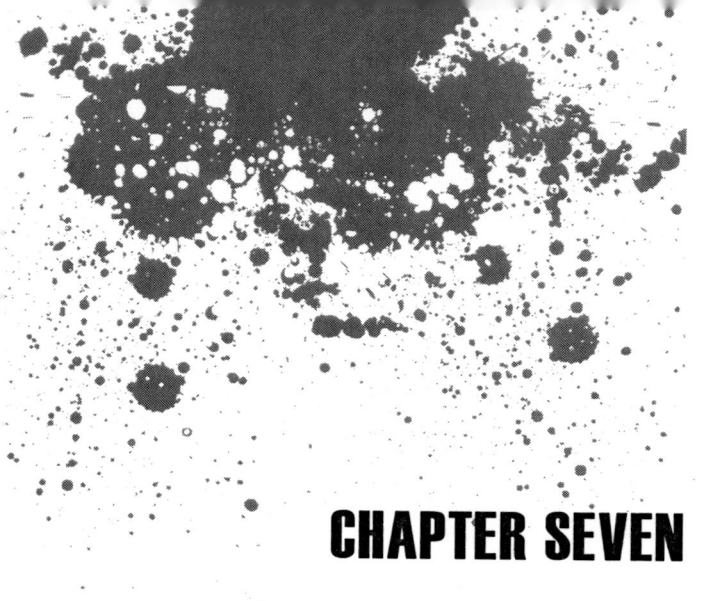

"STUPID COW."

Hannah shoves and punches the black beast, but it refuses to move. It takes little interest in the weak blows to its side, instead focusing on chewing the green leaves of a tomato plant.

"Ewwww." Hannah throws her shoulder against the monster using all her weight and still no movement.

She shoves even harder with her full body weight but gets no reaction. "I'm going to be in so much trouble."

A farm truck speeds up. Before the driver slams it into park, a boy about her age from the passenger side hops out.

"Gotonoutofhere!" he hollers.

The cow jerks its head still with a mouth full of tomato plant and scampers off.

"Sorry about that."

"Why are you apologizing?" She rubs her jeans with her palms in an attempt to clean them.

"That's one of the cows from my dad's farm. We just up and moved here and the cows don't know the boundaries yet."

"It would help if we had some fence." Nick slams the truck door.

Excited, Hannah jumps into his arms. Her blonde ponytail cracking him in the face like a whip.

"Good to see you too." He sets her down in his soldier mode, rubbing his cheek.

"They went to get fence to solve this problem. The cattle don't need to roam freely anyway. We need to fence in a small pasture. Let them clean it off and fertilize it then move them to a new pasture and repeat. It's easily done with some electric wire," the farm boy explains.

"Just because I'm brown doesn't mean I give a flip shit about farming. I was born in Detroit." Nick adds, "Jim Bob," as insultingly redneck as he can slur.

Hannah quickly changes the subject. "Electricity's something we've got plenty of."

"For sure." Jim Bob takes a .22 rifle from the truck. "You never realize how much you miss it until it's gone." He ignores Nick.

"I thought you were assigned to guard the dam?" she asks Nick.

"With all the new people to find jobs for, they just decided to leave everyone where they were and use the new soldiers to help place them in their new camp occupations. I've been with Simon getting anyone who needs checked out on weapons."

"Am I last?" *Finally. This was just an attempt to keep behind the fence. Dad's orders I'm sure.*

"You weren't a priority for gun clearance like the soldiers were. Jim Bob will take over your guard station."

"I can't move a cow," Hannah huffs.

Jim Bob leans against one of cattle panels running halfway around the field of tomatoes. "I've been doing it all my life, so it's no big deal. I'll keep them out of here and we'll have plenty of tomatoes to preserve for the winter. My mom's good at canning food."

"Is that all you farmers do is watch stuff grow?" Nick asks.

Hannah slugs him for being a jerk. Her punch has no more effect on him than it did the cow.

"Corporal, the day I stop watching stuff grow is the day you grow hungry." Jim Bob points to the rows of staked tomato vines. "You take that plant over here; if it wilts anymore, it needs to come out before it dies and harms any of the other plants. And even if it's just a weaker plant, removing it moves precious nutrients and water to go to the other plants allowing them to grow even stronger and make better tomatoes."

"I get it, you've got an important task. You keep us fed. I keep us safe. Seems like a good arrangement." Nick climbs into the truck.

"It does."

Hannah must slam the truck door on her second attempt to close it. Nick fires up the engine.

"You don't have to be such a d-bag."

"He's just some farm kid."

"I had a pretty easy life before the biters. I had no idea what goes into keeping food on our table," Hannah admits.

"Maybe you'll shoot well enough to be a guard over a farmer," Nick says.

"Maybe. If I could've moved that cow, I wouldn't feel bad about being assigned to protecting our food supply." She flips her ponytail. "Besides, being out in the sun so much has made my hair even blonder."

"Be careful you don't burn. There's a little aloe vera in the medical unit, and no sun screen, pasty white girl."

"I'll tan, just not as good as you."

He smiles at her, and then summons up the courage to ask, "Do you want to go out?"

"You mean like be your girlfriend?"

"No," falls out of his mouth way too quick. Nick backpedals, "I don't know what there is to do. Bowling is out and movies are possible, but I meant go on a date."

"You figure out what kind of *date* we can have, and I'll go with you."

"Would you consider shooting biters from a high vantage point a date?"

"You're not going to win any girl with that as your first date. Maybe a second, but definitely not the first." Hannah smiles.

"I'll find something special."

"What every girl wants to experience on her first date."

Nick parks outside the elementary school turned community center of the colony. He races around the truck to open the door for Hannah.

An older man with a grandfatherly face in military fatigues beats him to it. He introduces himself, "Chief Petty Officer Simon, US Navy retired. Small Arms Marksmanship Instructor."

"I remember meeting you at Fort Wood," Hannah says.

"Your father's status as base commander won't win you any Kewpie dolls here. You're going to have to shoot like everyone else."

Hannah nods.

"Right, now, soldier," he speaks to Nick, "I'm commandeering your vehicle."

CHAPTER EIGHT

AUSTIN DRAWS HIS finger over the edge of a badly faded Wal-Mart cash card. He releases it.

Catches it.

Releases it.

Catches it before it falls the twelve feet to the ground. He flips it again having worn the blue label from the plastic. Sighing, he repeats, releasing the card to catch it again. Earning his place on the gate as a crack shot does nothing to detract from the boredom of waiting for a passing biter or the never occurring survivor seeking sanctuary. The new group has military personnel; maybe he'll give his spot on the gate and transfer to a security detail on a scavenger detail. Get an opportunity to extinguish many undead.

He pockets his useless fully-loaded cash card. The rattle of a truck engine echoes for miles. Now without ambient noise sound travels further which means he'll get a chance to knock off a few undead before the end of his shift. As he unslings his rifle, he notes the speed of the truck. Too fast for a resident. They would know to slow as the road ends in the sally port gate system, allowing all who enter to submit for inspection.

He tracks the scope down the road until capturing the glint of windshield glass in the sun. His focus divides between the truck and the now eastbound approaching scavenging team. He slips his left hand from the rifle barrel to snap his fingers. If his counterpart on the opposite cargo trailer hasn't spotted all the approaching vehicles, the bone click should make her glance his way. He won't take his rifle off the unknown truck. The scavenging team's early return is not unusual if they ran into problems.

Kelsey calls down to the guards patrolling the base of the sally port before she draws a bead on the unknown truck. "One driver visible in the cab. The bed's covered in a tarp."

Austin uses this moment to swing his rifle toward the convoy of scavengers. The flatbed loaded with few fence pieces and a team, weapons exposed, sit on the back. From the visible team members, they are short a few dozen members.

"Team coming in. Alert medical staff!"

Knowing a scavenging team was retrieving large amounts of supplies, other *farm* workers would be prepared to assist in unloading and distributing supplies to necessary stations. Farm workers has become the code for any member of the community unskilled for jobs necessary to keep the colony operations. Two were lawyers before the apocalypse. Highly valued in the old world, but paper pushers no longer serve a function. Here, manual labor ensures being fed.

Austin lowers his rifle but remains vigilant. "Prepare for the team's return and a second visitor," he hollers. "You got the truck, Kelsey?"

"Give the word and the driver's brains paint the bed." She smiles.

"Not my call. Just keep him in your sights. I've got the scavenger team covered."

"You let them in first, in case this lone truck's a vanguard for an attack."

"I hear ya, Kelsey."

Danziger spots the top of a moving semi-trailer through the tree lines. He presses the brake.

The road crossing Highway 19 ends in a wall of cargo trailers and concertina wire, transformed onto a medieval castle gate system. Guard towers with snipers and dog runs stretch out from the structure. Primitive—it appears secure.

The semi reaches the entrance.

Danziger slows before a house in the process of being disassembled. He spots the riflemen on the cargo containers, knowing then the snipers have had him in their sights for yards. He speculates this must be the camp the wounded man directed him toward. Several people sport clean military uniforms. Not being his strongest skill, he avoids calculating the odds of accidentally discovering the convey Levin escaped to.

"This was a grand cluster fuck." Becky slips her sports bra into place.

The rest of the fence team dresses around them in the center of the sally port. None of them are allowed inside Acheron until they were fully inspected and cleared of bites. The two tractor trailers have been pulled through to be unloaded and inspected. An EMT crew examines Amie off to the side of the entrance. Another medical team loads Clay into ambulance.

Kenneth laces his boots from the bench besides her. "It wasn't her fault."

"Which part wasn't? We've both worked outside the fence and dealt with more biters than she has. This is what happens when you put a newb in charge. Ethan's never done it before."

"I didn't realize you cared so much about Bruce."

"I don't. He was a fucking sheep fucker, idiot, and was bound to get us killed...eventually. Better he go now. He was a waste of our food supply." Becky glares at the applauded face Kenneth gives her. "Don't even. You know as well as I he was a waste of air."

"Remind me never to piss you off."

"Just don't do it while I'm fucking guarding tomato plants." She shoots her glance at the flatbed where a team of people offload what little fences they procured. "We were to get enough of those cattle fence panels to surround the garden and keep the cattle from trampling the vegetables.· How many are scattered along the road between her and the farm store? I hate guarding plants."

Kenneth secures his gun belt. "There's not much else we can do. I never got to go to engineering school or you nursing."

"Pharmacology. Now I'm stuck as a guard—forever. Bullshit! I won't be forty and guarding a fucking tomato plant." Becky marches away from Kenneth without a gun strapped to her hip. "At least you can drive the trucks," she mumbles at him.

"Where are you going?" he asks.

Becky waves at the guard to open the inside gate so she can enter the compound. "To give that woman a piece of my mind." She stomps toward the ambulance.

Doctor Baker examines Amie's wounded leg. "It won't require surgery, but I'll have to stitch it up. Have them prep the operating room. If no one else is wounded let's get her back to the community building."

"That was a grand fuckup you got us into today," Becky scolds her.

EMT Victor steps between the fuming Becky and Amie. She's not sure how this clumsy guy passed his medical course, but she's willing to bet he wasn't on duty the day the outbreak went global.

"I'm sorry about Bruce," Amie offers, knowing these people have been surviving together for ten months.

"I don't care about that dumb nut. He was a fucktard and better he went alone than the rest of us." Becky asks, "How is Clay?"

"He'll need X-rays."

"Becky, she needs surgery to repair the damage," Dr. Baker lies to prevent a fight. "We need to go. You'll have a chance to discuss it with her later."

"You cost us a lot." Becky's tone shifts, "But your plan did save us. No matter how mad we all are, no one could have predicted a herd."

Kenneth catches up with her, carrying Becky's gun belt.

The metallic whirl of winches and pulleys echo as the outer gates to the sally port close behind the beat-up Chevy.

Austin orders Danziger, "You want past the first airlock? We've specific procedures to follow. Surrender all weapons. You can have them back once we qualify you to carry them."

Danziger steps from the truck. *I was a cop. I'm more qualified to carry them than you.* Danziger keeps that fact to himself. The metal cage prevents his escape or retreat. Attack from above gives the guards advantage and even if the truck exploded it would take a tank to advance further. Shiny metal beams through bullet holes riddling the left cargo trailer. Someone has tried to get past the first gate and failed.

"You and anyone with you must remove all articles of clothing and stand for inspection for bites."

"I've a wounded man with me. He has no bites, but I can't undress him myself. He said I need to see Windquy."

Austin lowers his rifle. Unless it's a ruse, to allow this guy inside as some kind of siege strategy, there is only one person still outside the fence who knows about Wanikiya. The man who brought them together to form this community. The man who saved each of their lives. All of them speculate now their leader is badly hurt or dead and how they will make this new man pay if he is.

Kelsey levels her rifle at Danziger.

Austin moves to the end of the cargo trailer in order to peer cleanly into the truck bed. "Who sent you?"

Danziger knows he has to reveal who he's transporting in the truck bed. He considered showing them their man outside the gate before they had a chance to lock him in. An escape route might be better for his health. Out there he could run if he had to. They may not believe he had nothing to do with the beating. If he were in their shoes he would believe this to be a trick. No, he needs trust. He pulls back the blanket.

Austin thinks he recognizes the swollen faced man lying there. "Get Wanikiya. NOW!"

"You want to get docked half a meal for not having this? You can't afford to not eat as skinny as you are." Kenneth flashes his sparkly teeth.

She gives him a playful "fuck-off" look before wrapping the belt around her waist. "I've the cup size of a ten-year-old boy and you couldn't take your eyes from my flat chest. You wouldn't know what to do if I gained weight."

"You didn't beat her bloody?"

"It wasn't Amie's fault. No one knew a herd was coming. I just hate guarding tomatoes with more important stuff to do. I don't know what I want to do with my life. I know I don't want guard duty forever." Becky adjusts her holster for easy draw.

"You think what we're doing right now is what we'll be doing the rest of our lives? How depressing."

"What did you think was going to happen? You'd wake up one day to all the biters being gone? Shanking the undead is our life now."

"I never thought about it," Kenneth admits.

"The military's gone, and the people left are scattered, barely surviving."

"And you're bitchin' because you have to guard tomatoes. How many people out there would kill for your job and enjoy the tomatoes?"

"Keeping the cattle from the vegetables might be important, it just isn't my career choice. You were going to engineering school?" Becky asks.

"One semester," Kenneth admits.

"Why aren't you working at the power plant?"

"I never mentioned it. I had a CDL and they needed truck drivers."

"You shoot good, too, but we have to keep the power plant operation and lot of those guys running it are old," Becky says.

"I'll check with—" Kenneth doesn't get to finish before guards yell at the main gate.

"Survivors?" Becky asks.

"There was a pickup on the highway," Kenneth says.

"As long as they aren't like the religious zealots that shot the place up weeks ago."

"Not everyone who has survived out there for this long has to be crazy."

"It helps."

The pair trot to the gate system. Guards unsling rifles or draw pistols. An unfriendly gesture to ensure compound security. The EMTs load Amie into the bus; Doctor Baker hops inside to wait in case needed.

Becky reaches the inner sally port gate to witness a man raise both arms in the air and release his grip on a shiny Taurus .357, letting it dangle from one finger to show he means no harm.

Kenneth laces his fingers in the chain link, "You ever see a gun like that before?"

"Looks like the boss's gun. He keeps it extra shiny."

"What are the chances of there being two shiny guns like that?" Kenneth asks.

Becky can't believe her ears or her own preceding thoughts. *The gun belongs to the man who built Acheron and brought us into the safety of her walls.* "No way that guy took it from Ethan."

Danziger eases the gun onto the hood of the truck before stepping away. He makes a couple of paces forward. "I was told to see Windquy. Win-a-qui. He's a big tall Indian."

"What business do you have with Wanikiya?" Austin corrects.

Through the windshield, Becky spots a tarp move in the truck bed. She breaks into a sprint around the cargo trailers. Kenneth chases after her.

Supervising the unloading of supplies from the semi her team retrieved, Barlock directs what little new equipment goes where in the camp.

Huffing for breath, Becky grabs Barlock's arm. "Something's... in his...truck bed," she pants.

"I'm sure he has some supplies."

Catching her breath, she insists, "Something moved."

"He's asking for Wanikiya by name. You think the boss sent him?" Kenneth asks.

"Austin have him covered?" Barlock asks.

"He's got a gun just like the boss," Becky protests.

"Let's get this guy stripped and inside. Simon records the serial numbers. He can check once this guy's where I can control him. Kenneth, pass the word to Austin. After we've locked this guy down, scan the tree line just in case he has friends."

Kenneth nods before climbing the ladder to the top of a cargo trailer.

Barlock waves to the EMTs. "Let's get these trucks out of here!" He glances at Becky. "You need to move back. You're not on duty. Go get some chow." He grabs Victor by the arm, lowering his voice. "Too many vehicles too close together. Get them stowed in the event this is an attack."

"If he's a problem, you'll need everyone," Becky protests.

"I don't need *extras* getting in the way."

Danziger sticks his arms through the bars.

The military doctor snips at the shredded shirt torn into bandages. He peels back the feminine pads revealing a goopy mess of puss and blood.

"How long have you had a fever?"

"Two, three days. Been taking Tylenol. Cleaned them a few times. Once with boiled tap water."

"At least they aren't bites."

"You a real doctor?" Danziger asks.

"Captain Sterling. Recently of Fort Leonard Wood."

"I just thought most of the medical personnel were gone in the first wave of DK infections."

"They call them biters around here. The military designation was vectors. I was on base and was spared. Too many hospitals across the country went dark within the first twenty-four hours." He twists Danziger's wrists in all directions in order to inspect every gash. Cuts and scrapes into the muscle tissue has festered into infection. "Do you remember your last tetanus shot?"

"Been years."

"We have some." He drops his voice because of the new trigger word he will use. "You are infected and bordering on blood poisoning. There are rusty flakes in here."

Danziger refuses to lock eyes with the doctor. *I've no idea what kind of survivors I've stumbled into. The fact they have full medical staff complete with an ambulance team scares me. If these people are from Fort Wood, they picked up Levin. If I spout off about how a beaten and tortured man is a serial killer, they might lock me up instead.* "Lot of people out there won't just straight up kill you for your supplies. They want to ring something else out of you first. Break you."

"It gives them the semblance of control. People make their own support groups and they have lost them and all control they felt they had over life." Dr. Sterling cleans each laceration to ensure none of them were caused by bites. "Too many of these need stitches but it's too late now."

Danziger nods. "In a former life I was a cop. I saw way too many men beat up on women to exert their control."

"I want to move you to infirmary."

"How's your leader?" Danziger asks.

"The man you brought in? Built like a brick shit house."

"They gave him a beating that would kill a normal man," Danziger reports.

"It still might." Dr. Sterling lacks the admiration the others surrounding the gate have for the beaten man. He just met him.

"Then what happens to me?"

"Depends on your health insurance coverage." Dr. Sterling's smile lasts half a second. "I doubt these people will punish you for his death. You tried to save him. You brought him back to them."

"Aren't you their doctor? You should know them."

"I just arrived here a week ago. Dr. Baker has been caring for them for months. He's with Ethan now."

Two doctors! Fence strong enough to keep out DKs, well-fed guards, laundered clothes—this place is a heaven.

CHAPTER NINE

MEDICS STRIP DOWN Ethan. They should cut off his clothes but his size garments aren't found in regular stores. They work as fast as possible without bringing him more discomfort.

Wanikiya remains a bystander from inside the compound as the EMTs do their job within the confines of the metal airlock gate systems. *Rules. Ethan's rules. They must follow them.* Ethan would never allow them to bring anyone inside until they know if they have been bitten. People linger—almost normal—for days with a bite.

He has witnessed it personally in the first group of survivors he teamed with. One was bit and kept it to themselves out of fear. Then when he finally died from the bite and turned he killed several before they all were destroyed.

Two guards stand on opposite sides of a naked Danziger.

Danziger notes the guard holding the bottom of a well-worn credit card between his thumb and forefinger, releasing it, catching the top corner before it falls. He flips the card over and repeats the process. The strange behavior interests Danziger only as far as to have something to do as the people around him clear the area. They have yet to remove him from the sally port or return his clothes.

Despite the humiliation of being stripped and inspected, the brilliance of the security measure prevents any single person with a bite from reaching the inside. Here they die in the sally port and the community remains protected.

If Levin lived to be brought inside this compound, then they locked him up until they knew if his wounds weren't bites. He might still be secured because the wounds won't have healed enough in the last few days.

This airlock gate is brilliant. Since everyone outside must strip for inspection. No one—absolutely no one—gets in who is bit or with contraband. Anyone with a suspicious bite can be observed inside the pen until deemed safe or destroyed.

The giant Native American runs his thumb over the tomahawk blade looped through his belt as he marches toward the truck. To top off the racist stereotype, the man has war paint streaked across his cheeks.

Danziger can't help himself. "They let you run this place, Tonto?"

"I am no fool, nor am I a Potawatomie. What I am is Sioux, and the current leader of this tribe."

"I'm lost. I thought the man in the truck was your leader."

"Until he regains consciousness, my word is law. As for most white people, you don't understand the foundation of your racism. *Tonto* means 'fool' in Spanish and he was part of the Potawatomie tribes in what was once the state of Michigan."

"Once?"

"I figure state lines mean little any more. As does the fact we spent thousands of years killing each other over our skin pigments. The biters don't care if you kneel before Allah or if you have red skin. We're all cattle to them."

"I brought your leader back. A group of survivors ambushed him." Danziger considers letting these people keep their mythos about their leader and his herculean skills. "It was a bad beating. As a cop, I've never seen anyone endure so much and live."

"If he dies. I'll give you back your clothes and a few days' worth of supplies and send you on your way. If he vouches for you. Stay or leave, your choice."

"I was helping your friend. He said to bring him to you," Danziger reports.

"I want to believe you."

"It's the truth. He was attacked, and I saved him."

"There had to be a lot of them for him to succumb to a beating," Wanikiya says.

"When I arrived, they already had him down. I don't know how they ambushed him. He had killed some of them already," Danziger says.

"What were you doing?"

The question causes Danziger to withdraw. He's not sure he wants to tell them of his quest to find the man that killed his daughter. "I was hunting supplies."

"For your group?"

"For my wounds. I've been alone since—" *A pause in my answer will hurt my case. These people will think I'm making up a lie.* "The last caravan of people left St. Louis for Ft. Wood. We were overrun by a herd." *Not a total lie.* "Can I get my clothes?"

"Becky, are you on duty?" Wanikiya glances at the woman half hiding by the edge of the gate complex. Like most of those living in Acheron she has an undying loyalty to the man who saved her life.

"No, just returned from a run. I want to know who he is," she demands.

"Get one of the garment boxes so he can pick out some fresh clothes." He turns to Danziger. "Your others are ruined."

"I was a cop. Do you treat everyone that shows up at your door like this?"

Wanikiya's answer—a hard yes.

"Open the gate," calls Dr. Baker. They carry Ethan secured to a backboard to a waiting gurney. "No bites on him!" he informs Wanikiya. "He'll need X-rays to check for broken bones. I don't know how anyone could make it through a beating like that."

Danziger steps from the sally port. He doesn't bother to count the number guns on him or those ready to draw on him.

Dr. Baker continues, "Dr. Baker continues, "It's too early to tell, but I think he'll live. However, even if he has no internal bleeding, it will still take a long time for him to recover." They load Ethan into the ambulance.

Wanikiya can't tell if that's a lie to make them all feel better or the truth. "Get him back to the medical ward, Dr. Baker."

"You have an X-ray machine and run ambulances?" Danziger asks.

"We have a society here. The man you returned to us built it all. The people living here—he rescued them," Becky says.

From the gather of people around the gate, Danziger understands if Ethan dies he would pass onto martyrdom—they don't need that. They need a living hero to protect them.

A team of people has moved into the airlock gate and inspects the truck. Becky sets a tote before Danziger allowing him to select some clean underwear.

Barlock reports to Wanikiya, "It's clean. We found all the boss's weapons and usual supplies. Nothing explosive on the truck and not enough gas for it to function as a bomb."

"What the fuck? You thought I was a suicide bomber?" Danziger protests.

"We don't know who you are. But we have a functioning society complete with electricity. Not for one moment do I think some group wouldn't try to take that from us," Wanikiya says.

"You don't let people in?"

"We bring in survivors as we find them, as long as they agree to adhere to our rules."

"I appreciate the medical attention and fresh clothes, but I've got a mission to continue," Danziger doesn't want to be here if their leader dies.

"He hasn't worked to earn any food," Becky squeals.

"He brought back Ethan. That has earned him a meal or two, young lady," Wanikiya says.

"I take it that's a rule," Danziger says. *I do need to feed this fever. I need to cure this fever.*

"Our biggest. You don't work you don't eat. But I will feed you, until the boss tells us his side of the story."

Even if I am welcome they aren't ready to accept me yet. "It could take days for him to wake," Danziger says. *I realize they don't trust me yet. If it turns out I hurt their leader they'll end me. I need to heal. I need to see if Levin is here.*

"Wanikiya, we don't have a holding cell. You know how the boss handles criminals," Becky protests.

"This man's not a criminal. He's a guest. He needs medical attention. Put him in one of the empty classrooms and place a guard detail on him."

"I'll pull my weight for a meal," Danziger volunteers.

Dr. Sterling secures his gear. "Not today. We need to heal your arms first. He may have to sleep with an ankle cuff."

"This man is a guest until I say otherwise. If he ends up with one bruise or mark on him, I will personally strip and exile the individual responsible. We don't know what happened. All we know is he brought Ethan back to us," Wanikiya speaks so all the milling people understand. Even without Twitter he knows his words will spread on the wind.

The guards escort Danziger to a truck.

Becky waits until Danziger is out of earshot before saying, "As much as I want interrogate him immediately, he did to bring back—"

Wanikiya cuts her off, "No need. The facts are he brought back Ethan. The truth is there are still decent people outside the fence. We need to find them and bring them in here before they turn into those who beat, steal, and kill."

"I want to confess something," Becky says. "Orscheln's was a complete cluster fuck, and I blamed Amie, but her quick thinking saved us. A herd. No one could have done any better. Not with a herd that size. It had to have moved through after Karen scouted the location."

"Would you go outside the fence under her command again?" he asks.

"I would. Until I get my own team to lead."

Dr. Baker slips the nasal cannula over Ethan's ears before guiding the prongs in his nose.

Victor adjusts the airflow. Ethan raises his arm to jerk at the tubes.

Dr. Baker and Victor both grab Ethan's hand to prevent him from removing the tines.

"We need to leave that in, Sir. No charge for the oxygen," Victor jokes as Ethan wraps his fingers like a vice grip smashing his digits together, threatening to break them.

"Take me to my house," Ethan orders.

"You need medical treatment. X-rays," protests Dr. Baker.

"I'm awake and competent. I refuse transport."

"Someone knows the rules," says Victor. Catching a disapproving glance from Dr. Baker, who fumes at Ethan, trashing old world rules at every turn.

"Take me home." Ethan pushes up on one elbow in an attempt to get off the gurney.

"Just take it easy. Let me speak to Wanikiya," Dr. Baker crawls out of the side door of the bus.

Ethan waits until the doctor's out of his view to collapse. Glad his bluff wasn't called.

"I'd rather keep him in the medical unit," Dr. Baker hates craning up to speak to the Sioux.

"How bad is it?"

"I've performed a cursory examination. I don't know how any man, even one in Kevlar, withstood such a beating. No way his chest was fully healed from the bullet impacts. He needs all the care our limited medical supplies will provide."

"Take him to his house," Wanikiya insists. "There'll be enough talk from the guards about how bad he was beaten. I don't want him seen just yet. It will disturb the hope he gives our people."

"He needs to be in the hospital. I'll need to X-ray his entire body."

"We can't have everyone see their leader like this. Rumors would cause enough despair. Take him to his house," Wanikiya orders.

"I'm begging you. I can't give him the care he needs unless he's at the hospital."

"What care will he get at the hospital you can't give him in his own bed?"

The smell of freshly-cooked eggs permeates the living room.

Even with Wanikiya on the end of the gurney, it takes five men to move their leader into the farmhouse. Wanikiya ducks under the door frame as he shuffle-steps to cross the threshold.

The noise brings the young Dartagnan from the kitchen. His expression dissolves into confusion. He howls, spotting Ethan strapped to the board.

Maneuvering the stretcher toward the staircase involves a catty-corner shift, causing one of the EMTs to bump the living room tables displaying the miniature model Dartagnan constructed of the compound.

Dartagnan's ear-splitting guttural squeals of warning puncture everyone's eardrums. Dartagnan drops to his butt, hugs his knees, and rocks back-and-forth, never ceasing his cries.

As miniature figurines and trees fall over—one crashing onto the floor—the young boy increases the wail to its maximum pitch.

The struggles to get the gurney up the narrow stairs only compound the child's distress. The men bang against the wall, with no room to maneuver, as they climb the stairs.

The rattling, heavy thumping, and boot stomps on the second floor send a waterfall of dust from the ceiling.

Dartagnan rocks faster.

Wanikiya tromps down the stairs having to slouch the entire trip.

"Ethan's going to be okay. You've seen him in action. He's a tough cookie." The man's comfort does nothing to cease the screams.

Wanikiya contemplates how the boy survived outside the fence before Ethan found him. Once the kid's mother passed he was left to fend for himself. One outburst like this would have attracted the biters. The kid may be able to cook eggs, build realistic models, and complete complicated math in his head, but he lacks the fortitude to defend against the undead.

"Dartagnan. I need you to lower your voice. The medics need quiet to fix Ethan." Even keeping his voice low and soft, Wanikiya's demeanor fails to calm the boy.

Voices carry from upstairs even over the screaming.

"He's stable."

"I've never seen skin purple like this."

"Do we ice the swelling?"

"It's impossible for a person to live through a beating like this."

"You're all trained medical personnel. Do your jobs," Dr. Baker snaps.

Two of the EMTs bound down the stairs with the empty gurney.

"Do you want to sedate him?" asks the EMT.

"Absolutely not. I'm no child specialist, but in this new world he's going to have to deal," Wanikiya says.

"He'll scream himself hoarse," Victor says.

"I'm worried he'll damage his vocal cords," the second EMT adds. "And if Ethan wakes again he'll try to get out of bed to check on the kid."

"When," Wanikiya corrects. He marches into the kitchen, flipping on the CB radio placed on top of the refrigerator. He clicks the mic button. "Chief Petty Officer Simon." No other Simon lives at the camp, but the retired gentlemen responds to his rank—the kind of soldier who never retires until forced. The end of the world provided him the outlet he needed to continue being Chief.

CHAPTER TEN

BLINDFOLDED, CHIEF PETTY Officer Simon snaps the barrel back into the weapon he reassembled before snagging the radio from its cradle. "Simon—"
 "Are you at HQ?"
 Simon slides off the blindfold. Not a single leftover gun part rests on the table. He locks the weapon in the drawer of his station.
 If not on the range, where else would I be? He considers answering in his best jarhead tone, but relents to respecting those above in command even if they aren't military. "Affirmative." *My twenty.* He should have asked. *Civvies never want to learn proper code.*
 "Bring Emily to the corner farm," Wanikiya's voice crackles.
 Simon was fully aware of the scrambled medical teams. When he's not certifying Acheron residence to carry or assist in the armory duties, he keeps a watchful eye on the camp. Including daily runs outside the fence. *So, why do I need to play chauffeur to a fifteen-year-old girl whose only skill is guarding books?* Simon's thoughts shift to practicality. *The must need help with Dartagnan. Never a good idea to leave such a special kid alone. I don't care how he survived outside, he needs constant looking after.*
 Emily leaps from the truck before Simon slams it into park. She knows the howls from inside the farmhouse are Dartagnan's. She skips every other step as she races up the stoop.

Simon parks, careful to give the two ambulances—one military and one civilian—access to leave the scene with ease. A few of the scheduled main gate guards gather outside.

He almost screams 'attention' but none of them survived basic. A bulldog snap should suffice. "Why aren't you at your posts?"

"Someone brought the boss back."

It takes Simon a second to remember Noah's name. *Another late teen kid Ethan rescued. A lot of near twenty-something kids survived being eaten. Most likely they could run.*

Upset, this kid tells more with his shaking than his words.

"Barlock, get these people back to their posts." Even with no authority to bark orders, the camp respects the veteran warrior.

"Someone beat him near to death."

Simon holds his best poker face. "Who?"

"We don't know. He came in with a lone stranger. Says he found Ethan.

"He may have. Where is this man?" Simon asks.

"We have him under guard at the sally port."

"Then get back there. Best way to breach our defenses is to draw guards away from the main gate." *Half true. Any one group could just cut a hole in the fence and get in,* but Simon leaves off his tactical assessment. "Get back to your stations where you'll be the most helpful." He adds, "Keep the boss's condition to yourself." *I won't panic the camp the way Dartagnan's panicked.* From the high-pitched wails, he knows the boy's upset by what he's witnessed.

"In fact, we should all return to our duties. I have another resident to certify. If you aren't directly involved here, return to work."

Emily knows Simon will worm information out of the gate guards milling about the farmhouse porch. She'd like to stay and find out what had happened to Ethan, but Dartagnan's howls of distress echo dangerously, loud enough to attract biters. Ethan explained how he'd found the special boy. He survived where so many normal people didn't, including the kid's mother. She had operated through painstaking patience, training the kid to function as normal children do. Mom had kept a journal of major disturbances, detailing how she'd controlled them and taught Dartagnan to handle them. Emily read a few pages and knows about the chair.

Dartagnan rocks on his buttocks. His arms hugging his knees. He touches each of the five watches on his left arm. Rocks five times and touches each watch, repeating the pattern. Opera singer lungs howl a constant, painful-pitched note. Never ceasing to take in gulps of air keep his face a bright red.

"Who did this to the model?" she asks.

"He's been screaming for twenty minutes."

"No wonder he's so upset," Emily blasts with disgust. "You destroyed the model." She scoops up a tree from the floor. "This is his whole world." His screaming wears on her young and sensitive ears. She snaps, "Dartagnan, you want to sit in the chair? Dartagnan!" It worked for Ethan.

He doesn't recognize her authority.

She bulls up, sucking in as much air as her lungs will allow and belts out her words i n what will become her most commanding mom voice. "Dartagnan, you stop and go sit in your chair. Right now!"

The boy's head snaps at the high back chair in the corner. Fear consumes his face. The one place he doesn't want to be sentenced to is the chair. From the notes, Emily knows it's a simple time out location, but somehow it's devastating to his socially inadequate mind.

Dartagnan freezes. Emily sucks in another full breath. "I said the chair." Stern but not mean. She can't back down from the contest.

Dartagnan hops to his quivering legs.

"Now."

Each baby step he inches toward the chair pains Emily. None of this is his fault. Even if she's in the wrong about punishing him she's on a path she must follow or he'll never listen to her again.

Once he places his bottom in the chair, Emily forces back her own tears at the sight of Dartagnan's.

In a sweet-as-she-can-sound voice, she asks, "What happened?"

He points to the model with all the tiny trees knocked over and crashed buildings.

Earthquake damage, she considers. *Nothing unrepairable but to a child with his condition—Mom never recorded what his actual diagnosis was—it is devastating.*

Blubbering, Dartagnan explains, "They destroyed the table carrying sleepy Ethan upstairs. Sleeping like my mom was when Ethan found me."

Emily's eyes flame. She'll howl herself if Ethan's hurt. "Who knocked over the table?"

"Victor," Wanikiya answers.

Even with his extra-long arms, he's unable to restrain her as Emily bolts up the stairs.

She pushes through the remaining medical staff, about to tear into them them for upsetting Dartagnan, when she spots Dr. Baker examining a deep bruise on Ethan's chest. Tunnel vision consumes her. Her world narrows to the purpling body of the man who'd broken her heart.

"You don't need to be up here, Emily." Dr. Baker's words restore her to reality.

Despite her tiny frame, she grabs Victor with enough force to knock him off balance when she grabs his arm.

"What the fuck!"

"Listen here, Victor. Go downstairs right now and apologize to Dartagnan."

"I never said a word to the boy," Victor says.

"Your ass bumped the table. You damaged his model. You go tell him how sorry you are," Emily demands with the ferocity of a mother bulldog.

"Are you serious, girl?"

"The one thing he has stable in this world is his model work. Now march down there and apologize to him." Emily, surprised at her own burst of authority, thanks her stars she didn't say "March, mister." She knows she would have lost all credibility with these men.

Dr. Baker nods.

Wanikiya speaks having followed her, "Emily's correct, Victor. The boy needs it. And she needs to go back downstairs as well."

"Is Ethan going to die?" She jerks her shoulder from Wanikiya's hand.

"Not if I have any say in it." Dr. Baker confidently adds, "He's the strongest person I know. Some of these marks would mean broken bones for anyone else, but it was Ethan who took the hits. I need to complete my examination and you seem to be the one with a handle on Dartagnan."

Once Emily's last footfall leaves the stairs, Wanikiya asks the doctor, "Are we able to speak with him?"

"He's out. I'd let him sleep. Without x-rays, we'll need to handle him carefully. Any discoloration in the urine or blood and I will have to move him. Now we need to find an unbruised vein for an IV."

Emily waits for Victor next to Dartagnan's chair.

Victor kneels before the boy. "I'm sorry. I didn't mean to damage your model."

Dartagnan halts his bellowing.

Emily gives Victor a shooing nod; much more explaining might set Dartagnan to screaming again.

The EMT heads for the door.

Wanikiya ducks down the stairs again. "Stay here, Emily. Keep an eye on Dartagnan. I'll send relief. I'm sure medical staff will be in and out, but let's not speak of his condition."

She knows he doesn't mean Dartagnan.

CHAPTER ELEVEN

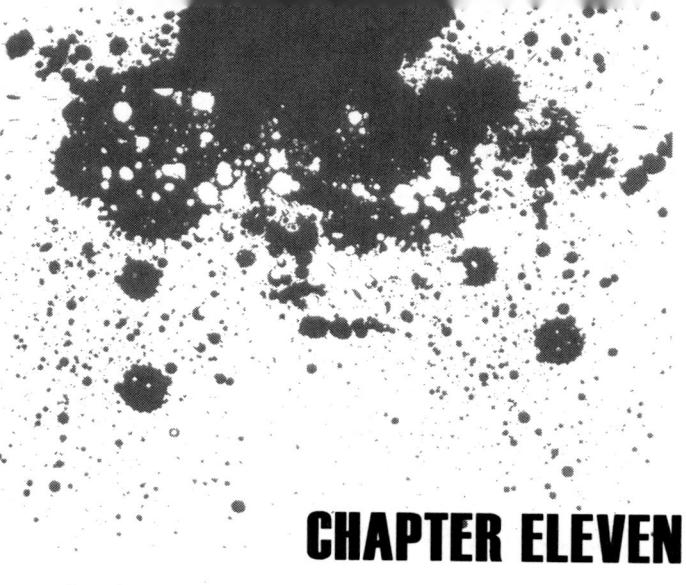

HANNAH RAISES THE pistol. Holding her breath, she peers down the sights.

Exhale.

Pop.

The coagulated spatter explodes out the chest of a biter, painting more of the creatures in a tarry goop. The bullet stops in an arm of the creature behind the one she hit.

"I'm no good with this thing." Hannah lowers the gun, releasing the clip before racking the slide to unload the chambered round. She places them on the table.

"One shot is not enough to assess your capabilities," Simon says.

"I'm no good with a pistol." She picks up the Mossberg 464 Lever Action rifle loading 30-30 rounds. Raising the weapon with the recoil pad tight into her shoulder, she moves the lever with the smoothness of a pro. The shell slides into the breach and she takes aim.

Bam.

Smooth hands move the lever action, ejecting a spent casing with a half second, she blows open the skull of a second biter, then a third.

Five rounds.

Five shots all in the center forehead of the undead.

"Fuck me, Annie Oakley." Nick is aghast. The girl he likes shoots better than him a trained US Soldier.

She lowers the weapon. "The Colonel had a Navy SEAL sniper instruct me a few summers ago. I still can't hit shit with a pistol."

"With your skill, you'll be useful on scavenging patrols." Simon adds, "I'll inform Wanikiya of your skill."

"I want one of these rifles. If not this one." She caresses her palm over the hand grip. "The recoil wasn't bad and my short fingers reach the trigger without effort."

"I will assign it to you after you complete the pistol test."

"I said I don't shoot them well."

"Rifles aren't usually carried," Simon says. "But I'll arrange it, due only to your level of skill. But my duty requires you shoot the pistol even if you miss."

Dr. Sterling holds up an X-ray of Amie's leg. "Nothing's broken."

Kayla uncuffs Amie's left hand from the medical bed.

"I'm not sure how the truck door cut you open this bad through your boot. I made the stitches as small as I could but I had to use a few staples, and without a plastic surgeon I won't prevent all the scarring."

"And my dancing career?"

"It will take a while before you can perform the Jarabe dance." Dr. Sterling adds, "You'll need to keep weight off it for a few days. Until the wound has healed, not traveling outside the fence. We may not know much about the vectors, but we do know blood attracts them."

"I've never seen anything like it except the time I went deep sea fishing and they chummed the water. I didn't think they were able to maintain smell," Amie says.

"We know so little about how they function."

"I wouldn't want one in here even to study," Kayla says.

"Valuable information and insight are needed in our understanding of the creature," Dr. Sterling says.

"Our camp remains safe and not ready to have a lab full of biters," Wanikiya says as he ducks to enter the examination room. "One day, maybe, but we are far from ready." He lowers his eyes to look at Amie's stitched leg. "Will you be okay, Private?"

"Am I still in the military, sir?" she asks.

"Respectfully, we all serve now."

"She'll be ready for duty in a week and back outside the fence in two. They smell blood."

Wanikiya nods. "Dr. Sterling, Dr. Baker examined Ethan at the farm house. Prepare a medical rotation to keep vigil over our leader."

"Ethan's hurt?" Amie knew of the commotion at the gate but not how Ethan was involved. She met Ethan when he blasted his way off Fort Wood killing the eldest Bowlin brother—a man needing permanent death after his abuses of so many women. Ethan's skill with a gun amazed her as if John Wayne stepped from the movies and drew. "How bad is it?"

"I think we should discuss this in the office," Dr. Sterling suggests. "Unless we've negated patient privacy?"

"Our rules on dealing with the biters does hinder people having a right to privacy," Kayla adds.

"Beyond bites, individual treatment should remain personal between the patient and the doctor," Dr. Sterling says.

"Since resources are limited, some treatments may involve a group decision on how we spend what medical supplies we have. And once some drugs are no longer salvageable, hard choices will be before us," Wanikiya says.

"Hey! Not that figuring out how to vaccinate future babies isn't important, what about Ethan?" Amie demands.

"Calm yourself, honey, you'll tear your stitches," Kayla warns.

"Scavengers beat him. We'll maintain a constant watch."

"He should be here," Dr. Sterling stresses. "Along with Clay and Levin."

"You see the reaction Sanchez just had to the news. I don't want anyone outside the medical staff around him," Wanikiya says.

"I'll consult Dr. Baker and prepare the medical staff to stay with him," Dr. Sterling says.

"Does it have to be a trained medic?" Amie asks.

"I would say tonight. The first twenty-four are crucial to ensure he's healthy," Dr. Sterling explains, having not examined Ethan in person.

"Get me some crutches and I'll take a shift. Unless there is a reason I shouldn't sit in a chair and watch him breath. I can't work the fences until I heal and I want to earn my keep," Amie says.

"You rest in here tonight," Kayla says.

"Add her to the rotation after Ethan's stable. Lack of round-the-clock medical care would assure the camp he's just resting," Wanikiya says.

"Being new here and not one of the few Ethan personally saved, I know my attachment to him is not as strong, but hanging your camp stability on one man..." Dr. Sterling says.

"He's our leader," Wanikiya's tone speaks finality.

Smashed between the two guards in the cab of the truck, Danziger's police training reminds him he should educate these people in proper transport of a prisoner. It concerns him. It means Levin could be running around free.

He had doubts the man he rescued will die. *He could still hemorrhage from internal bleeding, but a day after the beating he has no blood in his urine—a positive sign. Then again, my medical training doesn't extend past the mandatory police CPR class.*

"You guys have names?" Danziger asks.

"Hal. I was a copy clerk at the office supply store before," says the driver.

"Wade, something the fucking III. I hated that III shit. When you have a name that ends in *The III* you shouldn't be cleaning the grease traps at the Chicken Wing Barn. Thirty-seven delicious flavors of wings and that doesn't include our variety of mild through nine-alarm hot wings."

"That kind of makes me want some wings," Danziger says.

"I skip chicken night. Can't stand it. Wanikiya will serve me up a peanut butter sandwich."

"You get a lot of chicken for dinner."

"More eggs." Hal explains, "We're trying to build up our poultry population, before we butcher many. Chicken will be a nice change of pace when we get it. You better like beef. We eat a lot."

"Steak sounds delightful."

"Cattle roam the countryside and we've brought in a lot of them. One steer feeds a lot."

"They use a lot of the animal parts, too," Wade adds. "You don't know how to tan hides, do you? We need someone who can turn the cow skin into leather."

"Sorry, I was a cop. Never tanned animal hides before. There are no deer hunters in your group?"

"Lots, but like most people they turned the hides over to someone else."

"Stop the car!" Danziger orders.

Hal slams on the breaks. All three of them brace themselves to prevent impacting on the dashboard.

Danziger wants out, but he can't get past the two men.

"What's wrong, mister?"

In the parking lot before the school, functioning as the survivor's community center, are military trucks including a personnel carrier, ambulance, and tow truck.

"I spotted a convoy with vehicles just like those." Danziger swallows hard. *Speaking of Levin will make me sound crazy. The odds of it being the same group seem astronomical. But the odds must increase since I did chase an identical group north. I need to warn them. Will they believe me? Will I cause a panic? Will they exile me for being mental? How do I warn these people about Levin without seeming like a stark raving mad lunatic?* "I need to speak to Wanikiya."

"He'll check on you later."

"It's important. It pertains to those vehicles. He'll want to know immediately," Danziger says.

"We've got to lock you in the holding room and we'll call him," Hal says.

"Yeah. We've got to lock you up. I won't miss dinner because we didn't," Wade says.

"I won't cause you to miss dinner," Danziger assures.

"Not locking you up will. They told you the rules?"

"Yes."

"You work or you don't eat. It's a real punishment," Hal says as if he were a five-year-old avoiding punishment.

"There's no Mac Arches to get a burger if you aren't fed. Not many break rules more than once."

"Number one disciplinary action for failure to comply with camp rules or orders is a meal dock." Hal presses the accelerator.

CHAPTER TWELVE

SO MANY WOMEN. None of them are the correct age. And mostly brunette. Levin has no idea how to quell his mind. His thoughts. His passion—perversion, according to society. Now only a perverse society exists. *I should be ruler of this new world. These people should bring me the blonde girl, Emily, as tribute.* He rubs his hand over the top of the blanket. The thoughts of Emily stiffen his member. He sniffs at the book she brought him. Mostly paper musk but a trace of her scent hangs on the pages. It will linger in his mind long enough.

Commotion in the corridor makes him shift his hips so that anyone entering the room doesn't notice the mound at his waist. The concrete brick wall has empty screw holes where a blackboard used to be attached. Faded tape patches in the shape of the alphabet inform him the building was once full of happy children. Children who would have grown into teens. Teens like—

When it happened.

He was no older than his victim.

She wasn't a victim—she was his canvas. A living work of art. He prepared her body and her screams—

Maybe in this new world he'll allow these people to witness his work. It was satisfying to perform for Danziger. Only he lacked all his tools. He will have all he needs. These people will understand when they grow to desire what he has—the way he did—only they won't be forced.

Cocking his head in order to peek at the door without moving his body, he spots men escorting a prisoner with bandaged forearms.
Danziger.
The cop never glanced in the room.
One thing's for sure, he hasn't said anything about me. Fool. He must want to finish what he started in the barn. I should have taken his hands. No. He might have bled out. I wanted—needed him to witness. They all must witness my art. If not, they will never know.
Emily carries a paperback book in each hand as she enters the medical ward room.
Levin sits up to greet her better.
"I hope these two are more to your liking," she says.
"Have you not read *Gone with the Wind*?" Levin asks.
"I wasn't much into books before. I have found a few I like."
"What have you read?" Levin's eyes follow her blonde hair to the roots, which are corn in color not brown like so many *blondes* he's investigated.
"It's a little childish."
"Don't be shy. I won't judge."
She cocks her head to hide embarrassment, "*The Fault in our Stars.*"
"I haven't read it, but I was afraid you were going to say *Twilight.*"
"With all the dead returning to walk the earth, sparkling vampires are still the craziest thing I've ever heard of," Emily says.
"At least you have taste."
"So, I think I watched like a part of the movie," she touches the book.
Levin explains, "Scarlet was a rather timid girl in the ways of the world, but she was a free thinker and passionate. She would go after what wanted in life. She desired a certain boy and when he was to marry another her passion incensed until she could no longer stand it. As the war between the states encroaches she is forced to develop into a strong woman and do whatever she must in order to survive."
"Did she ever win the man she loves?"
"You will need to read the book."

"Why do adults always say that?" Emily ponders.

"Not much point if I only tell you the ending. You must discover the journey for yourself," Levin says.

"I should get back to the library."

"Do you have a lot of books to check out?"

"No. During the day it's pretty slow. Most people work a day shift. Evening before dinner rush I get a few. Most people want DVDs over books," she says.

"For a culture to move forward they must inscribe their works in tomes."

"I don't get it," she says.

Levin moves his hand, causing his handcuffed wrist to clink metal against metal.

"They still have you secure?" she asks. "Why?"

"Not because I'm dangerous." He flips the sheet off his abdomen. Hints of blood emerge on a large bandage. "This wound concerns them."

"Is it gross?" she asks.

"Want to see?" Levin edges his thumbnail under the corner of the bandage tape.

Emily steps closer in order to get a clear view.

Levin pulls slow at the tape.

Emily eases within arm's reach.

Levin flips his wrist releasing the handcuff to grab Emily. His hand clamps around her neck. He pulls her toward him clasping her mouth with his other hand. He slides off the bed backing her toward the door.

Too in shock to resist, he controls her movements like a dog catcher with a catch-pole. He peeks into the hall before closing the door. She had one full second to scream but her brain never focuses long enough to allow her mouth to open. He drags her back to the bed, cuffing her face down. He presses gauze against her lips, but she refuses to open her mouth. He pinches the loose skin on the back of her arm until she screams, allowing him to shove her cheeks full of cotton. Before she spits it all out, he tears a sheet and tightens a gag around her head. Ripping more cloth, he binds her other hand and then her ankles to the bed frame.

"You disappoint. Most girls struggle. I like it when you struggle. And scream. Can't have you screaming in here, so your muffled noises will have to do."

He opens a cabinet door.

She hears the clank of metal on the counter.

"Such tools. Even when I operated in my own home I never got some of these of such quality," Levin lies. He had the finest of surgical tools to perform his task, but mental torment stimulates their trauma and enhances his pleasure.

The *sher-chunk* of scissors cutting fills her ears. Then the tug at her shirt and more snips shred her top. Cold air covers her now exposed skin. He unclasps the single hook of her bra. "I never understood why you girls with no discernible breasts bothered to invest in bras. Why spend forty dollars on something serving you no purpose?" He cuts the shoulder straps. He rolls his thumb and forefinger over the lacey cup. "You don't even have a padded one to enhance your appeal to men who seek curvier women."

The cold steel slides against the curve of her rump as he dissects her jeans.

He leaves her exposed. "I miss having my camera to document my work. You, my child, are a blank canvas. And I'm going to paint my masterpiece." His hand touches the small of her back. Pinching his fingers together, he tugs at the tiny blonde hairs there. "First, I must cleanse you of imperfections. We'll start with your hair. They so obstruct the female form." He draws a scalpel blade over her skin leaving behind nothing but smooth shorn flesh.

"You take such pride in your toes and yet you fail to groom the proper areas a woman should take pride in." He draws the blade again. "Even if you only share yourself with your man you must keep yourself free of such blemishes."

Emily jerks against her bonds for the first time only because the razor edge of the scalpel sinks into the cleavage of her buttocks.

Never, not even his first victim whom he took with unsteady hands, did he draw blood. The bright crimson mushroom bursts forth, speeding across her curves and down her legs to soak the bed.

The blood will ruin his masterpiece. As he slaps a cloth over the gash, it sprays his side in a fountain of warm. It dribbles down his side—warm. So warm. So wet.

Warm moist drops roll down Levin's side. The deeper cut across his chest leaks. Excited with passion, his blood pumps fast enough to open the wound. His dream has fired more than his fantasy of killing the teen librarian.

He has no way to hide what he detects rolling down his side. He's done nothing wrong. What he did he dreamt of in his head. None of these people know of his secret pleasures. He was just resting and the wound opened. Maybe he stretched too far when hoeing the garden. Nothing to give away his plans to assume control of this camp and continue with his work.

Levin lifts the blanket. Blood from the knife wound soaks through the bandage. His thumping heart rattles his chest. More bright red blood flushes through the bandage. He didn't move fast enough to break open the wound. Danziger's attack was slashing to enhance pain instead of stabbing for damage. Still, this deep gorge wound might have reached something vital. Bright red means a fresh blood flow. He slides toward the edge of the mattress, but the biting pain forces him to freeze.

"Nurse." No one has wired the beds with call buttons.

"Nurse." He raises his voice. Blood flows from under the bandage. "Nurse!"

Kayla closes the door. "You don't have to yell."

"Are you the only nurse?" Levin asks.

"No. There are two doctors, five EMTs, and two more nurses. But with limited medical emergencies one of the other nurses works the fence line as a guard. She shoots better than most here. Did you call me in here to ask about the staff?"

"No." He flips off the sheet.

Even in all her medical training she jumps at the growing puddle of blood. Pulling on latex gloves, she yells out the door for Dr. Sterling. She folds a clean towel, placing it over the wound and pressing down. "What did you do?"

"Nothing. It's just bleeding. I was near asleep. Other than some morning supervised therapy I've stayed in bed."

Dr. Sterling enters. "What is it?"

"One of his wounds has broken open. I'm keeping pressure."

"What were you doing, Levin?" the doctor asks.

"It just opened. I was just laying her. Rolled over to sleep."

"You may have twisted wrong and damaged what was already mended. You may have been up and around too soon."

Kayla peels back the blood-soaked bandages."

Dr. Sterling orders, "Get the suture kit. I'll try and restitch this."

CHAPTER THIRTEEN

AMIE TAPS EMILY'S shoulder, motioning for her to follow from Ethan's bedroom into the hall. Kayla warms the metal bell and chest piece in her palms before performing a cursory examination of the slumbering mass.

"You can go back to the community center, get some food, there's no need for you to wait here," Amie whispers.

"I have to know if he's okay." Emily leans against the door frame, never taking her eyes from the sleeping mass in the bed.

"Emily, I can't tell you what to do, but I'll make sure he's fine."

Emily glares at the crutches and the woman demanding to take her spot. "You don't understand." *I love him.*

Amie knows many of the people in Acheron worship Ethan. He saved so many of them from death. Protected them from the biters. He has even risked himself to find some of their family. He's earned reverence. He's earned a peaceful rest.

Ethan earned her respect when she drove him from Fort Wood and he killed Kade Bowlin. The base commander Colonel Travis trusted Ethan with his only daughter, Hannah. If the Colonel entrusted her safety to this man, he must—

"You've never been outside the fence. I've never lived outside the fence. The time I was—"

"I just led a team out," Amie corrects her.

"The gathering mission didn't go so well for you." Emily points at Amie's bandaged foot.

"You love him," Amie realizes.

"I would just die if something happened to him. And not in some 'stupid teenage girl die' way. Without him, this place will collapse. He keeps it together. Protects us."

"For a man to take that kind of beating...I don't want to meet what would kill him," Amie says.

Kayla steps from Ethan's bedroom flipping her stethoscope around her neck. "He seems fine. Did he wake up at all in the night?"

"No. He never moved," Emily reports.

"He just needs to sleep and rest. The first sign of any blood in his stool and we move him to the medical ward. Until then, let him rest. We should change his sheets this afternoon."

"We'll do it," Amie volunteers.

"You don't need to put weight on your foot. Dr. Baker will be here after lunch."

"Why didn't he come this morning? He doesn't have a ward full of patients," Emily asks.

"He has three. Amie, you should be at the hospital with the other two."

"Three?"

"Clay fell off the truck. Banged up pretty bad. The doctor is checking over all the team on your mission, so far only minor bruises and hearing issues. Scavenging teams need to dawn ear protection before a firefight."

"Then they won't hear the biters," Amie protests.

"Catch 22, but if you lose your hearing you'll only be able to smell them if you are upwind of their approach," Kayla says.

"How long were you outside?" Emily inquires.

"Long enough. My boyfriend-slash-fuck boy—when he wasn't being a verbally abusive asshole—surprised me with a getaway weekend to Vegas. I think he had aspirations of being married by Elvis."

"Sounds romantic," Amie's tone lacks approval.

"His idea of romance was supersizing my French fries. Women should find reasons to date men besides their ability to perform like a stallion."

"I've dated one or two of those," Amie admits.

Emily refocuses the conversation since he has no similar experience to contribute. "How did you get from Vegas to here?"

"I'm from here. We never made it to the airport. The morning it started, we were on our way and never even made it into the city. I tried to help people hurt in accidents on the highway."

"They locked down Fort Wood after accepting much of the City of Rolla and other communities inside. Then nothing," Amie adds.

"Radio stayed on. Nothing too local. Stations that broadcast those pre-recorded music programs made it sound as if civilization was fine, but local news—nothing. Not even the Emergency Broadcast System. Ambulance, Fire, and Rescue never showed to assist at the accidents. The boyfriend. He threw me over his shoulder and carried me from the scene. I'd have been bit if he hadn't. Maybe the only decent act he performed. Some of the hurt people died and didn't reanimate. Then as if at a snap of fingers, others stood up."

Amie seems at a loss to imagine the terror of seeing a mangled body from a car accident get up. She nearly pissed herself the first time rotten corpses approached the base fence, but she knew they were out there. Kayla had no advanced notice as to what was happening.

"After I got done hating him for preventing me from helping, we found an emergency rescue station set up in the basement of a church. It was about half full of people from the highway. The locals wanted to seal the doors to anyone not from the town, but by the time they determined it was the best course of action there were too many outsiders inside to enforce."

Amie hobbles to the chair in the hall. Her foot throbs from being suspended in the air.

"Panic overtook these people quickly. First, they let too many inside."

"The same thing happened at Fort Wood." *It just took longer.* Amie leans her crutches against the wall.

"People naturally want to help each other," Emily says.

"Not anymore. The survivors now are those who are willing to forgo their humanity and do whatever to sustain living," Kayla says.

"We still help people," Emily says. "Ethan still saves people."

"Does he?" Kayla glances at both women. "You've both seen him kill."

"To protect—"

"To protect his own agenda," Kayla cuts Emily off. "About two months after judgment day, I was with a new group. Since I was a nurse, the other six kept me relatively safe. We encounter Ethan loading supplies into a truck. Now the leader of our group was the 'take what he wanted' type. Me having medical skills, he restrained himself. He wanted Ethan's truck, gear, and the shiny gun on his hip."

Emily understands the attraction the silver magnum has for people. People watch the hand cannon over what Ethan does with his fingers. She hopes none of his speed reduces once he heals.

"I've never seen a man move so fast. It wasn't like a quick draw in a Western, but more like the speedy superhero guy. Ethan didn't ask, or question, or give warning. He just...man. The guy told Ethan to drop his gear and step away. Ethan threw back his coat and two thunderclaps boomed."

"He did the same with the four men after the assault on me," Emily says.

Kade Bowlin needed to die. The first man Amie witnessed Ethan kill embodied evil. Nothing in either story changes my mind about a man who kills to defend himself or his surrogate family.

"Ethan then made us an offer we couldn't refuse. He had us discard our guns. We had him outnumbered and none of us wanted to test his speed, especially since he had a second gun to draw."

"He brought you back here."

"He had electricity and part of the premotor fence complete around this farmhouse. The five of us decided to stay and follow his rules. They are all still alive here and working."

"Six. You said your group had six and you, so with the leader dead you were six."

"On the way back, one in the group—which I had no attachment to outside of being safe—questioned Ethan and his ability to lead. One member of our group had been a carpenter. So, Ethan protected him and me, but this other guy, was some city council insurance salesman. He got a little too big for his britches and Ethan just shot him."

"In cold blood?"

"It wasn't direct self-defense," Kayla says.

"As I've seen it, if the death of a few sustains the rest of us then that expands the definition of self-defense," Amie says.

"Ethan's important. You've just never seen him as I have. He dishes out punishment like some medieval king," Kayla flips her right wrist over to glance at her watch. "We might as well all three change the sheets.

Amie draws the quilt off Ethan's slumbering frame. She sniffs the moist sheet underneath. It smells of sweat, not urine.

Kayla unhooks the fitted sheet, shoving it up against Ethan's abdomen, careful not to disturb him as he sleeps.

Emily clamps her hand over her mouth to muffle the anguished cry of shock. So much of Ethan's skin is purple or darkening purple whelps. She finds it difficult to locate a spot to place her palms in order to avoid discomfort when she rolls him enough to allow Kayla to yank out the sheet.

Between the three of them they finally get the bed stripped of all linens.

Amie takes a pillowcase and lays it over his exposed crotch.

"You embarrassed?" Emily teases.

"You're fifteen and don't need to see a grown man nude," she whispers.

"I've seen it before. We came in together. I think that social convention went out the window with the necessity to check everyone entering the compound for bites."

"Shhhh!" Kayla hisses.

"Despite segregation of male and female soldiers on base, isn't modesty lost on the battlefield?" Emily adds.

Amie bats the dirty bed clothes toward the hallway door with a crutch. Even if her grandmother said she blossomed into womanhood at age fifteen she would have peed herself to encounter a naked man then.

Emily's experience with boys was limited before the world fell apart and as far as Amie knows it has not changed since Ethan saved her from a brutal attack, he's older—not too old—and experienced. He interacts with Emily and all the women in the camp like a father figure. Three things instantly send many teen girls into a flaming infatuation. Not to mention, he's ruggedly handsome for a white boy.

"Most girls don't want to see it," Amie says.

Kayla nods in agreement as she tucks in a clean sheet over the corner.

"But men kill each other to peek at what women have between their legs," Emily says.

"Men are wired that way. Women instinctively look for a man that will be a good protector. His broad shoulders should draw your attention more than anything. He will give you strong healthy children." Kayla checks the IV. Irritated with their lack of assistance, she asks, "What did you want to do before you enlisted?"

"A psychologist, but my family made too much money for me to go to college without a lot of loans. Just because people make a dollar more than the cutoff line for income doesn't mean they afford more shit. I had a couple of semesters in before I enlisted. I put in for medic since several of my classes were along those lines. I didn't get much in the way of training before the biters happened."

"You were on the military base for nine months. Why didn't you get your training?"

"Training priority became shooting and a lot more guard duty." Amie shifts on her crutches.

Kayla moves like a linebacker, pushing her shoulder against him to roll Ethan enough to slide the clean sheet under him. She hates changing the linen so frequently but the farm house is not as sterile as the hospital room.

He barks a small grunt.

Emily slaps Kayla's arm. "Don't hurt him."

"I'm not. Why don't you help?" Kayla snaps.

Emily reaches under him, grasping the sheet. "He feels weird."

"What do you mean?" Kayla doubts the girl is anything but scared. She doesn't want to miss anything meaningful to a diagnosis.

"His skin feels different."

Amie speculates on how Emily knows. She just didn't figure on him being the kind of man to take advantage of such a helpless young girl. As the respect she had for him wanes, she has to ask, "How do you know what his skin feels like?"

Emily's pale skin flushes red.

"Have you slept with him?" Kayla asks.

"*No*," immediately pops out of her mouth.

"Do you want to?" Amie asks, teasing.

Emily turns beet red before lowering her head to hide her embarrassment. "He says I'm too young."

Amie respect returns. "How does he feel different?"

"He feels so dry. You know, like he needs to moisturize his skin."

"He's dehydrated. He needs more fluids," Kayla says.

CHAPTER FOURTEEN

IT'S NOT MUCH *of a holding cell.* Danziger scans the elementary classroom. *Levin is somewhere in this compound, and if the rest of their internal security is this lax he's freely moving around.* "I'm telling you I must meet your leader."

"He's unavailable," Hal says.

"I know, I brought him back to you. I need to talk to whoever's in charge when he travels outside your compound."

"You spoke to Wanikiya. They're dealing with things and...stuff. You just got to wait."

Those were the military trucks. These people rescued Levin. Danziger knows he'll appear a stark raving mad lunatic. *And I cut up Levin. From cop eyes, I'll appear to be the villain. I hurt him. Not enough. The cuts were deep but not deep enough. I wanted him to suffer. Suffer how I've suffered when he took my little girl. I get the chance again—I'll put a bullet in his brain.*

Swift.

Quick.

Clean.

Over.

If I find him, I'll just take a gun from one of the guards. They all carry one. They'll shoot me, but Levin will be gone, Danziger reflects. *Must qualify to carry, they said. Means everyone in this camp has been trained to shoot and hit a target. If I take a gun by force, I may* not get the chance to shoot Levin. Better to explain to Ethan. Saving his life should give me some credibility. If he wakes. No human should survive such a beating. Inside, he should have every organ turned to mush. He may not be pissing blood but he should be. He should be dead but he seems to be some god damn real life Captain America. *They have hospital equipment here, but it could take weeks for him to wake.* Danziger shakes his head. *Weeks is too long for him to be coherent. Levin will have killed a blonde teen by then. I saw one when they brought me into the building. And I bet there are a few more quartered here. I won't let another girl die. It won't take Levin long before he must quench his hunger.*

Hal flips a chair around, sitting backward to face Danziger. "How did you end up here?"

"St. Louis didn't experience the kind of undead growth as other major cities. No one cares about the fly-over states. The city organized a defensive plan. We kept order for months, but it didn't stop thousands from attempting to flee, blocking all the major highways for miles. As food stores ran low, people organized a caravan to reach Fort Leonard Wood." Danziger leaves out how he wasn't a part of this plan. "A massive herd swept over the caravan survivors scattering them. I met a man. Tom. He went one direction to assist; I went in the other direction."

"Were you able to help anyone?"

Danziger lowers his head. "The herd—"

"Yeah," Hal agrees, "I've seen what a group of those things do."

"Did I hear you say there was a shower?" Showering is the last thing he wants to do, but if he cleans up and appears calm it might be more convincing for the second-in-command. He runs his forefinger and thumb over his stubbly chin. *A less patchy growth would make me appear less insane. I can't be the first raving lunatic they will have seen. I have to appear normal. Too bad I lost my badge; it would add to my credibility.*

Wanikiya chops peppers on a cutting board.

"She needs to be on guard duty at least, if not out protecting those working outside the fence," Simon demands.

"No." Wanikiya shakes his head. "Ethan cut a deal with her father. All the supplies, military trucks, and personnel for her safety. Even the tanks on the dam we got months before. I don't know if the army will ever ride in to save us, but Colonel Travis left in a helicopter with the expectation to find his daughter alive and well. Outside this group, he is the only living person who knows we commandeered the dam and have power. Those tanks guarding our electrical source are due to him." He slides the peppers off the cutting board into a plastic sealable container.

"You can't put her to scrubbing garbage cans. It won't sell your established rules," Simon says.

The Sioux contemplates the ramification of his choice before rendering the verdict. "Simon, I value your perspective and wisdom. No outside patrol work or gate duty puts her at ill-advised risk. But if she is as skilled as you say, I must use her. Put her on the roaming fence patrol." He slices a loaf of homemade bread.

"Popping biters through the fence, checking for human invaders still has risk," Simon says.

"Living is risk. But we do nobody any favors by hiding them in a hole. Even Dartagnan pulls his weight. Unless Hannah has a more useful skill, she's on roaming patrol tomorrow." Wanikiya marks it down in a notebook. He chews his bottom lip. More people guard than run other operations. They need more residences.

"The horse-backed team?" Simon asks.

"If she's able to ride." Wanikiya completes the sandwich with mayo on the side in a dipping cup. He places a factory-sealed orange juice carton on a tray. "Our guest needs lunch. They say his arms are healing. Did you see them?"

"No. Deep gashes according to the gate guards."

"Someone didn't want him to escape without losing a hand. The question is why?"

"With all the sickos out there...I would bet food."

"Ethan warned of such people." Wanikiya carries the tray from the kitchen.

Hal keeps one hand on his holstered pistol. He has little trust for this man if Ethan is unable to vouch for him. Wanikiya places the tray on the floor just out of Danziger's reach. "You'll forgive my precautions."

"Fully understandable. You've converted some of these rooms; why not make a jail?" Danziger rubs his smooth chin. Fresh clothes and clean bandages cover his frame.

"Up until now, secure punishment was not necessary. Most of the time rule infractions are dealt with by cutting food rations. No one here wants to go hungry. Serious issues are met with banishment."

"I'm your first prisoner?" Danziger takes a bite of the beef sandwich.

"If you've survived this long then you know trust is no longer granted."

"I get it. Thanks for the lunch and the shower."

"He keeps requesting to meet with our leader," Hal says.

"I'm just concerned." Danziger coughs. He spits up his food bite.

"Danziger, are you okay?" Wanikiya asks.

"No. I feel woozy." Danziger catches himself on the bed.

Wanikiya hands his firearm and tomahawk to Hal before stepping in to help Danziger to the bed. Danziger sweats with fever.

"Get the doctor," Wanikiya orders.

CHAPTER FIFTEEN

THE WAIL STARTLES Amie enough she has to grab the arm of the chair in order to prevent her from tumbling to the floor. She finally fell asleep. *How Emily curls up like a cat I can't figure. The girl's almost as tall as me. With thinner thighs.* The stiff high-back chair stopped being comfortable for her two days ago.

Ethan tosses and mumbles in his sleep.

Amie strains her ear, but the name he mumbles is inaudible.

The scent of wet grass drifts in the open window.

Amie fishes in her blanket for her flashlight, but the moonlight brightens the room and allows her to witness Ethan tumbling from one side of the bed to the other. His fists pound the mattress squeaking the springs.

In the last three days, they have had to move him manually every few hours to prevent bed sores. Now his violent attack threatens to jolt him to the bed. She knows with one good leg she doesn't have the leverage to help him from the floor.

If Ethan wasn't a mass of bruises my cuddling next to him might pacify his dreams.

Amie hops to the bed using only one crutch. She leans in an attempt to understand the mumblings. Ethan paws at the sheets. Amie worries the IV will be torn loose. She reaches out to pin the flailing arm. The other hand tightens in her hair so swiftly she becomes discombobulated on top of him. She stretches her wounded foot out off of the mattress so if she falls she'll be able to keep it suspended in the air.

The force he uses to jerk Amie around drains his strength. Ethan maneuvers her next to him as if he's comforting a small child. He babbles as he caresses her head. Long after he settles and the mumbling halts, Amie slips her tee-shirt off pressing her bare back against his chest in order to be as comfortable as possible. She adjusts his left arm so she doesn't bump the IV. She draws her legs up so if he thrashes again he won't strike her foot. She takes his right hand wrapping it around her so he cups one of her breasts. As soon as he grips her breast, his arm constricts and Ethan instinctively pulls her tight against him as if to never release her.

Amie drifts off to sleep faster than she ever remembers, knowing she's never felt safer in her life.

Morning birds chirp with the sun peeking in the window. Amie's comfort keeps her from moving even if his member pokes into her back. She slides her hand down her back, reaching behind her and gripping the morning stiffness. She smiles as she wraps her fingers around it. She works her hand along the shaft. A pleasured grunt escapes from his lips. Her work is met with a pulse of desire, but he remains asleep. She pulls her arm back to unclamp his hand from her breasts. As she slides from under the covers to retrieve her t-shirt, her eyes meet with Emily.

CHAPTER SIXTEEN

DANZIGER REMEMBERS THE sting. He's sure he felt a needle jab his right side. It was too clear and sharp a pain to have been a dream. Now in his groggy state, he resists the manhandling of his limbs.

"*Fucking murderer,*" a voice screams.

Danziger has no idea what's happening until handcuffs bite into his wrist. They sting from more than just the cuff pressure.

They want to restrain me. Naturally, I resist, but that may not be the best option. If I could clear my head, I wouldn't have fought them. They didn't have to drug me. I would have cuffed up to meet with Ethan.

No screams of "fucking murderer" taint his ears again.

They think I killed someone.

He has put up little resistance. Danziger needs to clear his mind before he—

The slam against the wall with the pressure still on his chest jars him enough to be able to open his eyes.

His fever. They brought him food. His wrists burned. *What happened?*

Wanikiya—not a trained fighter. His towering size and strength allows him to toss much smaller men around. The Sioux, in full warrior mode, pins Danziger to the wall with his boot while he secures a man in a headlock with his left arm and holds a second man to the bars with his gleaming tomahawk.

"We are civilized," Wanikiya reminds them. He drops the breathless man to the floor.

Danziger's fingers are stuck together. Something has congealed over them. He needs to eat something. That might help him to metabolize the drug from that needle stick.

"We have our rules."

The man on the floor pants for breath. "He's covered in her blood."

Fuck. That's what's sticky. Levin. He has killed and framed me. It's the only logical explanation. He set me up. Now any claim I make against him will only make me the crazy one. Okay, Danziger, you have to clear your head and think about this. They clearly have due process they want to follow, but it has little room for reasonable doubt when you are covered in the victim's blood.

"Cuff his hands," Wanikiya orders. "And back out of here, Ryan."

Danziger holds up his arms to allow to be cuffed. Once he feels the bite on both wrists, the pressure on his chest relinquishes.

"Get me Dr. Baker and then Dr. Sterling. Be quick and quiet. You announce murder and I won't feed you for a week."

Going to bed without supper. Before Danziger blows off that threatened punishment, he ponders that a week without food would be severe. *There's no place to get more food. And if they are willing to be that harsh then I could be put to death with no trial.*

"As for you, Ty, I should leave you a nice scar to remind everyone of your inability to follow the rules. But I won't." Wanikiya lowers the axe.

"You haven't seen Kayla's body or you'd want him dead, too." Ty rubs the red mark on his neck where the blade could have severed his aorta.

"I want justice. This place won't work if we turn to lynching. And this man was locked in this room."

"He's covered in her blood," Ty protests.

"Compelling evidence, I agree."

Ryan returns with Dr. Baker.

"What's going on?"

Wanikiya nudges Ty with his boot, promoting him to answer.

"Our patrol this morning found a hand sticking from a shallow grave in the herb garden. It was nurse Kayla."

Dr. Baker notes the blood all over Danziger. "So, you find this newcomer and drug him in here to beat a confession out of him?"

"No. We found him in here sleeping, covered in her blood."

Dr. Baker kneels to be eye level with Ty. "How do you know it was her blood?"

"I don't."

"If this man committed murder we have to be sure before we take action. We won't allow such a savage act to turn us into savages." Dr. Baker rises. He witnesses firsthand how Ethan handles a rape conviction. He's not keen on frontier justice even for murder. "We need to photograph the body and him before any more evidence is destroyed. I'll test the blood on him and her and see if they are the same type."

"That will be a start."

Wanikiya and the doctor both glare at Danziger.

"I was locked in here all night." His only defense.

"The door?" Wanikiya nudges Ty with his boot again.

"It was locked and he was in a deep sleep," Ty says.

"If you're going to gather evidence, then you should examine at my side. Last night I felt something jab me. Here." He points to the spot.

"Lie down," Dr. Baker orders.

Danziger complies. *He seems to want reasonable doubt or at least to compile evidence before they execute me.*

Dr. Baker palpates the skin. "Take a picture of that. It's a needle stick."

"Why would anyone here set this man up?" Wanikiya asks.

Time for the insanity defense. "I told you I was a cop. I was tracking a serial killer. I think the military convoy trucks I saw parked outside rescued him. I think he saw me before I could prove he was here."

"So, he sets you up to take the fall for his murders. Why not tell us as soon as you arrived?" Wanikiya asks.

"I have been asking to speak with Ethan. I didn't want to alert this killer I was here, and I didn't want to come across as a lunatic. Levin has wounds, and I caused them." *A risk to admit but I need to restore some credibility.*

"You passed out three days ago from your fever. Cop or not, why keep chasing this guy? It gains you nothing in a world where you can't even eat every day."

"One of his victims was my daughter."

CHAPTER SEVENTEEN

KALE BOWLIN, THE youngest of five brothers, kicks his way past empty beer cans and liquor bottles. Forced to step over stoned, naked people who just collapsed to sleep when finished with their throws of raw animal passion. A drug fueled orgy of decadence—it sickens him.

Being the youngest, he knows, or knew full well, of the fetish depravities of his older brothers. Those urges cost three of them their lives. If he doesn't stop the remaining one, they won't have the supplies survive now Fort Wood's been destroyed. His march across the minefield of passed out drunks concludes at a recliner where a brunette bobs her head up and down at brother number four's crouch.

Kale laces his fingers into her hair and pulls her up. Her dirty face is marked with slobbers of spittle. He flings her to the floor.

Kaleb's eyes flash open. "Why'd you stop, bitch?" He rears up, ready to slap her when he spots his youngest brother. "What the fuck you think you're doing interrupting me?"

As much as he forces his eyes not to, they spot his brother's flaccid manhood.

"She's been fucking sucking all night; I was about to get hard."

"Maybe you should lay off the meth," Kale advises.

"You should try fucking on that shit, little bro."

"I see the results for myself." Kale tosses a throw pillow over his brother. "It has left you enfeebled. Now, since you're unable to rise—get out of the chair and find your pants."

"You fuckin' can't order me around; I'm older than you. Kade left me in charge."

"And in the week of your rule you've allowed half a year's food to be devoured. Kade would never allow this to go on. Now get up. Quit worrying about your penis and rule this camp, or it won't matter if you can get hard or not."

Kaleb trips over his own pants as he lunges for Kale. He falls onto a slumbering couple. In their drug-induced state, they take little notice except to grunt from the impact.

Kale marches to the door. "This ends now."

Kaleb staggers onto the porch covering his eyes from the morning sunlight. "I need to eat first, you little shit."

"I'm sure food in your stomach would help you to metabolize the drugs in your system, but more than likely you'd just vomit and waste what little food we have left." He visually surveys the farm. "There are no guards at the gate and with everyone passed out from your *parties*, because I lack the vernacular to describe what goes on in there, anyone could drive up and steal what diminutive amounts we have left."

"Little bro, the world has ended and, well... It's time to par-tay." He makes the rock-n-roll sign with his right hand and flicks his Gene Simmons tongue at him.

"The world has not ended. It has been reborn, and we're here at its inception. We build what we want it to be."

"I want it to be an orgy." Kaleb sniffs at the back of his hand as if he were drawing in coke.

"Which you have done. When the people figure out you have no food supply, how much longer do you think they will follow you? Any of those girls will pleasure you orally if you don't have meat scraps to throw them?"

"Why don't you just say 'fuck'?"

"The use of inappropriate social language shows a lack of creative intelligence. Despite our hillbilly upbringing, I utilize my education. Not only would I have been the first Bowlin to attend college, I was prepared to graduate in three years with a Master's."

"Mommy said you were the smart one. It took her five tries, but you got some brains."

"Mother, may she rest in peace, was correct. Despite Father's ruined sperm count after years of drinking, I retain the highest of intelligence," Kale says.

"Then use it to fix our food problem."

"Since many of these men were loyal to Kade, they look to you for leadership. I will tell you what to do. You'll lead these people and we will rebuild this world as we want it to be."

"I want pussy."

"If you are good I'll allow rewards." He waves a blister pack of four blue pills before Kaleb.

As Kaleb reaches for them, Kale jerks them out of reach. "Only after we get this camp functional. I'd wager half those women we brought here as sex slaves are now with child. We're not equipped to raise children."

"What do we do first, little bro?"

"First, find someone with enough sobriety to stand guard at the main gate. Then you and I are going to interrogate the agent assigned here by FEMA. After what our brother did to her, I'm sure she'll answer all my questions."

Why would a government agency want to use this farm as a staging point to help people during a disaster? Converting the barn into a loading bay to pull semi-trucks completely inside to hide them from aerial view while they unload makes little sense for an agency mandated to assist in disaster relief. FEMA never got a chance to finish stocking this place with provisions. The location's too far out of the way from major cities for effective distribution of emergency supplies. Unless there was a reason for it I have yet to uncover, Kale wonders.

Metal cattle panels line the inside of a horse stall to prevent any escape. Naked and bruised, the dirt-stained woman scampers into the far corner as Kale opens the door. Bare skin grips her ribs. She cowers in the fetal position, prepared to be assaulted again.

"I'm here to keep you from further harm." He drops his tone to one of being pleasant and friendly.

Her eyes blankly stare at the light from the door.

"Which is true. I don't see violence as a viable solution, but it can be necessary to quickly obtain what information one wants."

She twists away from him. Covering her back are bandages crusted with dried blood.

"What I will say is, don't make me use violence to achieve what I want." Kale smells the stale sex forced upon her. He contemplates this woman might respond to a bath or other methods including cleaning wounds festering with infection.

Kaleb blocks the doorway as he eats from an MRE package.

No matter what kind of government training she had, Lindsey no longer has the control she once did. Her eyes glare at only the food pouch.

Kale contemplates from the smells; no one has bothered to clean the stall in days or logically feed her either. *How desperate for food will she be?*

"Lindsey? That is your name, correct?" Kale snaps his fingers in her face. "Focus on me."

Her mouth salivates with the last bit of hydration she can produce.

"I can't do anything to make up for all the pain inflicted upon you, but if you cooperate, I can promise no one else will hurt you." He adds, "I am nothing like my brothers."

Lindsey's eyes reveal how unconvinced she is by his words.

"For sure. You even fucked a girl, bro." Kaleb munches on his MRE.

Kale waves for Kaleb to step closer so he can snatch the MRE bag. "Why don't you eat?" He holds out the pouch as far as his arm will stretch toward Lindsey. "I'll see if I can find some of the girls to come clean you up. And then we'll talk."

She grabs it, but he refuses to let go.

"I know you're starving, but eat slow or it will make you sick."

CHAPTER EIGHTEEN

AMIE SLIPS FROM under the cover, replacing Ethan's warmth against her with the morning chill. It perks her nipples, giving a false impression of arousal. As she reaches for her t-shirt, Emily steps in, food tray in hand. Broth steams in a bowl.

"What the fuck?" Emily demands.

"He's asleep. Lower your voice." Amie hops on one foot to reach her crutches. She scans the floor for her missing shirt.

"He's in no condition for you to..." Emily fights everything inside her not to throw the food tray or smash it against the floor. Her pale skin flushes red.

"He's a man. If he is breathing—he's capable."

Amie tosses her shirt out the door past Emily before taking the quivering food tray from Emily's hands before she drops it. She places it on the table and backs the teen out the door with her naked chest as a buffer. Closing the door behind her, she uses the end of a crutch to flip the shirt into her hand. "It's not what you think."

"If it quacks—"

"I just wanted to sleep next to someone. Maybe you haven't experienced the desire to hold someone, but I needed some contact. There was no sex. He never woke up." Amie doesn't want to explain Ethan's night terrors. Later, she must inform the doctor.

"Everyone thinks I'm too young to understand. I get you're a lying whore. You said...I trusted you."

"Keep your voice down. You'll disturb Dartagnan."

"It's okay to upset me. I held vigil over him when they brought him back. I took care of him. You moved in like some scabby bush monkey and stole him from me."

Scabby bush monkey? Amie's never heard such an insult before. *I'll skip being offended until I know what one is.*

Emily almost laughs. "I was reading about monkeys to David, the new boy. I don't know where—"

"I get you're upset. I didn't take advantage of Ethan in his present condition. I don't think I could have even if I had wanted to," Amie lies. Even beaten to near death with no damage to his manhood, he was maintaining a full salute and she could have done all the work.

"You're trying to take him from me."

Amie holds in an eye roll. The last issue Amie wants to deal with is the frustrations of a teenage girl.

"He doesn't want either of us. He wasn't awake to know I was even there."

"Maybe he just doesn't want *you*."

"He turned you down too, twice. You said so." Amie gives in to her nature and fences with Emily.

"He's just waiting until I'm older. I don't want you to ruin him."

"He's a man. And if he was half as charismatic before the apocalypse as he is now then more than one women ruined him long before you were born."

"He's not that old." Soured by the age factor, the fight drains from Emily.

"You need to feed him. I need to make a report."

"I'm sure you'll leave out you rubbed your titties all over him." Emily marches from the room. Before she reaches the stairs, she kicks the military duffle bag stations outside the second bedroom door. She pushes it open. The bed sports fresh sheets. Amie would not be allowed to just take the room as all beds are assigned.

Emily wishes she had been given the room next to Ethan. With Amie close to him on a daily basis when he is in camp, she might steal him away with her ample bosom. She runs her hand across her own chest. Maybe she has the build of a teen boy, but no one would live for him like she would.

Dartagnan pushes between the two women as if they are not even there. "Wrong time to be in the kitchen. You two should not be in the kitchen. I need brown. Did Ethan bring me brown paint?"

Amie slips her hand into the outside pocket on her BDUs. She was able to get most of the blood out and next she needs to sew the torn pant leg. "He brought you this." She holds out a model paint vial.

Dartagnan snatches it. He examines it as if it were a newborn baby. "Green. I've got green. I need brown."

Amie shifts into her commanding mother voice. "What do you say, Dartagnan?" The Latina scold in her tone makes the boy jump.

"Thank you, Miss Amie."

"You're welcome."

"Please, can I see the new fences they are building," Dartagnan pleads.

"I'll take you in a little while," she says.

Dartagnan scampers off to his replica of the compound.

"See, you'll need me to watch Ethan if you drive Dartagnan around," Emily says.

"You could take him," Amie suggests.

"I never got a license, and you handle Dartagnan almost as good as me. Better than I've even seen Ethan."

"He was raised only by his mother. Wanikiya said be harsh or he won't listen. But even if Mom was harsh, her tone would show how much she loved him."

Emily whispers, "How did you know about the paint?"

"Ethan always brings back model paint for him to use on his recreation of the compound. Only he doesn't always find more paint every time he goes out. Wanikiya gave me a few vials from a hidden stash to help me appease Dartagnan."

"They say Dartagnan's calculations keep us fed," Emily says.

"I've heard. He keeps it all in his head."

"He just thinks numbers."

"I can't make you leave, but you should report back to your job," Amie says.

"I had to stretch my legs for a minute and I'm going right back up there. Don't worry, I won't eat any of the food. I haven't earned since I'm not working."

"You just don't know how long he will be out." Amie stuffs a bundle of bed sheets into the washer. "You shouldn't try so hard."

"What are you talking about?" Emily sniffs the freshly dried clothes before she folds them.

"Trying to give yourself to Ethan."

Emily drops her head. She knows her pale face reddened with embarrassment. Then the red deepens with anger. "Who are you to tell me—"

"You're not a jilted school girl anymore, but yet you don't have the experience to read men."

"Is this where you dispense advice like in a badly written Romcom?"

"It's not that you don't arouse him, but something in his real brain holds him back." Amie fishes for an answer as to what caused Ethan's night terror. He spent days with Emily outside the fence. He may have mentioned something. Emily would never tell her under direct examination.

"He doesn't want to defile a fifteen-year-old."

"Noble, makes him desirable in itself, but there's something else. He could have his pick of women in this camp. He's saved most of them. I'm sure there is a line of women who would thank him with their favors, but he pushes them all back. He has put together a safe zone that has amenities. We couldn't keep hot water on the military base. Even with that and the duties of governing us, he still journeys outside."

"He wants to save people. Find people to make us stronger."

"At first he could find the people he needed to run the camp. Now it's just any survivors. Picking and choosing has reached an impasse if the community is to grow. Anyone can go outside and gather people. Why does he have to keep going out there?"

"You've strayed from your original question of why he won't sleep with either one of us." Emily enjoys the jab. Even if Amie had crawled in next to him just as comfort, she could have left her shirt on.

Amie knows the barb was meant to hurt. She propositioned her new commanding officer and had been rejected. "Now both answers are the same. Whatever pushes him to go out there keeps him from picking a mate in here."

"You're callous. You don't know Ethan."

"I know since he doesn't desire us there are still other options in Acheron. You with your budding breasts and willingness to open your legs can have a choice of men in this compound. Those kids you eat lunch with, those boys want you. Why not have a go with them?" Amie asks

"I don't like them."

"Why not? Why do you want a man approaching the age of your father?"

"I don't know."

"Nature. If for no other reason. Your body wants the best provider and strongest DNA to be passed on to any offspring you produce. He has by far proven himself to be the alpha male in this camp. The major reason why so many women want him."

"You're crazy."

"I studied this, and I know my own desires. In times of disaster, women have natural urges to want to reproduce. That's why so many babies were born nine months after the Haitian earthquake. Biology demands the rebuilding of the species and nature wants us to do it with the best possible DNA," Amie explains.

"Even if that's correct, it doesn't explain why he chooses to turn down every woman in the compound."

"Maybe he likes men," Amie wonders. "It would explain his over macho-ness."

"No."

"Maybe he can't perform anymore." Amie knows that is a lie.

"No. I've known that's not true." Emily remembers that night she offered herself to him after her first shower in this farmhouse. She wanted Ethan so badly she wettened until it ran down her legs and he swelled fully. How he controlled himself she'll never understand.

"Then he's protecting himself," Amie says.

"From what?"

"Everyone who survives has lost most everyone they care about. Some people have had to do unspeakable actions to endure. Maybe he had to kill someone who he loved and can't stand the thought of having to do it again. Those feelings could overpower a man's desires to deflower a pretty girl."

"Well, a Hispanic hoochie mama isn't to his liking either."

CHAPTER NINETEEN

LEVIN SLIPS FROM his bed. Hot needles puncture his side. The wound requires more days of rest to heal. Danziger's presence in the camp means he's lost his advantage over these peasants. Better to put his plan in motion now and lead them toward his wisdom later. He fishes under the mattress for the paperclip he hid. The bent metal will allow him to free his left hand from the handcuffs.

He waits until they ship the man named Clay out of the other bed. Whoever decided curtains provided a wall of privacy was a moron. They kept Clay two days to make sure he didn't die from his fall. He was banged up but not as bad as all the scrapes made him appear. And they seemed to make constant inspections of him when he slept. Levin wonders if Kayla did the same to him while he slept. When he sleeps.

The guards roaming patrols of the school-turned-community-building lack any formal structure or regulated pattern. Perhaps planned, but most likely unregulated guards never having any formal security training.

Levin moves quickly not knowing if the guards could return in five minutes or five hours. Creeping in the hall, he flattens around a darkened corner allowing him to witness the guards round up some people sneaking off to fuck. They wrangle then return them toward the gym allowing him to reach the kitchen. He jiggles the handle—locked. Levin races back to his room. Now with patients in the hospital ward they keep a watchful eye on it but don't bother to lock the door.

Logic dictates he should just sneak in and kill Danziger before the man decides he must tell these people about his past actions. Danziger's cuts could cause a fatal infection. The former cop's unwise in not revealing how Levin kills. Wanting to murder Levin personally is foolish. He doubts these people would bat an eye, and since he's not a part of their community yet, they might just banish the detective. They seem big on threatening banishment.

Maybe Danziger's presence works to his advantage. He has one use while breathing. Danziger tracked in order to kill him and fuck him bloody.

Levin shivers at that thought. *I may kill and pleasure young girls, but I'm no homo.*

No homo.

It takes Levin a second to pounce. Kayla might have reached her gun had she expected the attack from a living patient. Or the gun wasn't around her ankle. The gun clinks on the floor. Levin kicks it out of her reach as he wraps his arm around her throat.

She won't go down without a struggle. Kayla puts all her strength into an elbow thrust strong enough to tear open his cut.

The air rushes from Levin, but he keeps her entangled, driving her to the floor.

The elbow impact hurt and had she placed it on the other side of his chest he'd be near death. But in the confusion, she struck the unwounded side of his body. As he cuts off her air he drives a scalpel blade into her neck. Blood squirts. As the fight slips from Kayla he slides a bucket from under the bed. He catches as much of her blood as possible.

The assault should have excited him, but this woman—too old for his taste—did nothing to arouse him. She's key to his plan.

The classroom next to this has been transformed into offices and a more useful medical supply storage. He knows the medications are secured. Antibiotics and other meds will keep many people alive. The poor souls who need insulin or kidney drugs have long since become the demon at the gates. He uses Kayla's keys to open the locked cabinets. They should post a guard over the meds besides just securing them. They are valuable. These people have established a society and they must feel safer knowing there are meds when they need them. He wonders how they will feel when they are all gone.

If he could control his urge. He knows how to make a basic penicillin. An antibiotic would make him a rich man in this world. *Rich how? Money's no good, and they won't trade one life of teen girl for him to enjoy. Or would they? If I healed them would make me their leader.*

Everything is labeled and charted on a clipboard. In a drawer, he discovers his luckiest find. He scoops up the gun from the drawer. Its breach open, he can see it has a place for a dart—tranquilizers.

CHAPTER TWENTY

"YOU BELIEVE THAT bitch?" snarls Kaleb. "Just kill her. One less mouth you're worried about feeding."

"She's not from the area. All these back roads appear the same to anyone not familiar with them." Kale spreads a highway map across the kitchen table. "We're down here in Dent County. I think you should take a crew into Rolla."

"You...think I should, little brother." Kaleb's head throbs. His body transitions into hangover mode.

"When these inebriated meth-heads wake, you must whip them into shape before we completely run out of supplies. Kade led supply runs. People respect leaders who aren't afraid to jump into the trenches. You want them to follow you the way they did Kade, don't you?"

"Well, yeah. So, I lead a group into Rolla."

"Go to the courthouse and in the assessor's office there should be a giant county map. I need it, so we can track our search patterns. We will clean every farm and small town for supplies."

"Why not just start here?"

"Phelps County had a larger population, theoretically there will be more supplies to gather. A lot of those people were evacuated in the first days to Fort Wood and left their homes intact."

A light bulb clicks for Kaleb. "We should send a team to the military base. See what's left."

"Good idea." Kale placates his brother. "Most of the area was picked over by those fleeing the base after the soldiers scuttled it. But some supplies may have survived."

Kaleb smiles. His smarter, younger brother likes his idea.

"We need seed. Corn, and not hybrid corn. We need to plant a crop even if it's getting too late for a full fall harvest."

"We going to need copper pipe for a still."

"We're going to need corn to eat and feed cattle." Kale quickly realizes he could be overstepping his authority. "And some whiskey."

Kaleb grins.

"But we can't make it through winter on liquor alone."

"Winter's seven months from now."

"Did Mother never read to you?" Kale inquires.

"Like she had time to read shitting out five kids."

"I'll get you a copy of the allegory *The Ant and the Grasshopper*," Kale says.

"Bro, does it have pictures?"

"Seven months gives us plenty of time to stock supplies. Canned food only lasts so long. Most of the boxed stuff will be reaching its expiration dates by now. Gasoline will sour and rust out car tanks. We have to prepare."

"I say we beat that Lindsey girl 'til she tells us where the other FEMA trucks are."

"We could. She might know, but food will expire and there's no guarantee someone else hasn't raided the trucks already. We must establish ourselves."

"We just raid for supplies."

"I just explained to you how that will only work for a little while longer."

"You want to turn us all into farmers?" Kaleb spits.

"I've calculated without a gas supply in two years we'll be plowing the field with oxen."

"These men won't go for that. They'll leave."

"I realize they would rather face death in the unknown than perform manual labor."

"Then who's going to work it, slaves?" Kaleb asks.

"I know your redneck IQ demands you believe in the South rising again, but a slave system won't work. If you paid more attention in history class you'd understand slavery brought the end to the South. I propose we use feudalism."

Kaleb's eyes go blank.

"Don't stop to think, you won't start again. You, Kaleb, will function as the lord of the manor. We won't use the term 'king', but you, as our *Lord and Protector*, will do just that. These men we have now will become your vassals. They will bring in survivors and we will make them—"

Kaleb interrupts, "Slaves."

"Serfs. We'll make use of Serfdom."

"What's that?"

"You did complete the eighth grade. You studied manorialism, the cornerstone of feudal society in the high middle ages."

Kaleb retains his deer-in-the-headlights stare.

"I'll keep it simple. You find people. You bring them back here. They agree to farm the land and you and your men protect them. No rape. No beatings. No abuse."

"What if they don't want to farm?"

"Then when you go out on your next supply run you drop them off. They'll stay and work to feed their protectors."

"That sounds like a pretty good system. Why'd they stop doing it?"

"Democracy."

"We won't have none of that."

"No. You're the Lord and your word is law, but, Kaleb, you can't abuse the serfs. We need them as much as they need us. And we need to find a doctor or we'll have to employ the horse-has-a-broken-leg method."

"Execute our wounded."

"From now on, anyone hurt badly enough to die will return and we can't have them attacking anyone. Now, put together a crew and take two trucks. I need the map, and find a feed store."

"What are you going to do?"

"Determine which fields are best to plow for planting."

Maybe some Latin painted above the farm gate—Survival First. Not that I remember much Latin. The motto will serve as a reminder. I'll keep this camp secure and my brother under control. Infected shouldn't be a major issue. Swarms of the undead have no reason to travel this far from the interstate and steadier food supplies. A cattle herd may attract attention. We will have to build a stock yard and pen them up at night. Once my survival projects are underway, I'll focus Kaleb on my true agenda, Kale plots.

Finding and personally killing the unnamed man who murdered Kade and Kani. He won't let his brothers' deaths go unavenged. Reports have the military convoy going west after Fort Wood exploded. An irrational vengeance should send him scouring to the west and even raid the military base. Foolish actions, and he understands that. No, the man killing Kade was smart. Not as smart as him, but smart. He faked going west. At some point, he doubles back and his camp is somewhere in the east. He will send Kaleb on a county-by-county search until they find him. It will take time but a brother never forgets.

Kale decided to add motivation to his brother's mission.

Kale leads Kaleb to a small white utility shed behind the farmhouse. The hum of the generator permeates the air.

"Once food supplies and security has been established, you have one final task to perform as the head of our family."

Inside, a hospital bed contains a man shackled to the rails. Medical monitors chirp and beep with the patient's vitals. Charred and burnt chunks of skin cover exposed chest, arms and bald head. Regulating his breathing through oxygen tubes taped over the hole where the nose once was. Intravenous fluids and other medical devices monitor his vitals.

"You're concerned with dwindling resources and my meth parties and you keep *this...thing* alive."

"Take a closer look at the *thing* in the bed," Kale orders

"Looks like a charcoal briquette."

"It's Hale. Kade's wingman."

"He failed my brother and you're keeping him alive. What the fuck for?" He flicks open his knife blade.

"He's been in and out of a coma. My intention was not to waste needed medicine, but to learn Kade's fate."

"He has tubes down his throat, and I didn't think coma patients could talk."

"I will explain this for your fifth-grade education."

"I'm not stupid, just not book smart."

"After we abandoned Fort Leonard Wood, I waited for people to flee the Infected drawn to the base by the explosions. I took a team back to scavenge. I found Hale in a smoldering building. He had crawled there bleeding from multiple bullet wounds. He used the fire to cauterize the bleeding. The pain overwhelms him and he passed out still on fire," Kale explains.

"Put a bullet in him and end his pain. He's earned sleep and not returning."

"His brain still functions unlike yours. It has taken me all week, but with the work of a sketch artist I have a composite of the man who killed our brother." Kale takes a plastic-covered paper from the table next to the bed. "This man left the base with a caravan of military supplies and people with specific skills needed to survive in this new world."

"In a month, they would all be used up."

"Not if they have a compound and ration the supplies. Only a fool parties away a year's worth of emergency rations in a week. This man will have a colony and have more than just these supplies. He went north. After we secure our camp, we hunt him and take what he loves." Kale flips a light switch, cutting power to the medical equipment before handing Kaleb a sketch of Ethan.

CHAPTER TWENTY-ONE

STATUESQUE IN A prone position, Levin lies across the barn rafters. None of those who enter the open framed structure bother to glance up—until he pounces.

Levin tackles George.

The attack hinders Sam from escaping. She finds herself unable to scream. Her brain, powerless to handle another attack, relives the moment when Kyle grabbed her. He forced himself on top of her and then into her. Equally horrifying was Ethan's interrogation of her about the assault. As much as she wanted Kyle punished, she understood why so many women never reported rape. Telling about it was worse. Nearly worse than the original brutalization. Ethan's punishment was beyond the Old Testament from Sunday school. Or was it? Kyle took something from her, and as retribution, Ethan removed something of Kyle's.

She trusted the doctors when they said she had to go back into the barn in order to deal with her assault. She backs up against the wall. Her eyes widen as Levin's blade slashes into the cowering George.

The dark-headed George annoyed her, but he never made her insecure about being alone with him. He lacked an imposing demeanor being shorter than her. Best he could do in a fight was bite someone in the kneecap.

The scalpel dulls with each slash. Levin makes no wide arching swings; all his cuts are precision. When he ceases, blood splatters cover him and decorate the hay like a child's first finger painting. Dealt dozens of cuts, George moans on the ground. As Levin steps toward her, George finds one last bit of strength to grab Levin's ankle. Levin merely kicks the man in the ribs, sending concussive coughs through him.

Somewhere in Sam's mind she wonders why this crazed lunatic leaves George to bleed out. She should be figuring out a way to escape. George moans a puppy whimper. He reaches out his arm and digs his finger through the straw, pushing into the dirt. With a firm grip, he drags himself toward the door. Inching forward, he only moves about the length of his hand before Levin slashes off his pinky finger. George whines.

Nothing Sam does prevents the flood of her emotions. The terror of her previous assault melts her knees. Her mind overlaps this attack with what Kyle did to her. Her mixing thoughts of both events makes it impossible for her to know what reality she sinks into. Something inside Sam demands she screams. Another part remembers what Kyle said, *She'd live if she just let it happen.* If she screamed he'd snap her neck. She'll return as a biter. He'd shoot her and no one would ever know. They'd assume she fell in the barn.

George groans.

Pain means he lives, but Sam has no chance of rescue from him. She wishes he'd die. As a biter, he might be able to help her. Near death offers no hope. Sam needs George to die. If he's dead she might be able to run while the new biter distracts her assailant. Run. She forgot how to run. His hot breath radiates goose flesh down her back as he breathes on her neck.

"You're almost too old."

Seventeen.

She's only seventeen. Ripe for plucking in the old world even if she's still built like a scarecrow. He's even more sick than she realized if he wants younger girls. Sam's thoughts betray her desire to escape.

Memories of Kyle's assault overshadows the touch of this man's cupping her left breast. Her nipple stiffens then falls, collapsing in. The impact on the ground forces all the air from her lungs. She has no fight in her.

"Please don't cut me," she whimpers.

He yanks her to her shaking legs by her dirty blonde hair. Marching her from the barn, she gets five feet before her legs give out. Levin drags her like a caveman's trophy wife.

Pain.

Needles puncture her skullcap as all the hair follicles fight being torn loose. Sam opens her mouth. She must scream. She believed resisting Kyle's violation of her womanhood meant death. She realizes this maniac intends to kill her whether she cooperates or if she struggles. Some new fire flickers in her soul. Better in her last few moments to live standing than to be the frightened girl forced to endure a second assault.

Stepping closer toward him reduces the pull he maintains on her hair. His firm grip doesn't relax, but Levin didn't expect her to move toward him. Giving Sam a moment—half a second at best—to execute a plan of resistance. She swings. The last few weeks of farm work added to her musculature. The battering ram punch bends the bulge in Levin's pants. Enough to cause instant flaccidness and a whimper. He folds onto his butt.

Success, but Levin never released the grip on her hair. Sam finds her face raked over the gravel. Wet scrapes burn.

CHAPTER TWENTY-TWO

HANNAH SLIDES THE rifle into the leather scabbard secured to the saddle. She checks her synch strap before flipping down the stirrup.

"I didn't know you could ride," Nick says.

"Privileged white girl syndrome I don't have. Maybe you thought I needed an English saddle."

"No. Military bases no longer have a cavalry."

"Shouldn't you be working?" she asks.

"Give you a gun and you're a different girl."

She slips her foot from the stirrup. "Maybe so, but you know they wanted to put me in the kitchen. Besides the woman's place bullshit, my father wants me protected." She puts her arm around his waist. "I get to do inside fence patrols and I plan to keep this job. Prove I don't need a nursemaid." She kisses his cheek. The stubble scrapes her lips. She wishes for Chapstick. "You need a shave."

Nick rubs his bewhiskered chin. "I thought I'd grow a beard. I don't have to answer to military protocol anymore."

"If I don't like it, you'll have to shave it." She grabs the saddle horn.

"I don't answer to you."

Hannah whispers next to his ear, "If you want to do more than kiss me, you'll be smooth faced." She pulls herself onto the saddle.

"You be careful out there." Nick pats the horse's rump. "I'll see you at dinner."

"Clean shaven?" she calls after him as he returns to his vehicle.

Hannah adjusts herself in the saddle before choking up on the reins. She gives her mount a kiss-click with her tongue in order to trot it forward. She forces herself not to glance back at Nick. She wants to but enjoys making him sweat when it comes to their fledgling relationship.

"How does this work?" she asks the redhead on the painted mare.

"Jessica, and not Rabbit." She offers Hannah sunblock. "You might want this."

Hannah takes the tube.

Before she asks, the taller man says, "Forgive the ginger. She thinks everyone watched *Who Framed Roger Rabbit*. I'm Bert, by the way."

"I missed that film," Hannah admits.

"It's a classic."

"What do we do?" Hannah asks again.

"The fence stretches for miles and every few weeks expands. Giving us a nice protected territory," Bert says.

"The undead keep us on a reservation," Jessica says.

"We ride the fence line checking for breaches. Enough undead are capable of making holes. Simple holes, I have wire to fix. I have ribbon to tie as a marker for large issues we report and send a team back to repair," Bert says.

"If there's a danger. A biter got in or will. We'll stay and secure the problem," Jessica says.

"So, we just ride the fence line?" Hannah asks.

"We change our pattern, just in case."

"In case of what?" Hannah asks.

"We've got a great home here. Eventually, someone will want to take it from us," Bert adds.

"It's not like you don't take people in."

"We do. The military group was the largest. We just have to be careful our growth matches our food supply," Jessica says.

"Where do we patrol today?"

"Newbie's choice," Bert says.

"How about the lake?" Hannah asks.

"We do sweep the shoreline. A biter corpse washed up once, and someone could paddle over from the side of the lake we don't control."

"It will change our routine," Jessica says. "We never start there."

Emily stomps up the stairs until she realizes she rattles the house. She wants Ethan awake but not at the expense of the rest he needs. She takes the next step almost at a tiptoe. Reaching the bedroom, she slips inside wanting to slide into the bed next to him the way she caught Amie.

Ethan rolls to his side. Her lips draw into a smile. It's the first time he's moved under his own power since he was brought here. She creeps closer as not to startle him.

"Genoveva," tumbles from his lips. Upon realizing he spoke as if revealing his most guarded secret, Ethan wakes. He grunts from the stiffened pain of movement. Between atrophy and healing bruises, his entire body twinges.

Has to be what a bed of nails feels like. Little pricks decorate his skin. Jabbing him in waves.

He lifts his arm, but the weight of the cover sends it back to the bed. Every move hurts but every move releases the tension built from days of sleep. "Did someone get the number of that bus?"

"Do you feel like eating?" *What the fuck kind of question is that? He just woke. Dumb girl.* "I'm so glad you're alive."

"Me, too," he grunts.

"I don't know where to start. After three days, you must need food. More than the IV gives you."

"I hate needles." The dark purple marks on his arm have dimmed, turning a green-gray around the edges.

"What do you need, Ethan?" she asks. It's all she has not to ask who *Genoveva* is.

"I need you to be calm. I need to get up—move." He shifts to his elbows, but falls back. "Maybe not."

"You have no reason to get up. I'll get whatever you need. Just heal." Uncontrollable tears race down her cheeks. "Just don't die."

"I'm not going to die." He moves half an inch with pain-grunts. "Okay. I'll eat. How about some bacon?"

"I've got some bacon and chicken. Protein. You need it. To heal."

"In between painting your toenails and missing your iPod, did you learn to cook?"

She has socks on and he's not moved his head enough to even glance at her feet. So she knows he's guessing she has on a fresh coat of polish. "Private Sanchez isn't bad in front of the stove." *Plus, bacon will force her to keep her shirt on.*

"Sounds good. When I don't move, the pain I have may be hunger. Better get Dr. Baker and Wanikiya. They need to know I've returned to the living."

CHAPTER TWENTY-THREE

TOM'S NOT SURE what one-horse town he stumbled into, but it's at least large enough to have a corner drug store. His stomach flip-flops as it notes it's one of those ole-timey places with the soda fountains. The kind of place operating as a general store, but now is filled with useless crafts and novelties, cheap ice cream, and with any luck, an unraided drug counter. More important, he needs pain meds for his broken left arm and maybe some antibiotics to sway any infection growing.

His fireman experience reminds him that normally these buildings have apartments on the floors above the stores, so he could find a safe place to secure and sleep.

Exploring the outside of the building, he discovers the front door opens with the ringing of a bell. He snags the bobbing metal above him and jerks, breaking the bell from its hanger. Tom spins around letting the door close behind him. He glances up and down the street.

If he were in an old western, he'd expect a tumbleweed to drift past as lone flute music signified a ghost town. He pauses a moment longer. His brief glance inside gave no indication for disheveled shelves. He finds it strange so many places seem so untouched by looters. Approaching a year since the plague spread the undead across the country, he assumed every business, home and outhouse would have been plundered for supplies, yet he keeps finding so many places untouched except for gathering dust.

Confident the bell alerted nothing outside the building and anything dead inside should have crawled into view by now. He swings the door wide, keeping it propped with his foot while he draws a flashlight with his only working arm. He holds the light between his teeth, drawing his weapon. First chance he gets he'll duct tape the light to the barrel. It's going to be a long six to eight weeks with only one functioning arm, if he doesn't need physical therapy to make it work again. Danziger did a number when he broke it so they could escape the new breed of Manson family.

Tom makes a mental note to search for water, food, safe place to sleep, bullets, physical therapist who specialize in limbs. He wants to laugh. There's not much else he can do. Stale food reeks near the counter plastered in retro five-cent milkshake signs. Flare. They would call that. Tom feels teased. Not only because he has a nickel, but he'd kill for a milkshake.

His boot sticks as he lifts it to step. Ice cream or something else from the inoperable freezer has leaked across the floor in an attempt to glue him in place with dried sticky gel. It makes his rubber sole echo with each step. Some of the shelves have been raided. Blank spots exist between items. He will have to inspect each shelf for useful gear, but first he needs painkillers. Someone has been swiping items, but only what they needed. *Some decent people are left in the world*, Tom contemplates. *At least there were.* From the dust in the empty spots it's if they haven't been back in a long time.

He kicks open the half door of the pharmacy counter. Now, this place is more of what he expected. Completely bare shelves, ramshackle bottles, and broken glass. A pile of hypodermic needles still in plastic scattered on the floor from a ripped open box. Someone desperately needed an injection of something.

The empty shelf of narcotics doesn't surprise Tom. He searches the shelf and finds a bottle of Elavil. He puts the gun down and pockets the antidepressant, glad he aced the limited medical medication training. So many cites wanted firemen to double and function as medics. Knowing what drugs found on-scene during an emergency saves lives. Under the pharmacy counter he snags a box of dust-soaked protein bars overlooked by everyone in a hurry to steal drugs.

Through the "staff only" door, he finds stairs leading both up and down. He won't enter the dark and foreboding basement with only a flashlight.

Upstairs, he finds apartments. Tom checks each tiny room before shoving the couch to the entry door to block it.

He plops down and rips open a protein bar wrapper with his teeth. He's not sure what they tasted like fresh, but shit is not a flavor he craved. He needs something in his stomach to help metabolize the antidepressant containing chemicals to help numb the pain. That's what he needs. Hydroxyzine helps itching, maybe it will also with certain infections. He knows this to be true. What he doesn't know is if these drugs have an interaction and by mixing them they will cause horrible side effects such as death.

He swallows the Elavil risking a chance to sleep without pain.

People.

Voices of living people jar Tom from his deep slumber. Not sure how long he slept, the stiffness of his body stabs agony into him. He knows full well he needed the safe rest with the medication. His arm throbs, but he dare not take any more pills. He doesn't know how they will affect him and a drowsy state could be detrimental to his health.

He crawls to the window.

A half a block down the street, a group of people beat an undead with bats. Some have guns, but they appear to be going for a silent attack forgetting their war yells and screams attract just as much attention as a rifle shot.

One of them pokes the now lifeless corpse with his bat. Satisfied it's dead, they traipse onward toward the drug store. Tom now has a life-changing decision to make. Does he let these people know he's here or does he just hide and let them pass? They are not heavily equipped for a long journey, so they are either scavenging for a larger camp, or could be they fled the caravan and are in desperate need of supplies. They reach the optimum distance to fire upon for clean quick hits. He must decide now. *Trust has vanished from the world. Time to make the effort.*

The window sticks as he raises it with only one hand. The group freezes at the rattling for the sash. They unsling their rifles. No undead would open a window.

Tom gets it high enough to stick his head out. "Hold up. Hold up," he calls. He beats on the drooping side of the window to get it to move.

Of the five people, one dashes for cover behind a blue mailbox.

Tom sticks his head out. "Are you from the caravan?"

Direct question—he hopes it will lead to a dialogue.

The group hangs silent for a moment. They could fire and hit him before he could go back inside and operate a weapon. Maybe there are others in other windows ready to ambush them. They have nothing but guns and a few rounds but still, that's enough. Maybe they won't shoot everyone. Maybe just the three males. Women have become a commodity all to themselves.

"I'm Dusty," the tallest man says. "We barely escaped the hoard."

"Tom." *How much do I say?* "I was one of the guards holding the ending point of the caravan. I was helping search the caravan for..." *What do I call Levin?* "A *friend* who knew the person he was looking for was on his way to Fort Wood when the swarm hit." *Not completely the truth.*

"Do you have water?" Dusty asks.

"Look, kid, I'm just going to trust you. I've a broken arm. I found this place yesterday and needed to rest. I've not looked for a thing but some pain meds." Tom takes the risk; after all, they could shoot him before he gets back inside.

"There are still drugs," the ginger-haired girl retorts.

"Calm down, Danielle," Dusty snaps.

Tom wonders about her. She had some face piercing at one point and could have done some illegal drugs. "It's been picked over, but there are some meds and some other supplies."

The man leans over the mailbox. He holds his weapon at his side ready to bring it to a firing position. "How do you want to handle this old man?"

Tom knows he's older than these twenty-somethings, but despite the arm pain, he's far from old.

"I say we find some backpacks, load them with supplies, and pick a direction. We try for the military base or go back to St. Louis."

"No going back," the second girl shouts. She's got brown hair and couldn't be out of her teens. Her doe eyes calmer with the fear of what she's seen. Tom knows she doesn't need a handgun with that trigger-happy fear covering her face.

"Forgive Darcy. She watched a lot of people not escape the hoard," Dusty explains. "Tom, if we partner up with you, you'll mess up our group." He pats the third man on the shoulder. "This is Dakota. And the fool behind the mailbox is Dave. We've been calling ourselves the 'Ds'."

Humor's good, kid. It will help keep you going, Tom considers. "Not much I can do about being a Tom."

Tom steps outside the drugstore entrance unarmed. He hopes to build trust with these people.

"Where's your weapon?"

"Upstairs, along with a box of the most cardboard tasting food bars. I can't search for supplies and hold a gun with only one arm." He gentlemanly holds the door. "This floor and the apartment I stayed in are clear. I don't know about the other apartment or the basement."

"Watch out for undead," Dustin orders.

"If you find a map, we need it."

"What town are we in?" Dakota places his rifle on the food bar counter searching for anything edible.

"When we are ready to move, we need to figure out so we know what direction to head."

"We continue on to the military base. That's the safest place."

"What about the DKs?" Panic fills Darcy's voice.

"We'll avoid them. That swarm headed south. We must go west," Dustin assures her.

Danielle examines bottle after bottle of pills. When she finds one she likes, she stuffs it into a plastic bag. "They fuckin' cleaned out the good meds."

"Take what's useful."

"Tradable, you mean. We use this shit for currency, but it has to be useful for something."

"Take the antidepressants," Tom offers.

"I admit this world's a banquet of depressive shit but—"

"Some have other uses, like pain suppressants," Tom interrupts.

"How?" she asks him. "All the good pain meds are gone."

"I was a fireman with some medical training."

"I was in pharmacy school. The world ended. Do you see a PDR? There should be a few back here," Danielle says.

"I didn't look for a Physician's Desk Reference. I had too much pain," Tom admits.

Danielle shoves all the antidepressants into the plastic bag. "Dusty, find me a backpack. We have a lot we can take and trade with other survivors."

"You want this cutie's pink water bottle that reads 'You go, Gurl'?"

"Fuck you, Dakota."

Tom theories Danielle might just be one of the boys after all. "I'm going to get my gun and those food bars."

"I'll go with you," Dusty volunteers. "Maybe whoever lived in that apartment had a gym bag or suit case. We can't carry this stuff in plastic bags."

Can't blame the kid for not trusting me. But this group seems decent.

"Tom and the D's," Tom climbs the stairs.

"What?" Dusty follows, hanging back a few steps out of Tom's reach.

"What you can call yourself."

"Sounds like a bad fifties rock band."

"Guess it does," Tom says.

"You always bring people so easily into your circle?" Dusty asks.

"Kid, I'm in too much pain. You want to kill me—go for it."

"I need to know my group's safe."

Danziger, my new friend. You may be on your own. Then again what purpose do we have in this new world other than survival? A worthy goal might be what we need. Tom keeps a 9mm Glock in his right hand. His left arm now properly set and secured in a shoulder sling to rest immovable against his chest. Danielle doctored him.

The six move between the cars, inspecting for any useful supplies.

"Your two best buddies ran off with a military incursion team designated to destroy bridges over the river," Dusty says.

"About the gist of it," Tom says.

"We've all lost friends. Would you know this serial killer if you saw him again?" Darcy questions.

"Danziger had a photo. I'd know the guy if I saw him," Tom says.

"We've barely been able to stay alive and this guy still hunts teen girls."

"His survival depends on filling whatever void the killing satisfies inside him," Dave adds. He opens a car door, removing a bottle of water. He examines the seal.

"When did you become an expert?"

"A few semesters of psychology and ten seasons of *Criminal Minds* doesn't mean you understand the mind of a killer," Dusty adds.

"I thought about profiling as a career."

"Not a promising choice now." Danielle dumps a beach bag, scooping up a tube of sunscreen. She squirts a handful before offering, "Anyone else need tanning lotion?"

Dusty's skin's already dark from the sun. "You need the entire tube to protect your ginger skin."

"Keep it up. Each freckle is a soul I stole," she hisses at him.

"You let this cop break your arm?"

"Once away from the caravan, people have done whatever to survive," Tom says.

"It wasn't survival those people couldn't accept but the death of their loved ones from what you told us about."

"We just need to find someplace safe," Darcy says.

"You vote for the military base?" Dusty asks.

"St. Louis is overrun and there are no bridges to cross the river. I vote the military base."

A garden rake brains Danielle, cleaving open her face and snagging on her nose ring and extracting it.

Prepared for undead, the group never expected to encounter the living mixed in among the abandoned cars of the caravan.

Dakota has his rifle butt to his shoulder the fastest.

Tom raises the 9mm Glock.

Danielle's ginger hair deepens its natural red with spraying blood from her nose and scalp.

Dusty, shocked more than anyone, fumbles with his holstered weapon.

Danielle gets a second blow to the back before shoved toward her friends. The attacker bolts, ducking between cars.

None of the Ds act. They revert to being lost in a crisis.

The attacker races from the breakdown lane to the tree line.

Tom with his firefighter training knows to remain calm and assess the situation. Keeping his cool, he waits until Dusty's face requests his guidance.

"Draw your weapons. There could be more."

Unsettled, they all brandish their weapons.

"Dave, work your way to Danielle. Dakota, keep him covered," Tom orders. "Dusty, move toward Danielle and sweep the cars for rotters or the living. Darcy, move toward me. We need to find a first-aid kit."

"What do we do until you find a kit?"

"Get a towel or blanket. Support her head and put pressure on the head wound."

Dakota sweeps his rifle, making sure no other attackers are near Danielle. Dave tears a bed sheet holding the shreds against the gash. He gulps back down the bile jutting into his throat from the missing half of Danielle's nose.

CHAPTER TWENTY-FOUR

"YOU KNEW OF this killer?" Dr. Baker says.

"We should kill him for not telling us," Wade demands.

Major Ellsberg scowls. "Exile's not enough. Not when one of us has been murdered. He's just as responsible for Kayla's death."

Wanikiya raises a hand, calling for silence. "A proper judicial recourse will follow, after we have facts and Kayla's murderer stands for punishment."

"I was tracking Levin. I suspected he was in your camp." Danziger carefully selects his recollection of the past events. "I was a homicide cop and was assigned to his case. The newspapers called him the *Blonde Teen Slasher*."

He allows the information to sink in. *People in this state would have seen news reports daily for months during Levin's prime hunting even if the end of the world made them forget.* "Levin kidnapped and murdered my daughter. I was removed from the case."

"You knew what a threat he was to us and you said nothing," Wanikiya says.

"I had a fever and wasn't sure my story would even be accepted. I said nothing because after St. Louis fell to the biters I pursued Levin out of the city. I found him and did to him what he did to the little girls. He escaped before I could end him. He was wounded and my story makes me the crazed killer, not him. People don't understand; these killers, they are not hideous demons under the bed. They are the nicest, sometimes handsome, but charismatic people you'll meet. You'd trust them with your baby and you might even forgive them after they eat it because they are so charming."

None of them speak. Wanikiya accepts the argument. They would have sided with the wounded Levin. An angry father spews crazy talk and they might have thrown him out leaving Levin to murder in secret. "Logic dictates I keep you locked up and once we find Levin we exile you," Wanikiya says.

"Once he's dead. You do what you want with me—after Levin's dead. Right now, you're giving him what he wants. Time. While you interrogate me, he hunts a fresh victim. One who meets his needs. Kayla was a distraction. In no way was she killed by his ritual."

"You think he'll take one of us hostage?"

"He doesn't take hostages. He takes mementos. You're a small enough community and most of you eat together. How many fifteen-year-old blonde girls are in this camp?" Danziger asks.

"Hal. Find Simon. Send him to stay with Hannah." Wanikiya's priority must keep Ethan's oath to protect her. "Wade, get Sam. Dr. Baker. Emily—if she's in the library, and any other teenage girls, bring them to the gym. Keep them there under guard."

Wade races from the room.

"Try and do it without creating a panic," Wanikiya calls after him.

"I'll find him." Danziger raises his cuffed hand. "Then you exile me or execute me. But I will see Levin dead first."

"Emily was at Ethan's farm house last," Dr. Baker says.

"Once she is safe, I'll consider your assistance," Wanikiya says. The radio on his hip crackles.

"Wanikiya, come in."

He raises the CB mic to his mouth, "Wanikiya here."

"Ethan requests your presence," Emily says.

He's awake. Alive. At least she didn't scream he's finally awake. I've been able to quell most rumors about Ethan's condition to level peoples' concern. Even Victor felt he would be fine after a nap. The beast of a man has taken bullets to chest armor, airbags to the face, and a beating bad enough to drop a rhino. No telling what other dangers he's stared down since the undead devastated society and strolled away.

"I'm on my way, over." *I need to remember to follow the radio protocol. Even with the Levin issue I must meet with Ethan. Witness for myself my friend's alive. With the power his resurrection will have over the group I'm going to have to convince Ethan to remain here and lead. The group has grown enough; there are plenty of others to scavenge outside the fence.*

"Sorry, Barlock, I know it was your off time," Wanikiya says. He misses his kitchen. He's made more trips from the school-turned-community-building to the gate and Ethan's farm in the last few days than he has his entire time at Acheron. *We're growing too big for one man to rule this place. And when gas goes, communication dwindles.*

"Gate guards are never released from protecting the camp. Besides, Becky and Kenneth are available to assist in my absence," Barlock says.

"We should be making supply runs every day. Some necessities have a shelf life," Becky says.

Barlock admires the young girl's spunk, but she's a little too quick on the trigger to be outside the fence. *I don't make the rotations.*

Wanikiya gives her an evaluative glance.

"We've a multitude of pressing matters," Wanikiya says. He places his hand on the window frame of the truck so Danziger and the others all hear him. "Right now, you are still my guest, but get out of this truck or do anything questionable—" he shifts his gaze to Barlock "—and they are granted permission to shoot you."

Becky wants to ask what's going on but doesn't question the camp's second-in-command when his eyes reveal his intention to scalp someone.

"What doesn't kill us makes us stronger." Wanikiya steps through the bedroom door.

"They leave out the fact it *almost* kills you." Ethan struggles to sit up. His exposed skin now a dull purple with blotches of green.

"Are you competent enough to deal with our current crisis?" Wanikiya asks, not wanting to involve his friend, but he must.

"Emily was quick to rat out Amie losing someone on a failed supply run."

"We'll debate your inability to travel and protect every group going outside the fence later." Wanikiya's face maintains a constant lack of emotion under most circumstances.

Ethan detects a facial tick giving him concern. "How bad is it?"

"The wounded man you recovered on the way back from Fort Wood, is a serial killer."

Questions—too many—Ethan asks, "How many are dead?"

"So far one."

Ethan swings a leg from under the covers. From mid-calf down bares few marks from the attack. Wanikiya bars him from getting up.

"We're dealing with this. The man who found you after the attack, *do* you trust him?"

Ethan forgot about him. *He did save me with no motivating reasons. I trusted him enough to give him directions to Acheron. However, in delouse or desperation, I accepted any bedfellow to live.* "At the time, he seemed reliable."

"He was a cop and was pursuing the killer who took his daughter."

"Then he should be a wealth of information. Don't spend time speaking to me, drill him," Ethan orders.

"The killer murdered Kayla. He's free in the camp. I've dispatched patrols without creating a panic, but the cop, Danziger—"

Danziger. That was his name, Ethan's memory flashes to being placed in the truck bed. He shared a hidden stash location with this man.

"... wants me to let him loose on the compound to finish Levin."

Ethan doesn't need any more explanation. He understands why the man he found was cut to pieces.

"Release Danziger. Give him a gun."

"We discovered Danziger covered in Kayla's blood." Wanikiya wants a complete picture painted.

Ethan gets the second leg on the floor. "Did he kill her?"

"Speculation and circumstance would point to him being framed to give Levin time to escape."

"Give him a gun with one clip." Ethan slides as far to the edge of the bed as he dares. "If he's an expert in this killer, let him work."

Emily carries a tray with steaming food into the bedroom. "Where do you think you're going?"

"After a killer. Wanikiya, get a couple of guys to help me down the stairs." Ethan scoops up his Beretta from the table. "Give this to the cop. If he can't kill in ten rounds he's no good to us."

Wanikiya accepts the gun, pulling the slide enough to spot a shiny brass casing.

"Make sure he knows I want my gun back." Ethan orders, "Emily, find my M&P."

"You need to eat," she protests.

"You stay here, Ethan. You're unable to walk," Wanikiya says.

"I'll stay in the truck. We're in a crisis and the camp needs me up and dealing with it."

"Ethan, it's time you allow the rest of us to help."

Ethan staggers to the truck where Danziger remains in the passenger seat. He catches himself on the frame of the open window. He finds the cliché of every bone in his body hurts to be true.

"I'm no doctor, but I doubt you should be out of bed." Danziger caught the end of the beating they gave this man. By every law of nature, he should be dead.

"Glad no one around here's a doctor. Why did you help me out?" Ethan never takes his eyes from Danziger's.

"It wasn't to help. Not out of any kindness. Like your attackers, I felt you were too clean—too well equipped. I interfered in the hopes someone as well supplied as you might have seen or been a part of the military trucks helping Levin. And there was chance you had fever meds." Danziger holds up his bandaged wrists.

Ethan opens the door using it as a crutch to step back. "Barlock, cut him loose."

"Whatever you say, Boss." The man jingles a janitor-sized ring of keys.

Barlock's voice always brings the Cool Hand Luke mantra to Ethan's thoughts.

Wanikiya and Barlock's radio both crackle with a voice, "Wanikiya, we've found George at The Barn."

The Barn, the title for the hay storage building the group commandeered when first building the compound.

"Condition?" Wanikiya asks.

"We've called for medics. Sam was assigned to work with him. No sign of her."

Ethan wishes someone less panic stricken was on the radio. He raises his hand for Barlock's radio. "Secure The Barn. And keep everyone in sight of each other. Over."

"Ethan?" the voice questions.

"Yes. Do as I order." *That will give the camp something to talk about.* He explains to Danziger, "Sam was a little blond girl. She's been assaulted before."

"How old is she?" Danziger wants to rub his wrists from the tight cuff restraint but doesn't to avoid breaking open any of the healing.

"Seventeen," Barlock answers.

"This guy like young girls?" Becky no longer keeps quiet.

"He loves them. You don't want to know how," Danziger says. "If I'm free to act. Then I need to get to this barn. You people might mess up a sign I'll need to track him by."

Wanikiya holds the Beretta by the barrel. "Ethan wants his gun back."

Danziger takes the weapon and the separate ten-shot clip. "Point me to this barn."

"I'll take him," Becky offers.

Ethan replaces Danziger in the truck. "Drive. Danziger in the back. Wanikiya, stay here and keep an eye on Emily. Barlock, secure the main sally port. Kenneth, warn those at the dam."

Becky fires up the truck.

Ethan glances through eyes unaccustomed to the sun at the tan-skinned girl. "Did I save you?"

"How many blows to the head did you take?" She mashes the accelerator.

"Too many." Ethan smirks.

"You're still mostly purple. I don't know how you got out of bed. You saved us once. You don't have to keep being Superman."

"I would never be Superman. Trumped up ideals and defeated by a rock. That's about as bad as Kate Beckinsale dying in that piece of crap werewolf/vampire movie where she fell over a couch. No, girl, I'm more Captain America; at least he had super strength with a realistic view of the world. If not Cap then—" Ethan shifts his voice into a gravel guttural octave. "I'm Batman."

Ethan doesn't want to remain in the truck like some two-year-old while mother runs into the convenience store, but all the jarring has aggravated every bruise. *Part of me is amazed I didn't pass out from the pain. No, not in front of a girl. Got to remain manly.*

He spots the blood-soaked blanket covering what must be George. *We're supposed to be safe in here. After I punished Kyle for sexual assault no one would dare now. Minor infractions, a day of sluffing off work, are easily corrected by cutting food rations. We had such a healthy growing community. I have to keep finding people. Most out there are damaged. So many mentally sick people seem to have survived. We have to grow. The people who live here have to be better than those living out there.*

Becky leans against his truck door so as not to obscure his view. "They put George down."

Her remark, a bit too casual about the event, assures Ethan they have to be keep striving to be better than the outside world.

"He sliced him up. Left him to die," she snaps.

"A mask."

"What?"

"A disguise."

"I know what a mask is," Becky says.

"A distraction then. He wanted us to deal with a biter, but let George bleed out so Levin had time to escape with Sam, and of course the threat that if she didn't cooperate he'd do the same to her."

"But he will anyway."

"Correct, Pandora, but people want to believe."

"Pandora?" Becky asks.

"A Greek—"

"I know. She released all the evils into the world. Why did you call me Pandora?" she asks.

"Because she prevented Hope from escaping, but Hope is a cruel mistress. Sam hopes if she does what this Levin says she'll live. Hope suppresses the brain from knowing he's going to kill her no matter what. Hope is what people cling to even when they see Death swing his scythe."

"Were you always this pragmatic?" she asks.

"It keeps me alive."

Danziger marches to the truck.

"How do we organize this man hunt?" Ethan asks.

Danziger cranes his arm to demonstrate. "Bring your people in an arcing formation, tell them to stay in sight of one another as they swing in driving him toward the dam. I heard someone say tanks were there."

"Lot of forest, too; it was a National Park area."

"It'll force him to keep moving," Danziger says.

"He could still cut through the fence and escape."

"He'd be outside. The rest of your people would be safe. You send scavenging teams out under guard. You just have to watch for him." Danziger considers. "No, he'll stay here."

"People could still climb over the fence."

"What about Sam?" Becky asks.

"I'm going to follow his trail. I'll do what's necessary," Danziger says.

"What does that mean?" Becky demands.

"Once cornered, he'll kill Sam," Ethan says, cold as ice.

"There has to be some way to stop—" Becky protests.

"Not without risking more lives," Ethan says.

"If I get to him I might be able to stop him. This Sam sounds like the girls he performs his ritual on. I was forced to witness. Nothing in the woods will provide him the opportunity to live out his fantasy with her."

"Just save her, Danziger." Ethan holds out his radio. "Take this and take Keanu. He's a good shot and has been through this area to check the deer population."

"I'm going to kill Levin," Danziger says.

"I ain't sending the kid to prevent you, I'm sending him to assure it."

CHAPTER TWENTY-FIVE

DAVE SHOVES ALL the boxes out of the back seat of the car. Personal household items spill over the blacktop. Placing Danielle on the inside, he slides in next to her and clamps a towel over her bleeding nose. Careful not to smother her, he applies pressure.

"How bad is she?" Tom calls out. He sweeps his gun combat style toward the tree line, prepared for an attack. Ignoring the pain, the jerk radiates through his bound arm.

"Lot of blood. I don't know how to stop it. A piece of her nose is gone," Dave hollers.

Dusty keeps his rifle ready, "Maybe he thought we were a threat and just wanted to get away."

"Maybe. No one behaves rationally anymore." Tom keeps scanning the trees.

"Should we go after him?" Dakota asks.

Tom issues a resounding, "*No.* Re-sweep the cars around us. Then we stay around Danielle. We move once we have her bleeding under control."

Darcy digs through the scattered family items. Dave spills out into the road. She shreds clothes to make bandages.

"The bleeding won't stop!" Panic hangs in Dave's voice.

Tom holsters his weapon. He takes a loose round from his pocket and fishes out a Leatherman multi-tool. "Dusty, remove the bullet from the brass without spilling any of the powder."

"You going to perform some *Rambo* shit?" Dusty asks.

"We're too exposed here. We may be surrounded and a herd went through here days ago. Dozens, if not hundreds, of undead are still around, and we're making enough racket. I want to move."

Dusty crimps the bullet, twisting the wrench until he breaks free the copper hollow point. Pocketing the round.

"How do I do this?"

"Sprinkle about half of the tube on the wound. You got any cigarettes?"

"Search the cars," Dusty orders. "Find some smokes."

Darcy smashes a truck window, reaches in, and flips down the visor. She gives the generic brand of cigars to Dusty.

"I'm not much of a smoker."

Tom takes one and fumbles with the plastic wrapper. "I enjoy a good cigar once in a while. Light me."

Dusty flicks a lighter.

Tom puffs the cigar until the tip cherries.

Dave sprinkles the whole tube of gun powder onto Danielle's chunk of missing nose. Tom hands him the cigar.

Her howl, strong enough to shatter glass, ends as she succumbs to the burn. Dave dribbles water onto a rag and dabs at the blood to clean her face. "I never thought I'd ever burn a wound closed."

"Cauterizing it should staunch all blood and kill any infection." Tom takes back the cigar.

"Those things will kill you."

"It's a slow death. A lot faster ways to die today." Tom puffs.

"Poor girl. She had such a pretty face," Darcy says.

"She's alive. Let her sleep for a while," Tom suggests. "Where to now, Dusty?"

"I don't know where we are. These cars all have family possessions. Your caravan was loaded with useful gear. I still want to find it."

"Come, Darcy, we'll scout east until we find a mile marker. Figure out where we are." Tom crushes out the cigar before drawing his pistol. Hating being one handed.

"Don't be gone too far."

"Two tenths of a mile at most. One thing Missouri does well is mark all the highways every tenth of a mile or so. Gave the inmates something to make in prison, I assume."

"We have to be close to the Merrimac River," Darcy says.

"The caravan never made it that far. It was around Exit 266. A Route 66 Museum is located there."

"So, we are going to have to head toward the city and the hoard?"

"The trucks had guns, fuel, and food. I don't know where we're going, but we'd have more than we can carry."

"Why didn't the caravan get further?" she asks.

"I was planning on staying in the city. Kept hearing about problems clearing the road. Cars were twenty wide in places, took weeks to clear. Every time they'd inch forward they'd halt again."

Tom glances up at the mile marker. "265. A mile or less to the river and then more than a few to the caravan's lead."

"Too bad they are still boxed in; we could just take a car full of gear."

"I hear ya. Walking is killing my arm." Tom heads back toward the group.

"Why'd you ask me to come along?" she asks.

"You were turning green after seeing Danielle's nose. Thought you should get some air."

"There's no way to fix her nose anymore?"

"A good plastic surgeon might be busy fixing more basic damage."

"I'm glad you knew how to save her." She smiles.

"I wouldn't want to break up Tom and the Ds."

Dakota jogs toward them. "How long do we let her sleep? I killed two rotters."

"The bridge is this direction and then a few miles through the maze of cars to the caravan. I don't think we should carry her. We need to be able to avoid any undead under a car."

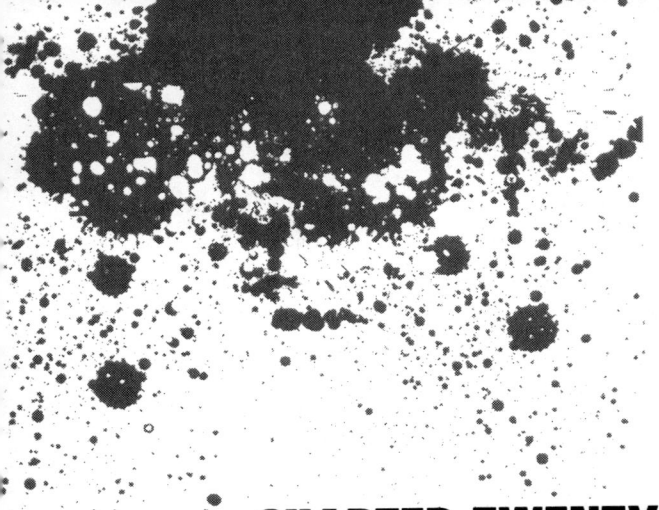

CHAPTER TWENTY-SIX

"STOP THE TRUCK." Kaleb flings open the door before the pickup still rolls. "Hold your fire," he orders the men in the bed. They all point rifles at a minivan parked angular in the lane.

"Please, Brothers." The man in the straw hat raises his arms. "We travel under God's protection."

"I see he took real good care of your tires." Kaleb sneers, "You *God will light your way* types are all same."

"He did bring us you, Brother."

One of the men in the truck swings his rifle to the trees. "Movement, Kaleb."

"Easy, Garth." He flicks the safety on his own rifle. "You got friends, mister?"

"I have many brothers and sisters."

"If they are hiding in the woods—" he raises his voice "—they need to come on out!"

Four people stumble from the trees. A middle-aged woman—Kaleb would consider her a MILF once she cleaned up—stumbles out. Her ripped dress shows dark hairs sprouting on her shapely legs. She tows a boy about nine behind her. Two more men in tattered suits carrying golf clubs follow her.

"That it?"

"Yes, we are traveling to Springfield. We understand God protects his worthy children there."

"And you decided to try the back roads to reach there?" Kale hates his brother's words. They need serfs.

"We didn't realize finding more gas would be so difficult."

"Guess God doesn't provide the worth with fuel."

"Why are we messing with these people?" Garth asks.

"Kale wants to build our population with workers." He keeps his finger on the trigger. "We have a camp and food."

"We wish to join the other faithful in Springfield."

"Then start walking. Or we'll place you under our protection."

"What does your *protection* mean?" the woman asks.

"You have a name?" Kaleb asks.

"Mary."

Fuck'n religious nuts always have Bible names. "Of course it is. He your boy?"

"My kids have joined God. Josiah, we saved."

"Well, Mary, under our new order, you do the work and we keep the rotters from eating you," Kaleb says.

"We should just kill them and take what they have," Garth says.

"No. I'm full agreement with Kale and our needs. We have to consider long term. No more drugs, no more rape, no more pillaging from the living."

"We will pass on your protection," the man in the straw hat proclaims.

Kaleb twirls his index finger in the air, signaling the two trucks to drive around the van.

"Wait," Mary says. "You promise no ill to befall me?"

"We will protect all in our stead from biters and anyone wishing to harm you," Kaleb swears.

"Then I wish to join your commune. We don't even know if Springfield has a human population."

"Josiah, you want to come with me?"

The boy nods his head.

Kaleb lifts Mary onto the tailgate, placing her bottom on the metal. Slipping his hand up her dress to grip her smooth inner thigh. He doesn't push too high as he massages the muscle. She smiles at his advance. She leans over to hug him in thanks. "If you want my pleasures, then I expect you to honor me. Make me your queen," she whispers.

"How do you know I am not married already?" Kaleb asks.

"A man like you may keep a harem, but you have no bride." She never raises her voice above a tone just for him to hear.

"We have a lot of struggle ahead and my men have been able to take what they want from whoever they wish until today."

"Make me your queen and you'll never want to desire another woman again. Claiming me will set an example for your men and allow you to lead and survive."

"I'm not much for God worshiping, Mary."

She moves her leg reminding him he still has her thigh in her grip. "I'll be the only God you need to follow."

The trucks leave the straw-hat man and two companions next to a gasless van.

CHAPTER TWENTY-SEVEN

LISTED TO ONE side, like a discarded beer can, the 7407 would have tipped completely over if not for the wing. The straight stretch of interstate made a perfect substitute runway when the plane was forced into an emergency alternative to crashing. Sprawled across the southbound lane, the plane appears to have landed intact. Fools attempted to clean the road of the behemoth, jerking free the forward landing gear, stranding the craft forever.

"I've never been on a plane before," Darcy says.

"It could be clear of rotters." Dave points at the tatters of inflated emergency slide dangling from the open door.

"Walking up those aisles at such a steep angle will be murder on the calves, and if you encounter an undead you have no space to move." Tom sounds more like a preparing father than a watchful companion.

"I'll take a look around," Dusty volunteers. "May be something useful in the overhead compartments."

"Count me out." Danielle fumbles with a car door handle. Upon finding it locked, she smashes the window with a pry bar tool. She uses it to brush glass from the seat in order to rest comfortably. Before she climbs into the car, she smashes the side view mirror.

Tom wishes he had a Halligan pry bar. The high carbon steel was made to destroy door, cars, anything in order to gain entry to put out a fire or perform a rescue. About twelve pounds, it would be the perfect combination tool/weapon. The spiked end allows for building entry or destroying a rotter. *Next firetruck I find I'll snag one.*

"How is your pain?"

"Manageable. I want to see it...and I don't," she says.

Tom doesn't know how to respond. He leans against the back door. "Be careful," he hollers after Darcy and Dusty.

Dave drops a truck tailgate, plopping down and jerking off his shoe to rub his foot. "How far do you think the caravan is?"

"A few miles," Tom guesses. "So many cars. This caravan was never going to clear this mess."

"So, they lied to the people trying to escape?'

"Yes."

"Why?" Danielle asks.

"My best guess would be to give people something to do, prevent a panic and provide hope for a future," Tom says. "If the herd hadn't scattered everyone they'd still be clearing this mess."

"Will it come back?"

Tom should lie. "I don't know what motivates such a mass of undead." Not a lie, but anything could swing them in any direction at any time. "Most people ran south and the herd followed."

Dave replaces his shoe. He digs through a cardboard box ruined by rain. He tosses aside DVDs, Christmas decorations, and a blow dryer. "Why did people pack this crap?"

"We were obsessed with things and stuff," Tom says. "In the wake of this disaster, we now understand what's truly important."

"I don't see the world any different. I'm still deprived of quality health care, I'm poor, but not poor enough for government assistance, and my vote still doesn't count," Danielle says.

"There is no more government," Dave says.

"Doesn't matter. They didn't help before. My mom made too much money for assistance, but not enough to feed everyone," Danielle adds.

"Quiet, you two." Tom raises his gun.

Staggering among the abandoned vehicles are more and more undead. Their numbers grow, but Tom doesn't spot where they originate from. "Where's Dakota?"

He scans the tops of the cars counting twelve DKs. "I don't know. Should we get in the plane?"

"Go," Tom agrees. The rotters move toward him but not in a swift enough pace to acknowledge they know of the group's presence.

"Dakota," Dave yells in his loudest whisper.

Danielle climbs onto the hood of the truck under the plane door. Tom backs himself up against the truck.

"Climb up," she demands.

"Not with my arm," Tom says.

"There are too many of them." From her new vantage, she spots a small herd—maybe fifty.

Dave joins her, picking her up in order for her to reach the bottom of the door frame.

"Just get inside," Tom orders.

The undead scurry forth, moving toward the plane, but still not aware of the group.

"Does this mean they don't smell us?" Dave asks.

"They like blood and noise, maybe something stronger is gravitating them this way, but not enough to excite them," Tom speculates.

Dakota blunders from between the cars. A short metal tube is poised between his lips. He puffs full against it. "Hey, guys. I found this whistle, but it doesn't work."

"Fuck me! How old are you?" Danielle scolds him.

"Never mind, stop blowing. It's a dog whistle. You're attracting them," Tom says, wanting to slap it out of his mouth.

"What?" Dakota seems confused.

"I'll shoot the dumb-nut," Danielle offers.

"Too much noise," Tom says.

The rotters shamble toward the plane. Tom fingers the gun's safety.

"Tom, Dakota and I will lift you into the plane. We should just wait them out inside," Dave suggests.

"I think you're right." Tom flips the safety on holstering the weapon. "Hiding is the better part of valor."

Rotters mill around the cars. Most seem confused—trapped—unsure how to escape and continue wandering. Many bounce off of a car or fall over a trunk only to create noise and draw a few other rotters toward them.

Dakota aims his rifle from the plane door. "I just want to pick a few of them off."

"They've thinned out. You ping a few and we'll have a small herd again," Dusty says. He has changed into fresh, slightly baggy, clothes. "We'll give it another half hour and then make a break for it."

"Where to?"

"Caravan, but I think we head south off the interstate and then come back up. Less chance of a rotter or a person hiding under a car," Tom suggests.

"I agree. Find anything useful besides fresh clothes?"

"Dude, I'm digging the clean underwear," Dusty says. "Usual carry-on items. No bodies. Wouldn't mind checking the cargo hold. Bet those suitcases have treasure, but none of us know how to get in the plane's belly."

"Even with the plane tilting to one side, this location is defendable. We locate a ladder and some tools, we could set up a base. If the caravan has all food and weapons for thousands. We could stockpile. We could remain here for months and be safe," Dakota says.

"Until winter. No way to heat this thing."

"We pack the best car and gear. Clear a road path and when summer ends we head to Florida."

"Nice plan, boys," Tom says.

"You approve, Tom?"

"I agree it's safe here. Still thousands of undead in the city. If we get trapped or cut off from the plane. It could be bad."

"No place is safe. But I'd get a good night's sleep up here."

"I like the idea of using the plane as base as we scavenge as much as possible from the caravan," Tom says. "Even if it's for a few days."

"Then we need to reach the caravan."

CHAPTER TWENTY-EIGHT

SAM'S NEVER FELT a lover's gentle touch against her skin, as the fingers push her shirt over her head to expose her back. Fear shudders over her as her blubbers are captured in the gag.

"I don't like to gag my girls. It distorts your beautiful faces. You already damaged your perfect skin when you forced me to injure you with the gravel." He tugs at the gag. "I don't want interruptions. I know you understand. I know you desire the transformation I'm giving you."

His push against her skin sends a ripple of goose flesh. She's peed enough to wet her underwear. The cold metal of his blade lies across her neck, and with the flick of surgical control he—

"Women should not have the burden of body hair. The skin must be smooth."

His warm breath blows away any hairs sheared by the blade. The pressure of each swipe brings fear of a cut, but his skill leaves no marks. The heat from lungs causes her a shudder, then a tickle. Warm air on her neck and the gentle fingers on her shoulders frighten her as her body betrays her. Never would she think she'd be aroused by a man going to murder her.

"If I were you, this—" his fingers tug, giving her notice of where he fondles "—mole needs checked out by a doctor. It's the wrong color for a girl of your mild complexions. I know they've worked you outside. A girl as lovely as you was never meant to be a workhorse."

The blade edges against the mole. He takes the razor edge around it.

"You will end in perfection."

Her left eye flows with a constant stream of tears. Part of her cries because no one has ever taken such interest in her—to handle her with such delicacy, as if she were a newborn. Yet she knows this man prepares her with the intent to kill.

Could she talk her way out of it if he removed the gag? Promise him anything—do anything to find reprieve. No. He's too practiced for the pleadings of a damaged girl to win her freedom. He has heard all these promises of complete submissiveness before.

His breath tickles her spine. No man has ever touched her like this. Why does it have to be her executioner? Why does it have to be like this?

"I need my makeup kit." He traces the line of her skin where the sun has darkened pigment and her tank top have protected the white. "You have three shirts you wear to sweat in."

She does. The skin tones must show three different levels of tan before he kisses what must be her white skin.

The wet of his lips sends her into shudders. The erotic touch might have stimulated her, but the kiss churns her stomach. Kyle kissed her. Pinning her down, he kissed and kissed. Maybe he thought it would change her mind before he—

She convulses from the pain her body remembers of the assault.

Levin rolls her shirt back down. Helping her to her feet, he brushes the dirt from the back of her legs and bottom as a parent does to a small child. "You've rested enough." Consideration in his tone, as if he hasn't bound her wrists and drags her through the woods to end her.

He loosens the gag, leaving the balled knot in her mouth. "Scream and I won't be able to finish turning you into a perfection. You've already damaged the palette when you fell in the gravel." He touches the dried blood on her cheek.

Tipping a canteen, he lets water splash into her mouth. Just enough to wet her lips.

Before he seals her mouth again, she asks, "Why do you do this?"

He takes her by the arm. She marches, no longer resisting.

"You want the story of my life? You want insight as to why I kill? You're not educated enough in psychology to hope I will reveal something you can use to convince me to allow you to escape. You know, if I were to guess, you're the kind of girl who never escapes the trailer park. Pretty—maybe even selected as a homecoming queen candidate—but you came by your dress third hand. You started off with a handsome boyfriend, but he strayed. Not because you wouldn't open your legs, but you always choose men who use you. Gaining you the reputation as easy. You got no substance in your relationships." His grip on her arm keeps her in step. "I'd bet you got accepted to the school of your choice, even if you knew there was no money to attend. Instead, you got a job at the local quickie-mart and didn't even take classes at the area community college. You smoke to cover up your weekend use of Mary Jane. The greatest moment is your life will be stolen from you by the end of the world. Being a victim of the Blonde Teen Slasher, you'd live forever, but no one's left to record or care anymore. Even I won't be a footnote in history."

He jerks her against an oak. Beyond the tree line, across a field, construction teams dig with backhoes earthen fortifications against cargo containers placed as if medieval castle walls. Beyond the wall a cave entrance hollowed enough for a Caterpillar haul truck to fit. The bottom layer of cargo trailers have been driven long end into the ground and are filled with the granite from the haul trucks.

Four guards, all with scoped rifles, protect the workers. Mostly the noise attracts biters, but they never make it past the outer fence, but even with the gate security a few could be inside. And Levin did create a new biter this morning.

Valuable fuel and manpower resources are going in and out of the cave. Considered what Levin has seen of this compound and how smooth they operate, these people are wasting themselves on such a secure area.

He drags the girl along, staying in the shadows. The backhoe noise allows him to shuffle her faster through the underbrush, drowning out their movement.

Danziger rolls the powder from the wet earth in between his thumb and forefinger. It is clear two people sat here recently. Small blonde nubs of hair scatter among the white powder.

"What is that?" Asks the kid with the rifle.

"Dead skin," Danziger stands.

"No blood?"

"None."

"What does it mean?" Keanu asks.

Danziger flicks his finger to shake loose the dust. "Serial killers establish a ritualistic ceremony when they kill. It's part of what makes them serial killers instead of just mass murderers. Levin's ritual—he shaves the woman of all hair except on the head."

"That's a lot of dead skin with no blood. I can't shave my face without getting a cut."

"Don't allow him to get close with a blade, kid. He knows how to use it."

"I see him, he won't even get a chance to turn." He pats the rifle stock.

Danziger fights the urge to scratch his forearm. They have healed under a doctor's care, but he'll always sport off-colored flesh and scars from being suspended in a bear trap. He'll accept his entire body being permanently scarred if it means killing the man who murdered his daughter. He clicks the walky-talky on.

"Danziger to base, over."

"Report, over."

"Located recent indication of Levin with girl, over."

"Acknowledged."

Danziger twists off the radio. Levin could be in earshot and he doesn't want him to know the outer search parties will close in on this position. He should forego the reports. It was a foolish thought. Others might find Levin first, but no reporting might allow his escape. If he reaches an outer fence and cuts through...

Danziger will end the chase of his daughter's killer here.

He follows the disturbed ground. "How long you been in this compound, kid?"

"Last November. It had snowed. I was with a group who decided to head south to get away from the cold. Even if you found an unlooted store, they had summer gear, nothing winter."

Keanu tenses at Danziger drawing his pistol at the diesel engine noise.

"Ethan found us. The biters move slower in the snow, but so did we. He brought us food and blankets. Some still went south. Five of us left with him. He had a van and drove us here."

"Did the group split off know he had a running car?" Danziger peeks through the trees at the Caterpillar haul truck.

"It never came up. We assumed we'd have to hoof it. He made no promises other than if we went with him and worked, we'd eat."

"What's going on there?" Danziger points to the construction.

"It's a fall back point kind of a Helm's Deep if the walls fell in. Still a real chance biters could overrun us."

"It's guarded." Danziger scans the ground for signs. "I doubt Levin would risk heading across the open field." He finds some broken branches on a bush. "So why keep working if the fences are secure?"

"Peace of mind. No one says, what do we do if the fences fall? We know to head here."

Danziger nods.

Instinct consumes him at the *crackle* of the gun. The wind of a bullet buzzed his ear. He drops, landing on a rock.

Gurgling.

Danziger slides back on his stomach, crawling on his elbows to the dying kid. He must keep a visual on the direction the bullet originated from. Even if the compound hospital has a surgeon, he'll be among the walking undead before they reach it. Blood fountains from a hole just below the throat. Danziger presses his gun against Keanu's temple and fires. He confiscates the rifle.

"I'm just going to kill you, Levin!" If not for the girl he'd fire blindly into the trees. It might be a waste of valuable ammo but it would keep Levin from circling around and stealing a loaded rifle. Danziger doesn't want to carry it. He needs to move fast.

Two shots should bring the search parties if they head them over to the bulldozer. Danziger locks the bolt on the rifle. The well-trained Keanu carried it open for safety—a well-trained dead kid.

Danziger keeps low in the bush. Levin would be foolish to wait for him unless he's trapped or the girl's dead.

His preparation was interrupted and he has no way to dress and photograph her. All part of his ritual. If his obsession requires—

Wait. He skipped the photos at the barn, but not the makeup. Or did he. I can't remember. So busy trying to escape the bear trap. The deepest cut itches. It will heal; physical wounds do. Killing Levin will restore the mental ones driven into his brain when he witnessed firsthand the work of the Blonde Teen Slasher.

He uses the rifle scope to scan the trees. Levin won't be decked out in camo. He won't have supplies. He should have a struggling girl with him. Even if she complies with his wishes he must move with her and she won't be attempting to remain as hidden as he does. He's bound her wrists so she won't step smoothly. Unless Levin just kills her to escape.

When he does, four people will have died because I didn't just kill Levin in the barn. I'm just as much the reason they are dead as their murderer. These people have built a community, and even with some still dying on outside missions, those inside the fence were safe.

"I'm going to kill you, Levin!" Somehow the useless and position revealing scream restores Danziger's. He has to keep a cool head to succeed.

He stays as low to the ground as possible and still run. The rocky outcropping provides cover enough for him to move higher and see more of the forest.

Save the girl. You should attempt to save her.

Didn't I try and do so before? I thought about the girl in the barn. I should have broken into the captain's office and gotten those suspects names and did my best to be Charles Bronson.

Redeem all those dead girls by saving this one.

The scope catches the glint of blonde hair. Danziger stretches his pointer finger as far from the trigger as possible without loosening his grip on the weapon.

He follows the top of her head. Levin used her as a shield or a distraction.

Danziger drops the scope, spotting Sam's center mass bob through the branches.

If you shoot her Levin won't be able to use her.

Fuck you.

You're still allowing her to suffer. You're still using her even if to slow Levin down. End her pain.

Gray-brown flashes over the scope.

Danziger fires wild.

Sam's screams muffle through her gag.

"Fuck." He moves, having to vacate his position so Levin doesn't know where he stalks from.

A deer bounds away through the woods. She must have nearly stepped on the creature before it decided to flee.

Sam's muffled screams continue.

Her panic has reached a point where she loses control of her body. He doubts no matter how much Levin threatens her, she has no control over her vocals.

"Fuck it." Danziger charges. Tree branches slap him but he doesn't slow his bolt. He reaches Sam. Before he raises the rifle, Levin slits her throat.

She doesn't notice the blade inch over her vocal cords. The crimson dripping down to her chest. The open mouth but no sound.

The rifle stock catches Levin across the scapula. He tumbles.

Danziger smashes the rifle butt into Levin's forearm, shattering the bone. He tosses the weapon out of reach in order to draw the Berretta.

No words.

No statements of judgments.

No reconciliations for his soul.

Danziger levels the gun at Levin's face and pulls the trigger until the weapon dry fires a half dozen times.

He lowers the weapons. The mushy mess that was once a human face couldn't be identified even with dental records.

Staggering back, Danziger legs are numb. Justice. Revenge. Satisfied. Nothing will bring back his daughter. No trial—triumph. His legs give out. He told himself he would be saving so many more. For a full second, he wishes he had saved one bullet.

His kid wouldn't want him to end his life. She was proud of Daddy being a cop and helping people. Plenty of people to help now.

CHAPTER TWENTY-NINE

ETHAN WOBBLES FROM his bedroom. Two more days of rest has only stiffened his bad leg to where he's unable to bend it. One bruise has disappeared from his arm. Most have transformed into a green-gray color. No shimmer purple anymore. Amie carries a bundle of bed sheets in her arms from the other bedroom, her bronze muscular legs emerging from underneath a long, lacy camisole.

"When did you move in?" he asks as a joke.

"Wanikiya felt you needed a woman to keep you and Dartagnan in line. Emily's been keeping vigil over you. She begged for the empty room, but he didn't think you found her age-appropriate for living next to you. I wanted out of the community sleeping quarters."

"I doubt you'd run around in that thing in the gym."

She lowers the blankets purposely revealing the low-cut top and the top of her well-rounded breasts. Ethan does little to avert his eyes considering the pain he would cause to crane his neck even if the polite thing to do would be to glance at her eyes. *Then again, she displayed herself on purpose whether it be an intentional tease or just a reminder she was a real woman and not a fifteen-year-old girl. Sanchez could be trying to learn just what kind of man she has taken residence with.*

"I saved her from the Bowlin brothers."

"Explains her loyalty to you. You saved a lot of women when you killed Kade," Sanchez says.

"She feels she needs to repay her rescue."
"And you think you should keep her honor intact?"
"Something like that."

Sanchez carries the bundle to the top of the stairs. "Would you like something to eat. I'll bring it to you so you don't have to traverse the stairs."

"I would appreciate it. I'm going to attempt to shower."

Ethan stumbles into the bathroom now filled with the collection of products only a woman would add. *Shit. Now I remember why I didn't want to share a bathroom. Men care nothing about, nor understand why a woman needs, five pairs of tweezers now on the back splash.* He uses the sink counter as a brace and lowers himself onto the toilet. Most of his body has turned a sullen gray-green tint. The beating was unlike anything he's ever gone through. *Whatever doesn't kill us makes us stronger—only they forget to mention* it almost kills you.

Even taking three bullets to a chest covered in Kevlar doesn't compare to the pain of each fading purple welt. Not a single bone broken or even cracked. Being in a cast in this new world would mean certain death. And despite some weight loss and being healthier now that McDonald's doesn't beckon, he figures some malnourishment in certain vitamins and minerals will plague everyone. It's a long hike to Florida if he ever wants to have an orange again.

What a girl, to sit down to pee. I've no choice. I can't stand long and everything hurts. He glances at the yellow liquid. *No blood. That's good.* He flushes. The worst mistake a person makes before getting in the shower. Now it will take a minute for the water temp to rebalance. *At least the water will be warm by the time I crawl in.* He adjusts the temperature. He must pick one leg up and set it in the tub. *Alive and I can barely move and those rotten dead people move around like they're in a marathon.*

He stays in the heated water until it chills. It loosens the stiffness, but not enough to make the arduous journey to his bed any less pain stricken.

He falls on the bed unable to move without pain.

Sanchez carries a tray with two water bottles and two brown MRE packages. She has put on jeans but left the camisole on.

He hurts too bad to notice or care if she just hasn't finished dressing yet or is purposefully displaying herself. *Why was it before the end of the world so difficult to attract a date and now they line up at my door?*

She sets the tray down and grabs his legs to help him swing onto the bed.

"I don't need a nurse maid," Ethan moans.

"It will take you all day to get into bed otherwise." She covers his legs with the blankets noting the scars on his left leg. They seem to be a mix of burnt tissue and lacerations. "Next time you get up, tell me and I'll strip the sheets."

"You're a Private in the military—not my nanny."

"I *was* a Private and I was everyone's maid. That's what Private means. Have a shit job, get a Private."

"I'm not a shit assignment," Ethan snaps. He detests being helpless.

"No, you're a good man who needs some assistance until he heals. You've saved all these people. None of them will think less of you if you give yourself a few days to heal."

"It does my leg no good to lay in bed. It stiffens and hurts more. I need to move."

"Fine, walk." She plops in a high-back chair, placing her own damaged foot on an ottoman before peeling open her MRE.

Ethan lifts his legs and then drops them back to the bed. "Okay. It hurts too much."

"Sleep and rest. I'll be around if you need me, and once you're better I go back to guard duty, or I might drive for the fence building groups. Leading a team didn't work out so well."

"Is that what you want to do?" Ethan asks. He stares at the MRE packet inches from his face as if it is the lost grail across a vast ocean. Pain outweighs his hunger.

"I wanted a GI Bill to pay for me to be an elementary teacher. Not enough kids from my neighborhood had good Hispanic role models."

"You're Hispanic?"

"My last name's Sanchez."

"My last name's German. Doesn't make me a Nazi. I just thought you had a nice tan. You're bronzy colored; that's sexy."

She smiles, content he noticed her.

Ethan hobbles along the two-lane blacktop shoulder toward the overlook near the dam. Private Sanchez jogs along the opposite side.

"You shouldn't be out of bed yet," she huffs, her own foot still painful.

"Don't nag. I can't lie in that bed any longer." Ethan does little to hide his admiration for her figure in a wife beater tee and military issued shorts. "Are you getting darker?"

"In the summer, I get darker."

He counts three sports bra straps under her tee before shifting his eyes to the foot she favors back to her midriff. Despite his willingness to remain without a partner, his body still has urges and desires. Amie's bouncing chest doesn't curtail urges. "Find a handgun you like?" He points to the gun on her hip.

"It's Beretta M9, standard issue." Jogging in place, she paces herself with short steps next to him. It may be the only time her five-two height matches his towering stature.

"Finish your run. I don't need an escort."

"You don't want to talk about—"

"Your raid on Orscheln's, or you and Emily fighting over who gets to bed me?" He's regained enough strength to discuss their actions.

"You heard that?"

"I faded in and out. You both got loud. I'm flattered to be fought over, but I think both of you need to find a more age-appropriate male interest."

"You're not that old."

"I'm not interested in relationship."

"You're gay," she teases. "It explains everything."

"I'm not gay. I like boobs way too much."

"I noticed you couldn't take your eyes off mine." She flashes her bedroom eyes. "I'm of age and you're not my commanding officer."

"I thought your cuddling stunt with me was a dream not a cock blocking stunt."

So, I'm your cock block—for Emily? Why would you even tell me this? "I was lonely. And so are you. Half the women in this camp want to be with you. You keep them at a distance. Do you get a sick thrill out of turning them down?" Amie asks.

"I won't be with anyone."

"It's not from lack of working equipment." Amie grins.

"It happens when men sleep, don't be too flattered."

"I've had sleepovers. You're choosing to be emotionally unavailable. And not like men who can't comment." Amie considers. "She must have been one special woman."

"What woman?" he asks.

"The one you had to kill."

Ethan hobbles away from her without a verbal response.

Amie has not spent enough time to know Ethan, but she knows she deserves the spurn he gives her.

"Ethan—"

"I'll move you back to the community center and get you other quarters," he says.

Might as well fill in the pit I dug. "Then you're back in the same boat. Now those women will want to mend the broken heart they will think I gave you."

Silence hangs in the air as he hobbles further away.

"I'm sorry you had to do it." Amie's apology pleads him not to send her away.

"Don't assume. Maybe I don't want some future bride to deal with my death. Chances are, I'll die on a supply run."

"Not as long as you have bullets in your gun. I watched you eliminate Bowlin's men as if you were in a popcorn shooting gallery."

"And four meth-addicted vagrants beat me to near death. Love forces stupid choices upon you. The risks I must take to keep hot showers working mean I can't afford to be blinded by love."

"How can you be so callous."

"I have to be, so this world you now live in remains safe for everyone else."

"You sacrifice your humanity—"

"So the rest of you can keep yours," Ethan says.

"Why bother to save us if you can't be a part of it?"

"I believe in the greater good. Before the end everyone was worried about an individual's feelings getting hurt. But changing the rules for one person makes a lot of others unhappy and no one seems to have cared about the masses. Hell, our planetary population was out of control. We were years away from Mad Max water wars. Maybe this plague was nature's way of restoring balance to the planet. Limited science was out there on the undead before the internet went dark speculated on a virus. Maybe rabies finally mutated just enough to bring the dead back to life."

"It can't be a disease. You can cure disease," she assures herself.

"Not all of them."

"I don't think your theory belongs in the crazy old man category. Factory pollution has ceased."

"The planet will repair itself. Now we have to survive and outlast the undead long enough to build a better world."

"You don't think there is a place for you in this new world?" she asks.

"Someone has to make sacrifices to build the new world, and there is no place for what I have to do in it in order to create it."

Reflecting, Major Ellsberg displays reverance before the Vietnam War Memorial. The oversized sundial stands as a testament to those from this section of the state who fell during the conflict. The Major remains at attention. His silent prayer ends and he raises his right hand in a salute.

The triangular geometric black granite sundial remains untouched by any of the survivors. A piece of the old world still important to the living. Keeping with its prominence and reverence, the Acheron residents have placed water worn smooth stones around the perimeter creating their own commemorative honor the loved ones fallen to the undead.

The sundial rests on the overlook behind the Clearwater Dam along with a visitor's center, picnic area, and nature hiking trail. Across from what was the visitor's center, now home for the dam operators, Ethan leans his back against the roof support pole of a half circular amphitheater. Using his pants as a handle, he picks his left leg up to prop it on the seat. As the trees green with summer foliage, the view of the lake is tranquil enough to cause memory loss at the evil consuming the planet.

Ellsberg somberly marches for the pavilion. "You mind if I join you, Sir?"

"You've earned your rank, Major. I was never accepted into the service. You don't have to *sir* me."

"You've earned my respect with what you do for these people."

"I wasn't so sure after those poor girls—"

"We can't undo all we've witnessed. What you've accomplished here—"

"Doesn't make up for what has to be done to keep it safe," Ethan says.

"Becoming Moses, are you? Lead your people across the desert—not allowing yourself into your promised paradise."

"You military types are always so spiritual."

"There are no atheists in foxholes," Ellsberg says.

"God's not here. He split on us."

"When there's no room in hell, the dead shall walk the Earth," adds the Major.

"Not in the Bible," Ethan says.

"You've read The Book."

"And, Shakespeare, Lovecraft, Bryon, Poe, and King. I couldn't get off the first page of Meyers' books. Sparkling vampires—no one could believe in that shit."

"You've read His words."

"I read a history greatly altered through translation. I'm not much up for theology today," Ethan says.

"Sometimes it helps."

"Did you just want to inquire about my spiritual wellness or did you have a pressing concern?"

"You have two engineers. They live in your converted visiting center here by the dam. But you requested another engineer from Colonel Travis, why?"

"They are civilian engineers. I wanted a military assessment of our camp. We're far from secure in here," Ethan admits.

"The sally port gate where you strip everyone is a brilliant tactic. We should have employed something similar at Fort Leonard Wood. Prevents infection from getting inside. You keep your numbers manageable even if you ride above the limits of your resources. Was this your plan?"

"The gate system and checking for bites was logical. It solves other issues. Black market smuggling for one. Fights over hidden amenities," Ethan says.

"I'd reinforce areas of the fence where penetration points are likely by both living and the dead," Ellsberg says.

"You have your answer as to why I wanted you."

"Did you walk up here?"

"It was only a few miles."

"I'll drive you back." Major Ellsberg notes the heavy sweating Ethan experienced on his trek.

"I've got to heal. Get back out there."

"You need to prepare other scavenging teams. Tactically, a sound investment."

"I've considered it. I sent one team out on my last journey to Fort Wood," Ethan says.

"You brought out many civilians skilled in keeping this compound secure. I scanned the list for my engineer crew. You brought two counselors. One specialized in PTSD trauma."

"Is that who's been leaning against your Jeep? I wondered."

"You brought them here to help people cope," Ellsberg says.

"Emily, Karley—both nearly assaulted before me. Other women in here were brutalized. Everyone has had to abandon or kill turned loved ones. They need a professional to talk to."

"And you don't?"

"Where I'm going, I'd just have to come right back for another session," Ethan smiles.

"I respect you, Ethan. These people would do everything you asked. Hell, you could have a harem if you desired. When you came back beaten nearly to death it broke many of them. They deserve a leader not afraid to deal with his own trauma."

"My trauma makes me who I am. It's not for sharing," Ethan says.

"She'd like to thank you for saving her."

"I know that trick, Major. She thanks me, and she worms her head-shrinking fingers into my brain."

"You know a lot. How far did you reach in your education?" Ellsberg asks.

"I'm over educated. I figure the student loan people search for me right now. The only group more determined to take a hunk of flesh from my ass than the biters." A grunt rolls from his lips as he shifts his weight in the seat. "Send her down."

Ellsberg waves at her.

The woman's build strikes him as being off from other women he's encountered. She has an air about her. One he places when he recalls Eastern European women don't indulge in fast food the way girls do here. Her blonde hair bounces over her shoulders as she marches with purpose.

"Let me guess, you're not an American."

"I'm a US citizen, Ethan."

"I detect a hint of Russian accent. I thought you looked Eastern European."

"My name is Ulyana. We'll forget the doctor part. I was born in the Soviet Union before my parents defected. Did you read my dossier before Colonel Travis sent me here?"

"I worked a summer at an amusement park that imported foreign university students to work. I *met* several Ukrainian women. They just have a non-American look, like you."

"Not sure how I should receive your observations."

"Not in a negative connotation. They all were the most beautiful women I had ever met."

"Do you want to tell me about them?" Ulyana asks.

"Wouldn't I ruin the mystery if I tell?"

Ulyana shifts the topic. "I understand your collection of skilled workers. Welders, medical staff, concrete pours, even the dentist. You wanted two psychiatrists and one needed to specialize in PTSD."

Ethan holds out a finger with each name. "Working backwards, Karley, Sarah, and Leah were all attacked to varying degrees. They need your time. I want everyone to carry guns. Can't have them going postal on living members of the camp."

"You witnessed the same brutality as all three women and have seen much worse out there. We can't have the glue that holds us together break."

"Nice metaphor. Help the others. I'll deal with my pain," Ethan assures her.

"I'm available when you're ready."

"Have you spoken with Emily?"

"I know you've told the doctors they can't maintain the Hippocratic oath where infected bites are concerned, but do you expect me to share what I'm told in confidence during my session? I won't," Ulyana says.

"To help people, you must build a trusting rapport. They won't let go of feelings if they think you gossip about them or perceive you do. I get it. I only want to know if you feel someone is a danger to themselves or the camp. We can't figure out a suicide risk after they have turned."

"Agreed. But no other personal information," she says with the finality of a James Bond villain.

"I want Emily to desire a more age-appropriate companion." Ethan opens a door the headshrinker will attempt to enter.

"You have no desires for women?" Ulyana asks.

"No desires for a fifteen-year-old girl. And she's developing obsessive tendencies. Nothing near rabbit boiler level."

"She seeks your affection. It doesn't have to be physical. She's lost everyone she loved and she searches for new camaraderie. Intimacy doesn't mean sex."

"She seeks both." Ethan smiles. Being desired is flattering even if it must be prevented.

"At your age, you'd think you'd be flattered by young girls desiring you," she asks.

"I'm not that old. And my urges are not in question. It's the moral issue."

"Traditionally, she's well beyond consenting age if she's menstruating." Ulyana continues, "In 1275, the moral age was twelve. 1885, many recognized age sixteen as appropriate to marry."

"Aren't you defending the wrong angle?" Ethan asks.

"No, I'm not encouraging you to ravage a teenager at least half your age. She's attractive and desirable. You don't want to exploit her. I commend you in your choice. You're making the correct one. But it is okay to have these feelings. We have such desires. Not acting on them keeps your humanity."

"Compared to the number of people I've killed."

"Because you kill you should rape?" she asks.

"Have you killed a fellow living human being?" Ethan asks. She's pushing at the door he doesn't want her to enter. "Protection…survival. Nothing short of survival."

"Kade Bowlin was a horrible man," Ulyana says.

"I never lost sleep over anyone I've killed. When I see their faces when I close my eyes, then you and I will chat." He uses the walking stick as a crutch to stand. "I'm going to hike back. I've rested my leg enough."

"You have two teams scavenging for supplies. Allow your body to recover before you travel back out there," Ulyana suggests.

"I won't just sit here while others risk their lives."

"Take the fence team out. Sanchez failed to retrieve the necessary supplies," she suggests.

"I heard about the debacle. It happens sometimes. Biters herd."

"How many have you eliminated?"

"Not enough. I don't count. Wouldn't notching my gun be signs of a psychopath?"

"Not necessarily."

"The only number I care about is the 224 people alive inside this fence."
"225. Don't you count yourself?"
"I don't know if Danziger is staying."

CHAPTER THIRTY

"NOT ENOUGH FOOD. Not enough food. Not enough food," Dartagnan rants.

Ethan limps to the couch. "I don't have the strength to order you to your chair. What's wrong?"

"Not enough hay to feed cattle this winter." He taps three of the five watches on his left arm.

Ethan's never noticed him just tap three of them before. "According to your numbers—"

"No," Dartagnan snaps. "Old numbers. You brought back more from army camp. Numbers change. More people to feed. Need more cattle. Cattle need more feed. More hay for winter."

"Hay is easy. Plenty of fields to cut outside the fence. We send teams with cab covered tractors and sniper patrols to clean off biters. We harvest all the hay we need." Ethan asks his real concern, "How many more cattle?"

"Not enough grass. Requires more hay unless you expand."

"I get it. Give me the numbers. I'll make it happen. We'll get the cattle. We'll cut hay. Then we expand. It's nothing to get upset over. It's May. Worst comes to worst, we could scavenge deep freezers and slaughter and store the meat."

Dartagnan shifts his head slightly to the right; simultaneously, his eyes dart left. As he nods, he darts his eyes left and right almost as if his brain is stuck in a processing loop.

"Don't overthink it, little buddy. You keep telling me what we need and I'll get it."

"Not for four weeks three days," Dartagnan says.

Confused, Ethan asks, "Why so long?"

"Time it takes your body to recover from trauma. 744 hours needed to heal."

"Based on what variables?"

"Average time—"

"I'm far from average."

"You can't go. Heal first. Only healed 159 hours. Need 585 more hours to recover."

Ethan never saw fear in the boy before. He found the kid cooking scrambled eggs for his dead mother. Plates and plates of uneaten eggs and Dartagnan never batted an eye, but now Ethan spots fear. No matter how harsh he has been in order to help maintain a sociable conversation, this kid fears losing Ethan.

"I won't go until I'm healed—enough. I certainly won't go until I can grip my gun properly." *I intend to live by that proclamation.* His right-hand burns when he grips his M&P. *I have to be comfortable to pull the trigger. I can't shoot for shit with the left. Even when I pull, the super cool two-gun* Matrix *double draw I can't shoot for shit with the left hand, never mind the impossibility of aiming two guns at the same time. When I do, the left gun simply forces people to keep their heads down and besides the cool movie action gun slinging scares the hell out of potential attackers giving me an edge.*

Amie plops into Dartagnan's punishment chair. The kid nearly has a heart attack. Torn between knowing the seat is only for his punishment and dealing with a guest.

Ethan snaps his fingers. "Remove yourself from the chair."

"I'm not one to be snapped at like a dog."

"I'm going to put you out like one if you don't move—*now*," Ethan commands.

She hops to her feet. Never has such a tone been thrown at her, not even by a Drill Sergeant.

Dartagnan's red face loses its flush.

"The chair serves a purpose. On the way to bring Dartagnan here, I had to go back. I carried the damn thing for a few miles, until I found a truck with gas in the tank."

"Why?"

"Kids like Dartagnan required a structured environment. Even if I don't know his diagnosis, I figured out fast his mother used the chair as a time out. When he misbehaved, he had to sit in this chair."

"My mother was heavy handed." Amie glances at her boots.

"Both achieved a desired effect. You both behave well in public."

"I was being polite," Amie adds.

"The world has no place for timeouts anymore. Children don't need beatings, but swift and decisive punishment must be delivered."

"Like the kid accused of rape?" She sits on a chair on the far side of the room putting the model tables between them.

"You heard about it?"

"One of the first stories about your celebrity circulating the camp. After everyone wanting to know if I had any idea what you did before the apocalypse."

"I'm a favorite dinner topic." Ethan shifts gears. "How am I in bed?"

"You knew they'd assume we'd copulate since I moved in."

"Apparently, I'm popular among the damsels I rescued. Before the end of the world I couldn't get a date, now my dance card is overflowing." Ethan considers. "Actually selfish of me. Your presence might quell speculations about my personal life."

"I guess there are worst ways men have used me. It hurts Emily mostly. The child loves you. Beyond infatuation, she deeply loves you."

"Therapy should fix her. Or a boy her own age," Ethan adds.

"Those Bowlin brothers—even if half the camp rumors were true—were some bastards."

"Why didn't Colonel Travis put a stop to them?" Ethan asks.

"The government keep pulling out troops. Near the end, the Colonel was down to a few hundred soldiers. Bowlin ran a black market and a thousand civilians wanted what he had to offer. In the end, it was math."

"Even at the expense of a few dozen brutalized women?" Ethan draws his left leg up onto the coffee table. "Everything is a numbers game. I hate math."

"As long as you're running this place no one will be taken advantage of the way the Bowlins did. Maybe you should stay and lead. You should settle. Show them it's safe to start a family again," Amie says.

"We're years from being able to have pregnant women in droves around here. Anyone going outside the fence should stay away from building romantic loves."

She bites her lip at the corner of her mouth.

"Everything now is a risk of death."

He crushes her fantasy and doesn't even realize.

"You can't do what you have to do out there if you are worried about a wife or child back here."

"Others can operate outside the fence," she says.

"Like you did?"

"That stung."

"No one saw a herd coming. I lost one. I saved my team. But I am not leader material," she admits, believing he wants to hear her say it.

"Bruce certainly didn't need to have children. Some survivors are an enigma. I don't know how they lasted ten months. He was stupid and should have died first," Ethan says.

"Lucky. Like those of us at Fort Wood."

"Luck runs out. Time runs out."

"Becky wants to be put in charge of a scavenging team. She saved my bacon and she's skilled with her machete. Maybe you should let her lead the supply recovery team," Amie says.

"What task should I have Wanikiya assign you?"

"Having your babies, according to half the camp," Amie snips.

"Dartagnan says we need more hay. Cutting will last for weeks. We'll need people operating the tractors and fire teams on the parameter of the fields to snipe any biters attracted by the noise. Perfect job for trained US soldiers."

"You're going to run tractors outside the fence for hours at a time in one location. Even if you cut the grass you'll face an army of infected before you bail."

"Use the Humvee to run patrols—small team, crack shots. The only danger is when the tractor drivers have to exit the cab for any reason. Which should be almost none."

"Do you know what fields? I want to scout them," Amie says.

"You'll do fine handling this."

"Are you still moving me out of this house?"

"No. I opened up the room for livability. According to our rules, I have to put someone in there. Might as well be you. And this mission puts you back into command."

"She doesn't feel right." Whatever miracle preventing anything from being broken extracted a toll with the rest of the damage done to his body. Pain stings as Ethan curls his fingers around the gun handle. He flexes, releases, flexes and releases his fingers until they no longer stiff around the weapon.

"That's your gun. Serial numbers match. Danziger brought it back with you." Simon jams an orange foam plug into his ear.

"She doesn't feel the way she used to. Like a woman you've loved for years—you know her every curve."

"Your hands still retain some swelling," Danziger says.

"You took a beating no one should have lived through," Simon adds.

"Don't become a doctor, Danziger; you have no bedside manner." Ethan raises the M&P.

The shot guts a biter. Chunks of dead flesh spry other undead.

Simon lowers his binoculars. "Not bad."

"It was the worst shot I've ever made. I was aiming two biters over."

"You never miss." Nick slides up from the Jeep. "Everyone in this camp speaks about how you never miss."

Frenzied biters grab and yank at the reinforced wire in an attempt to reach the wind chimes on spinning weather vanes. The dog run stretching from the main sally port ends here as if a second gate was to be built, but instead, the cargo containers secure a pit of steel fence posts driven to snag anything propelling itself into the compound. On the end closest to the firing station a third cargo container rests across the top of the two containers forming an H. It would only take the moving of one of the bottom containers by a few inches to send the top one crashing to the ground effectively blocking entrance into the camp.

"It will be a long day of practice," Simon says. "I need to qualify Danziger before you eliminate all the targets."

"At my current accuracy rate, there's no danger in that happening," Ethan sulks.

"Not many people would be up moving about this soon after the beating you took. You'll be a dead-eye again in a few days," Simon says.

Ethan places the M&P on the table. He pushes his left thumb into skin between the right thumb and forefinger, massaging it with as much pressure as possible, hoping the pain means he loosens the rigid muscles. He winces as he steps aside. "Test your skill, Danziger."

"You know I haven't decided to stay and be a part of this community. Now that Levin's dead," Danziger says.

"You want to eat. And we have rules."

"Does hitting the damn ugly cupid dolls grant me guard duty?" Danziger slides a clip into a Glock.

"Most want guard duty over feeding cows," Nick says, having become more the community center's designated gofer over a clear duty.

"What job do you want?"

Danziger raises the weapon, drawing in a breath. "All I desired was finding the man who murdered my daughter. I'm responsible for four deaths inside this compound."

No one speaks.

Danziger exhales, squeezing the trigger. Eight shots. Five biters fall.

"How many must I hit?"

"No question you are capable with a weapon. Finish the clip," Simon instructs.

After dropping five more undead, he pops the clip and places the empty weapon on the table.

"Do you have a weapon preference?" Simon asks.

"A Glock will do."

"What about a job?" Ethan asks.

"The best way I will help is to join one of your scavenging teams for supplies. Part of me thinks you need to take over the bridge where I found you."

"It's sixty miles to Hermann," Ethan says.

"But the military blew the fuck out of bridges over the Mississippi. If you lose the only way to cross the Missouri, you're trapped North of the river. And the major areas to scavenge are south of the river."

Ethan returns to the table. "Your argument's sound, but we don't have the manpower to expand sixty miles south. Not yet. More pressing is hay for the winter and more cattle." Ethan clips the ear of a biter. "Fuck."

"A hair over and you'd have hit him," Simon suggests.

"Still not the one I'm aiming for," Ethan admits.

"Then we do need more scavenging teams to locate cattle and fence. It's no longer a one-man job. There are too many people here to sustain," Danziger says.

CHAPTER THIRTY-ONE

RUN, RUN, RUN as fast as you can you'll never escape the gingerbread man. Mike has no idea why the cadence repeats through his brain as he pants for breath. He still runs five miles every day since his honorable discharge from the military. His only life accomplishment was to reach honorable discharge status. It's not something he makes light of. He's proud of it and all his training. It has so far kept him alive as the undead swarm the woods.

Thousands of shambling corpses chase him and the other few survivors from the caravan. He's surpassed his daily five miles and kept well ahead of anyone else who escaped the carnage. Alone with no one living or dead within sight. He checks his M16. Everything appears functional. He considers his options. No returning to the caravan. He could keep wandering south until he finds a landmark, and then work his way toward Fort Wood. The group was traveling there for safety.

Mike's breathing calms. He notices the smell of piss. Hard, stinky piss. His pants are soaked from when he lost bladder control. In the Middle East, he was shot at and was even credited with one confirmed Iraqi kill. He knows it was confirmed; he blew open the man's chest. Chucks of lung and bits of heart spattered over the wall behind him. The man drew a gun on his platoon and Mike was quick to prevent any of his brother soldiers from being shot. Every morning before he opens his eyes he sees the bearded man. Now, if he lives until the morning, he'll see the herd of thousands of undead scampering over cars and devouring all those people. Losing control of his bladder was acceptable. He doubts many people could handle what he witnessed and not piss themselves. He knows blood and noise attract the dead. He wonders if piss does as well.

The rotten monsters stink of death and shit, not piss.

He's stuck in the pants until he finds someplace with fresh clothes. He certainly won't find a working laundry. Nothing requiring electricity functions. He likes these camo pants. The nylon threading cannot be bitten clean through. Not without being torn first. Armor to keep him alive.

Alive—something he questions. Why keep fighting and running from a force impossible to escape? He should just lean against a tree and kiss the end of his M16.

"Hey, mister," whispers from behind a tree.

Mike jumps at the voice, forgetting for a moment DKs don't speak. He swings the rifle around and remembers the voice has to be a live person before he jams down the trigger.

A young teenager steps from behind the tree. She sports a hodgepodge of tight clothes covering her upper body including what looks like a cheerleader top with the school emblem ripped off. Around her thin legs is an even thinner gingham skirt over cowboy boots.

"You running from those things?" she asks.

Something about her doesn't seem quite right. If he had to bet, Mike would bet she was in the slow classes in school.

"Yeah." He lowers his rifle. She can't hurt him over there.

"Are they close?"

"I think I outran them."

"You need something to drink?" she asks.

Mike slaps his waist. His canteen's gone. "It would be nice."

"I was hunting mushrooms. I've got water back at my camp. I'll share. But my daddy… He won't like that gun."

"I can't give up my weapon."

"Then you can have a quick drink, but can't stay."

"I accept that."

"I'm Casey." She smiles, reaching out an emaciated hand.

Mike shakes with her.

She keeps a hold of his hand, skipping along and pulling him behind her.

They reach a giant metal culvert converted into a living space. Scattered junk from homes and cars decorate the open space around the makeshift home. A few dead bodies rot at the edge of the camp. Casey seems unbothered by the smell. It's strong. Mike's empty stomach burbles, but his brain considers the smell might mask Casey's odor from the walking dead.

She lifts several canteens off a hook near the entrance and hands him a cloth-covered canteen.

Mike drinks deeply.

It works quick on him. So quick he can't even threaten Casey with his M16 before it slips from his hand. He wants to ask why.

She giggles.

Mike gazes at the cold blue sky. Darkness washes over him. A bird flits past his line of sight. His belt buckle jerks as Casey unhitches it.

"You pissed yourself." She kicks him.

Mike slips into dreamless sleep.

Throbs of a jackhammer drive against Mike's skull. Replacing the waking hangover is the burning sting covering his entire left side. He reaches for the stings of what stings like hundreds of angry wasps, but belts and ropes keep him hog tied to a metal pole. He gets a waft of cooked meat as he struggles to turn his head. He buries his face in the ground to muffle his own scream. From his arm pit to his thigh his skin down to the muscle has been fileted away like a fish.

The meat smell belongs to him.

Casey stomps into the culvert carrying Mike's pants. "You know how hard it is to get your piss smell out of this material? I've been scrubbing for an hour. Now they won't be dry by the time Daddy gets back and I wanted to surprise him."

"Why are you doing this?"

"'Cause my daddy needs new pants."

"Why are you cutting me?"

"We don't have a refrigerator and no way to store meat. So, I'll cut bits off you to eat until I can't. I'll bandage you, but I'm good. I cut without much blood."

She skips from the culvert. Mike's amygdala wants him to twist and squirm free and run, or beg and plead to be spared from death, while frontal cortex reasons he's not the first captive and she won't let her lunch go free. He has nothing of value to bargain. He must find an opportunity to escape before she cuts off a leg.

Mike's stomach wants to taste the succulent smelling meat sautéing in a mushroom sauce while his higher brain functions compete against his lizard brain screaming it's his own flesh cooking over the fire. He struggles against his bonds. The girl knows how to tie a person up. She must have had a lot of practice over the last few months.

Cries of "Daddy" come from behind him. He compliments her on the sweet-smelling dinner.

Mike has no idea how to wrench free. He feels a tug on his cock and the cold edge of metal on his scrotum.

"Look, Daddy. We'll be well fed for a week with this one. He's a lot of muscle. I didn't cut too deep."

The metal scrapes his leg. "A runner I'd wager."

The knife pricks his sack.

It takes every ounce Mike has not to move.

"You want a treat tonight, Daddy? I know how much you love prairie oysters."

She grips the top of his sack stretching his balls down to the bottom.

"Save them. I brought a treat we can both share tonight." He holds out two tin pudding cups.

"Been a long time since we've had chocolate." Casey releases the scrotum.

Mike breathes again.

"I'll scrounge some more tomorrow. A new group got stuck on the interstate and was eaten by rotters. They left all kinds of supplies."

"That's good, Daddy. I'll cook you something special tomorrow night. Too bad cooking his liver would kill him. I'd love that."

He pats her on her head.

"Before he's useless, I'll cut it out and cook in wild mushroom sauce you love, Daddy."

Mike wishes he could regurgitate whatever's in his churning stomach despite needing whatever nourishment he has in order to escape. Unless he finds something sharp, he stands no chance of getting free of his bonds. Maybe without Daddy around he can convince Casey to untie him or at least an arm. He could do the rest himself. He closes his eyes, setting his mind to work on escape.

The culvert darkens as the sun sets. Casey's boots ring on the poorly nailed wooden planks placed for a floor. She leans over the table, flipping her dress up, presenting her white rump like a dog in heat. Her daddy follows her and unbuttons his pants.

Daddy thrusts into her splashing wetness. The table thumps violently, harder with each pounding he gives her. Mike wonders why the noise doesn't attract attention especially with Casey's pleasure hoots of "Daddy! Daddy! Daddy!" When he finishes, Mike can see gobs of his seed dribble down Casey's thighs.

"Will that give me a baby, Daddy? I want a baby."

"We'll do this until it does." He buttons his pants, stepping from the culvert.

Casey stays in her assumed position until he leaves. She either doesn't know or doesn't understand he pulls out of her before he climaxes.

Disgusted, Mike contemplates how to use this information in his escape. Mike wonders if they are going to cut on him for the breakfast meal or if he's safe until supper.

CHAPTER THIRTY-TWO

MARY STRETCHES HER leg straight into the air, flexing her toes. Water and bubbles splash back into the tub. She admires her clean body. Her nostrils sucking her own scent lacking any rank order. Smooth from shaving only enhances her flexed muscles when she points her toes. She doesn't care so much about having a razor, but to ensure her control over Kaleb she must be a woman. Removing all the hair hides the age she's accumulated in the past few months. She rolls her foot down then points back into the air. The water has loosened so much tension. Being safe enough to relax in bath, not just sponge off in a creek, keeps her pointing and flexing her toes. The index toe sticks out further than even her big toe. She wiggles it. So thankful to be safe in a tub of warm water. The lavish fragrance of shampoo burns away the death smell hanging around her.

She extends her leg to twist the hot water on.

I won't go back to scavenging. When the last burst of warm water turns cold, she slips from the tub.

How long has it been since I could just stand naked, exposed to the world, and not be afraid? Mary understands she won't leave the room naked to entice any of the men. *It's been so long since I wasn't in fear for life. Now once I secure Kaleb I'll never fear anything again.* She sorts through the towels. Clean laundry will be a priority after Kaleb. She takes care not to rub, as she pats her skin dry; not sure where the sun-reddened skin meets the lobster red flesh from the ho water. The sun has darkened her already naturally light tanned skin.

Considering what a lack of personal care products and weather exposure has done to her body she has a new understanding why the average life expectancy was age thirty-five for so long throughout history.

The bedroom carpet may be outdated shag, but she curls her toes in the scrunchy fibers nevertheless. She recalls life before the end. Never again will she be without comfort.

Kaleb enters the bedroom, startled to find her out of the tub. She chooses not to cover herself. Instead, she keeps herself bare for him. "Hello, my love."

"Did you enjoy your bath?" he asks, not expecting a woman in her thirties to be so physically gorgeous under her clothes. Her natural breasts hover perky despite saying she had once had children. He would never have guessed with a tummy lacking a single stretch mark.

"I brought you some clothes."

"Thank you." She flutters her eyelashes.

He tosses the garments onto the bed so his hand is free to clamp on her breast. She grabs his wrist firmly but does not remove his fingers. "Have you never touched a woman, Kaleb?"

"I've fucked lots of women. I never counted." His eyes hunger.

Her chest heaves with each breath. "But have you touched a woman? Not groped as if you were moving a feed sack." She takes his hand placing the palm between her breast. Her beating heart quickens.

He attempts to move his hand.

"No," she commands, soft, but firm.

"I want you."

"Then take me, but it will be only once. Trust me...and you'll have me forever." She slides his hand up her chest away from her breasts. "I'm going to teach you how to make love to a woman." She sucks the tip of his middle finger. "What do you want to do?"

"I want to fuck you."

She falls back onto the bed lifting her legs into the air before spreading them. "Take it."

Kaleb strips his shirt off. He interrupts his own pounce. "What do you mean I'll only have you once?"

She lowers her legs propping herself up on her elbows. "I told you—make me your queen. I won't be a whore."

"How do I make you my queen?'

"First, marry me. Find a reverend and marry me. Once you do—" she reaches down with her right hand, covering her mons Venus "—You can have this whenever you desire."

"I take what I want," he sneers.

"What do you want?"

"You."

"Beyond me, Kaleb?" she asks.

"To party and fuck. Shoot the rotten ones."

"You don't need me for any of that."

"You sound like my younger brother. He wants me to rule these people."

I'll have to meet this brother. "Then marry me and we will rule. Trust me. Sex is so much better when the woman desires you."

Despite the farm being a facade for a FEMA warehouse, the agents maintained the property as if it were a functioning farm. Kale's discovery of brand new tractors are a godsend to his plans. He will keep his older brother as the muscle people follow while he plots his dominion.

Kale motions his fingers for the truck to back the camping trailer into the spot before a second trailer. Men standing by with steel posts drive them into the ground. Sledge hammers ring with each tap to create a spike trap in the gaps between campers. The wall of camp trailers extends the defensive perimeter of the farmhouse.

"Why does Kaleb want all these trailers?"

"Besides a second line of defense to protect the farmhouse..." Kale considers his answer. He knows explaining to the functionaries will cement his plans to secure a livable location. "We need a place for the working women."

"Whores?"

History was built on women. Seattle funded their city by taxing prostitution. "Everyone must work for this compound to flourish. People need sex and this will prevent unwanted physical attacks. If we are to build, we have maintained order."

Two men jump from the backed truck and unhook the trailer hitch.

Across the field lumbers a snarling undead. Kale pulls a bowie knife. The axe-like blade shatters most of the skull. "Another one for the entrance."

At the end of the lane, men string up rotting undead in some twisted form of Roman crucifixion.

"All those Vectors will stink."

"I hope so," Kale says. "Let me show you something, Deshaun." He marches into a riding pen.

"You going to want to call your boss, Boss?"

"No." Kale loops his leg over the top fence rail to support himself as he watches the inside of the corral. Men shove Brenton into the center. The man staggers unrecovered from his drug-induced hangover.

"We are going to have to cut back on the drug use," Kale says. He snaps his fingers.

Two men drag in an undead clamped to the end of fully extended dog catcher poles. A third man knocks Brenton to the ground. The two men drag the Vector over Brenton.

It snaps and snarls in failed attempts to bite. The third man guts the creature, spilling coagulated blood and half-digested organs over Brenton. Covered now in the undead entrails, the three men abandon the arena. They race for the fence and scale to the top, wanting to witness the test.

A panel truck backs up to the gate. A man hanging on the top pulls free the gate so a half dozen vectors escape. They stumble toward the blood-soaked Brenton. Heads bob as they smell him only to ignore him.

Brenton's jeans soak with piss as he leaps to his feet and bolts for the fence. The undead shamble to the fence after the clean men.

"End them," Kale orders.

"What about Brenton?"

Kale considers before answering, "Have him drag these bodies to the end of the lane." Kale explains if speaking to five-year-olds. "Bash the undead in the head and stake them on poles to create a windbreak to mask the smell of the living."

"But we'll have to live with the smell," Deshaun protests.

"You'll get used to it. Until we build a huge wall or other defenses," Kale says.

"I know Kaleb said to build a farm, but why can't we just scavenge and take from other survivors?"

"We must fold other survivors into our group and make us strong. Build a base of operations and defenses to prevent the undead from overwhelming us. We must be logical in our tactics. Barbaric raids and pillage techniques only work if there are people to replace what is plundered."

"I see why they send you to college. Kade was smart, but you know stuff," Deshaun says.

"I understand how human beings work and what must be done to stay alive in this brave new world."

"Whatever you say, Boss."

"End those Vectors, Hansman," Kale orders.

The man jumps into the corral, knifing the closest undead. The others turn and snarl at the approaching snack. Hansman has no grace in his clubbing thrusts, but he drives the knife through bone quick enough to eliminate all six rotters before they bite him.

Kale scribbles on a pocket notepad: Militia, trained.

"Kale, will this stringing up the dead ones work?"

"Will it keep them away? No. They will be attracted to noise, but their dead smell will mask much of ours. Nighttime when all is dark and quieter, some of the rotters may move on."

"Lot of work for little result."

"Scarecrows always serve a purpose. For now, it gives the boys something to do. We need more trucks and gas to scavenge for supplies. If they just sit here, they get bored. Bored men do drugs, drink—damage women. All that stops now."

"Mary, this is my brother Kale. He's been to college," Kaleb says.

Mary holds out her hand. She grips Kale's limp wristed handshake with the force of a labor worker.

"Kaleb just found you?"

"I was with a group heading to Springfield. Many people have heard it is a haven for those who are worthy," she says.

"Worthy of what?" Kale smells her ambition. And she could easily lead Kaleb around by his cock.

"Many people believe those without sin won't be bitten. The undead are here to punish the wicked and the unworthy."

"You don't believe—"

"I find my time with God to be a comfort, but the rotten ones are not a punishment."

"Kale, any of these people a reverend?" Kaleb asks.

"Are you finding religion, Brother?" *She starts by converting him. I knew I didn't like her.*

"No, baby bro, I'm going to get hitched. As soon as I find a preacher I will take Mary as my bride."

"I'm not sure what to say," Kale says.

"It's your idea. You want me to run this camp. Create normalcy. Not by drugs and forcing myself onto women. What better message than to take a bride?"

Fuck me. Fuck her and whatever logic she drilled into him. Older brother or not, he's too dumb to think of this on his own. "If we don't have one among us then we'll find one on the road. We'll have a wedding feast. Use up the last of beer."

"You want to have a dry camp?" Mary inquires.

"At first. I want to get this group under control. They celebrated the destruction of Fort Wood a little too hard," Kale says.

"We did party." Kaleb snakes his arm around Mary's waist and pulls her against him as to never let go. "Those days are over, baby. I'm going to build you a kingdom."

What the fuck? Who is this woman? Even if it is in my head this woman has debased me to cursing. "We will build the kingdom, Brother. Are you taking Mary on your supply runs?" *Better chance she is killed off the farm. To kill her here while he's gone would have to be handled delicately.*

"Once married she will run the show here. You'll still advise me."

Now would be the moment to throw a tantrum, but this woman may be an equal. I must embrace her. "Then I advise we keep the supply runs. I still need the maps from Rolla."

"Sorry I never made it to the town. We found those survivors and raided a few houses. I see you've been busy with getting campers," Kaleb says.

"Why?" Mary asks.

"Besides the added defensive measures, they will serve to house female companions."

"You're going to prostitute women?" Mary hisses.

Kale is unsure if her outrage is genuine or not, but Kaleb assumes her display of being offended. "I thought we were moving away from women as meat?"

"We are. They are part of the societal hierarchy I—" he corrects himself too late. Mary heard what he meant in the I. "*We* are building."

"I don't know, little brother."

Calm. "Kaleb, we have to reward the men who protect this place and risk their lives gathering supplies. All the women who work will be willing."

Kaleb glances at Mary, seeking her approval.

"Do you even know all your brother plans to do while you risk yourself on supply runs?"

"Well..." Kaleb stumbles over his words unable to answer.

"I think we need to iron out what you want. And while you're gone, I'll make sure it gets done," Mary says.

CHAPTER THIRTY-THREE

"I KNOW I spend a great deal of time outside the fence, but after the beating it's a bitch to get dressed, so if you dragged me out her— It better be good." Ethan must use his hands to pick his left leg up and place it out of the truck. His fingers remain swollen and he detests not being able to properly grip his weapon.

"Dartagnan's latest report demands more grazing land, even though we need more houses. We can't keep people cooped up in the community center," Wanikiya says. "The people from Fort Wood have left it overcrowded."

"You also need to have scavenging teams going out, which means they could bring back even more survivors," Major Ellsberg says.

"I get we need more homes and fields. How does stopping on railroad tracks twenty miles from the sally port solve those two issues?" Ethan asks as he stands. Once free of the cramped Humvee, he is able to stretch his legs and hobbles until his gait unstiffens.

"I have a proposal," Major Ellsberg explains. "We expand the compound to these tracks.

"We build holding pens for livestock, warehouses, and a quarantine gate. We requisition a locomotive and run it up and down on the tracks." He kicks the rail with the toe of his boot. "We travel with some livestock cars, storage cars, a flatbed with vehicles. We make it defensible from biters. The train travels near a town and acts as a model base for scavenging teams."

Ethan kicks at the metal rail.

"Before you bring up the noise factor—"

"I wasn't. You weld 'shields' to the cars and if a herd too large for them to deal with arrives, the train withdraws. A locomotive engine and five or six train cars will hit speeds faster than any undead hoard. You may want some cattle guard or battering ram imposed on the front." Ethan envisions the future.

"You like the idea?" Danziger asks.

"I wish I'd of thought of it. One thing I was never into was trains." Ethan contemplates. "It's twenty miles to Paris, Missouri. It takes a lot of fence because we still have to fence in around the lake. Biters don't swim but they do float. We don't have the people to patrol such a large area and build more fence"

"It solves our grazing issues," Wanikiya says, "and there are homes along the way."

"What's the village above that side of the lake?" Ethan asks.

Wanikiya takes map from Humvee. "I don't recall. We never focused north of the lake. Not enough scavengable home to bother with."

Ethan studies the paper.

"I've drawn better ones back at the school, but I didn't want my detailed notes about our location to be outside the compound," Ellsberg says.

"I keep my travel map in code." Ethan asks, "Who knows about trains?"

"There's an Amtrak station in St Louis, but I'm not ready to head back into the city," Danziger says.

"Washington also has an Amtrak station. We send a scout team. What do they need to hunt for?" Ethan says.

"Manuals. Maps," Major Ellsberg says.

"Would a train schedule help?" Nick has been a dutiful Corporal being seen and not heard until now.

"The trains don't run, so doubtful," Wanikiya says.

"Wait. It might tell us where some of the trains are housed or stopped." Ethan draws with his finger on the map. "If we expand to Highway 107 and turn fence north to the lake. We then build a fence straight across the peninsula. Ending up near Otter Creek. It keeps much of the lake at our backs and we hit the train tracks just before Stoutsville."

"You'll need another sally port. Means another team of guards," Wanikiya says.

"If Soutsville's a village, why not just appropriate all the structures and make the city our base of operations for the train?"

"We'll scout it, but it's north of the lake. We'd need more fences and we still must wall in the peninsula. We're talking about six miles from our main sally port before turning north and some eight miles give or take to Stoutsville, but we don't have to go as far," Ethan says.

"Fifteen miles of fence," Major Ellsberg says.

"It's going to take more people," Wanikiya says.

"At some point, we have to thin out the dead," Nick adds.

"Then the real danger begins. With fewer undead attacks we become complacent and lose our hyper-awareness to danger. More chance of stumbling into a nest of them," Major Ellsberg contemplates on the future.

"We're a long way from dealing with a few biters. The mission to Orscheln's proved how even current intel means little when a herd moves in overnight," Ethan says.

"The locomotive noise will attract them. We staff the train with sniper crews to pick them off while others search the towns. We armor the train cars so no undead can scale the flatbeds, leaving an easy retreat."

"And scavenging whole areas at once has to mean less risk to our personnel."

"I was thinking it might make us safer to the living vagrants; as we clean out areas others will avoid them knowing they are devoid of supplies," Ethan says.

"Are we not taking in new people we find?" Ellsberg asks. "This operation will take a few hundred more people."

"We will bring in anyone willing to conform to our rules. That is who we are until proven otherwise. After a time, some who remain out there will become completely feral," Ethan adds.

"From what you tell us, Ethan, many have fallen to the dark side and refuse to return," Wanikiya says.

"I wish we didn't have to keep having this conversation but survivors survive because they are willing to do the unspeakable. Once behind our safe walls, people return to being civilized."

"You can't protect everyone from what's out there. We know," Major Ellsberg says.

"Knowing what's in the darkness and facing it are two different things. You have to defeat it without becoming it," Ethan says.

"Nietzsche?" Wanikiya asks.

"If it is, it is poorly paraphrased. 'Beware that, when fighting monsters, you yourself do not become a monster.' In this case, literal."

"Those that live behind the protection of walls should learn to keep the counsel of those who wander without them," Ellsberg says.

"Is that biblical?" Nick asks.

"It may become so in time." Ethan hobbles down the track away from the Humvee. "We build the fence toward this location. It brings in the land we need and homes for our people. Construct the sally port and warehouse for offloading supplies. Figure out how we want to handle letting those on train missions back into the compound. Will the train sit outside the fence? It's a lot of fence to enclose train cars, and the further out we send them the longer the train will need to be."

"The warehouse is caged off. So, we don't have to check everyone unloading, but if they want into Acheron we search them." Major Ellsberg has prepped for his sales pitch.

"That puts warehouse workers at risk from someone hiding a bite," Wanikiya says.

"It does, but those assigned to warehouse duty will know the dangers."

"It's feasible since any attacker will consider the warehouse an entry point or a source for supplies," Nick says.

"Most edible goods won't remain. By the time this place is up and running, many canned goods will have expired. We'll be able to sustain ourselves with our own food sources by the time processed food is inedible," Major Ellsberg says.

"We've a new goal. I'll fill in Dartagnan, because these new numbers will send him to his chair," Ethan says.

"It's going to take more people. The distance alone means more fence patrols."

"More fence?"

"We need a corridor so when we expand past the tracks people don't have to be searched when they cross."

"I don't know if I want the train inside the fence. A biter could get stuck underneath the train, or even an invader. Eventually, some people will want to find a way to take what we have away from us. The train will attract more than undead attention," Major Ellsberg says. "Eventually, this may be the way to recover supplies from the major cities."

"We add train operators to our list of survivors to gather," Ethan says.

"Won't inquiring out such an occupation draw suspicion?" Danziger asks, recalling his failure searching the caravan for Levin.

"It might. But not more than when I was searching for a dentist," Ethan says. "Send Karen's team down this track. We'll need a train."

"And someone to tell us how to get from tracks to tracks. Can freight trains and commercial travel trains even operate on the same tracks?"

"We check the camp at the next town meeting. Someone may have experience or have a relative who knew something," Wanikiya says.

"I don't want to be a Debby Downer, but this will entail a lot of work to even get off the ground. The fence teams are nowhere near ready to bring the fence this far," Nick points out.

"We finish the last round of fence first?"

"I think you've got to go to Kansas City, but there are trains in Springfield. Where masses of survivors keep traveling. We could open a trade route. Get a refrigerator car. Stock it with beef. Trade for cargo we can use."

The reverberation of a car horn brings all of them to draw holstered weapons.

The Chevy truck rattles. Ethan has brought back a dozen of this model mostly for part usage so they have a few reliable working vehicles instead of twenty to be unsure of. The fool driving now has swiped one of the unreliable automobiles to locate them. The hole in the muffler alone will bring a half dozen undead.

"Major Ellsberg." Austin jumps from the truck cab as he slams it into park.

"What couldn't wait until we returned?" Ethan's hand grips his Berretta knowing the noise will bring biters—if they are lucky only *one*. "Shut the truck off! Your noise will bring attention to our position."

"Sorry, Boss." He twists the keys. "We got a radio message."

"A what?" Wanikiya gasps.

"From where?" Ethan asks.

"Memphis. A Center for Disease Control location," Austin says.

"I thought they were in Atlanta," Danziger says.

"There's an office location in Nashville—but not in Memphis," Major Ellsberg says.

"It's a trick or a trap."

"It's a testing location set up by the CDC and military to search for a cure," Austin says.

"Fort Leonard Wood was the last active military operation—"

"Or so they told Travis or he lied to you," Wanikiya says., interrupting Major Ellsberg.

"It's some four hundred miles to Graceland. A bit long for a trip to an overrated pharmacy."

"We find some more women and I could use some of those blue pills." Major Ellsberg smirks.

"Joke all you want. The voice on the radio was trying to reach Fort Wood. He specifically asked for you, Major Ellsberg. Said he could prove it was not a hoax," Austin says.

"Anyone can claim to be military, and a few words of lingo doesn't mean shit," Major Ellsberg spits.

"I agree, but this guy said he was Dr. Ellsberg. Your brother."

CHAPTER THIRTY-FOUR

"TRAVIS ASSURED ME none of the soldiers had family—" *To prevent this exact argument.* Ethan thumps his left middle finger on the library table. The gathering conclave of Acheron residences are more than Ethan cares to have in this discussion.

"Memphis fell. All were reported lost. Colonel Travis believed, as did I, my brother was dead along with everyone else," Major Ellsberg explains. "From his words, the complex can only sustain itself for a few more weeks. His research must be preserved."

"A cusp of a cure is not a solution for the plague," Ethan says.

"He's my brother. He's alive."

"No questions he is who he says he is?" Ethan asks, not sure why anyone would want to face a call to Fort Wood.

"None," Major Ellsberg assures.

"I can't stop you from going," Ethan says. *As much as I need you to stay here, it goes against our founding principles.* "It's not a ten-hour drive. More like three-week hike," Ethan considers.

"I'll take a boat," Major Ellsberg suggests.

"I've safety concerns about water travel and the attention it could bring. I want to scout an area to the south," Ethan says.

"You haven't healed."

"I need to move my legs. I wake up stiff. I consider four-hundred miles therapy. You can't follow main roads, nor is car travel reliable. You might get three miles and then find a road block. Did he indicate how long the base will function?"

"It was an open channel. A month with current operation staff levels. I'd say that was an overstatement to give the illusion they are stronger than they are. Two weeks, max," guesses the Major.

"Translation, as they lose people, the food will last. Major, I need you here." Ethan has to pick up his left leg to place it in the second chair he uses as an ottoman. "Your train plan is key to our long-term survival."

"If his research has any viability—"

"I get it. We should move quickly. The Mississippi River offers new dangers. Rumor has it some bridges have been blown up. I'll circumvent St. Louis. I don't want to find the river blocked by downed bridges and have to land in the city. Somewhere south of Cape Girardeau I'll use the waterway. I'll need to take someone with some boating experience. I'll bring your brother back. I've gone after lots of family members for those in this camp—should be a cakewalk. You know where he is and we know he's alive."

"You're going to have to travel close to several major cities. You may not see a herd coming," Wanikiya adds.

"Just give me the supplies and I'll go. He's my brother," Major Ellsberg says.

"No. We need our doctors and engineers to stay here. This is what I do."

"There is little need for a full medical team here," Dr. Sterling says.

"We're a gold mine. Most medically trained people are among the undead. They were bitten before anyone knew what was going on because everyone rushed loved ones to the hospitals," Ethan says.

"There is another reason. Vaccination," Major Ellsberg says.

"A cure?" Emily's jaw drops.

"No. There is no cure. Once you have risen from the grave you can't return to what you were."

"The transmission said they had a vaccine," Dr. Sterling says.

"So, if you get bit you don't wake up a walking corpse," Ethan says.

"Are you sure that you want to bring these scientists here? There's only one way to test a vaccine."

"Are we really the group to debate the morals of killing? None of us can cast any stones in this room, except maybe the doctor," Ethan says.

"My hands are far from clean. Decisions had to be made to protect the military base," Dr. Sterling says.

No one questions the doctor further. They all know. They have all killed. Not just the undead in order to remain in this nightmare.

"First, it's his brother. We save family. Second, it's a possible solution. A vaccine means real families without the same fear we have now. Third, I want to explore that direction. We've nearly picked over our little territory. Treks outside the fence will take longer and longer. We are self-sufficient on food if the crops don't fail, but there are still good medications out there and bullets. We need more fence and I'd like to bring in more cattle. We have refrigeration. We can slaughter if we can't graze what we find."

Major Ellsberg spreads out an unfolded highway map on the table. "If I had a flask I'd raise a glass to the man willing to take this risk."

"You just get me a train," Ethan says.

Wanikiya pours a thumb full of rum in glasses before adding Coke from a plastic bottle. "Sorry, this has to be neat. I had to remove from a hidden stash."

"Bacardi's not a cooking rum."

"It does in a pinch." Ethan takes a glass.

Emily pulls several atlases from a shelf. "It's just too dangerous for you to travel that far alone," she protests, finally brave enough to interject.

"It's too dangerous to go outside the front door, but it has to be done," Ethan says.

"With Karen and her team gone, who's going to scavenge for supplies?"

"It will take you weeks round trip. Do we send someone to find you if you don't—"

"When have I not come back? No sending out a rescue party."

"I don't want you to go alone. It's too far and too unknown. We know you have safe places to hide between here and Rolla, but this is new."

"Fine," he relents. "Who."

"Sanchez?"

"She's not popular after the Orscheln's fiasco," Emily's retort remains personal.

"From everyone's report, no one, not even me, could have seen that herd coming," Ethan says. "No. She's going to run the hay cutting teams."

"We don't have the acreage inside the compound," Wanikiya says.

"Outside," Ethan corrects. "Dartagnan's concerned about the animals' winter food supply. The hay won't last the winter. We cut grass without it being inside the fence as long as guard teams watch the fields. I'm going to put Sanchez in charge, and I still need you here to keep the military staff in line."

"If you find hay bales we should bring them in too. Save on our own resources."

"Danziger has proven himself, and his arms are healing," Dr. Sterling says.

"Get Danziger and give him a team. We'll head south until he splits off wanting to find this Tom and others from the caravan. We need a clear path to I-44. We raid those cars for guns and food, gas as well. I'll move on to scout below Cape Girardeau; use a boat if it's safe."

"Becky has proven herself," Wanikiya suggests.

"She's a teenager."

"And a soccer player. She can run, shoot, and follows orders," Emily says.

"When I get back we are going to have to establish the age we have adults among us," Ethan says.

"Being a teenager no longer applies," Emily snaps. She hates that Ethan still sees her as a child. "We have a nine-year-old packing heat. And I believe she's twenty," she adds.

"As well as how we plan to continue with keeping the children educated and not lose the engineers," Major Ellsberg says.

"We're chasing a rabbit—you need one more in your party."

"Anyone from that direction? Someone who might know a bit of the territory?" Ethan asks. "Make it a male and make sure he can shoot, or knows something about boats."

"Why boats?"

"As good a swimmer as I am. I can't swim the Mississippi. I said rumors. It was Danziger who said that he encountered a military tactical team whose job it was to destroy the bridges over the Mississippi."

"Why would they do that?"

"Military strategy to cut off the enemy. The vectors can't ford the river," Major Ellsberg says.

"Means there will be even more undead leaving St. Louis in our direction." *And living who may not want to conform to our rules.*

"Everyone remain calm. It's part of the military's plan to take back the country. We just need to survive until they get here," Major Ellsberg says.

"If they do it like we do, then we'll all be old men before they even get to the Mississippi."

"And a vaccine will help us to live to be old people."

Karen flings open the door to the library. It smashes against the inside wall; books crash from a shelf.

Everyone jumps. Ethan's M&P is halfway out of its holster before he realizes she didn't intend to burst into the room in a stampede.

"Someone needs to fix the door hinge thing," Emily says.

The Major marches over and reaches up to adjust the automatic door closing mechanism. After a minute of fiddling with it, he says, "Yep, it's busted."

"Somewhere there's a joke in all this about how you have an engineering degree to determine that," Ethan says.

"I don't care about the door." Karen tosses some of the displaced books on a shelf. "What the fuck."

Fading green-gray stale color bruises still outline Ethan's face and exposed arms, halting her thoughts of punching him. "Your wounds should have killed you."

"Greatly overexaggerated," Ethan waves off her lack of concern.

"What about this killer? Four dead. I just brought back two more people. Maybe we should stop searching for people," Karen says.

"Slow down. We had a tragedy, but we must still build our home. I'm glad you're back, Karen. We need your team. But you are home a few days early."

"It was just a quick run. Had to do something after they found you. Maybe even make up for the Orscheln's debacle."

"Shit happens."

"You're telling me." She flips the chair around in order to sit backward. "Poor Sam. She was a messed-up girl, but she didn't deserve this. Acheron is supposed to be safe."

"We'll screen the entry candidates from now on," Ethan half jokes.

"You better. We encountered another group searching for this holy land where biters only attack the unworthy. They think Springfield is a safe haven of God. They're being called there."

"A calling? You mean God sent them to Springfield, Missouri. Home of cashew chicken and a church on every corner. The fourth largest Bible reading city in the nation. Springfield?" Ethan asks.

"I've never been there," she says.

"Last I was there it had a population of 160,000. That makes for a lot of fucking biters."

"These people claim the city is well defended and clear of undead—"

"And?"

"Protected by God," she spits.

"It's entirely possible," Ellsberg says.

"God? Really, Major?" Ethan's quizzical gaze scorns Ellsberg. "I don't begrudge anyone their faith. In fact, 'And when he had opened the third seal, I heard the third beast say, Come and see. And I beheld, and lo a black horse; and he that sat on him had a pair of balances in his hand.' If I recall my King James correctly."

Taken aback, Karen asks, "You know the Bible?"

"All educated people should know the Bible. You can't condemn or condone anything unless you've read it. War pestilence, famine, and my personal favorite Revelations 6:8 'And I looked, and behold a pale horse: and his name that sat on him was Death, and Hell followed with him.' I can't quite figure out why they are not war, famine, pestilence, then Death. That order would make more sense, but I'm not here for a theology lesson."

"I don't doubt God's love. Being under fire in a fox hole and returning without a scratch is a testament to anyone's faith. The city could have fortified itself," Major Ellsberg says.

"St. Louis lasted for seven months before it went nova. If they lacked a major undead outbreak they may have had time to secure an area and hold out. Plenty of guns in the area. Bible thumpers do love their guns."

"Granted. Then again, educated people should have a gun. But we've gotten off track. Are these two people true believers?"

"No, but traveling in numbers has its advantages, and at this point in the world any port in the storm. The more fanatical of the group went on while these two chose my team—less bible study. Both twenty-somethings who have survived outside for months. No longer amateur campers; she was a real estate agent and he played music."

"We'll find a new career for both. You find anything else?" Ethan asks.

"No. Runs are going to get longer. We've picked over the immediate area."

"I want to go to Springfield," Karen says.

"To find your true calling?"

Her *no* has bite.

"If you think some family made it there, I understand. We've figured out a better way to scavenge."

"People are heading to Springfield and the promise of safety. I think we should check it out," Karen says.

"Karen, it was a two-hour drive before. How long do you think it will take to hike?"

"I'll be gone three weeks."

"What do you mean 'you'?"

"I won't take Kalvin or Frank unless they want to go."

"The risk's too great alone."

"You go everywhere alone," Emily bellows like a spoiled teenage brat.

"We saw what that got me," Ethan snaps.

"Springfield could be a source of relevant trade. A city that size is bound to have resources we don't." Karen won't relent.

"They have a coal power plant," Wanikiya says.

"Two of them," he corrects Wanikiya. "And access to the gas pipeline. If they cut power to most of the city except where they need it they could stretch their coal reserves."

"Do people think to cut power to things like stop lights?" Ethan says.

"We did, not that the places we've annexed had many," Wanikiya adds.

"We need to know what's going on. If they are rebuilding civilization," Karen says.

"The idea of trade appeals to our growth," Wanikiya says.

"What we have of value to trade we need," Major Ellsberg says.

"We annex more fields, grow larger crops, and trade food—beef. Even if they are only a few thousand, they will be struggling to keep that many fed," Wanikiya says.

"Karen, if I agree to this, you are not an envoy on this trip, just a scout," Ethan says.

"I understand."

"Once you've checked it out, we have other plans. On your way back, we'll need you to explore the rail lines."

"Train tracks?" Karen wonders.

"The Major suggests we could load grain cars with food and return with what we need."

"That will take time to build," Karen says.

"We're expanding toward the tracks now. By the time we reach them, we'll know how feasible it will be. But the idea of a mobile armored base and the ability to scavenge hundreds of miles will sustain us indefinitely," Major Ellsberg says.

"I'll bring back all the information possible," Karen says.

"And a train engineer," Major Ellsberg adds.

"If I find one," Karen says.

"Keep our plans to yourself, but promise the moon if you have to to get a locomotive expert to return," Ethan says.

CHAPTER THIRTY-FIVE

A FLY DANCES across the exposed muscle tissue. Worse, it tickles. The damn fly tickles. Mike jerks his body which scares the fly only to have it return. War—he has been in two firefights. Two live ammo exchanges with insurgents attempting to kill him. Twice he had to fire back. Twice he placed himself in a position to kill other humans. He was trained to shoot those beheading sons-of-bitches. Nothing in all those experiences in the sand prepared him to deal with this. A constant faucet of tears runs from his right eye.

Casey plops down next to him. She dribbles oil on a knife blade before drawing over a wet stone. "He's not my daddy, you know. He just likes me calling him daddy. It keeps him hard longer. Being with your real father is sick."

Begging for freedom won't get him anywhere, nor much else from this girl. Maybe the threat to her food supply will shake her. "The fly on me will ruin the meat."

"Flies aren't too bad yet. Wait. Of course, I'll cut out your liver before you die. I love liver."

I'm going to die.

She slaps his side, killing the fly.

Mike jumps. *I have to get a free hand. I might be able to snap her neck if I get my fingers around her throat. Tiny as she is, one hand should be enough.*

"Why don't you just take my liver? End it now. Not much left in life. I don't want to suffer my last few hours."

"We don't have a refrigerator. I'm going to need a few more meals out of you. People are getting difficult to capture. I'm going to need steady food when the baby comes." She pats her belly.

Do I kill a pregnant girl to escape? Do I let her eat my flesh? "When are you due?" *Make her speak about the baby—build a confidence.*

"I'm not pregnant yet. Daddy hasn't given me a baby, yet."

"He's not going to. He pulls out. Don't you realize?" *Dumb fuck. Make her feel stupid.*

"You're just trying to get me to cut you. Daddy loves me. He said he'd give me a baby." She pushes out her stomach, creating a baby bump.

"Not the way he makes love."

"You lie." She jabs the knife at his eye. "I'll cut out your eyes."

"Doesn't change what I've already seen. I saw him lose it on your back. You don't get pregnant unless he blows inside you," Mike huffs.

"Say it again. I'll carve out your eye." She pokes the honed edge at the pupil.

"Do it. You're going to kill me. So, I live a day without an eye. Keeps me from witnessing him not give you a baby." *What the fuck? You can't escape blind. Dumbass.*

She jerks down his underwear.

Fuck. Kill me. Don't take my balls.

She tugs and twists at his member. "Give me a baby and maybe I won't kill you."

Don't be afraid. Can't be afraid if I want to stiffen. Mike shifts his thoughts to his wanting to escape plan. *Not a bad last request,* he thinks as she clamps her hips around him.

She bounces three humps. "Roll over more. I'm not comfortable."

"I can't lay like that in cuffs. Cuff me in the front."

She fishes a necklace from down her shirt. She uses the tiny brass key to unlock one cuff. Mike's hand clenches her throat. He closes her trachea before she reaches her knife.

Casey has a foot flat on the ground and uses it to push up. Mike tightens his grip. She falls back on him, twisting his member, and smashes his balls. Mike fights his instinct to let go in the rush of pain. He holds on.

She melts into unconsciousness. He turns her neck to snap it.

A rifle barrel fills his face.

"I think you should release her," Dusty says.

CHAPTER THIRTY-SIX

"DON'T THINK I'M unaware of what you are plotting," Kale slides back the door to the horse stall.

"I don't know what you mean." Mary drops her eyes in a coy maneuver.

"This is Lindsey. She was a FEMA agent left here to secure this location for the end of days."

Haggard, the woman appears to have been freshly washed, but many of her wounds are ripe with infection.

"What did you do to her?" Mary asks.

"Our eldest brother, Kade, was a sadist. This woman may have been his masterpiece," Kale says. "I don't want to hurt her. I don't want anyone to hurt her. I don't know what she told Kade, but I do need to know all she does about this farm."

"What do you expect of me?" Mary asks.

"You want to help run our group. Tell me you don't want to know all about this place. It's not just Ma and Pa Kettles place, it was a FEMA safe house. The barn was converted into a loading bay for semi-trucks. Other buildings have brand new tractors to give an illusion it was still a working farm. Stupid government types should have bought some twenty-year-old John Deere if they wanted to sell the deception."

"You seem to know a lot about this place already," Mary observes.

"I don't think so. I'm not saying there is a hidden bunker of weapons, but I'm sure there's a hidden bunker. I thought maybe if you spoke to her she'd realize I don't want to bring her harm."

"You speak about this right in front of her. She's never going to trust me," Mary says.

"It's a challenge for you, not an impossibility." Kale marches away from the stall.

Mary slides down the wall opposite from where Lindsey cowers. "I don't even know where to start. I could give you the 'we are both women trying to survive in this new world' shit, but you're too smart to buy into such a cheap line."

"Get me out of here." Lindsey's voice wheezes as if she just recovered from an asthma attack.

"You're much safer in here. If they're feeding you," Mary says.

"My price is a doctor for my wound, gear, and I want out of here."

"I don't know if they have a doctor. I certainly will see you're released," Mary promises.

"I want the gear and clothes first."

"Do you know where you'll go? I've been in…five groups, I think. Luckily, I've never been raped, but a few times I opened my legs in order to live."

"Kade took me in ways I never thought possible." Lindsey's eyes widen, but she no longer has tears.

"He's dead. Some hotshot gunmen took him down and some twenty of his men single-handedly. Or so the story circulating around here is. They have a living witness or did. They actually—" She halts in mid thought. "They must have a doctor. Kale wants his brother's killer. There was a survivor from Fort Wood who was caught in the explosions when the base was scuttled. He was being cared for."

"Boats are scuttled," Lindsey corrects her.

"You still have spirit." Mary smiles at her. "You'll need it out there if you want to live."

"About this doctor?" Lindsey asks.

"The burns were third degree and put him in a coma, but they kept his henchmen alive. No field medic or nurse accomplished such a task," Mary speaks to herself. "I know you have no reason to trust me. I'm going to help you. Only to help me. Just so you know...I don't want there be any illusions between us. I'll see you off this farm with enough supplies, if what you provide improves my station."

"No good faith offering?"

"I'm going to show you good faith." Mary gets to her feet, brushing off the hay from her white dress. "I have to locate this doctor first."

CHAPTER THIRTY-SEVEN

DUSTY POINTS THE rifle barrel at Mike as Danielle bandages his filleted side. Even with his hand secured by cuffs, none of them understand Mike's situation.

He notes his saviors seem well-equipped, as if they were part of the caravan, but he never saw any of them before now.

Darcy checks the unconscious girl's pulse. "Should we tie her up, too?"

"Someone sure cut the fuck out of this guy," Danielle adds.

"You should kill her and her companion. He'll be back soon," Mike warns.

"None of the evidence points to either of you being innocent. You were in the throes of passion when we found you." Tom patrols the edge of the campground, never taking an eye off Mike.

Dave sniffs at an open canteen.

"Don't drink it. She's drugged them," Mike warns. "It's how she caught me."

Dave pours out the water. "It's a good canteen. I wonder how much washing it will take to remove any residue."

"Are we going to steal these people's stuff?" Dakota asks.

"Those are my pants." Mike cranes his neck toward his camo pants on the clothesline. "Just give me my M16 and I'll leave."

"You tried to murder that girl," Danielle says.

"You'll find me in her digestive tract. She was keeping me alive to eat me. Saving my liver for last," Mike says.

"Keep your voice down. No way the rotter herd completely vacated," Tom orders.

"What do we do with him, Tom?" Dusty asks.

"We can't leave her here unconscious," Darcy says, "but if she's developed a taste for human meat, I wouldn't want to fall asleep around her."

"Is this a real-life prisoner's dilemma situation?" Dusty asks.

"Not quite," Tom says, "but it's the biggest conundrum I've encountered."

"Why save either?" Dakota asks.

"What?" Dusty glances at his friend.

"We don't know these two. Both are trying to kill each other. Shoot them and be done with it."

"Because we just don't kill people," Dusty says.

"There are no rules anymore," Dakota says. "If we can't trust them, just give them mercy and we move on. We do whatever necessary to keep *our* family safe. Us."

"Are you discussing this? We don't just shoot a sleeping girl," Darcy protests.

"You six debate all you want, but she and her lover eat people. Cut me loose and I'm gone," Mike orders. He won't plead. "Or cut me loose and I'll finish her, and her mate, who knows when he'll return. He's not going to be happy."

"Keep your eyes open, Dave," Tom says. "Granted, your wound indicates torture, but why would you fuck a woman who was going to cook your liver?"

"Short version, she wanted a baby and her lover was working the pull and pray method. I convinced her to let me have a go."

"During the process, you got a free hand and went to snap her neck," Tom believes this part of the man's story. He did allow Danziger to break his arm so they could escape.

"Guys," Dakota calls from the far edge of the camp.

Downwind of the camp in a ravine, Tom finds seven bodies. All rotten as if dead from the screwdrivers in their cranium—not infected. Parts of each body have been gutted and stripped of meat.

Tom marches back, tearing the camo pants from the clothes line. "Cut him loose."

"You're picking a man over her?" Danielle questions. "I don't want him in my plane."

"You have a plane?" Mike asks.

Dave jerks Mike to his feet.

"He was abusing this girl. Even if she was a cannibal. I say we leave them both," Darcy votes.

"We haven't decided what to do with him," Danielle protests.

"Discuss it all you want away from here," Tom says.

"What about the girl?" Darcy asks.

"Shoot her or leave her, but she eats people. From the signs of this camp she has friends. We need to move," Tom commands.

"Why are we bringing this guy?" Dusty asks.

"I won't leave anyone to be eaten. We take him out of here and cut him loose. Where he goes after I don't care." Tom jerks the M16 from a blanket pile and sticks a second pistol he discovers into his belt.

"Tom, we need to discuss—" Dusty's eye explodes. White goop laced with blood showers Tom's vest as the spent round splinters a tree behind him.

CHAPTER THIRTY-EIGHT

BECKY JUGGLES A machete. She catches the weapon in her opposite hand, twirling it like she's in a karate movie. "It has balance. Find me another like it."

"You fancy yourself a swordswoman?" Chad asks.

"I took ballet for years. It's all about balance with a sword. I'm not fencing, I'm stabbing. I don't need lessons for that."

Becky straps a second machete behind the gun holster on her left hip. In the shorts and mid-calf hiking boots, she has the appearance of Lara Croft. Her costume would excite Chad more if she had a single front curve. Disappointed, he's in the company of such a pretty girl with a shapely bottom but no chest. He's yet to change next to her, but the shoulder holster she adjusts proves she has less of a chest than he has.

Becky finishes her attire with yellow tinted shooting glasses.

"Shooting goggles?"

"Safety first, Chad."

Nick places two cans of gas in the bed of the truck. Barlock puts two shotguns in the car.

Tony climbs into the back sporting black BDU pants, boots, and an oversized 2Pac t-shirt.

Kelsey unloads her rifle, placing it in the bed along with a single strap canvas rucksack.

Danziger places a backpack and a rifle in the truck bed. He notes Tony's military-issued boots. "Maybe you two shouldn't be going outside the fence at all. It's not a *Resident Evil* game out there."

Tony laughs. "We've fared a lot better than the military led group to the feed store. They weren't trained for this kind of war."

"Most of the soldiers were on the base and not in the field. I respect your skills," Danziger says.

"I've been living outside as part of a special defense squad. My time with you is my ticket inside the fence," Tony says. His arrangement with Ethan remains complicated.

"I was never in the military. Austin won't miss me. While I'm gone, he'll be the best marksman at Acheron," Kelsey adds.

"Having second thoughts, Danziger?" Wanikiya asks.

"Not about seeking my friend, just these kids as part of my team."

"No one is a kid anymore, Danziger," Wanikiya says.

"There's just no coming back from getting your ass handed to you out there." Danziger notes how clean his team is.

"We know people are desperate." Karen tosses her bag in the truck. "We've seen how desperate people are. It's not just the undead who have been munching on people's liver."

"With some fava beans and a nice chianti?" Tony rapidly sucks in his lip like Hannibal Lecter.

"You've encountered cannibals?" Danziger asks.

"We saw evidence," Karen says.

"I thought we were all infected. Wouldn't the meat be tainted?" Tony asks.

"Only one way to test. We have too much beef to cut up a person," Wanikiya agrees.

"There are still untouched stores. Why would people find it necessary to resort to eating each other?" Tony asks, second thoughts racing through his mind. He wants of the chain gang, complete his deal with Ethan, and get inside the fence but he had no idea how safe wrangling biters was.

"I don't want to know the answer."

"I'm up for visiting Memphis," Kelsey says. "I've never been anywhere."

"We aren't going to Graceland. We're going for Major Ellsberg's brother," Ethan says.

"Is his research into the sickness?" Tony asks.

"It doesn't matter. I'm not going to Memphis for a cure or to see Elvis. I've made a promise to this group to save family when possible," Ethan says.

"You don't believe there's a vaccine?" Kelsey asks.

"My medical training is limited, but for there to be a vaccine they need to know the cause," Frank says.

Becky shakes her head.

"Colonel Travis implied Fort Wood was the last operational military base. We need to know if there are more active troops," Ethan says.

"You think he lied?" Becky asks.

"No. The government may not have reported to him about other operating locations. Memphis is too far to travel for supplies, yet."

"You want to build a fence all the way to Memphis?"

"No, but eventually we should be able to open trade routes with locomotives over long distances."

"There are no trains."

"There have to be. Just none close. Actually, works for us. Fewer groups scavenging for the same supplies prevents conflict," Ethan says.

Danziger hops into the truck bed. "It's going to be cramped back here."

"Only for a while. Nick and Barlock will take us down the road to as close as possible to the Christopher S. Bond Bridge."

"Where's that?"

Ethan says, "Hermann. Where I first met Danziger."

CHAPTER THIRTY-NINE

WANIKIYA WAITS FOR the truck to disappear from the ground view of the sally port. Major Ellsberg and Austin both remain vigilant beside him.

"She's going to get a lot more practice popping biters out there without me. I'll never be able to outshoot her now," Austin muses.

"You seem distracted, Wanikiya," Major Ellsberg notices.

"Just a feeling."

"They've all come back before," Austin says.

"None of them have traveled this far into the unknown before," Wanikiya says.

"It's not unknown. Even I went to Memphis once," Austin says.

"Son, everything's unknown now," Major Ellsberg says. "Something else is bothering our Native American friend."

"Maybe Ethan should have explained to Danziger about Tony and his deal," Wanikiya considers.

The brakes on Dr. Baker's truck squeak. He hops out, a bottle of pills in hand. "Damn. They're gone."

"Just over the hill."

"I made up some pain pills for Ethan."

"He wouldn't have taken them anyway," Wanikiya says.

"They would have helped with the swelling," Dr. Baker adds.

"None of us would have stopped him even if he isn't fully healed," Austin says.

"I was thinking, one of the reasons I wasn't caught in the infected pool was I was working research and not at a hospital. I want permission to try something. Next time we slaughter a steer I want to collect the blood and leave it outside where I can watch it with a microscope," Dr. Baker says.

"That will attract biters," Austin says.

"We're safe. We have food, water, shelter, a community. We're safe enough to have a library. I want to study the undead. We must study them," Dr. Baker pleads.

"Never will you bring one inside," Wanikiya commands.

"I agree. That's not what I want to study. I want to understand them in the wild. There's a draw bringing them toward the living, and it doesn't seem to be basic human scent."

"Go on."

Dr. Baker explains, "We know noise attracts them. We've used loud sounds many times to draw them where we want them. I want to try blood. You just add it to the compost."

"How will witnessing them attack a bucket of blood help?" Ellsberg asks.

"I start with blood. I want to test a variety of sounds and scents. If I learn enough we might be able to build a decoy. Say a scent attractor to place it out beyond where the fence teams work. You put a guard watching the attractor and as biters gather he warns the group," Baker suggests.

"They do so now, doctor."

"They do and are experts at it but based on what happened at Orscheln's, it might give the team more warning. Those biters were on them before the guards sounded a warning."

"Until more people arrive and need to get certified to carry, Simon and Nick will set up whatever you want to observe outside the fence. You'll not be allowed outside and *never* will an undead be brought inside," Wanikiya says.

"Acceptable," Dr. Baker says.

"I never thought we'd want to attract those damn things," Ellsberg says.

CHAPTER FORTY

"I DON'T GET why you want to spend shoe leather?" Nick shifts into park. It seems to be his assigned task at Acheron.

"Boss finds hiking is safer and faster." Barlock rolls down the window and opens the door with the outside handle.

"The world has lost all ambient noise, kid. The sound of a running engine travels much further than people realize." Ethan has to scoot to the edge of the tailgate to step down.

"Why not get some bicycles?" Nick asks.

"They don't travel too well over land," Danziger notes.

"You can cover three times as much ground on a bike than hoofing it, and even weave around the permanently gridlocked traffic on the interstate," Tony says.

"They would weave in and out of abandoned cars with ease, but those same vehicles are ripe for traps. Ride a bike if you want. I prefer to stay off the road," Ethan says.

Barlock pours gas into the truck tank from one of the two cans.

Ethan unfolds and refolds a map before placing it in a waterproof map sleeve for hikers. "Danziger, you follow Highway 100 into Washington. Then from there to I-44, I would run parallel to the road. Keep over land. Prospective assailants are less likely to have booby traps in the middle of a field than in the middle of the road."

"You're the expert. Any other advice?"

"I travel different paths even when I return to the same location. I don't trust anyone I find out here. And even then, you witnessed what a second of trust cost me."

"You sure you want us to head to the train station first?" Danziger asks.

"Any survivors from the caravan not knowing Fort Wood is gone will head west. Your friend may be among them. Could be a longer trip to backtrack. We need train info."

Danziger nods.

Kelsey joins him. "We'll find what you need, Boss."

"Don't let me down, Tony," Ethan says.

"I want us to be even." Tony flashes a gang sign Ethan doesn't understand.

Ethan folds another paper map. "Karen. You're an expert at this."

"You're going to run out of maps if you want us to take a new one each trip," she says.

"I'm still interested in hiding our location. New maps have less wear. From my folds a smart someone might figure out the lake location and suspect we have electricity."

"I'd miss it," Kalvin says.

"I'll miss you showering, and no beans. His farts are so loud they bring the biters." Karen smiles.

Frank does a final check on his medical gear. "Any more advice for us, Ethan?"

"Every devout group we've encountered have been a danger. But so are those not preaching the undead only bite the unworthy. Just be careful. I want this train plan to work."

"We'll make all attempts not to offend the faithful."

"Hell, I'll convert if means not getting bit," Frank says.

"You'd be in confession for your sins for a month," Karen says.

"You guys be careful out there." Ethan hands her a map encased in plastic.

"You be careful, Boss. The Mississippi's unpredictable with all those undertows," Karen says.

"Chad's supposed to know boats on the river."

"Poker runs on the Merrimac are not the same," Frank warns.

"I'll navigate ol' Miss just fine," Chad says.

"Who the fuck calls it ol' Miss?" Ethan rolls his eyes. "As long as he puts it in the water without a trailer still attached, we'll be good."

CHAPTER FORTY-ONE

ON THE LEFT corner of a black top crossroads rests a general store with gas pumps.

"How did these places ever stay in business?" Chad asks.

"We are just far enough outside of a major town it's cheaper to pay a dollar more for a gallon of milk over driving another fifteen/twenty miles for a Walmart."

"Why don't you scout over the hill, Chad?" Ethan's suggestion is an order.

The young buck jogs up the hill.

Becky expects them to stop but Ethan marches up the road. "Doesn't it have supplies?"

"The last time I went this way it did. Too bad we are freshly stocked. Later when we need food we'll find nothing," Ethan says.

"Are we going to stop?" Becky asks.

"You need a break already?"

"No. Thought you'd want to investigate if it was still stocked," Becky says.

"I'd rather spend those ten minutes to get closer to Cuba."

Chad races back from the hill crest. "Ethan!" he calls as loud as he can without yelling. "*Herd.*"

He snaps his fingers at Becky. "The door was unlocked. Check inside for biters." Ethan's gait returns to a hobble as he run-steps toward the hill. He fails to reach it before dozens of undead shambles into view. Drawing his Berretta, Ethan laces his left hand over his right to steady his aim.

Chad dips and zags out of the line of fire.

The round clips the shoulder of an approaching biter. Clumps of dead flesh splatters behind the creature but does nothing to slow its advance.

Ethan huffs with annoyance. He calms his next breath. *Calm.* He exhales as he squeezes the trigger.

"Fuck."

The chest of a biter explodes.

Some fifty undead shift their mindless march toward the gas station.

"*Ethan. The store's clear,*" Becky yells.

"Ethan!" Chad reaches Ethan before turning to fire his rifle. "You're thinking there's only fifty—don't. There're more over the hill."

Ethan's strides move him to the gas station parking lot. "It's not about their numbers, kid."

"We'll just wait them out," Chad says.

Ethan elects not to explain the emasculating factor of missing twice. "Don't pop anymore. Maybe we'll only lose an hour before something distracts them away from the store."

"*Got ya,*" Chad screams. A little old lady biter bounces off his Kevlar vest. "Where did she—" He doesn't get to finish his question as the biter's teeth sink into Ethan's arm.

CHAPTER FORTY-TWO

TOM FAILS TO hold in a yip as his broken arm bangs a tree on his way to the ground. Breaking the bone was the only way to escape the survivors who were going to cut him up for their undead family members. Now the pain waters his eyes. He needs clear vision in order to locate the shooter.

The Ds lack training in firefight tactics and must be in full-blown panic mode with their adopted leader disfigured and dead on the ground. Witnessing Dusty being shot and knowing he's dead weighs heavily on them. The missing eye paints a horrific picture.

As a firefighter, Tom has seen mangled bodies before the end of the world. All his experience keeps him from panic, but the new awakened pain in his arm clouds his thoughts. *Get over the pain if you want to live. Where did the initial shot originate from? Some of the Ds have returned fire. This guy's killed before. The first human kill— damn difficult.*

Tom squirrels to the next tree.

Screams of his team to move drown in the gun fire.

Did we free the assaulted man already? If he's a soldier he would be valuable in this fire fight. Tom uses the tree as support to slide up to his feet. The bark scrapes his back, but he barely notices the pain over his throbbing arm.

If I live through this, I need to find some kind of doctor. Even a vet. He could reset the bone.

Tom jams the pistol barrel into the mouth of the staggering rotter. Distracted by all the shooting, he forgot the reverberating noise attracts them. The removal of its brain only adds to the noise.

Time to be Rambo.

Tom marches into the center of the camp. As soon as his group spots him they cease firing. The partner of the unconscious girl fires wild, caught off guard by anyone stupid enough to parade straight into gunfire.

Tom empties the gun. Bullets whiz past the attacker, but not all.

Two slugs splatter his stomach open. A third splinters the radial bone. Tom kicks the rifle from the man's hand. Pointing the steaming pistol at his face with the chamber wide open.

Dave crashes through the underbrush to reach Tom, "Did you get..." Seeing the bleeding, but an alive man, he forgoes his question.

"You want to finish him?" Tom asks with no malice in his tone. A simple request like "clean your plate" or "turn off your cell phone at the movies".

"He's still alive. He's unarmed. Isn't that murder?"

Tom presses his empty gun into Dave's hand. "Reload it."

Dave fumbles to eject the clip. Tom hands him a full one.

"This man just shot your friend. He shot at the rest of your friends. He was going to kill each of us. Yes, he is unarmed now, but his intent was clear." Tom takes the gun back, releasing the slide to pop into place, jerking a bullet into the chamber. "Worst of all, this bastard and his whore were eating people."

"Passing judgment is not—"

Tom puts a bullet into the attacker's face.

"From now on I shoot cannibals on sight," Tom says.

Before he reaches the comatose girl, Darcy drives the blade of her hunting knife into her skull. "I am in full agreement."

"Darcy. You just murdered—"

"A killer and human flesh eater." She waves the bloody point at Dave. "And I'll kill anyone who puts us in danger from now on."

"Including him?" Tom points at Mike.

"Let him go. If I ever see him again I'll just kill him." Darcy flicks the blood from her knife. Before she sheathes the blade, undead crash through the trees. Tom pops two. Dakota smashes the butt of his rifle into a rotter's face.

Tom pops a rotter approaching Danielle. "Get over here, girl! Everyone, circle up." With Dusty dead, Tom assumes command. If the group wants a different leader, voting will transpire if they survive the few dozen monsters lumbering toward them.

Mike scrambles for his M16. For a moment, he seems to forget how to remove the clip as pain burns from his side. He fumbles the tool he was trained to strip and rebuild blindfolded. He gets the magazines secure, arming the weapon. The skittering burst unleashed twenty rounds in twelve seconds. The burst of rapid pops brings down ten Vectors. Missing legs and arms, they continue to crawl toward the group, but with a reduced rate of speed, knives shatter brain pans with little threat.

Mike reloads. Any healing his wound experienced now wets with fresh blood.

"Machine guns are pointless, go semi-auto and make each shot count," Tom orders.

Grateful the threat has thinned, he has yet to determine how to deal with the soldier. Tom holsters his weapon to draw his knife, finishing off the last undead to lumber into the camp.

"What do we do with this motherfucker?" Dave asks.

"You said you have a plane. We fly out of here. Plenty of island where defense is possible better than Missouri," Mike suggests. Hoping this group will allow him to join them.

"I don't want you part of my family." Darcy wipes her blade again on the shirt of an undead corpse. "Take your gear and go."

"There is safety in numbers. We were all a part of the caravan," Mike pleads. "No one will survive alone out there."

"Sorry, this group has spoken." Tom places his hand on the top of his holstered pistol.

Mike slinks to the tent and grabs his gear.

Part of Tom wants to ask the man to stay. *We need numbers. It may be harder to feed but more people, more protection. We're down a man. Hell, this group has popped their cherry. They have fought and lived. Their trust is damaged. We will swing back to building a group.*

"Take anything useful," Tom orders. "We need to reach the caravan."

CHAPTER FORTY-THREE

TRAPPED IN THE barn since being brutally assaulted, Lindsey is prevented from gaining any of her strength back. Remaining on nimble toes, she takes each stair step one at a time into the room hidden under the barn.

"I was only down here once." Lindsey crosses a motion sensor.

Startled, Mary jerks her gun hand as the lights flicker on.

Behind sealed glass walls are plastic crates marked with the caduceus emblem. Other sections have rifle racks full of automatic weapons. Black drums marked "flammable" fill another storage area.

"This was a backup for what was to be brought in and stored in the barn," Lindsey explains.

Each glass partition has a key card slot to gain entry.

"Where are the keys?" Mary demands with her sweet demeanor.

"I don't know. I was never issued a security card."

Mary flings Lindsey against a glass partition. "I'm not like those men and what they did to you—was physical." Mary digs her nails into Lindsey's arm. The gun barrel into her neck. The carotid artery thumps against the Ruger's metal. "Your little holes will heal, but if you lie to me, I'll keep you alive. I'll get in your head. You'll beg for death and it will never be granted."

She pushes against Mary's arms to free her grip but fails. She has no strength to squirm during the attack. "I don't have the passkey," Lindsey pleads.

"Then I don't let you leave." She backs away; the gun barrel imprint on Lindsay's neck already darkening.

Lindsey slides down the glass into a fetal heap. "I don't know. I want out of here." Her tear ducts remain dry. "I wasn't in command. Gibbs was the lead agent. Check his pockets."

"I think you know they burnt the bodies of those agents when they took over this place."

Excitement replaces Lindsey's need to cry. "Did they use an accelerant?"

"I wasn't here then."

"It's a metal card. It wouldn't burn. It would take a strong fuel to melt the card. Unless soaked in gasoline," Lindsey says.

"And if there's no card?"

"It would have been against policy to leave it in the farmhouse."

Mary flicks the hidden switch in a hole behind a barn pole. The hatch in the floor closes.

"I wouldn't use it too many times. It has an emergency battery if the farm loses power. I don't think it was meant to be opened and closed more than once without recharging," Lindsey says.

"What about entering through the ceiling? Just dig up the rooms."

"Any attempt to tamper with the rooms will release a gas."

"You FEMA people are all heart." Mary marches Lindsey past the farm house. "Run and I'll plug you."

"What are you going to do to me?"

"They piled those agent bodies near the end of the land. They don't burn well. Still too juicy to turn to ash." She points to the tree line.

Soot blackens Lindsey's arms. Cooked flesh and bone still covered by melted cloth fragments and nylon gun holsters. Her friends. Some of them. All of them she knew. Her only reprieve is the bodies are charred enough she's unable to recognize which body is who. She knows it would destroy her if she figures out whose bodies she defiles. "What if they see us?"

"I will keep my word, as long as you deliver." Mary's confidence frightens Lindsey.

Never having been covered in ash before, Lindsey's not sure how, but the disgusting material paints her skin. Rubbing it seems to stain the cells. She scrubs her forearms but it only darkens the paste.

It will never wash off.

"Keep searching," Mary commands.

"Maybe knowing which body was which I might find the card faster." She grabs an arm and the cooked meaty muscle falls off into shreds of chewy pink meat. The raw rotten smell removes her first solid meal in weeks from her stomach.

Mary steps back. The acidy fumes are worse than the cooked undead bouquet.

Lindsey dumps a body from the top of the pile. She tosses a second away. The sun beats down, festering the unburnt flesh. As she must touch more of the skin, she notices it doesn't crumble as a body did before the apocalypse. At this point in the decomposition process, maggots should consume the remains. In fact, not a single insect swarms the body.

As her pile of unsearched cooked human bodies equals the pile of rummaged bodies, Lindsey clasps a crisp, cold metal card.

Mary jerks it from her with a red bandana. She wipes it clean. With the grime gone, she holds it into the light. "Appears undamaged."

"We had a deal."

Mary nods. She marches Lindsey past the growing wall of crucified undead at the lane entrance. Her retching has no food in her stomach to bring up. The dry heave bothers Mary more than the reek of rotten flesh. One of the undead lashed to a pole reaches for the women. Its spine snaps just above the small of its back. Intestine and internal organs splatter to the ground in a wet, gushy mass.

Across the road, Mary tosses a backpack over a barbed wire fence. "I would go south. The boys are scavenging north. There's nothing for some fifty miles south of here worth sending out groups. Homes are scattered around so you'll find supplies. Don't ever come back. If they find you out there. I'll not have any authority to protect you."

Lindsey climbs the fence. She wants to wash off her blackened arms and use Scope, but escaping is more important. She shoulders the heavy pack. She must trust Mary actually gave her useful gear. It will be miles before she risks inspecting it. "Thank you."

"Go. I didn't do it for you." Mary holds up the metal card. "I did it for me."

Mary waits alongside Kale for the trucks to park. Kaleb's men unload gear and bedraggled people.

Kaleb roughly drags a man in front of his brother and betrothed.

"Mary, this is the good Pastor John Milton. No relation to the writer dude. He has his Bible and would gladly marry us."

John stammers. Only Mary catches his off-kilter glance. "You understand it would not be legal without a certificate."

"People married long before a courthouse. We'll be married in the eyes of God," Mary says.

"Yes, you will," Pastor Milton says. "When will we have this happy occasion?"

"Right now," Kaleb says.

"Now?" Pastor Milton fails to hide his surprise. "I will entreat you both, but I need a few minutes to confer in private. I have to know this is what you want. Partnering together in this new world is even more important."

"Agreed," Kale says. "I'll gather some witnesses."

"Where may I meet with each of you in turn?" Pastor Milton asks.

"Use the truck cab." Kaleb points.

Mary climbs into the passenger seat, and as soon as Pastor Milton closes his door, she blasts him. "Minister? What kind of scam are you pulling?"

"*Mary,* wow. You are no virgin," he says.

"I'm pulling the same swindle as you—staying alive," she says.

"I'll call you Mary."

"Milton. Figuring on the country rubes not being familiar with *Paradise Lost*?" she asks.

"It was fitting."

"We are stuck again dealing with each other. Kaleb runs the show. As his wife, I will be his queen."

"Always knew you wanted to be royalty." He smirks.

"You keep quiet, and I'll make sure they don't put you out in the fields."

"Slave labor?"

"Serfdom," she corrects.

"Not any difference. You just make sure I'm well taken care of." Milton notes, "The brother-in-law was not thrilled about my arrival."

"No. I'm assuming his place as the power behind his brother. An honor he was bucking for. He's going to be a problem."

"Kill him," Milton says.

"No. He is super smart. And this new world needs super smart people. You just keep your mouth shut." Mary jumps from the cab and races to Kaleb.

"She certainly has no dissension in her marriage choice. You are lucky to find a valued partner after the rapture," Pastor Milton says.

He scoops her up into his arms. "I don't need a minute, I want her."

"It's customary for the pastor to counsel the couple." Milton works his pastor role.

"The world's no longer customary, and with so many undead it's even shorter. I want to marry this woman. Wed us," Kaleb orders.

"You may kiss—"

Before Milton completes his decree, Kaleb rams his tongue into Mary's mouth and picks her up into the air with both hands clamped on her butt cheeks.

When he finally releases her, he says, "I want no disturbances."

His men cheer.

Kale scowls. He has no trust from his sister-in-law.

Mary places her hand on his jowl as gentle as a mother touching a babe. "I have a gift for you first, my husband."

She takes his hand and kisses the back of it—leading him toward the barn.

"I want to fuck you in the bedroom."

"We will, but want to show you how much I love you," Mary says.

"I'm going to show you every way I love you." He slaps her ass cheek, resonating a pop.

She smiles. Mary knows she will have to force him to control himself. Make him go slow. Once she lords over him in the bed she will control him forever. She touches the hidden button. The floor hatch rolls open. "Now, baby. This will make you king." She leads him down the stairs."

"Fuck me." He beats on the glass. "How did... How do we open these? I'll beat it out of the government chick."

"When you allow me to handle—" she grabs his crotch through his jeans "—the more sensitive issues, nothing will stop you."

"You got Lindsey to tell you about this place?"

"Yes." She bats a coy eye.

"Where is she?"

"I released her."

Mary finds she's unable to breathe as fingers clamp her throat. He has no intention of forgiving her or listening to her. She holds up the metal key card.

Kaleb releases her, snatching the card.

Mary drops to her knees, submissive.

He raises his arm poised to backhand her. "You may be mine, but you never make decisions without me."

She coughs, catching her breath. Wheezing, she insists, "She had to trust me. Use the key. You have guns and gas. You have the power to rule. I love you. I did it to win you all this."

God please let the key work, or I'm dead.

Kaleb slides the key into the lock.

Nothing.

Mary has to clamp her legs in order to prevent wetting herself.

"May I try, baby?"

Her shaky fingers swipe the card in the lock. A green light flashes and the door seals break. Mary's face spreads into a full grin. From now on, she rules Kaleb.

CHAPTER FORTY-FOUR

DAKOTA KICKS OVER an infected skeleton more than a dead body.

"I thought they only ate a body until it turned?" Tom ponders.

The vehicles belonging to the caravan survivors now blends in with the abandoned cars stalled out on the original evacuation attempt of the city.

"There were so many in the herd when they caught a person they consumed them before they died," Darcy says.

"It moved like a Tsunami wave," Danielle adds.

"Thousands died, leaving behind their survival gear."

"Where do we start?" Dave asks.

"I don't know what cars carried what supplies. Let's search, take what's useful and move back to the plane," Tom suggests.

"Who decided Tom would lead us?" Dakota demands.

"Dusty's dead," Darcy says. "We need—"

"Why does it have to be him?" Dakota raises his voice, illustrating he demands the job.

Dave opens a car door. "If we go by experience, Tom has dealt not only with rotters more, but his time as a fireman means he's resilient in a crisis." He digs through a duffle bag, pulling out nothing but clothes. He drops the bag, selecting another one.

Danielle draws a brush through her hair. "Dakota, you're too hot tempered to lead. You want to rush in fast." She ties it back with some hair bands she takes from a purse.

"I patrolled the camp and Dusty still got shot. I won't make mistakes again. I should have shot those people," Tom says.

"How are we going to deal with new people?" Danielle drops a pistol into a backpack. She paws under the seat of the car she searches.

"We don't need a leader to decide how we want to handle future encounters." Dave pops a trunk. "Bingo." Cases of bottled water fill the back.

"How do we carry all those back?"

"Maybe we need to mark the useful cars for when we return," Darcy suggests.

"Maybe you should just drop your weapons and put your hands up," an unfamiliar voice demands.

Surrounding Tom and the Ds are two dozen black men all wearing police-issue tactical combat vests and bandanas for headbands—a combo of blue and red.

"Caught by gang members," Dakota mumbles.

"North side. West side. Doesn't matter anymore, white boy. We all food. Now put down your guns." He levels a 9mm at Dakota aiming to kill, foregoing the sideways wrist turn.

CHAPTER FORTY-FIVE

THE BITER'S TEETH sink into Ethan's arm. Never has he allowed an undead get so close. He's taken most out from afar. The beating has slowed more than his reflexes.

"Run!" he orders.

Becky swings her machete, cleaving off the top half the biter. Coagulated blood and bile covers his arm. She admires Ethan. He saved her. How could she end him? Her heart jumps into her throat. He must be the kind of person to end it himself.

Ethan discharges the Berretta. Hot brass pings across the pavement.

Blood, mud, and the oozing gelatinous goop fermenting inside each monster splatters across the gas pumps.

With a path clear they race inside the store. Ethan jams a fresh clip into the pistol. More biters fall.

Chad slams the door, wrapping a bicycle chain lock around the door handles.

"How bad is it?" A terrible question to ask. Becky knows even the most superficial bite leads to returning as living corpse.

Ethan chucks an object at her.

She fumbles the goop-covered shape. She grabs the mass, rubbing her thumb over the porcelain and scraping away biter snot. "False teeth!"

Ethan grabs a whiskey bottle from a shelf, smashing the tip. He splashes the brown liquor to cleanse his forearm. "No skin breakage. It would burn like hell. With a rotten mouth, the creature couldn't get a proper bite without Fixodent."

"I thought you were dead," Becky breathes again.

"It will take more than one old lady biter to kill me."

Becky reaches up and pulls down a roll of scratcher tickets. She rubs her knife across the sliver cover, sending gray confetti all over her lap and the floor.

"What are you doing?" Ethan leans over the counter.

"I'm going to win a fortune, so I never have to work again."

"Sounds great. The Powerball was up to like 240 million. See if we can get a couple of those as well," Ethan says.

Becky chortles, holding back a bubbled laugh. The milling biters outside answer in a chorus of moan-howls.

"What the hell was that?" Ethan asks.

"I don't know. You like to berate me over my desire to text and yet you're supporting my gambling habit. You're fucking insane. You just were bit and treat life like a fucking joke."

"I figured you need to blow off some steam. I'd rather have you playing scratch-off than hitting the liquor bottles." Ethan ignores her concern.

"I'm not old enough to drink."

"You're not old enough to buy lottery tickets." He points at the shelf before her. "Toss me one of those airplane bottles of whiskey."

She reaches for it. Tears cloud her vision. She tosses him the bottle.

"Why are you crying?"

"I'm never going to get to buy alcohol," she mumbles, "legally."

"Lottery was a tax on the poor anyway." Ethan swallows the entire shot of warm rotgut.

"Lottery money was to cover all that tuition I did for A+." She leans over the counter opposite him. "Why are you drinking?"

"I'm not. Whiskey kills what ails you. In the Old West, it was safer and cleaner to drink whiskey over the water. The liquor also killed mouth germs. I'm just helping out my immune system." He reaches over the counter and fumbles for a pint."

"Is that true?"

"That's why I chide you over your iPhone. You young ones don't know anything without having to look it up. Yes, it's true, but a little goes a long way." He cracks the seal on the bottle, and offers it to her. "Take a swig."

"You'll contribute to the delinquency of a minor with liquor, but you won't sleep with one?"

"I'll sleep just fine tonight knowing I gave you whiskey. Putting my dick into a girl just a few years older than my daughter—not something I can live with."

"You had a daughter?" Becky choke-coughs on both the burning fluid and the knowledge—no one in the camp knows about Ethan's past.

"See what alcohol does. You lose all control of your faculties. I've not shared that." He takes the bottle back and takes a swig before capping it. "And that's all you're learning about me today or ever."

He stuffs the bottle into meshing on the end of his pack. "Finish your scratch-offs. We move out as soon as the biters clear."

Chad props himself in the corner where he watches the door. "They've set up camp out there. We may be here for the night." He adds, "Since we have to kill time. What caused the undead to rise?"

"Why does it matter?"

"It matters a lot," Chad says.

"Chemical spill. Meteor crash, which actually would bring a virus. Viruses. Parasites infesting the brain. Mutated rabies. Neurogenesis of brain cell tissue, medical waste, global warming. The Rapture."

"The Rapture?" Becky's shocked Ethan would suggest Divine intervention.

"God releasing the unworthy from Hell. None of that matters. We lack the ability to fix it. None of the theories are within my control to prevent. And do you want to be in the control group that's going to inject a vaccine? Last time I checked, that involved injecting part of the diseases inside you. It matters not how it started only how it ends. How we endure the end."

"I want to know," Chad says.

"What if you find out the government did it? It's not like you're going to sue the soda company for giving you cancer," Becky snaps.

"There's no way to undo this plague. It's not a video game with a reset button. Best scenario would be a functioning vaccine," Ethan says.

"I know they say they have one, but I remember being five. Terrified in the health office. Skipping my loving mother's explanation of the torture they were to perform. They fucking shot dead measles into my arm," Becky says.

"How it works, your body attacks the dead measles by learning what they are and creating an army of antibodies to swim around inside you until the living measles attacks. Only to be met by a prepared army able to defeat them."

"We're on the same page of understanding. They are going to inject whatever makes the dead reanimate into you. No way am I being stuck with whatever creates the undead."

Becky spins her wrists, twirling both machetes. She sinks one into a biter. Most of the herd disappeared in the middle of the night. As the sun rises, Ethan and Chad fan out from the entrance. Ethan keeps his Beretta drawn but uses the hunting knife to smash through biter skulls.

"You know, a bat... A spiked bat would be perfect," Chad theorizes.

"Shut it." *Damn kid! We don't need noise bringing more back.* Each kill Ethan makes moves him closer to the road. Having lost half a day's travel, he will waste no more time on these biters. If the other side of the hill remains clear they will move on. *I have plans. I have a search I must make and still reach Memphis within the two-week window. I may have to break down and use cars.*

Ethan stabs another biter. *I've ended so many. How could anyone keep track of giving peace to so many?*

Becky's blow deflects off the skull of an undead. Without the death impact to slay it, the beast's rancid finger claws at her shirt. She panics. Her backpedaling sends her tumbling over her own boots. As she falls, the biter plummets on top of her. She maintains enough of her facilities to bite her own bottom lip to hold in a scream.

Chad tosses the beast off her. It rolls to a stop on the pavement. Ethan plants his boot on the biter's chest. Its limbs flail, attempting to reach him.

Ethan holsters his pistol. "Machete."

Chad tosses Becky's blade.

In one fluid motion, Ethan catches the handle and brings the weapon down to tap the skullcap.

Tink. Tink. Tink.

Chad pulls Becky to her feet.

"What the hell?"

Ethan flicks the blade, peeling off the top layer of skin. Covered in blackish blood, but still shiny is a metal plate.

"Metal?" Becky seems confused.

"I'm unable to tell from this face how old he was before death, but I thought they switched to ceramic plates to fix broken crowns." Ethan pushes down on the blade through the eye socket, puncturing the brain. The biter's limbs collapse to the ground.

"Will we run into many metal plates?"

"Doubtful. Don't lose your cool. If the blade won't go in the skull one angle, try another. Keep your head as you take theirs."

"Didn't you ever wonder what would have happened if all technology, fast food, and unnecessary material wealth just went away? Money hoarding should have been made illegal and spread around so everyone could attend college," Chad says.

"I like tweeting on my iPhone."

"I enjoy showers." Ethan ponders about Chad becoming a poor choice for this trek.

"Then why do you leave the camp so much?" Chad asks.

"You're our leader. It's a full-time job. You get back and are gone again in a day. You only stayed a week the last time because those raiders beat the hell out of you," Becky says.

"There are plenty of others who would take their turn scouting for supplies and bringing in survivors," Chad says.

"Not all those survivors have an intention of returning to civilization."

"You mean like the dude who cut off those poor girl's hands. You mean like him?"

"He was bad. How do you help people who have to have hands to function?" Chad asks.

"Dartagnan survived," Becky points out.

"Because they had a gas stove and chickens. He could cook eggs. I'd hate to check his cholesterol level. He cooked them for his dead mom, too. I found him preparing for her. I don't know how messed up he was before but I'm certain no human contact for five months didn't help him. I don't let him get away with his fits. I did have to give in and go back and get that damn chair. He had to sit in it when he misbehaved. After I figured it out he does what he should. He's super smart. He builds his model of the town to scale and he grows a garden and tends the chickens. He keeps enough eggs for him and sends the rest to the kitchen."

"What's wrong with him?" Becky asks.

"Nothing. He has one of those –tisms, but he's the exception to the rule. In ten months, I haven't seen even one paraplegic. Alzheimer's, bed-ridden, and children haven't made it."

"How could they?"

"I wonder how many people died trying to save relatives that were of no use. We spent a lot of money on people unproductive to society," Chad says.

"How can you say that?" Becky asks.

"I accept the harsh reality of it. Society spent millions on people who no longer served a purpose. They use up resources but do provided jobs for those who give them care," Chad says.

"Let me tell you, when I forget how to wipe my own ass or what boobs are for then it's *Old Yeller* time," Ethan breaks in to cut the tension.

Becky snickers.

"What's funny, little girl?" Ethan asks.

"You do think about boobs a lot."

"I'm a man. Of course," Ethan says.

"Then what's wrong with Emily?" Becky asks. "She has some. I don't."

"She doesn't have any," Chad points out.

"Did you tag along on this trip to try and hook me up with a fifteen-year-old girl? We're not passing notes in gym class. I'm not interested," Ethan says.

"Finding cans of cream corn isn't all you have to look forward to. There are no rules anymore. If Emily's too young, then Private Sanchez. Her eyes flash at you with a little more than respect," Becky says.

"It won't work."

"What?"

"Don't be coy. You're pressing the issue until I cave and tell you my reasons for not choosing a mate. Never worked on me in my old job."

"What was that?" Chad asks.

"There's a betting pool, you know, as to what you used to do before the end of the world," Becky says.

"Then it wouldn't be fair to tell you unless we split the kitty," Ethan points out.

"I'll give you the whole cash if you tell me why you don't want a girlfriend or wife," Becky says.

"I don't think it's an option anymore. Partners would be better. Maybe even something more tribal. Everyone in the group raises the kids. Maybe you don't even know who the daddy is and it's socially acceptable," Ethan says.

"Are you saying that everyone just sleeps with everyone?" Chad grins.

"The girls still have to want to sleep with you," Becky jabs.

"Open relationships might be better. Husband and wife teams could never patrol together. Love would get them killed."

"You're so cynical," Becky chides.

"I'm a realist. If trapped by a herd or forced into a hostage situation by the living, people will not be rational. They'll protect their mate even if the choice kills the group," Ethan says.

"People would still fall in love," Becky says.

"Don't have sex with anyone you don't want," Ethan says. "Love never lasts."

Chad chimes in, "If no one bothers to keep track then won't the next generation hook up with a brother or sister and not know it?"

"Does it bother you when he actually is insightful?" She smiles.

"A little."

"Make jokes even when I'm right," Chad pouts.

"Sounds like a problem for the next generation to hash out—if we even have one."

CHAPTER FORTY-SIX

THE BLACK MAN hands Tom a backpack. "A pistol and twenty rounds for each of you."

Tom grabs the bag.

The man jerks it back, refusing to release it. "Don't get any bright ideas. The rounds are still in a box. By the time you load one we'll be gone."

"Why hoard all the supplies but release us with guns?"

"We need everything to take back The Lou. We figure you'll kill a few Zone-heads, which only helps us. Head west, cracker, and stay away from the caravan," he warns.

"We could help each other. You said so, it's not a black/white thing anymore," Tom says.

"This ain't about race; this is about food for my homies. And your five we ain't feeding. We're going to take the city back block by block."

"I was a fireman in that city. I know those streets."

"You don't know shit. Now take the pack and go. Before I decide I need those one-hundred rounds. More than I need to be letting the living live." He releases the pack.

Tom joins his team as the black men back away, rifles pointed at them.

As Dakota digs in the bag for a pistol, the black man tosses a rag bundle at them before disappearing among the cars.

Darcy retrieves it. Using her knife, she cuts the string. Five clips spill out.

"Fucker sure didn't want us to be able to shoot back." Dakota tears open the cardboard ammo box.

"At least he got us within sight of the plane," Danielle points out.

"We do have some supplies there, but Tom was fucked without our gear and access to more."

"They fucked us good." Dakota racks the slide, loading the weapon. "I say we go fuck him."

"Go if you want, but those men were too organized to be run-of-the-mill bangers. Whoever leads them has top-notch military training and you will stand out among them with your lack of a tan. You kids do what you want. I'm heading west. Fort Wood remains an option and I'll be there in a week on foot, faster once I'm out of the suburbs and I find a running car."

"You're just going to leave us?" Darcy whines.

"You're invited." Tom struggles as he presses a round into a clip. "Too many rotters; too many survivors this close to the city. We need to leave."

Darcy loads her clip before Tom has his half complete. She trades him. "I'm going with you."

"Fort Wood would be safe with all those soldiers. Are you taking up the mantle of leadership, Tom?" Dave asks.

"Most decisions we should make as a group this size. If we have an opportunity to discuss. If we have to make battle choices, you do whatever I say."

"I'll live with that. Danielle?"

"I sure as fuck ain't staying with Dakota here to die," she says.

"What about it, Dakota?"

"It's like two-hundred miles. We need to find a car."

"Six Flags."

"What, Darcy?"

"We hoof it to Eureka. Six Flags is there. Got to be parking lot full of cars and the caravan jam up never reached it," she says.

"Get what we have stashed in the plane. Sounds like we have the start to a plan." Tom holsters his weapon.

CHAPTER FORTY-SEVEN

KALE SPREADS THE county map across the kitchen table. He inspects the lines and roads until he locates the FEMA farm placing a miniature house in the location. "You did good, Brother."

Mary carries in a folding chair. "What are we to do with the children like Josiah? You brought back several more in your last run. Many were from Fort Wood." She daintily places herself in the chair poised so her spine doesn't touch the back of the chair.

"I've been interviewing each one of them. Kale will job place them. I bet they'll work the fields," Kaleb says.

"Interviewing them, why?" Mary asks.

"It seems that bastard who killed our brothers did his own interviewing. He took people with certain skill sets."

Kale impatiently asks, "What kind of skills?"

"Engineers, electricians, welders, machinists, even a frogman. Where the fuck are you going to go diving in Missouri?"

Kale takes a highway map spreading over the county map knocking over the miniature horse. "They left by the front gate. Some evidence says they went toward Columbia." He taps the city on the map. "MU had a large population. They would have to fend off a lot of infected." He thinks a moment. "This man recruited people with building skills. Construction means noise." Kale snaps his fingers. "It has to be a more rural area."

"Contemplate it later. We must focus on building this farm." Mary touches Kaleb's arm.

Kale takes the road map from the table. He will bide his time until he removes this witch from his brother's ear. "We have fuel and weapons. The fuel will sour so we use it to gather supplies to sustain us through the winter. By next winter will have crops to supplement the last of any supplies. I calculate by then most buildings will be devoid of anything useful."

"How long before we take this area?" Kaleb taps the map.

"Those are housing developments," Kale explains.

"Rich housing developments—mansions. I want my wife to be in one of these homes."

"Feasibly? The distance requires too much security to hold down this area and those homes. We need to expand outward and protect these southern farms. We need the fields and we need to graze cattle," Kale explains.

"I want my baby to be housed like the queen she is."

"Foolish luxury will be our downfall. Those tolling in the dirt won't stand by while you live in splendor. Remember the Czars of Russia," Kale says.

"We need to reclaim homes. Why not these mansions?" Mary taps the map. "We take one as the government house and living space. The rest we use as boarding homes for the masses. The community is gated so it has a wall to protect it already. Use these houses as a central location, not some isolated farm."

"It's just outside Rolla. The city will have infected."

"No. It was clear. Most of the early Fort Wood civilians were directly evacuated from there. All personal effects left behind. The city is...El Dorado," Kaleb says.

"Your brother has his own plans, Kale. You must accept your plans are not the only options," Mary interjects.

"Kaleb, you are in command of our group. We must be unified to exist, but we also must make moves that make sense."

"There are still tons of Fort Wood people scattered in the area. If they figure out Rolla has been virtually untouched, we lose valuable supplies and those desperate people will loot and damage. So, we claim it first." Kale refuses to capitulate to Mary. He attempts to regain his beachhead thought defection. "What else did you learn from those you picked up from Fort Wood?"

"The dude never shared his name. But he was there for two days before the soldiers evacuated. Some say he had been there lots before and left with supplies and equipment each time. He was a giant, broad-shouldered fucker. Hard to miss with his limp. Dude was built like a mountain and carried a shiny .357."

"He must have stood out if people remember so much about him."

"His size, mostly, and the way he carried himself—no fear. One guy, a welder, said he was interviewed."

"You found a welder?" Mary interrupts.

"Yeah. He's pretty upset. Said he was interviewed by this dude—our unnamed brother's killer. When the welder declined his offer, they placed him in protective custody, so he couldn't tell anyone about the civilians being collected to leave the base."

"Travis knew the soldiers were abandoning and decided to save a select few," Kale says.

"Fucker did it to save that blonde bitch daughter. The one Kade should have fucked—interfering bitch."

The wheels in Kale's mind whirl. "You might have brought to the table the best clue to locating this man. Colonel Travis was ordered to leave behind all civilians, including his precious daughter." Kale rubs his baby smooth chin. "This unnamed man has a camp. A secure camp made more secure by military equipment and necessary personnel—hand selected personnel."

"What are you driving at?"

"The location we seek is not just some farm in a field with fence. No, this place is a fortress someplace to keep Travis's kid safe for years in case it takes that long for the military to retake the country."

"Prison."

"What?"

"Prisons would be the perfect fortresses. Walls, self-contained, sniper towers. Motor pools, machine shops. We should be storming a prison."

"You still need food and would have to constantly be sending out teams to gather supplies." Kale strikes a chord. "Besides, your *queen* would have to be housed in a cell. No mansions for her."

"We'd need a tank to bust into one of those places anyway if people already had it secure. We'll build our kingdom here," Kaleb decrees.

"You seem lost in thought." Mary glances at Kale.

"Basically, we've returned to a medieval agrarian society. Most people will have to return to farming. I may have designed our defenses incorrectly. I planned for overwhelming number of undead but perhaps we need to consider a siege mentality involving the living."

"What do you mean?" Mary asks.

"Once we have food and a sustainable community, people will want to take it from us."

"They can try," Kaleb boasts.

"What are you thinking, genius?" Mary asks.

"A walled community would still need added defenses." Kale drifts deep into thought.

"You'll get your mansion, baby." Kaleb drapes his arm over her shoulder.

"Being with you is all I need, Kaleb." She seductively caresses his hand. "Does he always strike-out like this?"

"He'll snap back with, like, the complete plans to the Death Star. Kid's fucking precocious."

"I'm not sure he likes me." She switches into her coy mode.

"When he has plans, and is heavy in thought, he doesn't like anyone."

"I want you to be careful out there. And promise no more rapes. You have to bring people into our fold and they have to trust they are safe." Mary leans her head against him.

Kale wakes from his trance. "A cave."

Both Mary and Kaleb remain quizzical.

"Missouri is the cave state. Caves would make secure strongholds. With little chance of penetration and one or two entrances to guard. Also, the known big ones are in state parks…lacking populated areas to draw too many infected."

"The most well know is Meramec Caverns," Mary says.

"Yes, and next to it is Onondaga Cave. Some think they connect, but they would be prime locations for an apocalyptic hideout."

"But is in the opposite direction as Columbia," Kaleb points out.

"The direction was a ruse. They backtracked at some point toward their true destination knowing some Fort Wood civilians would attempt to follow when the walls fell. Desperate people wouldn't think it was misleading," Kale explains.

Mary wonders, "Wouldn't they be dark?"

"People have been using them long before electricity. Some served as speakeasies."

"Then me and some of the boys are going to make a run to the caverns," Kaleb says.

"There are more important items to deal with here," Mary protests.

"Nothing's more important than avenging my brother," Kaleb voice raises in defiance of all her work to control him.

"Kale, if you follow these country roads you'll make good time. More importantly if people are there—do not engage. Scout it. We'll make battle plans. If you go in halfcocked we'll lose valuable men." He digs through a drawer of a corner desk. "In fact—" he hands him a new, still encased in plastic digital camera "—take pictures of the location. We'll develop a plan of attack," Kale instructs.

"I won't. There's no room for mistakes anymore. No reset. I get it. But if I get the chance, I'll bring you the fucker's head," Kaleb swears.

"Now what needs to be done to help prepare this farm to annex the gated community," Mary asks.

"I wanted to expand toward these farms for the land, but if we move this direction we can move north and assume the gated community. But I suggest we maintain our strength here until all the FEMA supplies are used," Kale suggests.

"The more people we bring in the harder it is to trust them."

Kale wonders what new wedge Mary places between him and his brother.

"Once you find this murderer, it may be best if you lead fewer saving missions and stay here. Keep those who question what must be done in line."

"We should control the people with our strength, not fear," Kale protests. "They won't respond to fear. They'll leave."

"Leave to where? There is no place left to go." Mary rises. "They will have no choice but to stay. As long as Kaleb keeps them safe they will relish being ruled by a king."

CHAPTER FORTY-EIGHT

"HAVE YOU SEEN Ethan check his map in the last two days?" Becky asks as she snatches her backpack from the truck bed. She rubs at her neck. Ethan bumped the tree he parked against a little harder than she felt necessary.

"Not today." Chad rests his rifle over his forearm as he marches across the field after Ethan.

"He seems to know where he's going for not having scouted this place before."

Ethan moves as if the beating never happened.

Becky, for the first time on this trip, has to step faster to keep up with her leader. "If I dropped you off in any of the fields we were traveling across yesterday, could you tell the difference than the field we're in now?"

"No." Chad ascribes this as an explanation to the order Simon screams constantly, "move like you have a purpose."

"This area is way south of anyplace where he's taken a scavenging team to collect supplies."

"I hadn't noticed," Chad says. "One tree looks the same to me."

"Don't you think you should be paying attention to our route? What if we get separated?"

"I ain't leaving Ethan. Most of these towns have the same style buildings and street names. Besides I was thinking about other—"

Ethan steps over a smashed fence. He hurdles the ditch making a beeline straight across the blacktop to climb the fence across the road.

"Anytime he finds a road, he checks the map," Becky says. "But not so much as a glance since we got in the truck this morning."

"What are you driving at?"

"Nice pun. I'm observing." She mashes down the wire fence to step over it. "We have to pay attention to everything now. Our first clue should have been using a vehicle."

"I thought he was making up time for our night in the convenience store."

Ethan marches with a fervor Becky has yet to encounter in their leader. His limp has dissipated completely as he picks up speed.

Chad snags his pant leg on a broken wire. Once free, he runs to catch up. "You guys were going to leave me." He jabs his index finger into the new hole in his jeans. "Damn, it isn't going to be easy finding a new pair."

As if he's forgotten about his companions, Ethan vaults a fence into the backyard of a saltbox house. Landing next to a jungle gym swing set he increases speed. Under one of the swings a pile of dirt marks a child-sized grave.

Ethan enters the back door.

Becky draws her gun at the sound of crashes. She sprints to the fence line. Angry yelps and more smashing noises echo.

"Set up a perimeter," she orders Chad. "Noise will attract biters."

"How do I do that?"

"Circle the house. Make sure the immediate area is clear."

Furniture and shelves have all been overturned. Ethan clamps his hands over his face.

Becky scans the room before holstering her pistol. Noise of this magnitude should bring out any hidden biters. She steps with caution toward her travel companion. She doesn't want him to instinctively reach for his gun. Even beaten near to death, she knows his speed is unmatched.

With every ounce of body control, she touches his shoulder with gentleness. She makes one guess with her question, "Was this *her* house?"

She's not sure if he cries under his covered face, and his nod was so subtle she might have mistaken it. *What do you say?* She glances over the smashed shelves. The items seconds ago, resting on it are mostly in a heap, but several picture frames stand out. She fights the urge to rush over and view one, through her palm she detects the body shiver of someone releasing tears even if their flow is silent.

Not knowing what to do or say, she stands there. The man was beaten to near death. He's killed more biters. He protects the camp and all who live inside not only from what is outside but within. Becky doesn't know what to say to the man who, if Acheron survives, will live in the memories of the people as a Beowulf figure.

Chad bursts through the front door. "Hey."

Becky waves for him to leave.

"Biters."

His single word response snaps Ethan to his feet. "Any of them children?"

"All adult size." Chad slips out the door.

"Ethan, who lived here?" Becky asks.

"Ghosts."

CHAPTER FORTY-NINE

"WHERE ARE WE?" Kalvin asks. He checks the metal shelves of the garage.

"Somewhere below Jefferson City and above Fort Word," Karen says. "Close to some town called Vienna."

"We're making good time." Frank drops his tools into a side pocket in his pack. "This truck won't start."

"I'm not Ethan. We don't have to hoof it all the way to the Queens City if we're not out scavenging supplies." Karen folds her map. "Let's find another truck to jump start."

"Trucks will get us there in days. You said we'd be gone a month."

"Safe guess," Karen says. "We don't know what we'll discover when we get closer to Springfield. And if the city has fallen we may have a couple thousand biters to escape."

"What a happy positive thought."

"Two interstates designed to bypass the city actually encircle it. If people organized quickly—"

Bam.

As if choreographed, they all three crouch as low as possible and still be on their feet—guns in hand.

"Where?" Karen whispers.

"Not sure. Not at us. The echo means it's close, but not sure of the direction," Kalvin speculates.

"We've gone all this time without a biter." Karen duck-walks to the garage door. Peering out, the rural road remains vacant. She signals Frank. He takes up position on the opposite side of the truck door. Kalvin races out the door low as possible reaching the tree in the yard's center.

Bam.

Kalvin raises to his full height, "It's a mile away at least."

Karen approaches the trees across the driveway still in caution mode. "We need to know who is shooting. We don't want scavengers jumping us."

Bam. Bam.

"Those reports are going to draw the undead," Kalvin warns.

Frank twirls a long-handled fire axe. "Keeps us in practice. I don't want to get soft."

"You're an EMT. You are supposed to save lives."

"I consider bashing in the skulls of the undead a mercy." Frank marches from the yard.

Karen peers through her binoculars. Across the field, a small farmhouse has three fresh undead scattered in the yard.

"There were four shots."

"Doesn't mean anything. They shot one twice." Karen moves the lenses toward the porch. "The open front door concerns me."

"The distance to the house bothers me. Super easy for a sniper to pick one of us off with no cover. If we go down there," Kalvin says.

"We don't have to. We have no obligation to investigate."

Bam. Bam. Bam.

Three lightning flashes streak the house windows. Seconds later, a person staggers from the house. The woman stumbles some twenty feet before face planting in the grass.

"Now you want to go," Frank huffs. "It's a bad idea, Karen. Unnecessary risk."

"The wood stacked beside the house is green. Fresh cut. People might need our help and so far, we still help people."

"I agree, but I'm staying here as a lookout," Kalvin says. "Why do you get to stay? I'm the one who doesn't want to go," Frank protests.

"People may be hurt, Frank, and you're a medic."

Frank checks the pulse of the fallen woman. He pockets the pistol the man carried before driving the axe into his skull. He joins Karen poised to burst through the open door. After he draws his weapon and nods his readiness, Karen swings inside. Two bodies bleed bright red blood on an overturned table. A third now lifeless biter rots between them.

"They let one in?" Frank drives the axe into one of the unturned bodies.

A rattle from the next room freezes them both.

Karen side-steps toward the back room, gun drawn. Ready to strike, Frank raises the axe and follows her.

Karen holsters her weapon kneeling, she opens her arms wide. "Are you alone in here?"

The pigtail little girl nods, snuggling tight against her teddy bear.

Karen uses her *comfort mom voice* or the voice she thinks she'll use if she becomes a mom. "Frank, why don't you deal with the mess in the other room while I speak with my new friend."

He doesn't agree. Betting one or more of the bodies is the girl's parent. But he stays out of the back room.

"Does your bear have a name?" Karen asks.

"Teddy." She raises the stuffed animal with her hand stuffed in a hidden pouch.

Karen recognizes the familiar click of a pistol hammer.

"Mother told me to shoot anyone I didn't know."

"I wish you wouldn't. When did your mother tell you this? I don't want you to not do what your mother said, but I don't want to be shot."

"You're not a bad person like those who hurt my mom?"

"I'm a good person. Me and my friends are out here helping people. We find people to take them back to our camp. We protect people from the undead. I won't be able to protect them if you shoot me."

The little girl runs into Karen's arms. "Bad men took my mommy."

Karen hugs the little girl. "Do you have a name?"

"Grace."

"Grace. I'm Karen. We...need to...uncock your gun."

"I don't know how. I'm not supposed to cock it unless I'm going to shoot."

"Do you want me to do it?"

She shakes her head, snapping the pig tails like whips.

"Okay, but you shouldn't point it at people." Karen holds the little girl. "How old are you?"

"Five."

"Five is a good age. Do you have a bag?"

"Why?"

"You want to bring your stuff when you come with me?"

"Are they dead?"

Karen pauses. *How much do I shield from this armed child?* "Yes."

"They shouldn't have let the sick man in. Mom says to stay away from sick people," Grace declares.

"Your mom gives good advice. Do you want to get your bag?" *I've got to unload the gun.* Karen loosens her grip.

Grace runs for a box at the foot of the bed, removing a pink pony backpack. "Escape gear. Clothes, food bars, and two bottles of water."

"You might want a coat. Some nights are still chilly." *No, but it sounds momish.*

Grace slips on her pack before retrieving a coat from a dresser drawer.

"Are you sure you don't want me to uncock your gun? I promise to give it back and your bear."

Grace places her bear on the bed and backs away. "Fix."

Karen reaches into the back of the bear where a battery pack used to be housed. She holds the hammer as she depresses the trigger of a two-shot derringer. She slips it back into the bear, leaving it on the bed before backing away. *Wow. I just gave a loaded gun to a five-year-old.*

Grace grabs her bear.

They hop past the pools of blood as if it were a twisted hop scotch board.

How many dead has Grace seen to act like this is normal? Karen ponders as she steps on the porch. Tied to the rail are four saddled horses.

"Sadie!" Grace races to the painted horse and rubs on its nose as it nuzzles against the little girl. "Are you going to take my horses?"

"If we don't there won't be anybody to care for them," Kalvin says as he packs his gear on the saddle.

"We're going to take you with us. So nothing happens to you," Karen says.

"Don't say that. Mommy said that. These people said that. The stinky ones that bite—" she drops her head and pouts "—they take everyone away."

CHAPTER FIFTY

CHAD EXAMINES THE building through binoculars. "It's got to be a trap. Who puts a gun store in the middle of nowhere?"

Across the field, a dilapidated former farmhouse once painted white now has barred windows and a giant sign with red letters screaming GUNS.

"It's Missouri. I've run across convenience stores, barns, and even gun shops in the middle of fields before the apocalypse. I've found even more in my travels. People open a business outside of a town's city limits to avoid taxes or some of the one-horse towns have gun and bait shops that sell food. With all the gun and survivalist camping stores in this state, I don't know how the undead weren't eradicated before their population exploded," Ethan says.

"People won't shoot their moms," Becky says. *Or their daughters.*

"I can't imagine staring down a barrel at my dad or sister," Chad says.

Becky punches Chad in the arm and shifts the subject. "How long are you going to watch this place?"

"You in a hurry?" Ethan asks

"Even you don't like to be out here—exposed," Becky says.

"Keep you on your toes, kiddos," Ethan flips open the cylinder on his .357. All eight rounds are live.

As they march across the unmowed field, Ethan gives orders. "Chad, swing around to my left and ease up under the side window. Becky, to my right. Stay off the porch and be prepared to shoot anything coming out the door." Ethan draws his Beretta. Normally, he'd opt to quick draw as his opponent stares at his Taurus but his shoulder remains swollen, dampening his speed.

As they inch closer, nothing seems alive at the structure.

"Remember the old adage about gifts being too good?" Ethan inspects the door. "What bothers me is what's missing." He raises his gun. "A Visa logo and a sheriff's star sticker signal it's a legit business. Never been in a gun store that doesn't take American Express."

"Someone could have peeled it off." Becky assumes her assigned spot.

Chad slips from around the side to join them. "Now that's silly. It's the end of world and you take time to peel door stickers."

"I say we leave it. We've got more supplies than we can carry right now. More guns would slow us down," Ethan says.

"If this place hasn't been cleaned out already, it sure as hell would be if we do need supplies," Becky says.

Ethan reaches with his left hand for the door knob. "Stay alert."

His vision swims as he flashes in and out of reality.

Becky's screams penetrate the air.

The pops of punctured flesh reaches Ethan's ears, and the stick of a Taser's electrodes stings.

Men laugh.

They zap Becky.

Ethan slumps into unconsciousness.

Ethan wakes to the low whine of girly whimpers. Bed springs squeak. He fights with his own desire to sleep. The barrage of shocks keeps him unbalanced. Sex. Bed springs squawk like someone in the throes of forced passion. Opening his eyes enough to have a thin line of vision, Ethan sums up his situation. Bound to a metal pole by zip ties, he works his wrist down and uses the metal band to saw through the plastic.

"Let go of me!" Becky demands.

Ethan recognizes sounds of a struggle. Preoccupied with her, they ignore him. The volts they shot through him would have rendered a normal-sized person dead. But his mass and the years of therapy on his left leg involved small amounts of electric shock to constrict the muscles to build up a mild immunity.

"Got him," the unknown voice says. "Fucker."

"Leave him alone." Becky now advocates for Chad.

A burly, "I'm next" cuts Becky off.

Must be at least four of them. Two on her and two to bring Chad to the bed. The zip tie snaps.

"Get his other hand."

"Just zap him again."

"No." The gruff voice says, "I like them awake."

Ethan slips his right arm as slow as possible to avoid detection over his empty magnum holster. He expected it to be vacant. He knows the Beretta was in his hand when they electrocuted him. Even if they foolishly left his M&P, it is under him and they might spot him flipping over. They stripped off his boots so they found four guns.

Punches, slaps, and more wrestling grunts haunt his ears. The jingle of loosening belts and pant zippers gnaw at the pit of his stomach. It signals Chad is secure to the bed.

"I don't know why you always get to go first. You'll kill the boy with your horse dong."

Ankle holsters are a given. People disarm three of his guns and never pat down right behind the Beretta holster. Ethan's Taurus .22 designed mostly for a woman to carry in purses sports nine shots and no slide or hammer to snag as its draw. His index finger loops through the trigger guard.

"Slap that ass."

Chad's screams turn into whimpers as stinging blows echo from his backside. The spanking assault continues. The men laugh.

Becky cries. Helpless, knowing what is about to occur and she is next. In a normal world, this assault would take years of therapy to recover from—if ever.

Dumb ass. The lack of the licensing sticker should have signaled a trap. You ignored a blatant clue. You're behind on your time table. You're failing Chad. You've failed those little girls. You should have never left Acheron.

"You better make it last and grope that boy's titties. They're bigger than this girly's." Ethan hears more slaps. The man must have grabbed Becky and she's got enough spunk to fight. *More distraction, girl.*

"How does such a sweet ass not have no tits?"

Ethan images the unwashed man pinching Becky's chin or her flat chest.

"Don't touch me!" Becky stomps.

"This one's got a nice ass."

Another stinging flesh slap.

"Just use him up. I want to spend my nights with her."

Taurus locked in his hand, Ethan waits until Chad banshee wails. He knew. He must live with allowing the boy to be penetrated—violated. Scarred forever with the assault, but he needs to know the click of the safety wouldn't be noticed. *If there are more than four—*

Burly voiced dude.

Molesting Becky dude.

Helper to hold Chad down dude.

And one more voice. Likely also touching Becky.

He ends the humping man first.

Fuck I missed.

The slug embeds in a shoulder tattoo of a wolf. It freezes all men.

Every joint in Ethan's body pops as he leaps to his feet. "Don't move."

"You don't have enough rounds in your pea shooter to stop us."

Ethan never negotiates, but with off-aim he can't risk hitting Becky. "Maybe, but who wants to be the one to die before you reach me?" *The idiots should rush. The alternative is all four die over one.*

Blood dribbles from the wolf tattoo. He halts his thrust inside Chad.

Ethan fires two rounds into the next biggest man. He collapses, leaving Becky to deal with only one. "Your attention. I've got six more shots."

Becky doesn't need an order, she breaks free of her captors and retrieves a gun for herself before slipping Ethan's M&P into his left hand.

Good thing they don't know I can't shoot for shit before the beating with my left.

"We're going to kill—"

Ethan pops another round into the guy with the wolf tattoo, hitting his thigh. The muscular man has more fading blue ink on his body signifying time in prison. He falls off Chad.

Becky cuts Chad's right hand free. It flies back, grabbing his ass too late to protect it. Freeing his second hand sends the boy into a blubbering fit. He curls about halfway fetal.

"You just going to let me bleed?" the burly man asks.

Becky raises her gun, "We're going to fucking shoot you."

Ethan trades guns. With his M&P in his right hand, he marches the men from the back of the store. The two help the bleeding man. Keeping himself between them and the front room, Ethan spots a rack of shotguns. He sends them out a side door into the yard.

"Move," he orders. Once they are further from the building, Ethan steps down a step. He takes each stair one at a time. Becky follows him, ready to fire on any one of the three tempted to rush them.

"Find a shovel," Ethan instructs her.

"What are you going to do—"

Ethan puts a round in the grass between the two unwounded men. It wasn't the spot he wanted to hit but effective nonetheless.

"I've encountered about every kind of abusive bastard alive in this world." Ethan plops onto the top step.

Becky returns with two shoves. She tosses them at their feet.

"Make sure the one I popped never turns. Check on Chad. Get him dressed." Ethan waves the gun at the trio. In his best Clint Eastwood, low, gravely masculine tone, he says. "You see, in this world there's two kinds of people, my friend: Those with loaded guns and those who dig. You dig."

Becky cracks a smile as she heads back inside. It fades as she hears a blubbering Chad.

"I'm bleeding," the wolf tattooed man protests. His hands clamped over two bleeding bullet holes.

"Your chance to live through this is to dig."

As the hole reaches a two-foot depth, a naked Chad bursts from the building, new shotgun in hand. He jerks the pump mechanism, racking a shell into the chamber and reducing the wolf tattooed guy's crotch to a fine red mist. He rolls around on the ground, howling in pain.

His next shot blows over the heads of the other two as Ethan knocks the barrel up. "Unless you want to dig, go back inside." He tugs the gun free.

In the passing second, the other two men drop their shovels and race from the building. Ethan fires his M&P. None of his three shots strike either man. The fools believe he intended to warn them. Ethan knows he missed.

"Fuck. I may have to start using this thing." He speaks about the shotgun so only Chad hears. "Back to work!"

Chad huffs, his anger prevents any words.

"No. I've no idea what it was like to go through what you just did. You want to finish the fucker or just let him bleed?"

"No, I'm better than them." Chad marches across the overgrown yard, jabs the smoking barrel into wolf tattoo man's mouth, smashing through his teeth before firing.

Ethan has no words.

Chad hands him the shotgun, slinking back to the door. "Don't think less of me."

"Never."

Becky drops Ethan's boots behind him, "What do we do with all these guns?"

Her question halts the two diggers.

Ethan points the shotgun. "Don't worry, the grave's not for you two."

Ethan drives a make-shift cross into the grave.

The swelling has overtaken Becky's face. "Do you think he'll travel?"

"He has to. This road must get some human traffic or else the trap was pointless."

Becky wonders, "Won't someone dig up this grave. They might have friends."

Ethan kicks the dead wolf tattoo man in the gut. "I'll leave him to decompose."

"You told the other two you wouldn't kill them."

"I didn't want to dig a hole." Ethan flings a shove as far as he possible into the grassy field. "Let someone dig. At three feet, down they find two bodies. Motivation to stop digging. Three feet under them and the guns are hidden."

Becky throws the second shovel in the crawl space under the building. "You just shot them."

"You do understand after they finished with Chad and me they would have used you for weeks."

"But the two who dug the hole—you shot them in cold blood," says Becky.

"Not when intent is evident. Would you have wanted me to wait until each of them put their dick in Chad before I determined if they were harmful to us? Fuck. I'll sleep just fine tonight knowing I kept us alive and once back from Memphis I'll have a whole cache of weapons to recover."

"You were correct about this place. You knew this place was a trap."

"I failed. I knew. But even my experience dealing with the new world no one has constructed such an elaborate trap to capture people. I wasn't ready for the electric shock."

"I say we burn it down." Chad flings open the door.

"Fire attracts too much attention and impossible to control," Ethan says.

"It will be a trap for others."

"Not with those four dead and no supplies inside. It's a safe place to sleep and nothing more."

Chad storms off the porch even if his thumping gait radiates pain.

"I've never seen him like this." Becky flings her pack over her shoulder.

"We'd better keep a close eye on him."

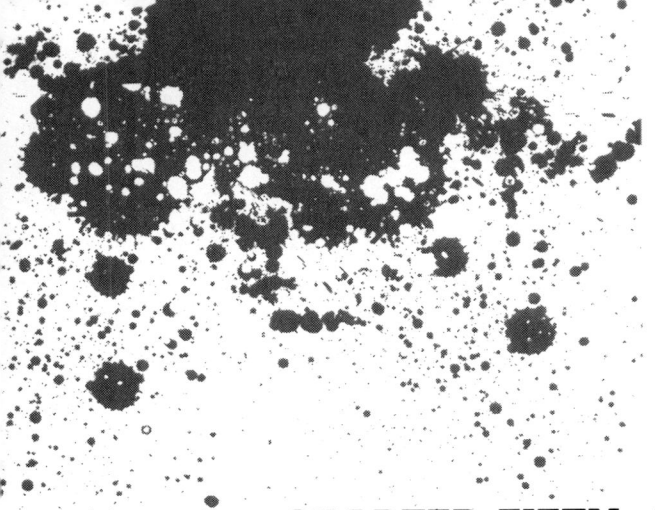

CHAPTER FIFTY-ONE

"SO, YOU WERE a cop?" Tony asks. He doesn't need much confirmation. He smells cops the way biters smell blood.

"Detective."

"Like Sherlock Holmes?" Kelsey jokes.

"No. I didn't wear a uniform or a damn tie. I didn't patrol, either. I compiled information and evidence for criminal cases. I had to pass a test and have some college to be a police detective."

"It means he's observant and smarter than those county guys who harassed me for open containers," Kelsey says.

"Must be nice to be bothered for something you did. I got pulled over—"

"Because you were black," Danziger completes Tony's rant. "It had nothing to do with being in an unregistered car, dressed in gang colors, or running from a building where a robbery just occurred."

"The world stopped being black and white when the undead decided to strut around. The dead don't care," Kelsey says. "We've got to trust each other."

"Some things are hard to get over," Tony admits.

"Then you better. I know this trip proves something to Ethan about you. You don't have to like each other, but we need to be a team," Kelsey says.

Tony and Danziger nod.

"So why are we heading so close to St. Louis?" Tony asks. "Got to be thousands of millions of those fuckers."

"There was a caravan of people enroute to Fort Wood. A herd forced them to abandon a lot of supplies, and in my search for Levin, I left a friend—Tom." Danziger asks, "Didn't they brief you on this?"

"I volunteered. Didn't care. I guess I should have. A couple of us owe Ethan a debt. One we had to work off to earn getting inside Acheron's fences. He said going with Danziger would accomplish it for me," Tony says.

"What were you in for?" Danziger's question shocks Kelsey more than Tony.

"Are you asking because he's black?" Kelsey asks.

"I'm just asking—cop intuition."

"Not supposed to speak on it, but, you want to trust. Ethan discovered us locked in a prison bus. A herd overturned it. Five us survived only because we were locked in cage. They couldn't reach us and we couldn't escape. Nor could we do anything while everyone one else was eaten around us. Ethan released us if we promised to protect the east area of Acheron. When he felt we earned our place, we could move inside."

A lightbulb clicks on for Kelsey. "Simon takes you food every day."

"That redneck fucker hates us."

"He's crotchety," Kelsey agrees. "I think it's just his age."

"We'll see how he treats a brother on the inside after I get him a locomotive."

"Not what we're doing," says Danziger.

"We're not after a train?" Tony asks.

"We're going to check the station in Washington and inspect the caravan," Danziger says.

"If we use a train, won't more biters be attracted by the noise?" Kelsey asks.

"Train cars will offer advantages and safety."

"A corpse won't derail a train like hitting a dozen in a car will," says Danziger.

"There's no direct route to Springfield from Acheron," says Kelsey.

"From the map, the train heads toward KC then south. I don't know anything about switching tracks, but if we find some train people we bring them back. Eventually, we could use the lines to move across the country. At least west of the Mississippi."

"Why only west? I'd want to go Washington DC; you know all those Senators are safe in some bunker," Tony says.

"The military was blowing bridges across the Mississippi River to slow the flow of undead," Danziger says. "I encountered a demolition team performing such actions."

"Why didn't you tell us?" Kelsey asks. "I think I jumped at this mission too quickly as well. I didn't realize there was so much missing information."

"We are scouts. It's our job to fill in the missing info. Wanikiya said you two were skilled. Kelsey you're a crack shot. I'm a cop who's been dealing with the undead. What did you do, Tony?"

"I'm an undead wrangler."

"Sounds like we've experts in the undead. Now we create the team."

"Nobody said how we determine when we encounter people if we offer to bring them back home," Kelsey points out.

"There's no training for selecting. We just play by our gut."

Moan-howls burble on the breeze. Danziger draws his pistol.

Kelsey raises her hand for him to stop, she shoulders her rifle while drawing her machete. "Don't draw noise attention for one." The blade cleaves the top of the skull exposing the brain. The biter collapse into a disheveled heap.

"They swarm to each other but for some reasons you do find loners."

"Has anyone studied them?" Danziger asks.

"You mean like scientifically? No fuck'n way. It's one thing to put makeup on chimps or carve up rats, but a lab mishap—"

"They don't move fast, but I had one charge me once. It sprinted," says Danziger.

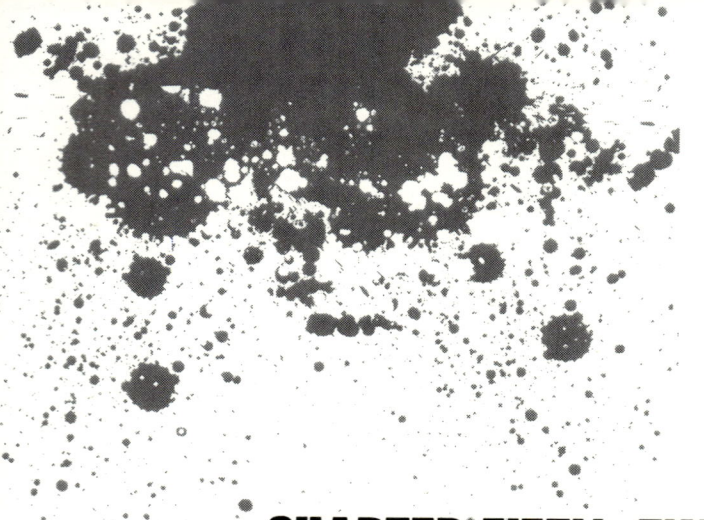

CHAPTER FIFTY-TWO

BECKY PUMPS A drop of hand lotion on her forefinger. She works it in circles over the garter tattoo on her right thigh. "Do you think we could recue a tattoo artist next?"

"The world ended and you want another tattoo," Chad unhooks his gun belt.

"I want to match," she slaps the inkless left leg.

"It gives you distinction," Ethan adjusts his supplies in his pack. "And, Chad, you're a moron. Don't argue with any girl that wants to show off her legs to you."

"He's still learning about women." Becky smiles at him.

"How the fuck are you two able to joke? Noon today, I was being made a prison bitch!" Chad flings the home's previous residents' personal items off the chest of drawers. "I took everything I had to just walk the rest of the day. That guy parked a bus in my ass." He shakes, not wanting to cry.

"But you did. You killed the bastard who touched you." Ethan flips open the cylinder on his magnum and dumps seven of the eight rounds. "If you're unable to deal with what happened...you have an option."

"What the fuck? No, Ethan. Chad, you aren't going to blow your brains out." Becky steps between them.

"There's no Dr. Phil on this trip." Ethan pulls his t-shirt over his head. Much of his chest still marred with gray bruises.

"I get it. You do have some understanding. I don't know how to just get over it," says Chad.

Ethan removes a pint of Bacardi from his pack. "I keep this for trade or medical. Kills a lot of germs in non-bite wounds. I'm not saying to start drinking, but a few shots tonight might help."

Becky takes the bottle and breaks the seal. She swills three gulps. "Woo-hoo! Dealing with you two will drive any girl to drink." She wipes her lips dry with the back of her hand before offering the bottle to Chad.

He swallows a finger's worth.

"Better."

"Yeah. Yeah. I feel more manly. As manly as you can getting your cherry popped by a dude."

Ethan seals the bottle, returning to his pack. "Sleepy time."

"Do you always stay on the second floor?" asks Becky.

"I have my madness." Ethan smiles. He would place bets on how to fix Chad, but he decides to keep his suggestion to himself. He reloads the magnum.

"How many times a day are you going to check your gun?"

"As many as it takes to keep me breathing. Remember to treat your gun like you do a woman—respect her, love her, never forget how dangerous she is."

"What makes you such an expert?" Chad asks.

"I know enough to know that as soon as I figure out a woman they hold a meeting and change all the rules."

"You're funny." Becky slips the hand lotion into a side pouch on her backpack.

"Keep it up girl and I'll give you the hose again."

"Is that some kind of women being a dog joke?" Becky snaps.

"No," Chad explains, "he referenced Hannibal Lector."

Ethan rolls his eyes. "Close enough." He flips open the cylinder on his magnum—eight rounds.

Chad flips the chest of drawers on its side to keep the door secure. "When do we find a boat?"

"Not today." Ethan lies on the bed, his magnum next to his right hand. He reaches to the nightstand, tapping the top of a Coleman lantern and it dims out, covering the room in blackness.

Ethan's finger touches his magnum handle. He keeps his eyes shut, recognizing the sounds. The low-grunts are not from the undead. Once sure what he hears is Becky releasing positive mumbles of pleasures, he drifts back to his own sexless dreams.

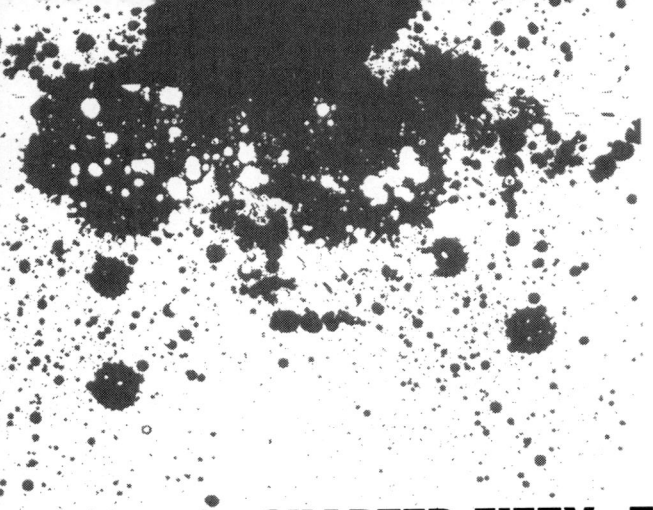

CHAPTER FIFTY-THREE

"I WANT TO attempt a small project," Wanikiya explains. "I read on the internet about Native American farming practices."

"You're a Sioux," Rad hammers in a post.

"Doesn't mean I know about farming practices. My people were hunters." Wanikiya scowls as he ties a string around the post. "Before the white man destroyed our way of life."

"Now the undead destroy everyone's." Rad hammers in another post about fifty feet from the first post.

"Quite the juxtaposition."

"Why do you educated types use such big words? Ethan does it a lot," Rad says.

"Knowledge will be what helps us survive. Now, from what I read, corn was planted." Wanikiya ties his string to the second post.

"Got plenty of corn seed." Rad marks off one-hundred paces before driving in a third post.

"Next plant beans. They'll use the corn as natural climbing poles. Finally, squash to choke out weeds."

"I'll say it seems logical. I'll plant a few acres as you requested. If it works next year, we'll do whole fields. It will be quite productive. What will we do with so much squash?"

"I know a squash casserole recipe," Wanikiya assures. "Pies."

"We will get to a point when we waste nothing. Wish my grandfather was alive. He grew up during the Great Depression. They re-used everything. He'd even find some use for all the cell phones lying around."

"We'll figure new uses for everything in time. We'll stick with using up what we have first. We need to learn to tan the cow hides. Some library somewhere must have a book on it."

"You think we'll return to wearing buckskin?" Rad asks.

"In the summer. It breathes and it stays cool, not like all the wool sweaters we're going to have to knit for winter," Wanikiya says.

"We've got a few people who knit. Once the fields no longer have to be weeded. Have you given much thought to the gas situation?"

"Lack of fuel is one reason Ethan chooses to hike. Retrieving what he recovers rates a higher use for fuel expenditures while it lasts," Wanikiya says.

"Even if we plant and harvest by hand, we still need tractors. No one is ready to yoke some oxen. And we don't have enough people to operate as field hands."

"We need more people to maintain our survival, but we have electric lights and plow our fields with mules. We will learn to do again what people have done for centuries."

"It's been too long now since we huddled in this farm house and built our first fence. Now we'll have to take who we find."

"Ethan brought people who helped to grow our community. Are you saying to stop screening who he encounters?" Wanikiya asks.

"As much as possible."

"The work for your food rule is effective. Now that you can't just go buy off the dollar menu, when some is caught slacking and goes to bed without supper they don't slack anymore," Wanikiya says.

"As it should be. We provide no free rides."

"We're going to have to worry about children. No way someone's not going to be pregnant—and soon."

"We do have some children now."

"A few."

"Plenty of educated people?"

"There's a few. Several hoe weeds because world history studies don't translate well to useful skills during an apocalypse."

"So much to do, and I must cook dinner," Wanikiya says.

"I enjoy your food. I've never had Mom's home cooking before you, but there are plenty who'll work the kitchen while you perform administrative duties. If our leader spends all his time outside the fence, then it's only right you run this place."

"Ethan's plans are sound," Wanikiya says.

"But he doesn't stay to enforce them," Rad reminds him.

"I think he knows one day his knee will give out and he doesn't want to be a burden on us. He wants to ensure his retirement."

"He could do so by keeping this place running successfully."

"My ideas might be even more radical than Ethan insisting on grade level reading and apprenticeship programs," Wanikiya says.

"Training people seems reasonable. What could be more radical?"

"Music. Reading expands the mind, and we need the next generation to be smart. Hell, if I find a music teacher, every one of those kids would learn to play an instrument. It improves the brain," Wanikiya says.

"Have Ethan add sheet music to the shopping list." Rad laughs. He tosses his hammer in the back of the truck. "I'll get your garden experiment going."

"Keep us focused on the practical Rad. Food growth and gate security is of upmost importance."

"Rebuilding a community is more than a strong wall. We must care how we rebuild as well. If we are to rebuild at all."

CHAPTER FIFTY-FOUR

"FUCK ME." DAKOTA hoists his foot onto the interstate highway guard rail overlooking Six Flag's parking lot.

"At least you were correct about the all the cars to choose from."

A layer of mud reaches the top of most of the car tires, trapping them.

"Without people here to stop it, the river flooded. It won't take Mother Nature long to reclaim what humans have done to her," Tom says.

"Then maybe we should just go extinct." Danielle pokes at her tender nose scar, causing her eyes to water.

"Your scar don't make you any less pretty than the hog ring you had in there before," Dakota says.

"Fuck you, small dick," Danielle quips.

Dakota grabs his crotch. "You know you want it."

"I've seen you pee, dude. I'm not impressed." Danielle rolls her eyes.

"Just wait. You'll want it."

"Not if we can find batteries," Danielle snaps.

Darcy smirks as does Tom.

"Dude, let it go," Dave says. "What 's our next move, Tom?"

"Even if any of the cars lacked enough water damage to allow the engine to turn over we've never dig one out. We move on to Fort

Wood. Look for homes with cars left in garages and for now none in low lying areas."

"You seem unsure, Tom," Darcy questions his saddened tone.

"I don't know anymore, kid. People should be helping each other. Times of crisis have always brought out the best in people."

"Tom, those people died helping," Dave says.

Dakota jerks open a car door, driving a knife into the skull of an infected trapped by the seat belt. He tosses the body onto the road, reaching into twist the keys. The engine sputters for one crank then nothing. Not one light or alarm beep. His kick crumples the fender. "I'm not hoofing some hundred miles."

"I've got to concur with short dick," Danielle says.

"Keep it up, you twiggy bitch. I'll show you how small it is when I fuck that gap you call a nose."

"I will cut it off." Danielle grips her dagger.

Tom steps closer to between the two of them. "It's going to be difficult if we can't get along."

"Dusty held us together," Danielle says.

At the sound of his name, Darcy collapses against a car and breaks into tears. "He promised he wouldn't die. Everyone in my life has died."

"Get over it. All our families are dead," says Dakota.

"You're a giant douche." Darcy throws a used fast food wrapper at him.

"Just get over it."

Even if Tom wants to punch him in the mouth right now his actions won't help. "Dakota, please."

"I'm not the bad guy here," he protests.

"Just scout west for a while."

"Fuck you all."

Darcy puts her arm around Danielle. "We're your family. I need you. Without you I've got to tell these men about my periods."

"I just can't." Danielle smiles as snot drips from her nose. "I don't want everyone left I know to die."

"I don't plan to die." Tom's bravado doesn't reassure her.

"You're hurt. You've one arm. You need surgery."

Darcy speaks, almost mousey, "We're going to find a safe place."

"Don't you get it. No place is safe!"

"Being with us. Your new family will keep you safe," Tom says.

"Why?"

"We have to live, Danielle. I don't want to turn into those things," Darcy says.

"What did you want in life, Darcy?"

"I don't know. My parents wanted college. I was afraid to leave high school. I didn't fill out a scholarship on purpose. The guidance counselor was sure I would get it. If I didn't do it, it meant I had no reason to go away. I don't want to go away." She hangs her head. "I should have done it. My mom...she would've been so proud. Had I done it. She'd still be dead, but I'd know she died proud of me."

"You'll never take it back, and with the way the world is you can't even spend the rest of your life making up for it by graduating college. It's all pointless now."

"Nothing pointless," Tom scolds. "Darcy, honor your mother by living. She would want you to go on. You just have to find your purpose in this new world. You'll make her proud."

"Don't feed her such bullshit. Just admit there is no reason to go on. The world is over. You said so yourself: Mother Nature is reclaiming the planet and soon we'll all be rotters." She claps her pistol.

Tom recognizes the glaze in Danielle's eyes. He has but seconds and lacks the speed to reach her. As the barrel presses against Danielle's temple, he reaches Darcy. He swings the girl, pulling her into a tight embrace, burying her face against her chest so she doesn't witness Danielle pulling the trigger.

CHAPTER FIFTY-FIVE

"YOU DO THAT in every house we sleep in?" Becky scoops a moleskin book from under the bed.

The sun dips below the tree line.

Ethan tips the dresser over, covering the bedroom door. "Consider it an early warning alarm. I still tend to sleep soundly. If biters find us at three AM they'll make lots of noise reaching us." He kicks his boots off and lies back on the bed. His M&P lays inches from his right hand.

Chad uses a beach towel as a pillow while Becky curls into ball in the frumpy chair they drug from another bedroom. She drops the journal into her pack.

"Any reason you always get the bed?" Chad flips over, unable to get comfortable.

"Besides I'm older, faster, tougher, and ruggedly handsome. Any day you're froggy enough to take the bed you go right ahead and try. Just remember to leave an address," Ethan says.

"Why an address?" Chad asks.

Becky answers, "In order to mail you back your balls." She pulls the blanket up to her neck.

Becky's attempt at being extra quiet makes more noise instinctively sending Ethan's fingers for his M&P for a second night in a row. He knows instantly what he hears could be more dangerous than any biter—two horny teenagers.

Ethan cracks an eye enough to find a room lit by some moonlight. *At least they waited until the middle of night hoping I was in REM sleep.*

Whispers echo louds.

"Damn it, Chad. You're... Just, let me put it in."

"Your legs are like sandpaper."

Great way to keep a woman wet.

"Just lie on your back," she commands.

Bodies shuffle.

Ethan has to smile. He was young once.

CHAPTER FIFTY-SIX

SHOVED FORWARD, TOM tugs against his duct taped wrist. His captors were kind enough not to bind his broken arm but they secured the free one extra tight.

Tears stain Darcy's face. Danielle's death hangs on her. Dave is shoved against her.

Tom's not sure where these people came from but bets Dakota must have been far enough down the road they missed him. *I guess we'll discover what kind of team player he is.*

These survivors have taken residence in a church adorned in ten-foot-tall stained glass windows depicting various biblical scenes.

Tom attempts to count the eyes glaring at them.

Before the pulpit, they have cut a ten-foot-wide hole over the basement. Tom doesn't have to peer over the edge to know the snarling below is coming from trapped undead.

The pastor, the only member in the congregation to be clean down to his freshly pressed suit raises his arms in the air. "Praise be to God to return our brothers."

"Praise to Him," all respond in unison.

"We have so few worthy left. Are you worthy, my friends?"

One of the men who captured them opens his mouth. "Pastor Isaac—"

He waves a silencing hand. "Let them speak."

"We just seek someplace safe," Tom says.

"You're safe. All those who are worthy of God's love are safe." Isaac waves his arm and two adults, body odor hanging around them like deflector screens, bring forth a young girl—maybe ten.

One pulls the child's arm tight while the other jerks back the sleeve covering bite marks.

Tom recognizes the gashes immediately. Firemen responded to more than just fires. Many a domestic disturbance and even a few kittens in trees, but numerous first responding calls to animal bites—especially dog. Someone let a dog munch on the girl's arm enough to scar. This man of God uses her to promote his trickery.

Tom makes a private vow to God.

"Those who follow his path and are worthy. Are shown his love." Isaac smiles.

I'm going to kill you.

"These two are not worthy. They just stood by as another in their group took her own life." Isaac steps to his pulpit. "Ezekiel 23:7—*Keep far from false charge, and do not slay the innocent and the righteous, for I will not acquit the wicked.* You're wicked, sir, to allow your companion to end her life."

"I alone did so. These two did not know. But you stretch your faith for the Bible does not speak of suicide," says Tom.

Isaac raises his arm as if to be Zeus casting a lightning bolt. "Christ himself commanded: *You have heard it said to men of old, 'You shall not kill; and whoever kills shall be liable to judgment.' But I say to you that everyone who is angry with his brother shall be liable to judgment.* You are to be judged, sir!"

"It's not your place," Tom rebuffs.

"Certain of that I am. God has sent his judgment method to us and those unworthy of his love will be your judge."

"Cast him in," chants the congregation.

Darcy screams in protest.

Dave struggles against his guards only to find a rifle butt bash the side of his face; as he loses consciousness on the way to the floor his eye photographs one single moment. Another eye peeking through a thin separated crack in the stain glass. He prays the pupil belongs to Dakota.

"God will test your worthiness," Pastor Isaac commands.

Tom finds himself falling into the dark basement. Wrists still bound to his side, he lands on his broken arm. *God, don't let me pass out.* Needles crawl up his arm like a thousand marching ants.

The rotters seem to take no notice of him at first, remaining in their mindless milling state. He tugs at the duct tape. No way he has the ability to tear free. *Pass out and you die. This will hurt.* He twists his secured wrist as high to reach his arm sling.

Not having casting supplies, he splinted the bone with the hard case of a hunting knife sheath. He selected this blade because it locks into place keeping the sheath even more rigid. His problem: The release must be sprung to draw the blade.

Tom contorts his body. He still has inches to reach the release on the hilt. He flips over to get a better angle and his flop on the floor alerts the rotters to his existence. They snarl and pounce.

CHAPTER FIFTY-SEVEN

"WHAT DID YOU do?" Kelsey asks.

"You never ask a convict what he did." Danziger keeps in step to the triangle formation; the group moves forward as they keep to the center of the highway.

Tony ignores her question, wanting the ex-cop's take on his history.

"Why not? He was incarcerated. He did something."

"You ask him what he's accused of. All people in prison are innocent," says Danziger.

"Not me. I'm guilty, just not for what they put me in there for. I don't do that."

"You're serious." Kelsey's not sure she's ever heard such twisted logic.

"As an over fifty-five white man's heart attack," says Tony.

"Then what did they accuse you of?"

"I don't remember," Tony says.

"At least you didn't say it was because you were black." Danziger halts, craning his neck to listen to a sound he thought he detected off in the distance.

"Even I know, officer, there ain't no black and white no more. I was no child rapist and Ethan promised us a do-over. He never even asked what we did."

"But he didn't let you inside the fence," Kelsey points out. Ethan has brought in so many without question, but not Tony and his group. It gives her pause and a reminder to keep one open eye when she sleeps.

"The camp was young and people were still scared of black folk. You whites get paranoid around us blacks from the city."

"Hey! I've black friends," Kelsey chirps.

"The mantra of the white trying not to sound racist. With the most racist comments possible." Danziger steps from the triangle formation signing *quiet*.

Kelsey flips her rifle to firing position her finger on the safety.

"I didn't mean it, white girl," Tony whispers.

Danziger shakes his head. "I thought it was a whimper."

"Do they whimper?"

"Never heard one do much beyond those moan-howl groans. And we wrangled a lot of them," Tony says.

Before Kelsey asks why, Danziger races toward the clear barking.

She keeps her finger on the safety and jobs after him. Dogs are rare. Of the three at Acheron, one refuses to approach living people. Simon leaves a bowl of food for it and it eats, but never if it smells anyone around.

Tony hangs back, drawing his pistol. Not sure of his new teammates or chasing after dogs in the woods.

Danziger bounds through the underbrush.

Kelsey considers his actions foolish.

Tony keeps his distance, not trusting barking from a stationary position. He smells trap. So should the experienced cop he follows.

Three undead reach clawed hands at the yapping beast who barks, leaps to one side of the creatures, barks and leaps to the other side. The constant changing sound confuses the three monsters while protecting a girl child. The golden-haired dog has done it so much its fur has developed a frothy foam. It won't last much longer.

Drawing a hunting knife, Danziger smashes the skull of a biter. Upon spotting this, the dog darts further to the left of the creatures causing them to stumble giving Danziger a clear path to the second biter. The blade drinks deep of the oily ink that was once blood.

Kelsey smashes the butt of her rifle into the third one's skull.

The dog races back to the girl, no older than eight, collapsing at her feet. Still with enough fight to growl at the strangers approaching his owner.

Kelsey steps toward the little girl. "Do you have a name, sweetheart?"

The dog growls at her.

Danziger cleans his blade. "The dog doesn't think much of you."

"It's tired and doesn't know us." Kelsey shoulders the rifle before kneeling to be eye level with the girl. "Where are you parents?"

"Dead." Not so much as a break in her emotions when she answers.

"Children will handle this world better than us. They'll never know any different than what there is now."

"Kids love me," Kelsey says.

"Not this kid," barks the little girl.

"We can't just leave you here." Kelsey steps forward, activating more dog growls.

"You got some place we can escort you to?" Danziger speaks to an equal; even if she's eight, she must deal with the world dangers the same as anyone else now. *No more childhoods. Maybe at Acheron—one day. For now, the world has two kinds of people in it.*

"Not so much for me, but Butch is tired and I can't carry him. Will you carry him, mister?"

"I will. Do you have a name?" Danziger asks.

"Lizbeth."

Danziger carries the retriever in his arms while Lizbeth holds tight to him riding piggyback.

Kelsey keeps a watchful eye as part of her wonders how easy the lost little girl routine would be perfect bait. *No wonder Ethan says to stay off the roads. Random traps in fields would be too complicated.* She keeps her concerns to herself trusting Danziger will snap the child's neck if she leads them into a snare. *I never knew there were so many fields in this state. Cows butt up against skyscrapers.*

Tony keeps behind the two following stealthily from house to house covering them as they stroll down the center of street.

Biter bodies lie scattered across several yards and two in the street. The door of every house Tony passes has been left open. He glances inside to find ransacked rooms. Someone has scavenged this neighborhood.

"How far did you get, Lizbeth?"

"Far. These houses have all been thieved. But it's best way to get home to the Caverns."

"Danziger." Kelsey cocks her head to point down an alley with a car. Two bodies are visible inside.

Danziger places the dog on the grass.

Lizbeth slides from his back. "Don't hurt Butch."

"I won't."

"Lizzy, step away from them," orders a voice.

Kelsey raises her arms, her finger still on the safety.

"Nobody's here to harm anyone." Danziger holds his arms away from his body, palms up.

"James. They protected me. Put away your gun. Auntie will be mad."

Both men step from the alley guns pointed at Danziger.

"You know who else would be mad?" Tony levels his pistol at James' skull. "Should have checked your flank. The dead make noise people have the ability to remain quiet." Tony's proud of his stealth. He waves his gun as an order for the two men to lower theirs.

James and the other man toss their guns into the grass.

Kelsey swings her rifle toward them, flicking the safety off.

"Lizbeth. Do you know these people?"

"James is my brother. He doesn't like it when I come here to play in my room."

"Mister, don't hurt my sister," James pleads.

"I'm not hurting anyone. Unless they're undead."

"We're just passing through," Kelsey says.

"Not much to scavenge here, minter. These houses have been stripped, and the closer you get to the city, the larger the herds. Your friend here would fit in."

"What does that mean?" Tony demands.

James defends his statement, "Nothing, just an army of black men. Well-armed, loud, and protecting supplies."

"We need to check it out for ourselves," says Tony.

"Your funeral, mister," the other man says.

"Lizbeth, do you want to go with your brother?" Danziger asks.

"I love him."

"James, why don't you take Lizbeth and Butch and we all go our separate ways?"

"You all seem well fed and supplied," James' companion says.

"The area north of the Missouri hasn't been scavenged as much. Go to Herman and keep traveling. The undead are scarcer there," Kelsey says.

"They can't swim so fewer dead's believable. Why head south if supplies are so good?"

Her glance at Danziger reveals she's not sure how to answer.

"You travel far enough you'll find people. People who will welcome you. Tony, get their guns."

"What do you want me to do with them?"

"You can't leave us without our guns," James yells.

"I'm not." Tony removes the clips and brings the pistols along. "We'll leave them at the end of the street before we head into the woods. Kelsey, cover us," Danziger commands. "You take care of Lizbeth, and if you want safety, you'll do as I said."

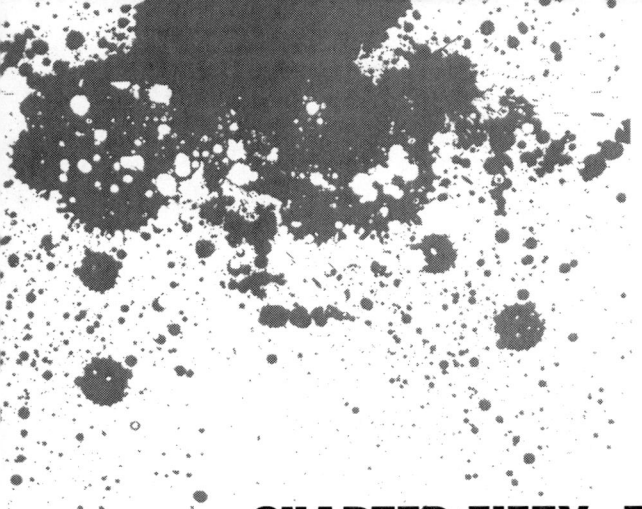

CHAPTER FIFTY-EIGHT

CHAD FIDDLES UNDER the hood of the rusty pick-up.

"If you can't fix it, move on. We could be down the road and found another car already. This is one reason I don't mess with cars." Ethan piles his gear next to a shirtless Becky.

She dangles her legs over the bridge.

"Give me fifteen more minutes. All I need to do is get this hose clamp to stay on," Chad calls out.

"He does have issues with his hose." Becky flips through the diary she found.

"I respect what you did the first night after what happened to him at the gun store. Men, no matter what level of homophobia they suppress, have to do something extra masculine to recover from emasculation," says Ethan.

"I thought he might do something stupid if he didn't remember what it was to be a man," Becky says.

"Most people don't handle control being stripped from them, but you don't have to perform every night."

"You heard us?" Becky soaking the sun into her bare back explains, "The second night was because I wanted it."

"You think you've got a career with Chad there?" Ethan asks.

She glances back before she answers to make sure Chad doesn't hear her, "Fuck no. He's a pretty boy. When we search houses, he pockets hair gel."

"He was pocketing something else last night."

Becky face grows wide with surprise at such a barb. "You're not going to try and make this weird, turn us into a father-daughter moment, are you?"

"No after school special between us. I just want you to be careful."

"We didn't exactly go to the drug store beforehand, but don't worry, I doubt I fuck him again."

"I know I'm going to regret this—why?"

"It was awful. He had no idea what do," she says. "

"Did you tell him?"

"No."

Ethan's tone churns. "Look, little girl, you need to explain to him how to pleasure you."

"Men don't want directions," Becky says.

"Men don't want you telling every other girl in the camp he's the worst fuck ever, either. I also don't need him distracted by thinking about why you don't want him to touch you anymore, so if you decide you want to try again, you explain to him what you want. Teach him. He doesn't know what to do and won't ask. You explain it to him. Guide him. Make him the kind of lover you want. Just saying, his future girlfriends will thank you." Ethan smiles.

"Are you for serious?" she asks.

"Yes. And any woman who says, 'for serious', is too young for sex. Use that sexy voice and guide him to what you want. He'll be receptive."

"Young guys aren't like that. They don't want a woman in control."

"No, they think that whatever they did the last time is what works unless you help them out and they will keep doing it. Don't nag. Guide." Ethan slips her a box of condoms.

"I couldn't have had this conversation with my dad," she says, stuffing the box in her pack.

"I'm not old enough to be your father," Ethan assures her.

"You should follow some of your own advice," Becky suggests. "Emily likes you a lot. Why not take her up on it?"

"She's fifteen."

"You're sitting next to a twenty-year-old with her ta-tas hanging out." Becky leans back showing off her flat chest with coffee-colored nipples. "She may not make it to seventeen. Two years is a long fucking time now. There's no laws anymore."

"We've made laws. We live by laws."

"You have laws on rape. She's willing. That's not rape."

"Maybe. Maybe not, but I've a personal moral code."

Becky sighs. "Wow, women do encounter men who are still noble. Just the fact you won't jump on her after she's made it clear she's so willing just makes you that much more attractive."

"Why don't you go for a swim. Cool off. We'll give Chad one more chance to fix the truck."

"You could go for a swim," she suggests.

"You could put a shirt on." He plops down next to her. "So, by not chasing a girl, I get other girls to chase me. The mind of women makes no sense."

"Women want to know how you're going to treat them based on how you treat other women. You took care of Emily. You respect women and you make no advances on those who you rule over. Who wouldn't want to be with a guy who takes cares of those in his charge?" Becky removes her shoes and socks.

"I reach an understanding of women after the world ends." Ethan smirks. "Figures."

"Why won't you date?"

"You know scavenging hunts are a privilege. Your questions might get you guarding a garden from the cows." He pushes himself up, struggling to stay on his bad leg. "I'll see if I can't get you stationed someplace else. Maybe carrot patrol. Plenty of rascally rabbits to shoot."

"Funny. Too bad the world ended. Your comedy career would have soared." Becky drops her shorts. She glances into his eyes before he turns his head to avoid staring at her ass. "You're still in pain?" She doesn't mean his leg. She steps over the bridge guard rail. "You're afraid of being hurt. You've been safe all this time afraid to live. By ur pain, it allows you to push everyone away and you nally safe." She hops to a rock below.

" out here every day risking my life to keep everyone safe. Having love back home would only put my choices into question. Anyone operating out here must not have distraction back home."

"Surviving is not enough, Ethan. You have to love." Becky draws her toes across the surface of the water.

"In this new world, in order for our group to succeed, some of us have to sacrifice their humanity."

"Why not love? Even if it's not Emily. You allow her age to be an excuse, but it's not anymore. Not in this world. She's no baby. There are plenty of other women who desire you. Let go of your fear. Don't be afraid to love." With that, she dives into the water.

Chad scouts the road ahead of his companions.

Becky matches pace with Ethan's limp. "How did you hurt yourself?" she asks.

"I had the sex talk with you and it was less uncomfortable for me than to explain what happened," says Ethan. "What's in the book?"

Becky flips through the pages of the diary. "Someone tried to document what happened."

"A kid?"

"An early teen. The first few pages are girl stuff." She turns into a tween. "Like Johnny's cute. Why aren't my boobs bigger? My dad wants to talk to me about sex and I just want to die. I wouldn't know what any of that's like."

"She wrote about *the talk*?"

"No."

"It would have to be a kid anyway. I doubt adults took time to write anything down," Ethan speculates.

"She didn't have time to write long entries."

"If humanity survives the next few years and thrives in some capacity, people will want to know what caused it."

"You said it does matter," Becky reminds him.

"It doesn't. It doesn't to us. People in the future will want to know for them to question the choices we make. People armchair history because they weren't alive at the time when those choices had to be made."

"Part of me wants to know and part of me doesn't. At first people claimed it was a plague released by our own government. I don't want to know if it's true," Becky says.

"I was busy surviving and trying to reach family in those first days."

Becky flips some pages. "She relabeled and stopped dating the entries. The cursive's so pretty and legible. I think she could have grown up to be an artist.

Day I

Not sure if this is day one of the outbreak. Mom calls it an outbreak. Terrifying Biblical End of Humanity would scare people too much. News has had concerns and alerts for three days now and everyone has been ordered to pack one carry-on sized bag and report to an evacuation center locations constantly scrolling across the TV screen and internet. Mom believes if it is plague then joining with other people will only help to spread the disease. Mom has never allowed dad to have his guns out in the house. I had no idea he had so many when he laid them all out on the kitchen table. I may get to learn to shoot. We've filled the tub with water and everything that will hold water. All of us sleeping in the living room like when the power goes out during a winter storm. Dad has boarded up the basement and stocking it with supplies. He thinks it's the safest place with only one entrance. As I write three TV channels I like have switched to twenty-four-hour news and two others are nothing but black now.

"The news should have reported what was happening."

"*'Dead Return to Life'.* No one would believe such a headline outside a horror movie," Ethan says.

"The government should have acted faster. Protected us." Becky's disgust in the system is evident when she nearly tears a page when she turns it.

"How old were you when Katrina happened? Waiting to act is what they do. What else did she write?"

"More dad fixes basement. More water collection. More orders to evacuate. Fewer and fewer television stations." She scans each page, "*All channels show news now and only stories about fighting in major cities.* Here we go—

Day IV

NO INTERNET!!!!!!!!!!!
How do I LIVE Without Snapchat!!!!!!!!!!!!!!!
Dad said this would be a final trip into town. I would never believed it if I hadn't witnessed it with my own eyes. The news said it's plague. Dad said a natural plague didn't work so fast. Mom and I stayed in the truck. Dad went into the hardware store. Mr. Danvers who taught my mom math and I would have him next school year, bit mom on the arm and wouldn't let go. Dad hit him so hard with a 2x4 the board broke. Mr. Danvers fell down, but he got back up trying to bite dad. Dad shot him. Three times in the chest. He just kept getting back up. Dad said he has rabies. We got mom home. Her bite won't co-agu-late. Just bleed and bleed a blackish blood. Parts of town are on fire. The glow even at the farm makes it like a sunset at 3AM.

Becky flips the page.

Day V

Bleeding stopped.
Mom is sick. The infected bite. Dads says she has rabies too. No TV. Dad says no hospitals to help her.
Dad was gone. All afternoon. I used the last of the ice to cool mom. When Dad came back he was muddy dirty. Told me to say good bye to mom.

Becky flips the pages; all the rest are blank.

"Not much of a history, everyone who still lives tells almost that story," says Ethan.

"He shot his wife."

"More than likely."

"Before she turned." *There were no bodies in the house. I never check basements for supplies—too dark. Too great a chance of a hidden biter. I'd bet he shot his daughter and then himself.*

"If he thought it was a disease he did it to protect his daughter. After shooting a man three times who was in his fifties and he remained standing, I'd put down any sick person I saw," says Ethan.

"You had to...didn't you?"

Ethan considers his answer might relieve him of the burden. "She'd already turned."

"You daughter?" Becky asks.

He nods. "I'm not sure what transpired. I was divorced. Living across the state for my job. They left the house for an evacuation shelter. I'd received messages when they arrived. Then I found one girl at the house." Ethan chokes on the emotions he swallows. "A note said they were going to a second rescue station. The evacuation centers were abandoned. I lost any trail."

"Why bounce around rescue stations?" Becky asks." If they were exposed, it would be at the stations."

"If people thought it was a plague they might conclude separation from people might prevent the spread. So, they went back home. Then one turned. I don't know."

"No disease spreads like this. All those cities around the world at once."

"Does if it was weaponized." Ethan's tone chills her.

"If they made it? It means a cure is possible." Becky flusters her thoughts as she considers the fate of the diary author.

"If it was something out of nature then maybe it's just our time. The planet finding a way to restore balance to herself."

"Like that M. Night Shyamalan movie with the plants killing people," Becky says.

"Something along those lines. I know I can do nothing about the cause. I doubt knowing the cause changes anything, but human curiosity does demand answers."

CHAPTER FIFTY-NINE

BEYOND TRAINING, DANZIGER has never been in the position he has placed dozens of perpetrators—on his knees with fingers laced on top of his head. Next to him, armed gunmen shove a shirtless Tony to his knees. His lip bleeds. They gave up without a struggle. Hindsight reveals shooting their way out was the correct choice. At the moment, the three trucks rolled up he thought better of speaking with the survivors than shooting. He knew they were lost. Too far east of the city. Helping the girl and her dog brought them too far south.

"What to do with these three?" Kaleb Bowlin whaps a metal poker into his left hand.

Men drag tree branches and broken lumber forming a tent of wood. Once completed, they build a fire in the center of the cylindrical pyramid.

"They had military-issued equipment." Garth holds up an olive bandoleer.

"Makes you wonder, Kaleb, if they know someone...someone who visited a military base recently."

"They don't smell too bad neither." Garth sniffs at a tuft of Kelsey's hair. "She's had a shampoo." He shoves her to her knees on the other side of Danziger. They patted down all three of them removing all weapons. The man seemed to take a little long inspecting her.

"Tie him down, naked," Kaleb orders, pointing the poker at Tony. The men jerk Tony to his feet.

Danziger protests, "Just take our gear. We have no quarrel with you. We're just scavenging for supplies like every survivor."

"We're doing more than scavenging. Your gear bags are all military issue and brand new. You haven't even snagged one on a fence yet." Kaleb waves the backpack in Danziger's face. "If you weren't at Fort Wood—you know someone who left there with truckloads of supplies."

Danziger has no idea what these men are searching for; if he did, he might be able to save his team.

The men hog tie Tony leaving his unclothed rump in the air.

Garth waves a paper sheathed in a plastic sleeve before Danziger. "So you know this man."

Danziger shows no reaction. Kelsey doesn't burst out an answer, but her surprised glance reveals she recognizes the image.

Kaleb whaps his hand with the metal rod. "Now, I know if I ask you, you'll lie out of loyalty to you master. You may not even know he murdered my brother. But you do know his current whereabouts. The question is how much pain must be endured before I believe your answer?"

"Do what you want. We won't tell you." Kelsey's resistance confirms she knows the image.

"I'm not starting with you." Kaleb draws the poker into a batting stance and smashes Tony's hams.

Even if he wanted to, Tony's unable to hold in a scream.

Garth draws his index and middle finger through her soft hair. "I know you promised your new bride we'd no longer rape, but some of the boys—"

"No. I gave my word to my queen." Kaleb drops the poker's pointed end into the campfire.

"I'm sure she meant only women," Garth says.

"Garth, I had no idea you enjoyed buggery."

"Not me, but of couple of the men did serve time and wouldn't mind trying a little black ass."

400 MILES TO GRACELAND

"Fuck you, cracker mother fuckers." Tony squirms but his bonds are too tight.

"What do you want to know? Just let them go and I'll tell you," Danziger offers.

Kaleb waves the drawing. "Where is this man?"

"I don't know," Danziger spits.

Kaleb snaps his fingers. His minions twist Danziger's neck, forcing him to view Tony.

"I'll torture your friends until you tell me, and I believe you. You get to watch. All nice and safe."

Garth hands Kaleb bolt cutters. "They say the threat of torture is more traumatic than the actual pain inflicted." He slips the jaws over one of Tony's finger's and crimps it off.

Tony's shrills cause to Danziger drops his eyes.

"Fuck you, cracker-ass mother fucker," he blubbers. Blood squirts in three quicks burst then dribbles out.

Without a word, Kaleb stirs the fire with the poker he placed in it. He removes the red hot top, searing closed the bleeding appendage.

Tony's shrieks turn to whimpers of pain. "My younger brother is a college nerd and book read. Not me. I never read much, but I did like reading about the Vlad Tepes dude. He like to impale his enemies. It would be a slow death and unstoppable. I doubt you'd talk knowing you'll die no matter what. The only reprieve I would offer would be a quick death." Kaleb sticks the cooling poker back into the fire.

"We don't know where he is at," Kelsey confirms.

"My brother, may he rest in peace, loved to inflict pain. I ask you again, where is the man who killed him!"

The only answer is Tony's blubbering.

"You know what's coming, don't you, girl. Your friend, he can't. He's just glad he not having a bus parked in his ass by my men. He knows we're cooking up something. He might want death. He'll beg for it. You tell me where my brother's killer is and I'll strip the three of you and leave you tied to a tree. You might escape."

"Fuck you!" Kelsey says.

He pulls out the white-hot metal. "Last chance." Kaleb touches the poker to the wrinkled skin of Tony's manhood.

Kelsey hears only the searing of meat like the time she dropped a frozen pork chop onto a hot skillet. Bile swills in her mouth and stomach acid burns her nose. Burt hair overwhelms her followed by the aroma of cooking meat. No matter how many people she's has seen die in the past few months pleading for help, the guttural sounds from Tony are the worst.

"Tell me where the man who killed my brother is." Kaleb rubs his bewhiskered chin. "What's your name, boy?"

Tony's defiance comes in a whimper, "Fuck you."

"What loyalty do you have to this man? He just cost you your balls."

Sizzling fat cooks under the charring flesh as he rolls the poker along Tony's backside.

Sometime during the screams, Tony passes out.

"Which one of you wants it next? If I were you, I'd be shitting myself wondering how much fire hurts." Kaleb jabs the poker back into the fire. "Tell me. I'll tie you to the tree and leave you. I'll tie up so you'll be able to work yourself free. No one will ever know you told me. Everyone will just think the infected got your leader."

Stoic Danziger and Kelsey refuse to answer.

"Strip the girl," he orders. "We'll see if he can stand her pretty skin burning."

As the men enjoy tugging and jerking at Kelsey's clothes, she breaks free. Danziger uses the momentary distraction to lunge at the captors. He knocks one down. Quickly overwhelmed, the men beat and club him until blood flows from his nose.

Dragging Kelsey by her hair, Kaleb flings her against the truck bed. He pins her with his full body weight. He controls his urge to smash her face. Letting loose his frustration for an answer in six kidney punches to her abdomen.

He flips her to the ground.

Kelsey has no struggle left.

Kaleb pulls on a heavy work glove before withdrawing the poker.

"Where is the man who murdered my brother?" Not giving time for her to answer, he whacks Kelsey across her back, kicks her over to flop flat on her back. "We play a game. I hit you back-front, back-front until you talk."

Kelsey's arms pull away from her shoulder sockets as her toes scrape the dirt searching for a surface to balance on. The burn welts refuse to allow her skin to stretch as it did before. If she could just get some leverage, she could pull herself up and work the rope knot. Warm liquid flows down her legs. The releasing pressure burns. She forces herself to glance down. A yellow-red pool puddled at her feet. She does have red pee.

Despite the pain, she should have held her pee. She'll need water soon. Once the mid-morning sun moves beyond the branch, she'll cook in the sun.

Kaleb kept his word—all three of them are alive—now he knows where Ethan travels. A man who saved her life—betrayed.

If she doesn't work free, her life will end with her dying of exposure, dehydration, or a passing biter.

Even if she does escape, they have no supplies, clothes, weapons, or medical attention. She doubts Tony will be able to move and she hasn't the strength to carry him. Even if her arms weren't dislocated under her hanging weight.

Even after Kaleb gained his information, he beat Danziger. She spots no movement from either of her companions.

Mid-afternoon sun and her white flesh has moved from pink in spots to full blown red.

If she doesn't twitch, her arms don't hurt.

Snarls.

Instinctually, she whips her head toward the moan-howl. Muscles twinge, bind, locking her head to the side as her body betrays her. Part of her wants to give up. Just let the monster take her. The part of her wanting to live and save her friends consumes her. She twists until she spots the gray mound of flesh shambling toward her. With any luck, he's a loner.

Everything she does in the next second will make her an old woman physically if she lives. Blood drips from her bindings as she lifts herself into the air, dropping her calf muscles onto the creature's shoulders. She locks her feet together keeping one leg under its jaw preventing a bite. She does sink into the gooey wet warm compost of flesh. Her body enjoys the release of pressure from being suspending for hours, but she has no time to relax. The crumpled undead body works as a step-stool allowing her to reach the branch with her fingers. She climbs into the tree avoiding teeth on her naked flesh.

"Danziger," she calls as loud as she dares. "Tony." As Kelsey works the knot lose, the branch cracks. She yelps as the branch cracks enough to dump her feet off the biter step-stool. She summons enough force to kick the creature's chest. A footprint imprints on its rotten pectoral muscle.

It claws at her.

"Hey! Fuck bag," Danziger screams at the monster.

More interested in the new noise, it lumbers away from Kelsey.

Forced to witness one last torture, Kelsey chomps her bottom lip to stifle her impotence as the creature face plants into Danziger's chest taking out a hunk of skin. He has no screams left or he keeps them back not wanting to draw anymore undead. Soon he will find an end to his pain.

The branch snaps as Kelsey works the knot loose. It falls, tree bark scraping her in a dozen places. The worst was the sharp splinters drawing across the fresh burns.

One habit of the dead is never finishing a large meal. Her fall draws the creatures toward her over the immovable feast. The biter claws at her but hasn't the reach to grab her before she slips her bound wrists over the end of the splintered branch. She flips the heavy branch over using it as ballast to knock the creature down. Once on its back, she lifts the end of the branch up, crashing it against the biter's skull three times before it caves in enough to kill it.

With careful skill, she grinds the rope against the monster's teeth, working frays into her bindings. Once free, she lies in the grass, her body refusing to move.

When muscle control returns to her, she calls out. "Danziger, are you alive?"

"I don't have much choice in the matter."

"You don't. When I move again—"

"You need to move before I turn. Where's Tony?"

Something crawls though the warm blood of her scratches. Insects march over her naked body. Kelsey works up onto her elbows.

Hemorrhaging blood covers Danziger like a robe from the chest down. The bite festers. "I hear Tony's breathing slowing."

Kelsey raises enough to survey the empty campsite—nothing. It takes her ten more minutes to get to her knees. Being barefoot or running around inside in socks is not the same as being outside in a field. The brutalization leaves her weak and her feet haven't built up calluses to withstand the impact of hard ground. Her muscles ache. Her skin hurts. Her thighs hurt. She must pee again.

She holds it.

"I don't want to be one of those things," Danziger begs.

Kelsey wants to curl up and cry. She has had everything taken from her and now she must kill a friend—maybe two—three. Ethan. She has murdered Ethan as well.

It takes all the strength she has left in her arm to tear free the thickest green branch off the branch she was tied to. It doesn't have enough heft for her purpose. She crawls to the remains of the fire. The only evidence of the attackers having been there—other than the burns on her chest and back. She drags a charred fence rail. It has the weight she desires.

Each step stings her feet. She's never been one for going shoeless. "Danziger?"

"Don't...don't let me become one of those things."

"You know what you ask?" She raises the board. Bringing it down with all her weight and energy she cracks it against the side of his skull splitting the ear open.

Danziger bites his lip.

Kelsey raises the board again. She slams it against his skull three times. Danziger still breathes, never calling out. Not wanting to leave her with guilt for her merciful actions.

She clubs Danziger more times than she counts until she breaks open his skull. She collapses on top of his lifeless body.

Kelsey's own finger raw from gripping the board, she has no choice but to crawl on her elbows to the tree where Tony's bound.

"I don't know how to cut you free."

"I don't know if I'll ever walk again," his voice now is high pitched.

"I won't leave you." She breaks down next to him.

"We need water and shelter and weeks in rehab. I need a burn unit. You..."

"You're not a medic." Just hold me. She nuzzles against him.

"You need to untie me."

"I need to just—" Kelsey whimpers without tears. "I just bludgeoned Danziger to death. It wasn't quick or painless like all the head shots I make. Kaleb needs to pay for every blow he forced on me."

"We haven't the luxury of comfort. If I'm going to live, I need to move. You need to move. We're going to stiffen and we need water," Tony scolds her.

"He should have killed us. Now I have to live with knowing I sold out our people." Ants crawl over her ankles.

"The camp wasn't sold out. Just Ethan. Even if they don't locate him on the way to Memphis, the camp will be safe."

"First, water. Shelter. Tomorrow do we go after Kaleb?" She works her bleeding fingers into the rope knot securing Tony.

"I need medical help. We lack the ability to travel. We're going to die," Tony says.

"If we go after Kaleb at least we die trying to correct betrayal."

"I wanted the pain to stop. I prayed we'd tell before he burnt me. It's on all of us."

She releases the knot. "I won't be much of a crutch."

He lies on his side, "I'm telling you, girl. I can't walk. You're going to have to go on alone."

Kelsey crawls close. The backs of both Tony's legs have been melted to the bone.

CHAPTER SIXTY

"CHAD, WHAT DID you do before?" Becky asks.

"Worked at the lumberyard. Stupid aspirations of saving money for college. I was never going to go. I'm not sure I wanted to, but if you didn't go right after school you were working to go. I felt better to say than I don't have any idea what to do with my life. Everyone thought I should make something of myself, but no one offered any real ideas."

"I didn't get much direction, either," Becky agrees. "Dental assistant school was my goal." She smiles.

"I played football, but not good enough for college. Grades were average. Some days I considered the military. There just wasn't any guidance on which direction to take in life."

"There never was," Ethan says.

"You're some kind of genus. You know so much."

"Near genius, but I never felt school gave me any guidance, either. I just had an idea of what I wanted to do."

"What was that?"

"Nice try. I know about the betting pool on my past career." Ethan smiles.

"Didn't I see that in a movie?" Becky asks.

"I'm sure if you watch enough films you'll encounter most of life's scenarios. Writers take from real life. Many from events they experience or witnessed. Sometimes things happen in real life you can't make up. Human survival is no new concept. The struggle to overcome never changes just the obstacles." Ethan halts, drawing his .357.

Becky unsheathes both her machetes. She's never known Ethan to draw the shiny weapon he uses to distract his enemies while he quick-draws his Berretta.

A lioness charges Ethan.

Before his brain asks how there is a lion in Missouri, his .357 booms eight thunderous detonations.

The Berretta sends seven more shots into the wild, African-born beast before the smoking magnum bounces on the pavement. The creature dies as it slides, still barreling toward him, skittering to a halt inches before it could leap and bring Ethan down.

"It's like running into Bill Murray in central Park—no one's going to believe this." He scoops up his magnum, flipping open the cylinder. He pockets the still smoking empty cartages.

"You just killed a fucking lion."

"Need a change of underwear?" Becky asks.

"Yeah." He drinks from his canteen. Ethan loads his magnum. "Must have escaped from a zoo or one of the several tiger sanctuaries in the state.

"That was a lion." Shock freezes Chad.

"They take in all big cats. Took my daughters once." He places a fresh clip in his Berretta and holsters the .357. Drawing a knife, he approaches the fallen beast. "She looks well fed. I wonder why she attacked us."

"That...was...a lion," Chad's brain stammers on one thought.

"Snap out of it," Becky scolds.

Chad swings his rifle from his shoulder, ready to fire in case the beast still breathes. "What the fuck are you doing?"

"I never believed in hunting for trophies. Food, yes, sport if the meat gets eaten. But never for trophies. It's wrong. But I just killed a lion. I want proof. We're too far from home to take the hide. I'll take a claw and we'll see what lion steaks taste like tonight."

"You're going to eat it." Becky face squints, grossed by the thought.

"I won't have killed it for nothing."

A horse bolts from the tree line. It gallops past at full speed. The shrills of birds pierce the air as flocks fill the sky in droves large enough to blot out the sun.

Ethan sheathes the blade.

"What the fuck's going on?" Chad raises his rifle to draw a bead on the buck bursting from the trees.

"Move!" Ethan races to the barbed wire fence protecting a field.

More deer—does, bucks and fawns charge past then leap the fence.

Ethan smashes down the top row of rusted wire and leaps into the field. His companions follow.

"What the fuck!"

Chasing the deer, a black bear sprints down the road. It mashes through the wire.

Ethan run-hop-steps away from all the trees around the field.

"Tell me what happening," Becky demands.

Cattle trot following the bear. More forest creatures. Foxes, squirrels, opossums, raccoons, deer whisk by bolting past animals that should be eating each other now move with a new-found brotherhood.

"You're not going to like the answer."

Dozens of dogs—most domesticated—dash by chased by hundreds of cats. The meows are nearly as deafening as the fainting bird squawks. Trailing the pack are thousands of rats and mice. They skitter at full speed. Chad hops from foot to foot eluding the gray river flowing past. The rodents take no notice of them, leaving the three to stand in a field of perfect calm. No squeaks or squawks, a moo or a whinny, and a bit of breeze to rustle a leaf.

Perfect stillness.

Ethan finds himself face down in the grass. The thunderous rattle of dozens of big trucks shakes them—only no passing trucks. The ground rolls like a wave cresting for a surfer then slams into the beach. Ethan and his companions are tossed into the air. They land on still shaking dirt. Becky crashes on top of Ethan.

Limbs snap.

Trees fall.

The cracking of a million eggs fills the air. The rumbling slows. As the jarring nears its end, a fireball fills the distant horizon.

Ethan counts.

When they finally hear the pop of the explosions he calculates that its more than twenty miles off.

The rubbles subside.

Ethan staggers to his feet.

"Was that—"

"Without a seismograph, I don't know, but I'm guessing that the last time anyone felt an earthquake like that in this state, church bells rang in Canada and the Mississippi ran backwards for eight hours."

CHAPTER SIXTY-ONE

ALL THREE DOGS in Acheron howl.
    Wanikiya dries his hand on a dish towel, stepping from the kitchen in time to witness all the horses bolting across the field.
    "What's the matter with the animals?" Nina asks.
    Wanikiya grabs her, pulling Nina away from the building. Before he drags her under the metal framed picnic table, the ground shivers.
    "What's..." Nina never finishes her question.
    The ground shakes. A car alarm blears in the distance. Muffled screams echo over the rumble.
    Wanikiya lost count holding on to the table, but no more than twelve seconds transpired. "Stay out of the building."
    Inside his kitchen, all pots and pans decorate the floor. *Thankfully, the food plates are plastic. Power remains on for the moment. First chance I get the dam gets a full inspection. The frogman gets to earn his keep.* Wanikiya flips off the stove burner before snagging the two radios from their cradles, maneuvering past the scattered mess.
    Nina emerges from the picnic table. "Why can't we go back inside? People have to be hurt."
    "They are." He raises the radio mic to his mouth. Before pressing the talk button, he adds, "Stay out here. There are bound to be aftershocks. Aftershocks kill more people than the initial quake." He speaks into the radio. "This is Wanikiya. Status report."

Resonating beeps chirp back as everyone seems to answer at once. Wanikiya accepts his mistake and orders, "Listen. Front gate report."

"We seem to be intact."

"Good. Open and shut the gates make sure they remain on their tracks. Stay off and away from any structure that could slip in an aftershock. Send a patrol to inspect the fence line. Breaches are a current priority. Dam report?"

"We've are inspecting the dam and cutting back generator power."

"Proceed." Wanikiya defers to the judgment of those engineers, but he knows those listening on the radios need everything to be under control. "Dam security?"

"No breaches. Already inspecting our fence line," Zeke responds.

"Affirmative. All farm hands and fence builders. Report to the community center. Bring any wounded. We'll organize inspections teams and account for everyone in the camp. Don't get cocky, people. Our fences have held, but a falling book case could have injured someone." Wanikiya hesitates, but he must warn his people, "Prepare for aftershocks. "

"What do we do here?" Nina asks

"We've never had a preparedness plan for this. The world ended and biters became the only natural disaster of consequence. We forgot about Nature and our relationship to the Great Spirit."

"I need to do something. People are hurt and I'm standing here." Nina fidgets.

"We get the census and evacuate this building. We need a check point to account for everyone."

"Bet we have a plan for the next disaster," she attempts humor, but still fidgets.

"Preparations for a harsh winter was underway."

"I don't want to imagine if this has occurred with two feet of snow on the ground," her fidgeting increases.

Emily stumbles out the door. A gash in her forehead drips blood. "I have to check on Dartagnan. He will be in full panic."

"Did you hit your head?" a question Wanikiya knows he'll be asking frequently.

"The counter, I think."

He escorts the teen to the picnic table. "I'll send a recovery team there first."

"He doesn't deal well with anyone else since Ethan's gone. Even Sanchez is outside the fence." Blood dribbles down the side of her face.

"You sit here. I'll get Dr. Baker to clear you and we'll get you to Dartagnan."

Wanikiya closes his eyes and draws in the deepest breath possible. Holding it, he accepts as leader he must protect his people. Fences are first. However, earthquakes turn animals wonky. He never studied the sciences beyond basic classes, and none of them would have a chapter on undead during a tremor, but earthquakes create noise and destroy structures creating more noise. The biters will be in more of a panic than any of his people.

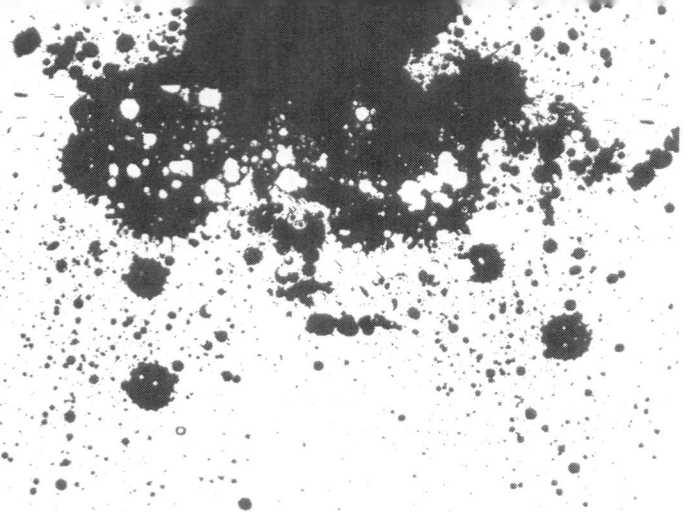

CHAPTER SIXTY-TWO

"HOW DID YOU get so lucky to get a room, Sanchez?" Private Combeth loads the belt into the 50-caliber machinegun atop the Humvee.

"What do you mean?" Amie asks. She scans the field through binoculars.

"Only a few of the soldiers got assigned actual rooms. The rest are housed in the gym at the bottom of the waiting list for private bedrooms. We're behind all those people already living here."

"I don't know. It was a single room."

"This is your second mission you're commanding. What's your secret?" Combeth asks.

"I'm not spreading my legs if that's what you're wondering," Amie snaps.

"Maybe you should. That Ethan cat runs this place. He's a fucking god to these people," he says.

She touches her chest at the top of her cleavage. The silver cross given to her during her Quinceañera remains under her uniform. "Don't blaspheme."

"I forgot you're a holy roller," says Combeth.

"I've faith. In these end times, we all should turn to God." She never pushes her faith on anyone but it seems good advice.

"The dead walking around is a great indication God split."

"It's all part of his plans." Amie hides her concern that this is no longer true. No God would create monsters to eat children.

"Was it part of His plan for you to get a bed while the rest of us have a fart saturated cot? Hell, the training barracks were more private than the gym. And smelt better."

"You want my room you're welcome to it, but I thought they separated some of us as part of their procedures. From the few people I've spoken with who've arrived in larger groups they separated them."

"To what purpose?" Combeth asks.

"Prevent infiltration of some group who would want to take over."

"I know guarding a hayfield is a bit soft duty, but this place is a paradise. With Fort Wood gone this is the only stronghold left west of the Mississippi."

"We got spoiled at Fort Wood. And we must be the only place left in the state still with electric power. People will do anything to have access," she says.

"I guess I've guarded worse than a bunch of hay cutting tractors."

"I'd rather be traveling to Memphis to recover the Major's brother." Amie waves to the Humvee across the field.

A tractor engine fires up. Backing off a flatbed trailer as soon as it rolls into the field the sickle drops and grass stalks fall.

"We've got noise. Be ready. It's not *if* it draws the undead—it's when and how many," She hopes that sounded like she was in total control of her command.

"I'm on it." Combeth swings the 50-Cal to get a better view of the tree line. "I'm not convinced the radio message was real. Fort Leonard Wood was the last bastion of military strength. Without it, I've no idea how the country will ever be taken from the dead."

"The military was not finished. Didn't the Colonel speak to you about this assignment?" Amie asks.

"I was given a choice of no room on the helicopters or the need to protect valued survivors," Combeth says.

"The alternative was a destroyed base and teaming with those Bowlins."

"Stories about them was worse than dealing with the undead," he says.

"Colonel Travis provided this place with supplies and some troops before he stocked our convoy."

"The Colonel was too good a man. He should've stopped taking in survivors and the base would have held longer. He took in everybody. Too many mouths to feed. This place has the right idea. Which is why I'm guarding a tractor cutting hay," Combeth says.

"They bring in plenty of survivors," Amie says. "Still might need a better screening process. Levin killed four. One a nurse. Not many trained medical people left. Those people should be kept under guard."

"Doctors and bullets are the new gold," Combeth says. "Spend a night in the gym. You'll learn much about this place. A few weeks ago, a group of religious nuts tried to shoot their way in and the gate guards killed them all. Your hero, Ethan, rescued some women from some nut job who was keeping them prisoners. All three girls had both hands removed and all three *died*, one at a time on the trail back."

"Ethan killed them?" Amie asks.

"The story goes one fell off a cliff and one was murdered by some bikers. Who Ethan killed and didn't invite back."

The man I share a house with would not murder the helpless. "How true are those stories?"

"If I didn't hear the same versions from different people, I'd question their accuracy, but everyone tells the same version with little embellishment."

"We both witnessed Ethan's exploits. You know he needs no embellishment of his actions. If we survive as a species, his stories will become the new legends."

"I plan to live forever," says Combeth.

"Don't worry, I'll put a bullet in your slobbering corpse." Amie smiles.

"Eventually they should rot?"

"They don't. Even after the head shot the body's slow to decompose." Amie finds herself staring at clouds covered in stars.

She jerks the way she does when someone shoves her as if shaking her awake.

The ground moves.

"Earthquake!" Combeth screams.

"No shit." Amie uses the Humvee to steady herself as the Earth's vibrations quell. "We need to get the mowing team into the Humvees and return to Acheron. We'll come back for the tractors later."

"I don't think we should leave the equipment."

"We need to be inside the fence and now. There's never just one earthquake," Amie scolds.

"I don't think we're going anywhere." Combeth points.

Amie lifts her binoculars. Staggering over the horizon all in a line as if protesting the living are thousands of undead.

CHAPTER SIXTY-THREE

MIKE RAISES THE M16, peering down the barrel to sight in the limping rotter. Dirty and blood stained, the naked woman moves away from him. He considered the ramification of a single rifle shot. He decides she's not worth the noise and the other undead it will attract. Since she staggers away from him, catching her across the field just to end her misery is also a pointless exercise.

Something about her gait keeps his eye focused on her. The blood covering her seems dry—fresh. Her body lacks bites. Maybe she opted out. Took pills to end it because despite the contusions, her skin seems fresh as if she just died.

He lowers the weapon. *One's not worth any risk.* Mike shoulders his pack.

Snarls echo as two more undead shamble across the field. They head toward the naked rotter. He praises his choice in not firing. He knew there were more around.

There are always more around.

He ignores them, not wanting to draw more attention to himself when the naked undead runs away from the two approaching rotters.

Mike scans through his current choices. All of them tell him to help this woman despite his growing distrust of other survivors. She could be a trap, but for who. No one would be traveling these fields or not enough people to set a trap. He would bet she was well-supplied and stripped of all her gear, left for dead by scavengers. Maybe she was the scavenger and some group did to her what she was going to do to them?

Tom's group. They were good people. They just didn't understand what was going on. They made a choice to protect themselves but not at his expense. Too bad a group with those morals won't last. What of my morals? My oaths. I swore to protect the constitution from all enemies... These rotters are destroying the American way of life.

Oh, hell, someone needs help and even if I'm wrong I did what's right.

He unsheathes a M7 bayonet locking it into place on the M16. Tom's group was honorable enough not to take his gear. He charges from the tree stabbing the first undead in the chest knocking it back to the ground. He swings the rifle more like a club whacking off half the second creature's head. Goopy brains splatter the greening grass. The first rotter flop like a beached fish attempting to return to its feet. Mike drives the blade into the first rotter's face.

He shifts the weapon behind his back as he assumes a parade rest stance before the woman. "I won't hurt you."

"Everyone says so." She keeps a healthy distance from him.

"I'd don't know what else to say. Do you want my assistance?"

Kelsey faints.

Mike holds his weapon, ready to fire as he twists the doorknob to the farm house. *Country people still never lock their doors.* It creaks open. He sweeps in, clearing the ground floor rooms one by one. A door in the kitchen leads to the basement. He jabs a chair under the handle to wedge it secure.

Once the ground floor is clear, he carries the unconscious girl to the couch from the porch swing where he left her. He covers her with the knitted afghan. Before moving up the stairs, he marches back to the front door and twists the lock.

Once securing the house—minus the dark basement—Mike cleans the girl's wounds, careful around the burns. The wrinkled skin requires grafts to repair it. He doubts she'll ever be normal again. She has a massive contusion on her left side. A bruise surrounding a seared burn on her back matches a duplicate one across her stomach.

Mike finds his own flayed skin throbs as he examines this poor woman.

Her feet are the worst. The rough terrain shredded the soles. She'll need to be able to walk if she is to live. She needs fluids too. I don't have any idea... Do I pour it down her throat?

After cleaning and dressing all her cuts, he covers her with a sheet, tucking it in around her, then lays a quilt over the top. He camps out in the stiff high-back chair, rifle across his lap. Kicking his boots off, Mike drifts off.

God, I hope she doesn't die in her sleep.

The orange sun splashing on the woman's face gives her a death glow. Her blankets rise and fall with each breath. Knowing she's alive relaxes him until his bladder cramps. The shadows growing across the floor inform Mike he's been asleep and now dusk creeps up on him.

He shoulders the M16 and sneaks to the porch. He undoes his fly to water the bushes. As the pressure leaves his crotch, Mike considers doing a sweep around the house. The dark soon will be pitch. Not like in the movies. This night he will have no visibility, and if he does ignite his flashlight, the beam will cut through the darkness alerting anyone living to his location. Better to hunker down and rest.

He wonders about the girl and who bushwhacked her. As he cleaned her, she didn't appear to be sexually violated. Why not just kill her? Stripping her of everything was as good as killing her. And when she does die then it's one more rotter to deal with. At some time, their numbers should be depleted.

Mike returns to his vigilant watch over the woman. *Until I figure out otherwise, I'll see she lives. I've got nothing better to do. Fort Wood remains my best option. The base isn't gone.*

Mike jerks awake. At first, the moans forming under the blankets bring his rifle to bear on the shifting mass, but he quickly lowers it as her cries are of a nightmare. He scoops the squirming girl up and sits on the couch so her head rests on his lap. He strokes her hair, lulling her back to a calming sleep. He doubts her cries aroused a rotter, but continual screams might.

Birds chirp as the sun rises. Mike never appreciated the noise so much as one signaling he remains among the living. Birds are also a strong indication no undead are around and certainly no living people are within range of the house. No matter how stealthy a person is, birds will flee.

As he lifts the woman's head up in order move his tingling leg, her eyes flash open.

"I won't hurt you."

She struggles against the tight sheet tucked in around her. Mike lays her head back down, fleeing to the chair. The quick movement breaks open his own healing wound. Warm wet drops dribble down his side. He notes the position of his M16. "Take your time. I'll just stay over here."

As she draws her arm up to escape the blanket, Kelsey finds bandages covering her flesh. "You cared for me?"

Mike nods. He should change his own dressings.

"Why?"

"Short answer—I'm still a decent person."

"Water?"

Mike reaches into his pack withdrawing a canteen. He stretches out his arm, keeping his body off balance and at a distance—least threatening as possible.

"I don't have much food. A few power bars," he offers.

She holds the water in her mouth letting the liquid soak into her cheek and tongue.

"Cottonmouth?"

She nods meaning "thank you."

"There are clothes upstairs. Whoever lived here didn't take much...but the food."

She induces needle stabs in her legs with just a movement of an inch. "I'm not sure I'm ready for stairs. How long have I been out?"

"I found you yesterday afternoon."

"I'll have lost the trail. I lost my friends. I lost the mission." She rattles her list, delirious with guilt.

"You were chasing something—I thought you were escaping."

Kelsey considers what information to reveal. Plenty of people will help her to learn about Acheron. "My group sent us out to scavenge for supplies. We encountered marauders. My leader killed their leader when Fort Wood was destroyed."

Somehow, of all she said, the only fact registering with Mike is Fort Wood is *gone*.

"Are you not listening to me?" Kelsey asks.

"Sorry...wow... My plan was to reach Fort Wood. Now I don't know what do in life," Mike sulks.

"If I had the energy, I'd scream at you for being so self-centered."

"What happened at the base? So many people are still trying to reach it."

"The military blew it up," Kelsey explains.

Minutes, maybe ten, transpire before Mike accepts what the woman says, "No way the military would give up a stronghold to the undead."

"Check for yourself. You won't find anything but charred structures. Anything left was looted by the civilians who they left behind."

"It was our job to protect the innocent when I was in the service. Something else had to have driven them off base."

"Believe or don't. I have to catch up with the men who left me for dead." Kelsey pushes up off the couch. As soon as she puts weight on her swollen feet, agony skirts up into her calves. She collapses. "Hurts."

Mike lifts her legs into the air to remove the pressure.

"Fuck me." Her burns radiate more pain through her.

"You won't be able to walk for days," Mike says. "I don't know how you got as far as you did. If you came from the base."

"I didn't. My team was ambushed. We headed toward St Louis to scout for supplies."

"It's too dangerous the closer you get. Now with Fort Wood gone I don't know where is safe." Mike's mind fogs.

"Dude, you gotta break out of this. My feet—too bad to walk. I need you to help me reach my leader," Kelsey commands.

"You want me to carry you?" Mike asks.

"Find a car. Drive me to Memphis."

"Girl, you're crazy."

"I have to warn Ethan. The Bowlin brothers know his destination."

Before Mike inquires further, the windows blow out. Kelsey drops to the floor as the house shakes. Mike dives toward the door. Cracks form in the walls as the convulsions quicken. The front porch collapses.

The fluctuations calm even as the building still sways.

"What the fuck? An Earthquake in Missouri?"

"The New Madrid fault is the largest. I just didn't think we'd feel it this far north." Mike gets to his feet as the house continues to quiver. "We need to get outside; this house wasn't designed—"

Thunderous cracks deafen the pair in the half second before the first floor collapses.

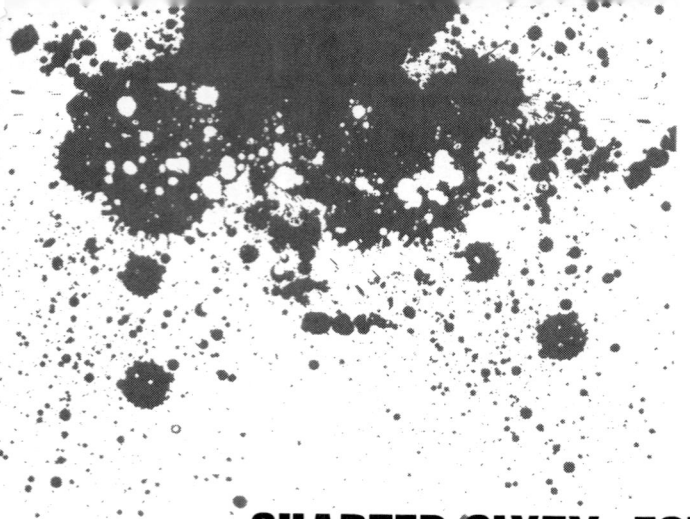

CHAPTER SIXTY-FOUR

ETHAN FLATTENS HIS palm against the ground. Rumbles like when his stomach growls permeating through his fingers. The vibration reminds him how the living planet plans to evict the remaining humans.

"Should we go back?" Chad asks.

"Memphis is closer," Ethan reasons.

Becky paces in circles. "What are we going to do?"

"We're going to remain calm."

"Going to be more aftershocks," she says.

"There's going to be a lot more, and crazy animals and biters, but if you don't keep your head about you then you're going to get hurt."

Her agitation accelerates. "We can't even go through buildings. They might fall on us."

"What do you want to do with her, Boss?" Chad asks

"Let her spazz out for a minute. Get it out of her system."

"Boss, I'm terrified," Chad admits.

"You start that shit and I'll punch you in the face. If you think I'm not bothered by this then you're crazy, but we must keep a cool head. There's no National Guard to bring us water and no Red Cross to pass out blankets. It's less than a hundred miles to Memphis and three hundred back. We go on. We find the Major's brother and maybe a vaccine."

Becky falls to the ground. She rocks on her butt. Her arms wrapped around her freshly-skinned knees.

Shit.

Blood. Cleaned her up. Ethan kneels before the girl. "Becky. You had your moment. We got to clean you up and move on."

She glances at him as if she were five and realized all adults have lied about Santa Clause. "Everyone's dead. Everything's gone." Tears stream down her cheeks. "I didn't get to say goodbye to any of my family. I didn't get to bury them. Nobody has fed my dog. He was an inside dog. Nobody let him out to even try and fend for himself. What are we doing? Why? Why are we even trying to go on?"

"Chad, scout the area." He opens a small first-aid pack for camper. "I don't have those answers. I go on because I'm not ready to quit."

She watches him tear open an alcohol pad to brush over her scrapes. She flinches but doesn't jerk away "Where are your kids?"

"What?"

"You treat us a lot like children...like you *had* children." An epiphany washes over her about the house with the grave under the swing set.

He covers the scrapes in Band-Aids.

She enunciates each word. "You protect us like your kids."

He struggles to get back to his feet. He winces from the knee pain but says nothing.

"When you go out, are you making amends for failing to save them?"

"Someone of lesser calm would smack you across the face for that. If I were to lose control you wouldn't have to worry about brushing anymore." Ethan meets with her brown eyes. "When I found the emergency evacuation point, it had been overrun."

"There were no clues in the house we searched?"

"Maybe not. But until I bury the other one, she is out there," Ethan says.

Becky understands why Ethan always scavenges for supplies. Always gone. Forever searching for his child.

He puts his hand flat against the ground, reminded of western films where they put an ear to the ground to learn of approaching horses. Detecting movement, Ethan announces, "Are not you moved, when all the sway of earth shakes like a thing unfirm? O Cicero, I have seen tempests, when the scolding winds have rived the knotty oaks, and I have seen the ambitious ocean swell and rage and foam, to be exalted with the threatening clouds: But never till to-night, never till now, Did I go through a tempest dropping fire. Either there is a civil strife in heaven, Or else the world, too saucy with the gods, incenses them to send destruction."

"You speak the speech," Becky says. "Shakespeare?"

Ethan continues, "I met a lion, who glared upon me, and went surly by, Without annoying me: and there were drawn upon a heap a hundred ghastly women, Transformed with their fear; who swore they saw Men all in fire walk up and down the streets."

"Were you an actor?" She calculates only a stage actor would quote Shakespeare.

"Because I know lines from *Julius Caesar*. You should've paid more attention to the words." Ethan marches to the king of beasts.

Becky keeps her finger near the trigger of her weapon. "How did you know an earthquake was about to happen?"

"I sure didn't when this lion charged us." He guts the creature. "She wasn't attacking she was fleeing. And we were in her way."

"But you knew. You got us away from all these trees. If they had fallen—"

"I grew up here. Not far south enough to detect the New Madrid fault all the time. But when we did it was like a big truck speeding too close to the house. Shook the dust off some light fixtures. What I've seen is horses dart across the field nearly leaping the fences to get away from the rumble that followed." He slices the hind quarters of the lioness. Not sure the proper technique to skin a lion, he treats it much like he would a deer.

"You're still going to eat that lion?"

"Yes. It would bother me to waste the carcass completely. It will stretch our food out for a meal and I've a feeling it's going to be harder to scrounge for supplies. I don't know the magnitude, but as strong as it felt, it leveled building and damaged gas lines setting the countryside aflame.

"How do you stay so calm?"

"Panic gets us nowhere." He drops chunks of red meat strips into a gallon Ziploc baggie. "Since we don't have a cooler we should find someplace to cook this soon. How much do you think you can eat?"

"I don't know that I can."

Ethan cracks a handful of twigs, sprinkling the pieces in the barbeque grill of the roadside park.

Chad carries a bundle of wood wrapped in plastic. "The roadside bait-shop has some campfire wood for sale. This was the least rotten." He drops it next to the grill. He removes a plastic bag dangling from his belt. "I thought this might serve."

"Hickory chips?"

"For the smoke flavor." Chad smiles.

"Anything useful in the building?" Ethan arranges the twigs.

"It had twisted off its foundation like a mashed cardboard box."

"Without any aftershocks, yet, I don't know how were going to sleep. I've a constant buzz every time I stand still. Thought I was going to fall over when I pissed," Ethan adds.

"I didn't go too far into the building," Chad admits.

"Science says there will be days of aftershocks. There has to be with a quake so large." He sprinkles some silver metal flakes from a baggie onto the pyramid of twigs. Ethan lights a match and the magnesium shaving flash and fire consumes the twigs. "We're going to have to be careful of every house and building we go into from now on."

"Do you think Acheron felt it?"

Ethan peels the bark from some larger twigs so the wood fibers catch fire easier. After he places a piece of the campfire wood on the flames, he takes out his map from inside his vest. "I've been trying not to, but yeah. They should inspect the fence and watch the power plant. All they can do."

"I'm ready to go on." Becky emerges from the trees. Calmer. She seals a toilet paper roll into a plastic baggie shoving into her pack. She spritzes hand sanitizer onto her fingers and rubs it in. "I vote we go back."

"I vote it's time for a boat ride," Chad says. He picks up the baggie containing the lion meat. Had he not known what it was, he doubts he would know the difference from beef.

Ethan skewers some meat cubes onto a sharpened stick. "It'd take a week or longer to go back—a lot longer if certain bridges are damaged. If they haven't got the camp secure by then we'll be of no help."

"But they are our family," Becky says.

"You want to explain to Major Ellsberg how we were miles from his brother and turned around?" Ethan examines the blacking meat before biting into a cube and pulling it his mouth.

Chad waits for Ethan to completely masticate. "How does it taste?"

"Like chewy pork." Ethan slips another cube onto the stick. "Now this is total guess work, but if you follow the main interstate you cut right above New Madrid. The town's located on the fault line we felt. Damage will be the worst there."

"We already avoid populated areas," Becky says. "Why go there?"

"Noise attacks them. I wonder if the epicenter of the quake will?" Ethan ponders.

"You want us to march into a town where the undead will gather into an army. No fuck'n way." Chad slams the meat bag down.

"Easily distracted or not they have a herd mentality. If a large enough group moves toward the epicenter, a few stragglers who watch a building fall over won't matter." Ethan slides another piece of wood on the fire.

"The earthquake could draw the largest herd ever seen together," Chad says.

"And we're heading right for it."

CHAPTER SIXTY-FIVE

NICK PARKS SIMON'S Jeep before the barn fully converted into a functioning stable. Someone in their wisdom made a fancy sign above the door: The Bridle Suite. He wonders how many will get the pun.

Spotting Hannah brushing her mount after the day's ride, he creeps into the barn, inching close to her without announcing his entrance.

He gets right behind her and tickles her right above her hips. She startles slapping him across the cheek with the brush.

"You're lucky I don't have a gun."

"Sorry." Nick massages the red spot.

Hannah rubs her horse's neck to calm her after the shriek startled the normally calm creature. "I don't know if sneaking up on people anymore is such a good idea. Had I a knife you'd have an extra orifice."

"I missed you." He leans in, placing his lips on hers, reaching around and placing a hand on her butt cheek—squeezing.

She pushes him away. "First, find a mint. Second, my ass is sore from riding all day,"

"Then maybe you need someone to massage it." He flashes her a conjugal smile.

"After you find a mint." She hugs him. "I've missed you."

He caresses the top of her left shoulder. It melts her against him.

"Did you have a good day?" he asks, focusing his attention away from the tingle growing in his pants.

"I think I rode half of Acheron today. Did you know they are constructing a cave—shelter. I guess."

"No." He reaches down, careful with his touch, sliding his hands along her thighs picking her into the air by them. He carries her into a stall, his lips on her neck. She manipulates her fingers through his dark hair.

He kisses down her neck to the cleft of her knit jersey top. He kneels, placing her on the ground as gently as possible while keeping his balance. He doesn't stop stimulating her. Giving her a second to protest and she might have him stop. The last thing he wants to do. Once she is safely on the ground his hands move up her body. One on top of her cupping a breast while the other fishes under the shirt then a bra cup. No matter how soft her skin the tender breast is even softer. He finds himself at full salute as he pushes up the top to find two budding breasts with pink nipples. He got this far once before.

She relented.

He respected her.

His mouth clamps on the tiny nipple.

Hooves smash and kick at the stall. Other horses clomp and stamp around whinnying to escape confinement. Some even throw themselves against the north walls.

"What did you do?" Hannah pushes him off her, jumping to her feet. She pulls her shirt down, forgoing adjusting the bra. Before she reaches the stall door, the building rattles, spiraling her into Nick. They collapse to the straw-covered floor with her on top of him.

"Fuck me," he says as they cease quivering. "That's going to wake the neighbors."

"If the dam cracks we'll lose our electricity." She rolls off him.

"I'd be more worried about a split in the fence. Biters get in we're fucked."

"Check the horses. Make sure none are hurt. Oh, and stay calm," she says more of a command to herself than to him.

Nick jogs from the barn.

"Hey, I said—"

He snags something from the Jeep. "I'm the official camp gofer. Shit job, but they give me a radio." He clicks the mic on. "Wanikiya, Nick reporting in from the stables."

"Put the horses in the outer pen and get to the sally port. Once everyone is accounted for we'll secure the fence line."

"The horses are nervous as fuck."

"We all are, kid." Wanikiya cuts out.

Hannah leads her mount from the barn. "Move, soldier. I doubt we'll be able to hold onto these nervous nellies when an aftershock hits."

Nick grabs a lead rope from a wall rack not wanting the girl he loves to be more of a man than him.

CHAPTER SIXTY-SIX

GRAYSON GETS OFF the floor of the lookout tower faster than he's moved before. It doesn't take having been in an earthquake before to know what put him on his ass. The closest experience was the prison bus flipping over a half dozen times. He cut a deal with the white boy to be let out of the cage and—just before a half second ago—when the ground moved his job of wrangling undead into cargo containers earning him three squares a day and cot was the best months of his life. Somehow protecting peoplemakes him human.

He did doubt Ethan would ever let them move inside the fence but with Tony gone earning his place he knew it would happen. He and his three friends continue to gather functioning undead. Ethan has some grand plan for such a large number of secure biters.

Now in the dozen secured trailers all biters inside in unison thump on the south wall—the same direction as the New Madrid fault. The beating much like a drum line percussion will attract more undead as it progressively gets louder. He's never seen a biter behave with a brain but as deafening as the thumps are, they are in unison.

Grayson gets to his feet. Being high in the ranger station fire lookout tower before he inspects the containers, he spots a line of undead moving toward the noise. If they reach his post he's going to regret Ethan saving him from the overturned prison bus.

The banging increases.

The straggling herd shifts toward the hammering.

Luckily, the cargo trailers are too heavy for even the sardine packed undead inside to tip over. Or a few hundred more would add to the growing thousand he spots.

Grayson yells out the window, "Gather anything important to you and make for the sally port."

"You know they ain't going to let a brother in!" Terry screams back.

Grayson yells over the pounding, "Then stay here, but there are going to be more biters than even you can wrangle!"

CHAPTER SIXTY-SEVEN

BARLOCK SCRATCHES DOWN names on a piece of paper. He has to know who he sends where. "I need each group to patrol the fence line. Any and I mean any chink and you report it."

No grumbles. Plenty of nods. Everyone knows what one biter inside means.

Austin calls from the top of the cargo trailer, "Barlock. Four men on foot are approaching."

"Do they appear threatening?"

Austin avoids the comment about their dark skin. "If I had to guess, they want to qualify for the Olympic track team."

"Let them in!" Barlock yells. Fully aware of the arrangement the five ex-prison inmates had with Ethan, their abandonment of their post means only one of two things: The biters they pen escaped or more biters than they could handle are heading to Acheron.

Barlock clicks his radio. "Wanikiya, I've got fence patrols moving out." He must keep panic from ensuing. Everyone who has access to a radio in the camp will have it on. He chooses his words to mask his own panic. "I need you to inspect the sally port."

"On my way to check on Dartagnan, over." Wanikiya's voice crackles.

"Affirmative." He forgets the radio etiquettes. Barlock holsters the radio to climb the ladder up the cargo trailer.

The truck doesn't seem to slow much as it rolls past allowing Wanikiya to leap out as it speeds toward Ethan's house. The Sioux wastes no time climbing the ladder to join Barlock. "Somehow being up here with impending aftershocks seems to negate the usefulness of my education."

Confused, Austin says, "What?"

"He said we're dumb asses for being up here, kid," Barlock explains.

"No argument there."

Wanikiya immediately recognizes the four men reaching the gate. "Let them in. Keep all search procedures in place."

"More problems, Barlock"

He forgets the skinny girl's name. She carries a compound bow and is not normally on gate duty. He knows she hunts. "What is it, Katniss?"

"Like I haven't heard that joke by everyone still alive." She scoffs, "I prefer Merida, it matches the strawberry in my hair better."

Wanikiya forgoes the banter he participates in when in his kitchen. "Report."

"Sanchez's Humvee." She points down the road.

Austin hands his binoculars to Barlock. "None of the tractors or trucks to haul them are behind them. Just the Humvee."

Wanikiya rubs the back of his top left central incisor with his tongue. "I don't think I'd risk loading a tractor in an earthquake. Ain't like it will get stolen."

The outer sally port gate opens. The four men race inside.

"Where's Simon?" Grayson hollers.

"I know who you are," Barlock instructs. "Remove all gear. Place it in the cubby and strip!"

"Strip?" Terry questions.

"They inspect everyone who enters for bites." Grayson pulls his shirt over his head.

"Make it quick we've got another team coming in hot," Barlock says.

"Not all you got coming in. We just outran a throng." He drops his pants.

"Throng?" Barlock muses.

"Bigger than a herd or a hoard," Wanikiya explains.

"Fuck me, like every biter in the world is going to ride right down on top of us. The ones in the capture trailers were pounding in unison to escape. When we get inside and redress I need some clean fucking underwear," Terry panics.

"Couldn't we lead them away from the gate? Make more racket than what is drawing them toward us?"

"Noise," Wanikiya contemplates. *Noise attracts them.* "Earthquakes travel in three types of waves."

"Fuck, is this where I should have paid more attention in science class?" Austin grumbles.

Wanikiya continues, "The above ground wave is sound."

"Shouldn't they be heading south toward the fault line in the Boot Heel?" Barlock asks.

The Humvee reaches the gate. The driver bleats the horn in two quick successions.

"They are. We're just in their way." Wanikiya orders Grayson and his team into the next section of airlocks securing the Humvee behind the fence.

Sanchez hops out. The other hay cutting crew also exit the cramped vehicle space immediately stripping.

"Report."

"We're fucked." Sanchez tears off her top.

Combeth jumps from the fifty cal. "Fucked without lube."

"Don't worry, these fuckers will kiss you on the neck first." Sanchez places her weapon on the hood. "I've never seen so many biters."

"Maybe they'll go on by," Merida hopes.

"Are you good with a rifle, girl?"

"No so much," Merida says.

Wanikiya keeps his cool. "Barlock, I want every sniper at the gate now."

"Wish Kelsey was here," Austin says.

"Now's your chance to rack up more kills than her," Barlock says.

"We'll all fill a quota by the time today is done." Wanikiya continues, "The fence patrols need to keep inspecting and a team to make repairs behind them. The rest of the camp needs to be here and now."

"How close do we let them get?" Austin lines his scope crosshairs onto an undead.

"Close enough no one misses," Wanikiya says. "Every bullet must count."

Behind the fence, Simon unloads rifles from a pickup placing them for easy access on folding tables. Ambulances behind those are now waiting triage stations.

"So far, no holes discovered in the fence," Barlock reports, "and the north gate team has had a rise in biter activity, but the dam remains clear."

"If we lose the dam, we blow the bridge over the lake and it ends any invasion. But it means no more dam access or electricity."

Bam.

A biter falls.

"Austin!"

"I didn't miss." He lines up for another shot.

Keeping the illusion he has control, Wanikiya calls out, "No one else fires unless ordered."

A low dull moan much like the clearing of a tuba reed hangs in the air.

Merida counts to herself. "Fuck me in the ass!" Her lips moving under the binoculars, "Hey, guys. I don't think we've enough bullets." She points to a second line of biters trailing the first.

Wanikiya draws in his breath. "These aren't thinking men, they're just brainless dolts. Even outnumbered we've the advantage."

"Yeah, but if we fall now, no one will write great stories about us the way they do the Spartans at Thermopylae or the Texans at Alamo," Austin says.

"Couldn't you pick an example where the outnumbered won?" Merida asks.

"The grand battle wouldn't be grand if the underdog won," Austin attempts to tease her, needing levity to keep from shitting his own pants.

The moan-howl cadence loudens.

"Many small forces have defeated grand armies. During the battle of Cannae Hannibal surrounded and destroyed the Romans. The grandest army in the known world had them outnumbered two to one," Wanikiya recalls.

"Great, but you got something a little more in the lines of twenty to one?" Merida asks.

"Some one-hundred-eight Australians fended off over two-thousand Vietcong defending their base at Nui Dat in the 1960s."

"How many Aussies died?" Austin asks.

"Seventeen."

Barlock seems impressed. "Our attackers don't shoot back. We'll clean up."

Austin pops another biter. "They're in range now, Wanikiya."

The Sioux nods. He looms over the two-hundred survivors gathering around the sally port. "Great battle speeches are remembered because their delivery inspires the men before being lead into battle. I have no such speech. I make only a promise." He raises his tomahawk in the air. Twisting it so the sun catches it just right. "I won't leave this battlefield until we are safe."

Guns and rifles of every denomination rise into air and the crowd howls in defiance, pumping the weapons,

"Ready." Wanikiya stuffs the disposable orange foam earplugs into his ears.

Acheron citizens line up along the fence. Those on the inside of the dog run section take aim with rifles. Where the dog run ends, those people have sharpened crowbars and metal poles to poke through the chain length. A second group of survivors hang back behind the first row ready to fill in any holes while someone reloads or replaces a weapon. Everyone knows the undead will be relentless.

Wanikiya draws his pistol.

Biters shamble onto the road.

He picks a target.

The head explodes.

It takes ten seconds before a gunpowder clouds hangs in the air strong enough for Wanikiya to taste it. Bodies stack along the center road line. A tactical maneuver providing sandbag like cover if the enemy cared about avoiding bullets.

Low moan-howls echo, trumping over the constant ring of gun fire.

Wanikiya drops the clips as he empties them. Once Merida expends the last of her arrows, she reloads empty clips.

Hot brass pings everywhere.

The wave of moan-howls grows over the thunder of reports.

Simon reloads clips. He hands off rifle and pistol ammo until his truck empties.

Nick stabs a biter thought the fence then steps back. Hannah pops one in the face. Nick bounds in to stabs another. They, with dozens of others, repeat this pattern until the undead stack so high they must scale the corpses to reach at the living.

"What happens if they reach the top of the fence?"

Nick reads her lips. Between the ear plugs and the expenditure of ammo he has no hearing. The answer beats in his head. "People die." He knows the area with the dog run provides more space to fill, but the single fence area they defend must not allow undead over or panic will cause catastrophic failure.

As the tower of undead against the fence reaches high enough, biters claw at the concertina wire protecting the top of the fence those citizens in the dog run are called to evacuate. They escape the severed limbs and a few dismembered heads raining inside. Despite the lack of military discipline, they reform the defense line along the inner fence line and stab at biters surviving the fall inside the dog run.

Finally out of ammo or to cool weapons too hot to reload, people retreat from the chain-link. Biter corpses carpet the road from the fence line all the way to opposite the tree line.

Simon dumps another box of ammo onto the table. Hands blackened from gun powder, blistered, and some bleeding from the repetitive shoving of bullets against the springs of the clips. The people tired, hot, and arm muscles tired from holding weapons are not ready to give up, but their persistence is trumped by the reduction in ammo reserves. All the Chief's combat experience demands he buy these people time.

More biters claw to the top of the pile of extinguished undead. This wave will make it over while everyone reloads what remains of his arsenal.

Simon slams the Humvee into park slipping into the 50-cal nest. He swings the weapon around unloading into the climbing wall of biters. He doesn't bother with head shots but without arms, legs, and torsos, the creatures lose the ability to scale the wall of fallen biters.

"Damn, Chief!" Nick scrapes out his ear plugs.

The 50-cal rounds incinerate so many undead. The armor puncturing rounds single-handedly drove back a wave of rotten flesh.

"You're going to spend the next month doing reloads, son," Simon says.

"How many were there?" Hannah asks.

"I doled out some five-thousand rounds."

Dripping with her own sweat, Sanchez holds her blistering palms open to the air.

Combeth slides down the wall of the cargo trail next to her. "You better report to medical."

"Gun got too hot. I just couldn't stop firing."

"It's a bad burn maybe enough to get you out of cleanup duty," Combeth jokes.

"In a minute. Have to be others worse than me." Sanchez pats him on the shoulder with the back of her hand. "Once we're dismissed, you want to go back to my room and fuck?"

"What?"

"We just lived through the worst shit I've ever seen. I want to be with someone. I want to be alive in the arms of man."

"You don't have to ask twice." Combeth gets to his feet, helping her up. "Let's get you to medical."

"I need a shower."

"We start in the shower." He smiles.

Wanikiya remains stoic.

The 50-cal ringing in his skull as the ear plugs offered no protection against the repeating explosions. He stands at attention and raises his right arm to salute the Chief Petty Officer. Now he must feed his people.

Merida reloads the last of the ammo she has and hands him a full clip.

"I might have to pray," Barlock says. "We lost no one."

"The Great Spirit watched over us." Wanikiya slides the clip into the pistol. He holds it out to let the air cool the heat radiating off it. "Ethan brought back small quantities of liquor to be used as medicine. I think I will get Dr. Baker to prescribe everyone a drink."

"Everyone?" Austin asks.

"Everyone."

Before anyone discovers energy to celebrate the victory, the second wave of biters pours through the trees.

CHAPTER SIXTY-EIGHT

"HOW LONG WILL gas last?" Becky asks.

"I didn't think this long. It stales." Ethan repacks his jumpstart.

Chad flips up the tarpaulin covering the boat. "Jackpot."

Six duct taped shut coolers are crammed into the floor area.

Becky raises up on her toe tips to peer inside. "You don't even know what's in those coolers."

"They taped them closed. They hold treasure." Chad smiles.

Ethan steps over the trailer hitch, sweeping the other side of the boat. "You don't know what those people thought were priceless—could be family wedding photos. A better question to ask yourself right now is where are the owners. These people prepped for an escape. This SUV's packed."

"They're dead, or there wouldn't be a boat."

"You haven't been paying attention, Chad. If they're dead, then we need to know they aren't going to crawl out from under the truck and bite us. Second, we don't need to be shot because they're hiding. They may have a safe place to go, but some people wait until other loved ones show up first before heading out."

"One thing for sure, people lose all reason in a crisis."

"Not you." Becky smiles. She admires Ethan's Clint Eastwood demeanor. She tosses her machete into the boat and climbs in.

"Don't be in a rush."

"I'll open it carefully." She slices the tape. "I remember you saying about the freezer full of unabashed heads."

"Seriously?"

"Guy was collecting them. The way he protected it I thought it was food," says Ethan.

Becky turns her head as she opens the lid. Rotten vegetable fumes burn her eyes.

"We know they had an escape plan."

"And been dead for a while." Becky turns her nose from the stench.

"Double check for bodies."

"I still don't get it?" Chad admits.

"They expected to eat perishables quickly. Something prevented them from leaving. I haven't lived this long by not being careful," Ethan lies. He takes plenty of risks, logic dictates something happened to the owner of this truck and with the supplies still in the boat he'd guess not marauders.

The next cooler holds canned and dry goods. "We eat well tonight."

"We take what we need and leave the rest."

"So some scavengers take it? I'm just talking about an extra tin of something."

"Eat what you want. We're not coming back this way," says Ethan.

"We're not?"

"We'll take a boat across the river and north to Hannibal and hike the twenty miles to the dam."

"Wait. If we hadn't had an earthquake we'd still be walking?"

"Does it matter, Chad?" she asks.

"I didn't sign on to walk four hundred miles and not even get to visit Graceland," Chad attempts to be funny.

Becky flashes Ethan a 'what the fuck' glare.

"Don't look at me. You the one riding him."

"There're limited choices."

"What the fuck does that mean?" Chad asks.

"It means, Chad, if it weren't for the fucking undead, you'd have to work harder to get in my pants."

"You mean like bring you chocolates."

"I don't like chocolate. I kind of like the shiny items."

"Don't complain, Chad, she sounds expensive." Ethan removes an unopened cooler from the boat.

"We're not going to find out what's inside?"

"Leave it."

"It could be guns."

"It could be a map to the lost city of Atlantis, but I don't want to know," Ethan says.

"I'd hate to leave something behind we know we needed."

"Won't you feel that way now?"

"No. We pass a lot of houses we don't search. I don't regret not going into them. Let's find a boat ramp and get across the Mississippi. We've got a doctor to locate."

Rounding the curve of the road, the truck enters the city limits of a village. Ethan slows as quick as possible with the boat trailer in tow.

"Wasn't expecting a town."

"Just keep driving," Chad suggests.

Ethan flips the gear into park, shutting down the engine, and leaving the keys. "Time to stretch the legs."

"I don't know why we don't just keep driving past this one-horse burg?"

Ethan makes a few limp-steps before he kneels. His face wrinkles as he holds back the scream from the bending left joint. A good orthopedic surgeon would be more valuable to him than a plague cure.

Chad who has been the observant scout when traveling on the tar loses all sensibilities in this Podunk berg. He blocks Chad's path with his arm.

"Hey, dude. It's just another abandoned town. I don't even see any biters. Most of these buildings appear to be still on their foundations."

"Lack of biters doesn't concern me. They're always around. Take a better look at this place."

"It's too clean." Becky draws her sidearm.

"Exactamundo. Rolla was the only town I've been in that was evacuated and left unscathed, but this place." Ethan points to a row of storefronts. "Many of those windows are smashed. And some have been boarded up with no glass fragments on the ground."

"Glass falls in when you smash a window." Chad, proud of his observation, laces his thumb behind his gun belt buckle.

"Don't get cocky, kid."

"Not a dead body or abandoned car on the street, either." Becky seeks confirmation, "Trap?"

"The world fell apart ten months ago, and everyone reduced to clubbing each other in the head for a few cans of dog food." Ethan rises not having to exaggerate his stiffness. "Becky, take the right. Chad, left."

"What are you going to do?"

"Ever see *City Heat* with Clint Eastwood."

"No," they answer in unison.

"I'll add it to my list of items to scavenge." Ethan marches down the center, flipping his duster coat behind the gleaming .357.

Becky hangs under a shop window sliding up enough to peek inside.

Chad tugs at a board over broken glass pans. He shakes his head signaling Ethan he's unable to spot any people.

Kid's going to get me shot. He better hope they do me in, or he gets my first bullet.

Three buildings down, extending from a second-story window, a rifle barrel appears.

Ethan snaps his finger.

Becky halts.

Ethan flicks his head as a signal.

Chad panics, diving behind a concrete flower pot.

Ethan would return fire, but the bullet smashing into the building high above Chad's position was the worst shot ever or just to scare the stupid kid. *If was a scare, maybe we can chat.* "We're just passing through. We don't want anything you have. We just—"

"We want what you got!" a voice from above calls out.

Ethan mumbles, "Of course you do. I didn't want to kill anybody today." A bullet splinters the asphalt at his feet. He remains statuesque.

"You're the only one going to die if you don't drop your weapons and supplies and run away."

Did she spot Becky? Ethan shifts his weight to his right leg to remove pressure from the left.

"Don't move, fuckwad!" the voice from the window screams.

Profanity used in an attempt to appear tough informs Ethan about his assailant. *Now how much assistance does this Sure Shot have? I hope Becky doesn't just rush the room in case she had two or three friends.*

"I'm not giving you my gear." Ethan's defiance brings pause to the voice.

"Nothing you have's worth dying for."

Ethan raises his voice to answer, "Funny. I was thinking the same thing."

Chad freaks behind the elongated flowerpot giving Ethan the 'what the fuck' face.

How many friends? No one person cleaned this street.

The rifle discharges as it falls from the window. The bullet kicks up roof tiles from the awning below the window.

Ethan draws the magnum at the scuffling sounds from inside. He catches a glimpse of Becky tangling with a woman.

"Move, Chad!" he orders.

The nineteen-year-old lags. Ethan beats him to the door of the shop below the window. Chad pushes past him, flying past resale clothing.

Too many good places to hide in here.

Ethan scopes out blind spots as he follows Chad to the door leading to the back.

Smashing glass quickens his pace. Ethan half wonders why Becky didn't just shoot the woman. Reaching the top of the stairs, he understands why.

Becky holds the top of her machete against the round belly of a pregnant woman. Her distraught face reveals to him she

400 MILES TO GRACELAND

would never hurt the unborn he just hopes the mom doesn't figure it out.

"Chad?"

"Scoping out the other rooms."

Becky pants. Blood trickles from fingernail scratches across her forehead. "You know how hard it is to punch a pregnant woman?"

Ethan waves his hand, ordering Becky to back away. "Don't try anything, lady."

"You'd harm a pregnant woman?" the woman asks.

Becky never expected Ethan capable, but she believes from his face he will.

"Lady, I shot my own mother," Ethan lies, but with no doubt his tone's believable because it was close to the truth.

"She has no bag or suitcase just the rifle. Not even a bottle of water," Becky huffs.

"Where's the rest of your group?"

"I'm alone."

"Then you just got alone. You're too hydrated for a pregnant woman to have gone long without water." Ethan gropes the round belly. His fingers palpate real flesh.

"You a doctor?"

"I know enough."

"Then don't fucking touch me." She kicks Ethan in the knee.

He goes down swifter than Girl Scout cookies at a Weight Watchers meeting.

Before Becky reacts, the woman reaches the shop door, snagging two bags she has strategically placed for a quick escape. Becky has the speed to catch her but her concern for Ethan slows her.

"Don't!" Ethan calls after Becky. "Trap."

"She's stealing the truck."

"Let it go." Ethan slides against the wall. "I smell a trap."

Truck door slams. The engine roars to life and tires squeal as it speeds off.

"She must have friends." Becky glances out the window. The boat disappears.

"I just wonder why they keep the town clean. If they were into trapping and stealing for passersby a dirty street would lure a false sense of abandonment."

Chad bounds down the stairs, "You okay, Ethan? Where's preggo?"

"Do me a favor, kid, and don't have children." Ethan forces himself to get up.

"Is it bad?" Becky asks.

"It will bruise and stiffen and hurt like fuck. Much like every other day of my life." He limps toward the door. "I've had worse."

CHAPTER SIXTY-NINE

GLOOPY, BLACKING BLOOD sprays from the arm Becky pins. "She's turned!" Slamming the woman's arm to the grass frenzies her struggle.

Information apparent to Ethan, he ignores the proper Captain Obvious retort while restraining the other arm with his leg to free his hands. His leg burns from where the pregnant woman kicked it.

"Shouldn't we just bash in her brains?" Chad asks. He fails to hide panic over being so close to chomping teeth without driving a machete through them.

"No!" Ethan and Becky scream simultaneously. Neither of them knowing how this will play out, they both must possess the same speculator theory.

"Just finish off her friends," Ethan orders.

Chad uses Becky's machete to splinter the skull of a man. All three collapsed bodies appear dragged through the meat grinder. The second he ends has dozens of little cuts like being flung through glass.

The third coughs up blood.

"He's not dead!"

"He will be. Unless you're a surgeon, end him and get over to hold her legs."

Chad hovers over the dying man.

The man uses his last bit of strength to nod yes.

Chad drives the machete into the skull.

"Hold her legs," Ethan orders.

Chad squats over the tantrum thrashing of limbs. The belly mound blues. The last of the woman's life transforms into undead existence.

Becky wonders if at some point had Ethan delivered a baby.

Ethan knows her unspoken question. *Admittedly, it was a plastic doll shot through a rubber vagina—in theory, I was certified for such action. The key was to drive the ambulance faster.* In this case, none of his training works in his favor. C-sections were invasive and he never secured the certification to move to that level.

He palpates the graying tummy. The bulbous navel and—

"She's completing the turn!" Chad panics.

Ethan calm, draws the hunting knife over the epidermis, splitting the skin. The yellowish layer of adipose tissue women collect while pregnant. Relieved to find yellow around the uterus satisfies him enough his rescue attempt is possible.

"Don't watch."

A warning to invite the gawking of his partners.

He interlaces all ten of his fingers into the gash. If ever an opportunity brought him to utter a prayer it would be now as he grips both sides of the uterine wall and flexes his upper body, pulling his arms apart.

Cracking bone echoes over the tears of meat.

Chad catches his lunch in his throat, preventing an exhalation.

Becky turns her face.

Ethan slips inside the cavity hallway to his elbows. He lifts them out cradling a baby filling one of his hands.

Becky doesn't wait for his order. She drives her second machete thought the forehead of the mother.

Ethan clears away placenta. "Chad, get me the newspaper."

"Dirty old paper."

Ethan forgoes the expiation he picked up during his training about the sterile nature of newspapers and it works for a baby swaddling when lacking a blanket. They have several, but he'd rather save them for later until the baby's clean.

Ethan loops some of the paracord he carries around the umbilical cord tying it off in two places. "You want to cut the cord?" he asks Becky.

She flips open a knife, slicing though the tissue between the cord. "The baby didn't turn." Becky smiles.

"The mother's last gift to her child. I read once were mothers with full blown AIDS didn't transfer the disease to their unborn even though they shared the same blood." As gently as possible, with giant finger he flicks clear the mucus plugging the baby's nose.

"Shouldn't we have boiled some water?" Chad asks, newspaper in hand. "In every movie, ever, they send someone to boil water."

"Because it gives some Podunk stressed moron something to do who would just be in the fucking way?" Ethan speaks in his lowest register to the baby. "Boiling water would be too hot for baby's soft skin." He pinches the baby's foot.

Pain gives way to life as the little girl cries.

Becky and Chad both give a flirtatious smile to each other. Chad's looses his happiness first. "Won't she attract biters."

Ethan bounces the baby in his arm until her cries turn to whimpers. Keeping his baby speaking tone, he says, "Then we'll just have to kill every last one of them." Ethan swaddles her in the newspaper and allows her to hold his index finger with her tiny hand as comfort. "She's going to need to eat.

"Mom's milk will have soured by now," Chad says.

"Don't look at me. I don't even have tits."

"Size of the breast isn't important. It's what they make and you don't have the colostrum this baby needs," Ethan says.

"Were do we find colostrum?" Becky asks.

"Goat's milk," Chad says.

Becky and Ethan both glance at him.

"Seriously. Where are we going to locate a goat?" Chad asks.

"We can't take this baby to Memphis," Becky protests.

"We find a new boat, drive up the river," Chad suggests.

"You're not serious about bringing the baby along to Memphis."

"You want to leave her here. Why don't you just bash her skull in with your boot, save her from growing up in this nightmare. It would be mercy, not murder." Ethan never changes from his father voice.

"Easy, Ethan, I just meant, I—"

"The best option is we find a car and you two head back to the colony. I'll head to Memphis."

"By yourself."

"I've been on my own plenty. It will take both of you to protect the baby. "

"She'll need to eat."

"Your instinct will be to search grocery stores, but you're more likely to encounter biters. It might be emotionally more difficult, but I'd check daycares; they'll have extra diapers and food and most people don't search them for supplies."

"I don't know the way back. Not without taking the interstate, and you said to stay off the interstate," Chad protests.

"I'll map you out a path—don't get in hurry," Ethan says.

"Are you worried she's not crying?"

"No. Not yet. She's warm and comfortable, and has a pleasing voice to sooth her."

Becky gathers their gear. "She was about to burst." As she stuffs items into her backpack. "If I were an expecting mother I'd have gathered baby items."

The baby tightens her grip on Ethan's pinky finger, closing its eyes. Ethan rocks her.

Chad reloads his weapon. He jerks the slide.

Ethan voice remains a calm, soothing whisper, "A diaper bag's feasible. You two track back the way they came. No more than half a mile. If they've been running longer you won't find it."

"You going to be fine?"

Ethan draws his M&P, placing on his bag inches from where he holds the baby. "Privacy will give me a chance to name this little girl."

Becky cleans the blood from her machete, dropping her pack next to Ethan. "Leave your gear," she orders Chad.

The boat rests on its trailer, wedged between two trees. Smoking further down the road, the SUV rests right side up. The crumpled roof bears the marks of several rollover impacts.

"She over corrected around the corner to fast while pulling the boat." Chad slides his pistol from its holster.

"How did she live long enough to crawl from where we found her?" Chad asks.

"A mother's will. She wanted to save her baby and so did those people." Becky rakes chunks shattered bloody glass from the window remains. Kneeling, she cranes her neck to peek inside. "Search the road. She was heading back to the ambush town. Maybe a diaper bag flung out during one of the roll overs."

Chad pats the back tire, full of air. He glances at the remaining three. "No blow out. Just speed caused the crash?"

Becky jerks a backpack wedged in the seats. "How is it important?"

"I don't know, but I thought it might be, if they were avoiding an obstacle like a biter herd."

She fishes in the pack—clothes, crunchy bars, knife—nothing useful for a newborn. "No fresh splatters on the front grill and we'd hear a herd."

"Funny."

"Find the diaper bag," she orders.

Annoyed with her bossiness toward him, Chad toddles along the shoulder scanning the grass for any man-made object.

Becky huffs out her breath. The SUV appears devoid of biters, but not of her bag lodged between seats. The only way to reach them is by crawling inside. A task she wanted to avoid.

Claustrophobia was never an issue for her until the world ended. Once halfway inside she'll be trapped and defenseless. She draws in a deep breath as if preparing to leap in a lake. She'd never tell Ethan her aversions to him trapping them in the bedroom at night when he seals the doors with overturned dressers. Cuddling with Chad was the only way she stayed sane.

Two bags. One of prenatal vitamins—expired. A second travel bag for the weekend camper.

She scrambles out from the wreckage.

Chad greats her with two satchel bags. "Any of this useful?"

Before she's able to pilfer, tire squelching brings her to her feet.

Spilling from the rust-red Chevy are three men in flannel, toting double barrel shotguns.

Becky considers the inferiority of the weapon against a herd. Reload time improves chances of a biter reaching you and at a distance the buckshot may not destroy enough of the brain. The weapons will, however, shred her and Chad before she kills more than one of the men. She's hasn't Ethan's quick draw speed. Even if Chad missed and she got one Ethan would pick off the others before they fire. His reflexes are inhuman—his X-man skill. Becky wishes she had just half his speed.

Her fingers brush over Chad's wrist, putting pressures to keep him from drawing his weapon. Talking's the only way out of this.

She raises her arms in the air, gunless, before the rednecks demand it.

"Where's the person who belongs to that bag?" demands the older one.

Becky points at the trail the traveled to reach the SVU. Her mind races. How much does she say to these men? What if the pregnant woman was running from them? What is the best response to keep her face free of buckshot? "The pregnant woman sent us for her baby supplies." Not a complete lie.

The younger man lowers his weapon racing for the path. "Sandra! Is she okay?"

Chad has the good sense to keep his mouth shut and let her speak. "She was hurt,"

This halts the younger man and causes the others to keep their raise weapons.

"She went into labor. The baby's with our friend."

"Two fingers, one at a time you place your weapons on the ground," the older man commands.

"Fuck you. The baby needs formula. Not you holding your dick while we disarm. Chad will walk the path. You follow to keep our friend from blowing his head off and I'll stay here with you pointing your guns on me until you know the baby's all right."

"Who do you think you are, little girl?"

"Someone who wants that baby girl to live." Becky never wanted so much for her words to be true. For the first time, she wants someone besides herself to make to tomorrow. The positive emotion overwhelms her and she knows now why Ethan does what he does.

Ethan unfolds his map. "Don't travel the major interstaters and avoid the cities. There are also clans of people killing, if you're lucky, for whatever you have."

"I didn't know people were capable of some of the shit I've seen," the old man adds, "and I was in 'Nam."

"I knew. I just didn't think I'd ever see it." Ethan taps the map. "Head to Cuba, Missouri. Take the scenic route as much as possible. Follow Highway 19 North after Cuba."

"For how long?" he asks

"Becky and Chad will accompany you back."

"The hell I will. We've got get to Memphis," Becky protests.

"Keep your voice down; you'll wake the baby," Ethan scolds.

"I'm going with you," she says.

"It's not like you were going to get to tour Graceland. I'll get the Major's brother and catch up with you."

"Ethan, you need us."

"I need you to protect this baby no matter what. She's the future of the next generation."

"How safe is your camp?" asks the old man.

"We have walls and doctors," Ethan says. "People willing to help. We've strict rules. You don't work—you don't eat."

"The way it should be," says the old man.

"We'll all go to Memphis. Leave them on the boat with the baby," Becky's protest falls on deaf ears.

"Get the baby home. We won't find formula on the river and we'll have same issue any town big enough to have supplies will be full of undead."

"We have a few supplies at our camp, the truck, and a well," says the old man.

"Healthy drinking water for a few days will be a welcome change," Becky says.

The old man kicks at a pebble with his boot. "Why are you all doing all this?"

"To stay human. I'm on a path to enlightenment." Ethan smiles.

"You'll make it, son. My granddaughter did you wrong and you did all you could for her and my great-grandbaby. One decent person left. Not like those people who cleared out our town."

"I doubt when Anubis weighs my heart against the feather I'll be found worthy. But maybe those survivors in the compound and your great-grandbaby won't ever have to worry or witness what I have witnessed." Ethan folds his map, sliding it into the waterproof sleeve. He hands it to Becky.

She throws her arms around him. "You better catch up, old man." She kisses him on the lips.

"You protect the baby. No matter what. Steer clear of the New Madrid area. Remember, no matter what."

CHAPTER SEVENTY

ETHAN CRANKS THE release on the trailer, dropping the Monterey 186 MS motorboat into the water. Momentum carries it into the swift current, sending it floating away from the launch. Realizing the craft will soon be out his reach he dives for the edge catching the tie rope.

No, I wasn't much of a sailor. Good thing no one was here to witness. I'd lose my reputation for knowing it all.

Ethan tosses in his gear bag and a baseball bat before flopping into the boat. He lands with less elegance than a fish flopping on the bank. His left leg doesn't allow for grace.

Taking a seat at the pilot station he wonders why the steering wheel is on the right side opposite American-made cars.

Great. Bluetooth and an interface for my iPad.

Caught in the swift current of the Mississippi River, the boat now floats far enough away from the bank to make it impossible for Ethan to safely swim back.

"You better start." Not thinking to grab an oar, Ethan cranks the engine. It turns over.

Ethan flips the accelerator. The boat jerks and had he been standing he'd have tumbled end over end to the back of the boat. He backs off the accelerator, not ready to drive at full speed. *Not quite like a car. Nothing like a motorcycle.* He turns the wheel. Even heading downstream, the boat moves against currents. Confident with his ability not to drive right up onto the bank Ethan points the boat downstream.

I know you're not supposed to swim in this river due to the hidden undertows. The quake has stirred it up worse. I had no idea this was so rough a ride. At least the river isn't running backward.

Keeping to the center of the river. Ethan never expected the current to be as curvy as backwater creek on the way to school.

He slows the boat. The skeletal remains of the Caruthersville Bridge rests shattered in the water. Between the stories of the military destroying bridges and the blackened remains of the girders, Ethan knows this wasn't caused by the earthquake. *Danziger's story was true.* He brings the boat close to pylon hoping not to snag on some metal beam hidden under the water's surface.

Ethan breaths. Not sure how long he held his breath. Once at a distance there should be no more hidden bridge sections. He guns the motor. *I wonder how many mph this thing gets. Do boats measure gas usage in mph? I'm going down stream. That has to use less gas than when I fight against to get back to Hannibal. I know nothing about boats.* The fuel gauge has not moved.

Maybe I should have thought this through better.

Ethan doesn't have to view the city skyline to know he's close. The smell of rot is worse than any biter. Digging inside his armor vest he slips from a hidden pocket a hard case. Cracking open the waterproof seal to protect a cell phone Ethan removes a military pocket GPS. Major Ellsberg said it would lead him right to Dr. Ellsberg. *Emily would never believe I'd have such a device. Or how much it terrifies me. For this GPS to operate someone somewhere must be in control of military satellites.*

It takes the device minutes to acquire a signal. A red dot flashes on the LED screen. Ethan hooks it to his Kevlar vest before accelerating down the river.

Reaching the shore some twenty miles above Memphis, he expected the dot to be closer to the city. He drives the boat onto the muddy shore. He debates a second about leaving the keys. He kicks them under the seat.

Ethan tosses the baseball bat from the boat. He again must undignifiedly flop off the bow to reach ground. Only a few hours on the water has left his knee unusable. He limps to the trees with the end of the tow line.

Retrieving the bat, he takes a few practice swings defeating air. What he notices is the stiffness in his arms has left him. He rolls his shoulder—no pain. Occupied with the trip he hasn't paid much attention to his recovery from the beating.

He switches the bat to his left hand and shifts into his gunfighter stance. Before a quick draw practice, the ground rumbles. He jabs the bat into the ground as a tripod to keep him on his feet.

When the shaking subsides, Ethan accepts there's nothing to do about it now but focus on the mission to find Dr. Ellsberg.

Consulting the GPS, he hobbles through the trees until his knee loosens enough to march forward. The tiny screen on the GPS doesn't convey distance. As he moves closer, toward his target, Ethan notes how it must be approximately twenty miles above Memphis. *So much for seeing Elvis.*

I actually miss Chad's bumbling.

Ethan tracks north of the city. The GPS flashes a dot. Ethan fiddles with the buttons on the side and the dot grows. Puzzled, he wonders why the tracker Major Ellsberg said his brother injected into himself is some eighteen miles North of Memphis. *If he's a biter. He covered a good distance. All this distance and I didn't succeed. If he is dead, I will do right by him.*

Ethan treks toward the flashing dot. *I like this thing. It's direct the one from my car had to be on a road to track positions, but this works through a forested area.*

Ethan dives behind a tree he hopes gives him cover as a series of explosions echo before shaking the trees. Crackling branches shatter as they fall, echoing more noise on top of the explosions. He stays crouched toward as close to the ground as possible and still hop away.

Chainsaws buzz.

People are working. Ethan considers the force of armed people needed to operate chainsaws with a city full of thousands of undead a few miles away. He would never risk his group in this manner even to create a killing field to waist biters.

The noise lies between him and the flashing red dot. He secures the GPS back in its hidden pocket.

Discovering teams of uniformed soldiers, Ethan raises his arms high and surrenders. They waste no time or questions on him. They strip him of his weapons including the Taurus .22, handcuff him and place in in a Humvee. As they do he notes the explosions brought down rows of trees not only creating kill zone but they chop them up for a barricade. Cables strung across the road trap any wondering biter. They fell more trees attempting to create a bottleneck. A noise source and a line of well-armed Marines in the center of the road could pick off an approaching herd. Which should be heading this way with all the aftershocks drawing them north.

CHAPTER SEVENTY-ONE

"WHY DID THE horses run off? Are we going to find them? Why did the ground shake?" Grace barrages Frank with questions as she rides on his shoulders.

"The quake scared them. Didn't the quake scare you?" Frank asks with a childish demanding tone. He won't admit how much it terrified him.

"Nope I wasn't scared," Grace beams. "Why'd it scare the horses?"

"Earthquakes make a noise only animals hear. It frightens them."

"Will the noise frighten the biters?" Grace asks.

Karen freezes at Grace's question. *From the mouth of babes.* "No, but the quake should attract them. Draw them toward the epicenter."

"What's that?" Grace asks.

"The starting point of the earthquake."

"A better question is where?" asks Frank. "I thought earthquakes were a Cali thing."

"The New Madrid Fault in the Boot Heel is larger than those in California. Missouri just doesn't get the press like a place about to fall off into the ocean," Karen explains. "The horses would have run away from the quake where biters would be attracted toward it. We may have an opportunity to trek right into Springfield."

"Will they notice the quake at Acheron?" Frank asks.

"I'm sure half the country felt it."

Karen draws a folded trenching shovel from her pack. "Frank, why don't you scout with Grace?"

"Dangerous to send her off with him alone. He has to hold her and fire. Just because we haven't seen a biter in days doesn't mean they aren't around," Kalvin says.

After they are gone, Karen drives the shovel into the earth. "We're about a mile from our destination. I don't know what we'll find, but I think we'd blend in better if we appear more desperate."

"I get it. We keep our gear safe in case we are not so welcome. Why send Frank off with Grace?"

"The question queen might ask in front of someone why we buried our gear. If she asks where it went we claim lost it." She scoops out more dirt. "One, we protect Grace. We bring her back to Acheron. These zealots crusading to Springfield have an unrealistic understanding of biters."

"You'll get no arguments. We're all unworthy when it comes to the undead."

"Another reason to stash some gear."

"We've a story to present? We're a little too nourished to have been lost for long."

"We were with a group. Doing well and then too many biters overran us."

"Everyone has that story."

"Which is why it works." She drives the shove into the loose soil.

At the overpass where Interstate 44 crosses Highway 65, a barricade of smashed cars lines the road along with men in rifle stations on the upper highway.

The four march forward until they are ordered to stop. Rifle barrels swing toward them. Karen raises her arms in the air keeping her finger off the trigger of the 38 special. She never cared much for the backup weapon. It fires high and to the right. Her feelings won't hurt if they confiscate it. But to be weaponless would raise more suspicion than lack of food or water.

"We seek sanctuary," Karen calls out.

The men with guns just stare at them.

"How do you want to handle this?" Kalvin whispers.

"If they build a barricade straight down those two highways then the entire city may be protected and intact. We need to ally ourselves with this group."

"Even if they are a bunch of religious nut jobs?" Kalvin asks.

Frank does his best to keep Grace out of earshot of their conversation.

"Just keep moving until they tell us to go away."

"And if they shoot us?"

The gate is just welded metal over chain link. Nothing fancy, nothing a V8 truck at thirty miles an hour couldn't crash through. Nor do these people strip and search for bites before allowing the living inside. Karen respects the security in Acheron. Ethan's methods keep out infected. She wonders if the biblical lines about seeing thy father's nakedness prevents a full out search. Blind faith will be their undoing as someone not yet turned will make it inside and rain havoc.

Two bearded men approach. "We need you to hand over your weapons."

Karen wonders how much protesting should she perform? "How do we know we'll be safe inside."

"I'm sure your God will protect you." The first bearded man holds out the weapon butt first.

"My faith has been shaken. Sounds like, so has yours," she probes, as she hands over her weapon.

"People of this town have had a healthy respect of faith. They still do, but somehow survivors beyond her borders have christened her a holy mecca. We're just trying to survive."

"People out there need something to believe in," Frank says, as he too gives up a twenty-two.

"You steal those pants or earn them," the second bearded man asks.

"I've a license. For all that matters now about paper. Most of my skills are useless since no one revives alive if they code."

"We'll feed you a meal or two and allow you to bunk for the night. We're developing a barter system. Most will trade labor for food. Medical training highly valuable. Earn you good meals. Maybe even some beer."

"You have beer?" Karen asks.

Her team perks wanting an answer.

"The distillers are almost as important as doctors and vets. I recommend if you trade for beer, you trade it for items you need rather than drink it. Its value rates over bullets."

Kalvin gives up two long hunting knifes. "Who runs the city?"

"Now you get complicated. Several of the more prominent churches seek a ruling council made up of representatives mostly of their branch of denomination. Most are in favor of an elected council to make decisions."

"Arguments are in abundance as to who should be on it. How appointed. It's a cluster."

"So, who put you gentlemen in charge of greeting strangers?" Karen asks, noting specific lax in their security already.

"We get a cut for protecting the city. Most don't want anything to do with popping the unworthy."

"People pay us to keep them safe and don't ask questions."

"Without outside resources food has to be getting scarce." Karen speculates.

"Direct all your questions to our leader. He holds final court over who stays and is cast out."

CHAPTER SEVENTY-TWO

"YOU'RE NOT MUCH of a talker, are you, Corporal?" Ethan flexes his writs. They didn't clamp the stainless steel as tight as they could, but his massive hands won't slip through the cuffs.

From the vehicle speed, Ethan deduces the road has been cleared.

The Humvee rattles from a small aftershock. Ethan wonders how bad Memphis was hit. Many of the buildings were wooded framed and never earthquake proofed. At the onset of the outbreak someone must have turned off the gas line or he'd have seen the smoke from the city burning. *Too bad cars can't be switched to run on natural gas. Lots of places to get natural gas. I need to find more scientists.*

"Was the city hit bad in the earthquake?"

The Marine ignores him.

He attempts another approach with the soldier, "How have you survived? Memphis has the largest population of people on the Mississippi River, some seven hundred thousand in the city limits alone."

"We are the US Military."

Still prideful. Possibilities. "I'm confused. The military at Fort Wood packed it in. Gave up. Never thought they'd tarnish my grandfather's memory by running. But the undead are nothing like the beaches of Normandy."

"Why didn't you serve?"

Ethan taps his leg. "Metal rod. They wouldn't take me. I tried. I couldn't be a Marine. I was in line for the Air Force."

"Simper Fi, mother fucker. Real men don't join the chair force." Ethan smiles to himself.

"Why didn't you say you wanted to be a Marine? Win my trust by creating a common bond. Saying Air Force makes me like you even less."

"Marines would be a lie. Catching me in a lie would end trust. I'm just here to bring a message to Dr. Ellsberg."

"You'll have to speak to the L.T. Not part of my detail."

He's not a tight-lipped soldier but he won't just spill information.

"I was expecting to locate Dr. Ellsberg in Memphis. When did you lose the city?"

"The compound is actually North of Millington at a National Guard Armory," says the Marine. "The compound has a medical facility and we brought all the CDC personnel there after Nashville fell. My boots never saw Memphis."

"They thought they had isolated the cause of the infection," Ethan brings up to prove he's not just a passerby who knows a name. He recognizes the purpose of the facility.

"What good does that do?"

"If you know what caused the disease, science can develop a cure," Ethan says.

"But people are dead. You can't heal them and why would you want to? Some of them are half rotten. Imagine restoring them to life with no skin left."

"So, a vaccine's not a priory for the military?"

"Not for this Marine."

"I thought a vaccine was worth the trip since Fort Wood fell."

The Marine taps the brake as if this is the first-time Ethan mentioned this fact. "Fort Wood's gone? No way?"

"I was there when the last transport evacuated troops. I've no reason to lie about it. If the base was still there then why isn't a platoon of rangers been sent here to locate Dr. Ellsberg? The soldiers remaining behind to demolish the base fled to my camp."

"They wouldn't send some half-crippled who fancies himself John Wayne with the shiny hand cannon he carries." The Marine slows the Humvee.

"Eastwood carried a magnum, and neither one of them had to deal with an earthquake."

The Corporal flashes the lights in a distinct pattern.

The guards have trouble pulling open the gate. Ethan speculates the earthquake knocked it off its runners. They get it open far enough to allow the Humvee to pass.

In the rearview mirror, Ethan witnesses the struggle to pull the gate shut. *Not going to be good. I wonder why the biters from the city haven't moved north toward the quake's epicenter.*

Ethan rubs his wrist, now free of the handcuffs. He likes the idea they consider him weak. "Does this mean I'm a guest? The food was palatable, but maid never came to turn down the bed. Two days. I sat in cell for two days."

The man in the lab coat ignores Ethan's banter.

"Dr. Ellsberg said whoever his brother send would have a code phrase. What is it?"

"It's for Dr. Ellsberg—only."

"We don't want to risk our top scientist if you aren't who you say you are. He's too close to curing this infection."

Ethan would lay odds this young man was a research assistant when the world ended and was never outside a fence for long to have to worry about his own survival. Something about such a person glazes his eyes over with disgust. Protecting people from the outside is one task he's accepted, but all those people he protects have firsthand experiences dealing with the problems the undead bring.

"Look. Kid, I'm here to speak with Dr. Ellsberg. If you're not going to introduce me to him then give me back my guns. I want to swing by Graceland and pick up some souvenirs before I head back to my home."

"Souvenirs? Have you lost your gourd? No one's going into the city. Even the Marines avoid it."

"Got to prove I was here to Major Ellsberg when I report back to him I wasn't allowed to meet with his brother," Ethan says.

A man who Ethan would believe related to Major Ellsberg holds the interrogation room door open to allow the young lab coat to exit.

"Are you trained in interrogations?" he asks.

"In manner of speaking, yes. My pre-apocalyptic career made demands on my ability to read people."

"And you won't tell me what you did before?"

"Not unless you want to split the kitty. I hear the betting pool has gotten quite high around my camp," says Ethan. "I'm something of a local celebrity."

"You played Dr. Seaseters, pretty good."

"The kid's a doctor?"

"Had his second master's by age fourteen."

"Neither one in people skills." Ethan smirks. "But as long as we are discussing it, you're not Dr. Ellsberg either."

"I'll give you the code phrase to prove—"

"Lift your shirt. Left side," Ethan orders.

"What?"

"You've got in an earpiece. So I'm going to assume—dangerous I know—the real doctor is feeding you information through it. The real Dr. Ellsberg has a scar where they would have removed his kidney. His father needed a transplant. Dr. Ellsberg volunteered without hesitation. While on the table, his father died before the transplant was complete. But not before the aborted surgery left him a healthy scar."

The next lab coated man bears a near identical to but aged face Major Ellsberg. He lifts his shirt.

Ethan nods at the pink scar. "You're one intelligent individual. Stupid people never survive these situations."

"I need to speak with Ethan, alone." Dr. Ellsberg opens the second door inviting Ethan to exit the integration room.

400 MILES TO GRACELAND

Once in the medical lab, Dr. Ellsberg seals the door. "I don't think they have been able to bug this room. If my brother trusts you...I know I can." He hands Ethan a tote with his guns inside.

"A bit too much cloak and dagger for the end of the world, don't you think?"

"You reason because the world ended things change. Nothing's changed. Do you know what they are having me do?"

"Injecting possible cures into people and then having them bitten to test if you have developed a vaccine," Ethan guesses.

"Are you a doctor?"

"No, but it's logical."

"I've murdered. I've murdered to stay alive. There are plenty of undesirables that would seek refuge at the base. I would test it on them. I overheard about the military base evacuations. Failure on my part would mean the military would leave the medical staff behind when they pulled out. Since Ft. Wood has fallen they have no contact with any other base," Dr. Ellsberg's confession spills from him.

"Did you find a way to prevent the spread of this *plague*?" Ethan desires his guns—badly.

"I need you to get me to my brother. I don't know why he's not on a ship in the Atlantic, but I'll bet he's in the safest place possible. This base has been damaged with all the aftershocks. The soldiers have been encountering more Vectors moving north and rampant panic consumes everyone. You're the only person I've meet who's been outside maintaining a cool head."

"Doc, I'm here to get you to your brother."

"This base is in the process of collapse. I no longer care what happens to me. My sins outweigh what I discovered. I need you to deliver a package to my brother."

"I'm here to retrieve you."

"Did you see many soldiers when they brought you in?" Dr. Ellsberg asks.

"A few struggled with the gate. It seemed bent. The rapid building of a barricade a few miles down the road won't hold long."

Dr. Ellsberg flips on a flat screen television mounted to the wall.

An aerial view of the base clears as the screen warms. "This is drone footage for half an hour ago." He presses play on a remote.

"The aftershocks brought down the back wall."

The image scrolls down along the road for miles to the solider adding to the barricade. As the drone zooms further, the lens fills with hundreds of biters.

"And you're wasting man power building a pointless barricade. Get these men to pack their gear. My home has a place for all of them."

"I don't have time to explain the politics involved here. Just trust me when I tell you if the current administration learns my vaccine research is succeeding they aren't going to administer it to anyone not surrendering to their new government."

Aftershocks rock the building.

CHAPTER SEVENTY-THREE

SALT AIR WHIPS over the bow of the *USS Harry S. Truman*. Colonel Travis glances through binoculars at the horizon.

Navy Helicopters hover over the luxury yacht. Sea water churns and bubbles as the blades drive down an air mass. Men rappel to the deck. With exact precision, the tactical team invades clearing the deck before moving in pairs inside.

The waves prevent the rapid-fire sound accompanying the muzzle flashes Travis catches in the windows. Men drag out rotten bodies dumping them into the ocean.

Popping a flare signals a retrieval boat. It speeds to the yacht. Gray fatigued sailors trade off with the assault team.

Travis lowers his binoculars. Wind ripples his battle fatigues. The salt in the air leaves a taste in his mouth reminding him has yet to earn his sea legs.

Lieutenant Browns marches to the edge of the air craft carrier saluting his superior before handing him a document. "They have prepared a meeting, sir. Your presence is required."

"I tire of meetings. I tire of finding civilian ships full of Vectors. We don't do something soon and there won't be anyone left to save."

"The troops are ready. Only the Navy wants to stay out on these *boats*."

Travis takes position behind his chair assuming parade rest while other officers enter the war room. Top brass from the Navy, Army, and Air Force file in. He expected at least one of them to be on the President's cabinet. As it stands, he doesn't know any of them. Nor has a single female officer been invited to this briefing.

"Gentlemen. We have much to cover, so we'll forgo formalities as rank dictates to move forward," the Army General says.

Travis notes the Army General has been promoted to five stars. A rank only granted in time of war. The last known attempt to even promote a general to five star was in respect to General Norman Schwarzkopf and it was unsuccessful. Not even the Global terrorism war inspired such a rank. Now this man must be the leader of the entire remaining military. For once, someone has been able to suppress indifference.

"There has been a restructuring of the United States political system. The remaining members of congress have voted a regime change. Until the American way of life is restored we operate as a Junta."

He quells the mumbles with a wave of his hand.

"You're tossing aside the Constitution," an Army Major protests.

"In time of war the Roman Republic would set aside personal freedom and give one man the power of absolute rule until the war was over. It was an effective system."

"Until Caesar refuses to abnegate his crown."

Travis wonders how long before this Major is shipped to the front lines.

"Currently, the United States is a democracy. We must expel these invader—"

"With all due respect, General, they are not invaders. They are our mothers, sons, sisters, aunts, our children," Travis speaks out.

"Colonel Travis, you have spent more time in the field than anyone in this room and dealt with the Vectors for nine months. We consider you an authority."

"You have plenty of men and women who have interacted with Vectors more than I have." Travis was just as safe at Fort Wood as these men are on the Atlantic.

"We already have an abundance of officers over enlisted men, but none with ten months of boots on the ground," says the General.

Stationed on a walled military base where I sent civilians contractors to deal with the undead more than my own soldiers. I'm no expert. "Hiding being a fence for nine months isn't experience."

The leaders have stayed hidden for ten months on the Atlantic Fleet. Travis hopes his words sting the men who forced him to abandon his daughter.

"We have lost our focus, we'll return to the Colonel and his necessity for being here. First, I am General Matt Powel appointed by the Senate to lead our combined armed forced." He allows his statement to sink in. "We are beyond declaring marshal law to save our beloved country. It must be reclaimed by force. In order to do so, all survivors from now on are considered conscripts."

"Clarification General, every person we rescue is automatically drafted?"

"Like there are no atheists in foxholes, there are no civilians in this war on the undead."

"Even children?"

"Until this crisis has abated, adolescents will train only." The General moves on before any protests surface. "Do we have current reports on the earthquake?"

Travis knows he has been kept from information briefings. Most officers have been given fragments of what occurs on the mainland. But no one outside of this room has learned of any earthquake. Those surviving will receive no federal assistance or Red Cross as no such organizations exists.

"The devastation might have been worse. Many gas and power companies had disconnected service as the plague worsened. Had cities like Memphis kept the gas on all the wooden structures would have burned. The damage remains extensive as aftershocks have not ceases."

"What are the magnitudes?" Travis asks. None of these men know his daughter has been ferreted away to safety. A safety now compromised if the earthquake damages the Cannon Dam.

"Unconfirmed at this time, but the initial earthquake was eight-one."

"Looks like we got your people out just in time, Colonel," General Powel says.

Travis has no idea where the control inside him emanates from to not leap the table and beat the general bloody.

"The number of civilian in the area means we are going to lose many living. We need to send recon," Travis says.

"You're too valuable to use for these search missions, Colonel."

"There is an overabundance of officers in this fleet and not enough enlisted to run missions. I'd be of more use getting my hands dirty." *Once back in mid-America I'd search for my daughter. I won't abandon her again.*

"Those people are going to have to fend for themselves. We have made your plan, Colonel Travis, a priority. I have ordered the fleet off Key West Florida on your recommendation."

One of the officers Travis doesn't know unrolls a map of the southern Florida peninsula on the table. "Travis if you will explain your proposal to us."

I borrowed this from Ethan. His ideas should be keeping Hannah safe if the earthquake didn't damage the fence he built.

"Thank you, Sir. Key West makes the best beachhead with it being an island. I have a three-pronged attack plan in place." He uncaps a marker. "Two small platoons along with construction team land on Highway 1. They secure the bridge and build a checkpoint a mile out from the city. After the check point is complete the second platoon will move in toward the city securing what we will later build as the main entrance. Anyone wanting in the city will undergo a complete full body inspection before being allowed to enter."

He dots the West side of the island. "The first major landing will be here with a second here." He dots the southernmost point of the island. The soldiers will line up and do a full march forward checking every block, building, room, closet and cabinet. Yes, gentlemen, every home every single cabinet. Eliminate any Vector with a headshot. The body to be drug into the street where a cleanup crew will gather and dispose of the bodies with fire. They'll also escort any survivors to the medical unit we will have first on the beach then in this hotel."

"You expect to find living."

"Any able-bodied adult without pertinent skills will be drafted, trained and added to the search team," General Powel reminds the room of his order.

"Why not start in Miami or another major city? We should take back the capital."

"We should start with farm lands and gather food stores. But that requires large open areas to fence in and patrol. With the ocean at our backs we have less chance of being overrun or losing the valuable ground we've gained to the undead. This is not like any military operation we've embarked on before. We don't attack Vectors the way we would living insurgents."

The General nods, "This why Coronel Travis will lead the mission to take back our country."

CHAPTER SEVENTY-FOUR

GLASS TWO INCHES thick secures cubical cells. In the final chamber an ashen woman's body slumps in a heap on the floor. Grayer than any undead epidermis Ethan's encountered he ponders if *the cure* changed her.

Dr. Ellsberg allowed Ethan into the chamber unaccompanied to win the trust of the experiment.

He taps the glass.

Nothing.

So much for a cure.

The emaciated girl twitches. Ethan's arm points the gun before his brain transfers the command to do so finding comfort with his speed returning.

Despite her dry and chapped lips, her eyes lacked the glazed cataracts of the undead. She adjusts the paper gown in a modest attempt to cover her private areas. Ethan's natural inclination to respect her privacy hangs with him a moment until he notices the healed bite marks tracking up her right arm.

"Do you understand me?" He taps the glass.

Amanda pulls herself using the wall as a leaning post. She reaches up with her long arm fumbling to clasp the phone receiver from its cradle. It falls whacking the glass. Ethan snatches the phone on his side.

She puts it to her ear. With a cough, her raspy voice lacks the moan-howl of the dead. "You're not one of the doctors," dry-throated she observes.

"Biters are overrunning the camp. Are you bit?"

"They tied me to a chair..." Tears should flow, if she wasn't dehydrated. "I knew I was dead. They injected me with something."

"It kept you from turning."

"It destroyed *all* bacteria in my body."

"Do you need water?" Ethan asks.

Moving as if her arm weighs fifty pounds, she points to the wall. "They filter the water...I drink, but without power to run the filter. it's not pure."

How do I save a cure unable to leave a clean room? "What about the stuff in your body to digest food?"

"Be glad you weren't here days ago—it hit me hard. They've been introducing small amounts of germs to rebuild my immune system."

"What happens if I open the doors?" Ethan asks.

"If I have enough built up immunity—I might live."

"You stay in this room and you die for sure."

"I should have died when I was bit. Whatever they did, I didn't turn. But I don't know if I'm the cure."

"If I find a way to open the door, do you want me to?" *Put it on her. It should be her choice while she still has life to make it.*

Amanda nods.

Ethan bursts through the door from the human laboratory cages to find Dr. Ellsberg ransacking a desk shoving papers and files into a duffle bag.

"We should take all this research with us." Dr. Ellsberg points to the chair by the door.

"What about the girl?" Ethan wraps his gun belt around his waist.

"All indications are she is immune to Vector bites. And has enough exposure to the germ-filled air to be safely released.

"We take her," Ethan checks each gun—fully loaded. Ellsberg hands him a keycard. "This will open her cell."

The key card gives Ethan access to the hall and the girl's room. He opens the door exposing her to all the germs in the world.

She uses the bed as a crutch. "Won't get far without water."

Ethan unsnaps his canteen swilling as much as he can before pouring the rest on the floor. "Put your fingers in your ears."

She complies.

Ethan uses his left index finger to close his right ear pumping two slugs into the wall mounted water dispenses. Liquid flows from the holes.

Amanda stumbles to the water.

He hands her his canteen. "Fill it and let's go."

"You exposed me to the air. And I'm not dead."

"You've been breathing it for a while. The generator operating the air filtration system cut out."

She drinks.

As she consumes more fluid, her skin pinks.

Not yet a healthy hue, but better than the corpse-gray she had minutes ago. Ethan leads her back into the office where he left Dr. Ellsberg.

When she spots the doctor, Amanda grabs an ink pen off the desk and stabs him in the stomach.

Dr. Ellsberg's shock prevents any reaction to the attack.

Ethan grabs her, tossing her into a chair, but not before she punctures two more holes in the doctor.

"I needed him."

"He did this to me," she holds up her bite scarred arm.

Ethan finds her evidence hard to dispute. He's killed for less.

Dr. Ellsberg collapses in the desk chair. "I think she hit something vital." He covers one gushing hole with his hand.

"You stay over there," he scolds the girl. Ethan slides the file cabinet over to block the door. It won't prevent a living person from entering, but the undead don't fiddle too long with blocked doors unless they know something is inside they want to eat.

"You don't need me. She's the key to a vaccine," says Dr. Ellsberg.

Ethan glances around the room. Regretting he ever embarked on this mission. *Damn pride.*

The far wall contains a paper map of the United States. Radiating dots cover a dozen major cities. Scrolled in black sharpie are dates and times. Allowing for the time zone differences Ethan calculates the outbreak of undead occurred in fourteen major US cities within a half hour of each other.

Flipping on a cell phone he waits for the chirping drum roll signaling its warming up.

"Improbable, to have been...a natural epidemic," Dr. Ellsberg admits, as blood pumps from the three holes.

"It doesn't excuse your testing on people. How many did you murder when the other vaccines didn't work!?" Amanda screams at him.

Ethan snaps a picture of the map before digging through the papers on the desk. "Is this all your research? It's a lot of hard copy."

"We searched for a cure. No disease has fourteen patient zeroes at the same time. Those are just the American ones. Other cities around the word reported outbreaks within an hour either side of those times."

"A coordinated terrorist act. What's it matter now?"

Dr. Ellsberg's breathing labors. "I don't want to be one of those things." He holds up a flash drive. "Everything is on this stick."

Ethan flips off the cell phone, returning it to the waterproof case along with the flash drive and military GPS.

Dr. Ellsberg holds up a blood-covered key card. His breathing labors, "This area gives access to the exit door past the cells. You'll find a motor pool." Ellsberg coughs blood. "You tell my brother all I wanted to do was stop our inevitable extinction."

"When you are willing to do what you did to me, it proves humans have no right to go on."

"I don't want to be one of those things," Dr. Ellsberg begs.

"I don't know if this will be painless or not." He takes hold of the man's forehead.

"Wait." Ellsberg genuflects, leaving behind a bloody cross on his lab coat, "God forgive me."

Ethan slams the knife thought the ear canal puncturing the brain. He wipes the blade clean on a clear spot of lab coat.

A door bolted with card key security blocks their escape.

Amanda twists the handle and it pops open. "Electronic sealed doors unlock when the power goes out in case of fire. Unless they are medically special, like my cell."

No matter how many times Ethan's encountered a group of undead feasting on a fallen body, it turns his stomach. He pushes the disgust from his thoughts. The first-round splatters more blood over the unfazed creatures. Engrossed in their duties, they ignore the noise. The second creature drops from a shot and now they turn their frenzy on its maker. Ethan dispatches two more. In quick rapid succession, three more fall. He spares the person being dined upon from returning from the dead with blow from his knife. Blood-covered key card dangles from the ring attached to his belt.

Ethan cuts free the keyring. "Just in case."

Still human. He pushes down bile. Being sick means he's still human. What about the woman?

They open doors searching for an escape. In a janitorial supply closet, Amanda grabs a jacket. She zips it up over her paper gown. Drinking from the canteen brightens her complexion revealing she has tan lines from being outdoors. "Do I get a gun?"

Ethan checks the clip in his Beretta, loading the missing rounds. "You've got eleven bullets. Make them count."

"Now I need a clothing store for some new clothes."

"I had a bad experience in mall with the undead, once." Ethan smiles.

"Lots of supplies," she says.

"I'll find you a whole wardrobe once we get out of here."

"I won't leave without knowing what happened to my companions. They brought three of us in here. I've got to know if my friends are dead."

"We'll search for them on the way out, but the earthquakes brought down the outer walls. This place is overrun with biters. And every resident of Memphis is about to arrive."

Gunfire.

At least the soldiers are still defending this place.

They burst through a door marked EXIT.

Ethan flings the cure behind him.

A soldier remaining at his post greets them.

Ethan would drop the Corporal, but the boy has his finger on the trigger allowing for final burst from his automatic.

"Whoa! Easy, Sir."

"Don't *Sir* me; I work for a living." Ethan recalls his grandfather's mantra. "Are you deserting your post, son?" Depending on his former level of patriotism, his words may sting the Corporal into assisting.

"The military's finished."

"Not an answer. But I might have one." Keeping the woman behind him, he pulls her arm so the Corporal sees it. "She has healed Vector bites. They injected her with something. Her blood contains the cure.

"There is no cure."

"Then explain her bites. They are healed and they are human." Ethan needs the kid to lower the rifle slightly to pick him off.

"It won't do any good. Half of Memphis is burning from the aftershock and quake draws them. Without this compound—"

"I have a base in...Northern Missouri near a hydroelectric dam. We've electricity, hot water, cattle, and walls." Ethan's never explained so much to anyone. "It's far enough north the earthquake won't have caused damage."

"Lies."

"No. Major Ellsberg is the doctor's brother. I came here to retrieve Dr. Ellsberg and take him back. He knew weeks ago this place was compromised—before the quake."

"Then the girl is a priority."

"I've a name," Amanda snaps.

"You've an extraction plan?" the Corporal asks.

"Get across the bridge. I've got some companions. We'll use a boat and head up river," He leaves out he has a boat and lacks a need to cross the Mississippi.

"Motor pool. The Jeeps are always fully gassed."

"Lead the way. I'll take the rear—keep the cure between us."

"I'm no damsel in distress."

"We need you alive." Ethan spanks her with his eyes. He may not trust the Corporal, but the boy knows the base layout and like them he has deep aspirations to not become a biter.

"You said you had a base." The Corporal sweeps his weapon, prepared to fire.

"And everyone works to support it. We protect each other like family."

The overwhelming gas/oil mix greets them as they enter the motor pool. Ethan draws in a breath through his nose.

"What are you doing?" Amanda inquires.

"Enjoying a smell not coated in dead people."

The Corporal pulls rings of keys from a peg board. "What's our next move?"

Time for trust. "Two Humvees. I take the first, smash through any barriers and the bulk of the biters. You follow with the cure in the second and pick me up. We head for the bridge."

"I cannot count the ways that's the most fucked plan I've ever heard," says the Corporal.

"I agree with the Marine," Amanda says.

"There are too many biters for one of us to get out and unlock the gate."

"Then we take one Humvee and ram it," says the Corporal.

"If the fence gets tangled in the wheel-well, were fucked," Ethan says.

"I see your angle." He tosses Ethan a set of keys. "Find the Humvee loaded with extra supplies. They keep one for emergencies."

"Ten-hut!"

The Corporal stumbles over his feet while snapping to attention.

Ethan whirls at the voice. A Sergeant, arm ripped to shreds by bite marks, lumbers into the motor pool. "I'll be taking that one. But I like your idea of ramming the gate. Put your weapons on the ground so you can drive." He points his gun at Ethan.

"How about we keep our guns and we take three Humvees? When we get across the bridge, I'll cure your bites," Ethan offers.

"There's no cure."

"What do you think they were working on in there? Her blood contains the cure." Ethan nods toward the woman's arm.

"How do you plan to get it into me?"

"I was an EMT-B. I'll transfer enough of her blood." Ethan hopes this guy doesn't know EMT-Bs aren't trained to do anything invasive.

"Do it before we leave. This building's secure."

"It may be, Sergeant, but my level of trust isn't," Ethan says.

Ethan slows the Humvee. Between his bad leg and being too tall to comfortably fit behind the wheel, he hopes he doesn't have to escape quickly from the cab. With a foot on the brake he keeps the vehicle in gear, halting behind a row of troops popping biter after biter at the barricade.

"Makes you proud. Those boys will stand their ground," beams the Sergeant. His satisfaction remains minute as he weakens.

"Until they're overrun. There are a few thousand more undead heading this way. Your brave men got enough ammo to deal with them? Or do you want to sit here and watch them die for their country?"

"I won't order them to retreat. Even I know there is no place for them to go."

"I have a place," *Fuck, there goes my boat escape.* "And they should be protecting the cure. That's not retreating that's a mission."

A soldier appears at the driver's door. "New orders, sir." He corrects himself, "Sorry, Sergeant. Orders?"

When the pause concerns the soldier, he questions, "Orders, Sergeant?"

"Get them on the Humvee. Protecting these two civilians is your new priority." His eyes pound Ethan with an "I need the blood now" glance.

The Marine races to retrieve those popping biters.

"I don't know how you plan to get to the bridge."

"The roads clear of obstacles, besides undead?" Ethan asks.

"We kept it clear," says the Sergeant.

Soldiers climb into every cranny on the Humvee.

"Hold on!" Ethan floors it.

The Humvee races off the road behind the barrier. It gives all those hitching a ride a moment to breath—reload.

"How far north of Memphis did you drop these trees?"

"Ten miles," calls out a soldier's voice.

Ten miles to the city. No way to stay in the trees for such a distance. The biters are drawn north. Maybe our two vehicles won't be the attraction the aftershocks are. Ethan weaves and bobs through the forest.

The barricade ends, giving way to trees too thick and too close together to navigate a wide Humvee through.

Short bursts of machine gun fire distracts the biters. Ethan punches the accelerator, flying over the ditch onto the road. Undead splatter over the grill as he waves across the center line in an attempt to hit as few as possible.

"Hey, Marine! Shoot the Vectors in front!"

Hot brass rains into the cab.

No more hearing. Ethan drops his eyes to the odometer. *Nine miles? Felt like so much further.*

The undead herd thins like an eye of a hurricane.

The Corporal voids the undead Ethan misses with the first Humvee. "Your savior is fucking nuts."

"I just met him," Amanda says.

"And you trust him to protect you?"

"I trusted your soldiers to keep me safe and I was fucking experimented on."

The Corporal unclips a grenade from his utility harness. "No way for me to make up for the way you were treated, but this will prevent anyone from hurting you again." He hands her the orb.

In the second the Corporal glances at Amanda to make sure she has the grenade before releasing it, he misses the first Humvee stalling just for a second as it climbs over a tree fallen across the road.

The impact flings the first Humvee forward doing little damage to either vehicle. A soldier holding onto the back of the Humvee flies across the hood flipping onto the roof. The fifty-caliber gun placement prevent him from reaching the pavement. A second soldier hanging on the back of Ethan's Humvee felt the full brunt of the impact when his legs crushed against the grill.

Screams for a Corpsman.

Ethan slows. Troops leap to secure the area. The Sergeant grabs Ethan as he attempts to get out to check on the fallen soldier.

"Leave him." Beading sweat drips from his forehead. "I need the cure."

"I need to make sure the back end will get the next seven miles," Ethan gets out.

Two Marines work the fallen soldier. His lower legs are gone. From the amount of crimson spilling onto the road, Ethan knows he's bleeding out.

Two others help the second Marine tossed against the fifty-cal in the impact.

Amanda hops from the Humvee.

"Get back inside!" Ethan scolds her.

"Why is she so important?" asks a Marine.

Ethan decides it's time to go for broke. "Her blood contains antibodies to prevent a Vector bite from and reanimating you."

"She's some kind of cure? We should be evacuating her to the Atlantic Fleet."

"You want to wait at the base for a helicopter?" Ethan asks.

"You have a second evacuation point?"

Ethan must be careful. The support of these Marines will ensure returning to Acheron with this girl. A woman whose name he has forgotten to ask. She's become a package not a person.

"I have military personnel at my camp. But it's four hundred miles to get there."

Before any answers forthcoming—

"He's gone," reports one of the Marines working the wounded."

"You need to do right by him," Ethan says.

"You mean put a bullet in him."

"If you're unable..." Ethan touches his Berretta. "I'll do it."

"No, Sir. I'll do it."

Ethan slows. The remains of a military checkpoint signal the edge of the city. "What happened here, Sergeant?" The barricades, concertina wire and metal walls charred black from an intense fire leave an opening large enough for the Humvee.

Ethan nudges the Sergeant's shoulder.

He jars from his slumber. "What? I'm far from dead?"

"What happened?" Ethan points at the firebombed military barricades.

"We kept them bottled in the city until the earthquake. Then a few good men blew all they could to hell."

"A few hundred thousand biters would be impossible for anyone to control. How do I get to the bridge from here?"

"Head down to the right. Follow the signs. We marked it when we thought we were going to defend it. There are obstacles on the bridge. You'll need time to get across without company." The Sergeant hollers out the window, "Hold this position. Until we clear the bridge. Then haul ass across!" He falls back inside in labored breath.

Ethan hops from his Humvee.

The Corporal escorts Amanda to him. "Get her across the bridge. We'll follow up."

Ethan drags her to his vehicle.

"I'm not some hunk of meat," she protests.

Bullets shatter the moment of stillness.

"You certainly are to those biters. I don't have time for politeness."

The Marines assume the checkpoints defensive potions opening fire on the Vectors.

"Corporal, I could use you as we cross the bridge." *Especially when I have to shoot the Sergeant.*

"I'll be right behind you. I'm after all the Vectors worst nightmare." He climbs behind the Humvee fifty-caliber. "A nineteen-year-old American with a machine gun."

Now Ethan uses all his strength to hold the snarling Sergeant at arm's length while he barrels through standing bodies. Ethan floors the accelerator. He doubts the stability of the Hernando de Soto Bridge after the earthquake. Limited options superseded his better judgment.

Undead splatter against the grill raining coagulated syrupy mess across the windshield.

Metal grinds on concert. The Humvee bounces off the barrier.

The windshield wipers clear enough cadaverous fluids from the glass for him to make out trucks on disjointed pavement parked across the bridge's center.

The Humvee sputters and dies in a jerk as if hitting a wall.

White smoke belches from the hood. Red and green fluid drip mixing with black goop. The smell of antifreeze overwhelms the rotten stench of stale blood for a second.

Copper soaks his tongue. Ethan tastes the blood. He must have busted open his lip on impact.

The heavy *ther-rump* of repeating 50-caliber rounds tells him the Corporal remains alive. Part of Ethan wants to go back for him.

"Just shoot him!" Amanda screams.

"Get out," he orders through clenched teeth.

Being fresh, the Sergeant maintains much of his human strength. Ethan stumbles from the driver's door. He drives his knife through the Sergeant's skull when he attempts to crawl after him.

"You should have just shot him."

"The Corporal's noise is keeping biters away from the bridge. I don't need them coming up here for a bullet shot."

"You're not much better than those doctors. You used those soldiers to ensure your escape," says Amanda.

"*Our* escape..."

She points. "But if you had friends on the bridge you—"

"Friends?" *I must have hit my head.*

They fired into the engine block. I was so occupied with the biter I missed them. Oh, fuck me!

A pick-up full of armed men blocks their escape. They have tied a naked woman across the hood like a trophy deer.

Outgunned even with his speed and at this range, Ethan won't get more than three before there automatic weapons cut him down. He doubts even his armored vest will stop enough bullets for him to kill a forth.

"*You killed my brothers,*" the unknown voice screams at him.

Ethan steps to the center of the bridge, gunslinger ready. "You're going to have to be more specific."

The truck rolls forward.

The fifty-caliber background noise fades followed by dying M16 fire.

The soldiers have been overrun. Got to get off this bridge. Ethan notes the face of the man swearing at him.

"Of all the people in all the world... How many fuck'n brothers do you have?"

Kaleb Bowlin cuts free the woman, dragging her from the hood, twisting her around to reveal her face.

She's been tied there long enough to burn her skin in the sun. Dried blood crusts her naked frame. Her broken face will require reconstructive surgery, but Ethan recognizes Becky.

Kaleb shoves her forward. She hobble-steps with her right foot pigeon-toed inward. Ethan guesses her hip has been disjointed. Becky didn't let them take her easily and they made her pay for her resistance.

She needs to move from before his target. Baby steps only move her a few inches forward and keeps her in the direct line of fire between him and Bowlin. Medically moving on her broken hip seem impossible. Compelled to escape keeps her on her feet.

"Which Bowlin Bastard are you?"

Kaleb beams. "You know who I am."

"I've killed enough of your brothers."

The bridge metal contorts in the wind.

"You mother must have never gotten off her back." Most rednecks can't abide mother insults even if they know she was worthless trash. Ethan needs this man angry, unthinking.

"I don't excite as easily as my brothers."

Damn. He noticed the hook.

"I take my time. Enjoy the moment. Make it last." He yanks Becky by the hair. The jerk sends her back into his arms. "This one knows I take a long time."

Where is the baby? Chad? The others?

"You've had your fun. I know you want me dead for killing your brothers. Before we relive the O.K. Corral on this bridge don't you want to know why you had to chase me all the way to Memphis? I didn't come here to scavenge for cans of beans. You and I both know there are plenty of neglected food marts in Missouri ripe for foraging."

Caught up in his thirst for revenge, Kaleb never considered why this man would lead people from Fort Wood in personnel carriers only to hike to Memphis. Kale would want to know. "You're stalling."

Damn right! You should have killed me the moment I stepped from the car. Don't play with your food. It never worked for the coyote. Once you're in range—I kill you.

Ethan lays all his cards on the table. "Scientists in Memphis were developing a vaccine against the biters. This woman's blood contains antibodies preventing an infected from turning you into the walking dead."

"There is no cure."

"I didn't say cure, you moron. I said vaccine, like for the measles. We can't cure, but we can prevent future outbreaks." Ethan won't pander to Bowlin, not now.

"Who taught you how to negotiate?" Amanda asks.

"I know what I'm doing," Ethan whispers. "Show your arm."

Amanda holds up her arm. Keeping the grenade behind her back with the one.

"She's been bitten and they've healed. She's not going to turn."

"You think I'm stupid. You want me to believe this girl survived a bite. Take her back to my camp and allow her to infect my people."

"Bites don't heal. But they did on her. The vaccine works."

BAM. BAM. BAM.

Bullets shred Amanda.

Blood bursts from her wounds.

Ethan's *no* allows splashes of a copper taste into his mouth.

He dives for cover. His first shot wild. Before he aims, he falls to the pavement.

Amanda uses her last ounce of life to propel a grenade at the truck. Ethan's drop prevents any reaction other than to scream Becky's name.

Unable to react, the explosion propels her against the center barrier. Helpless, Ethan witnesses her shatter against the concrete much like a crumpling rag doll does on the floor. Flames lick Becky's naked back from the ensuing fireball.

Screams of men on fire drown in the gas tank explosion.

Biters on both sides of the river cease their mindless droning, scuttling toward the loud excitement.

The pavement has yet to warm in the sun. Ethan has a second to formulate a new plan of escape.

Aftershock.

Or the expulsion destabilized the bridge. Either way Ethan's glad he's on the ground already. So much for the seismic retrofitting project.

The impact of Kaleb's tackle radiates through Ethan, reawakening the pain of the beating, and even the bruises from the bullets he took to the chest.

Old.

The first thought racing through him. *Hell, not even a twenty-something could take such a beating and not be traumatized even* if it's physical. The human body remembers. They say it forgets pain. But not the joints and tendons. They remember. They resist. They tire of fighting. The body gives in.

Ethan fights his body to move as much as with Kaleb. Why does a family he's never met before want to destroy all he's worked to build? He may have killed some of them but they were ravaging young women. Terrorists in the new age of undead. They represent the darkness overcoming so many. Ethan won't allow such people to exist in the new world he's created.

Now his mind betrays him. Time to throw in the towel. Give up. People are safe. Life will go on even without a vaccine.

The bridge shifts. The burning truck disappears through collapsing pavement plummeting toward the river.

The crash distracts Kaleb's advance on Ethan.

Nothing noble about Ethan's next move. His knife flashes red from the hole he punches in Kaleb's side. The little man squeals. Ethan summons every ounce of strength he has and heaves the man over his head. The shoulder press maneuver performed with ease becomes complicated when he tosses.

Kaleb skids across the pavement, not reaching the newly formed hole.

Undead shamble from both ends of the bridge. Their moan-howls attract more brethren.

Ethan scoops up his M&P. He raises the weapon. Kaleb smiles at him and rolls into the hole. Ethan hears the splash before he reaches the cavity. In his mind, Kaleb must have relished depriving Ethan of a kill as he fell to his death. He had seconds to consider his choice.

Ethan cradles Becky in his arms. With her one eye, she gives him the glance of a loving daughter. Tears cover Ethan's cheek. Even in a restored world with full medical facilities he doubts they could repair her broken body.

Before the moan-howls drown her words, Becky speaks through broken teeth and shattered jaw. "End...me—"

It's all he can do for her. No more pain. Not allowing her to turn. The bullet bounces around in her brain pan ensuring no reanimation.

Ethan checks the clip.

Twelve.

And one in the pipe.

Marching up both sides of the Hernando de Soto Bridge are more biters than he cares to count. They are a thinner group on the Arkansas side of the river, but even if it is the necessary direction he needs to travel there are more undead then even he'll be able to kill.

He slips a second full clip from his belt, placing it in his mouth, then grips the third full clip in his left hand ready to replace the first once he empties it.

ABOUT THE AUTHOR

William Schlichter has a Bachelor of Science in Education emphasizing English from Southeast Missouri State and a Masters of Arts in Theater from Missouri State University. With seventeen years of teaching English/Speech/Theater, he has returned to making writing his priority. Recent successes with scriptwriting earned him third place in the 2013 Broadcast Education Association National Festival of Media Arts for writing a TV Spec Script episode of *The Walking Dead*.

His full-length feature script, *Incinta*, was an officially selected finalist in the 2014 New Orleans Horror Film Festival. *Incinta* received recognition again by being selected as a finalist at the 2015 Beverly Hills Film Festival for a full-length feature. *Incinta* has advanced in several other script contests, including most recently being an Official Selected finalist in the 2016 Irvine Film Festival. His next life goal would be to see his film transferred from the pages to the screen.

Writing has always been his passion even through traveling, raising twin children, and educating teenagers. While he specializes in the phantasmagorical world of the undead and science fiction fantasy stories, William continues to teach acting, composition, and creative writing.

CPSIA information can be obtained
at www.ICGtesting.com
Printed in the USA
FFOW03n0819300118
44725067-44751FF